THE AINSWORTH ROYALS

RARE LONDON 2023

EMILY SILVER

Copyright © 2023 by Emily Silver

All rights reserved.

This is a work of fiction. Names, characters, places and incidents are either the product of the author's imagination or are use fictitiously. Any resemblance to actual persons, living or dead, businesses, companies, events or locations is entirely coincidental.

No part of this book may be reproduced in any form or by any electronic or mechanical means, including information storage and retrieval systems, without written permission from the author, except for the use of brief quotations in a book review. For more information, please email the author at authoremilysilver@gmail.com.

Cover Design by Angela Brindley

Editing by Happily Editing Anns

www.authoremilysilver.com

 Created with Vellum

A Note from the Author

Thank you so much for reading Royal Reckoning! I have taken some literary license when writing this book in regard to the royal world and the Succession to the Crown Act, passed in 2013. Prior to 2011, any second-born male could displace an older sister in line to the throne. Since this is my own royal world, this does not apply in this book.

Happy reading!

Royal Reckoning

AN AINSWORTH ROYALS STORY

ROYAL
reckoning

EMILY SILVER

TRAVELIN' HOOSIER BOOKS

For Tutu, a queen in her own right

Chapter One

ELLIE

"Eleanor, are you paying attention?"

The smack of papers in front of me pulls my attention away from the large windows of the palace. The London skies are a dull grey. A stern look from my advisor tells me that she has lost my attention, even though I heard every word she said. It's another endless cycle of luncheons, plays, and—

"Wait, what about the new after-school art programme?" It was a rare day when my granddad and I were to attend an event together. The new art school opening in Shoreditch was going to be the bright spot in my day.

"It's been pushed back. Not much detail was passed along, but I believe their funding fell through at the last hour. Now, after the luncheon and meeting with the Australian ambassador, you will have the new play opening tonight in the West End."

I should be used to the endless list of events, but it's frustrating that the one event I'm actually excited about gets canceled.

"You should enjoy the play. British history at its finest." Alice shows more enthusiasm about my events than I do. My eyes roll on their own at the thought of this new play I'll have to suffer through.

Her lips purse. "You will need to show more excitement when you show up."

My back straight as a steel rod, I take a sip of my now cool morning tea.

"British history has been drilled into my head since I was old enough to read. This is nothing I haven't heard before. Taking what wasn't ours, being kicked out. Battles. I will act appropriate for the event." I keep the sharp retort about being flayed by the paparazzi to myself, as they will no doubt be swarming the event this evening.

I give her a sharp eye, a sheepish look coming over her.

"Are you causing trouble in here?" The deep voice of my grandfather alleviates the annoyances of my morning.

"No more than you are." Smirking at him, I finish my tea and stand. Smoothing my hands down the plain fabric of my blue sheath dress, I walk over and give him a hug.

"Your Majesty." Everyone is quick to curtsy in front of the king.

"How are you this morning, Granddad?"

"Old. I hear that you and I no longer have our event today." The wrinkles in his old face cut deep.

"We don't. I was very much looking forward to spending the morning with you." I loop my arm through his as we walk out of my office.

"Shame. I always like the art programmes." Our pace is slow. He's more frail than someone his age should be. "What else is on the diary for the day, Wildflower?"

I smile at the familiar nickname. "Lunch with the Australian ambassador and then the new play opening tonight. I get to learn about British history in three hours this evening."

"Now, now." His hand claps down on top of mine where it's linked with his arm. "You may end up learning something."

"Okay, Granddad." I laugh at him as we turn into his private study. "I will be sure to let you know if I discover something new about us Brits."

"That's the spirit." His bones creak as he sits down into the old chair behind his ornate desk.

"And what will you do with your day now?"

"Might see your mum for lunch. We'll all be heading on holiday soon, so should see everyone while I still have time."

"No need to be so morose. It's not like you won't be around when the holidays are over."

"Forgive me, Eleanor. I just want to spend more time with those I love."

"Speaking of your favourites." The loud voice of my brother James carries through Granddad's office.

"No one said you were the favourite, Jamie." Life has always been easy for my twin brother. He was born seven minutes after me, forever sealing his fate as third in line to the British throne.

"I beg to differ. Morning, Granddad." He drops a kiss on his cheek before he comes to pull me out of my chair. "I need to borrow Ellie for a bit. I'll have her back before your big event today."

"It was canceled."

"Perfect. More time for me." I kiss my granddad goodbye as I trail behind Jamie, wondering what he wants with me.

"Sis. I'm so glad I caught you today." He pulls me close into his side as we make our way to his office through the gilded halls of the palace. The portraits of past kings and queens line the hall. Their regal stares are a stern reminder as to what will one day be my own legacy.

"What are your plans for this evening?" James is a mirror image of me, with dark hair and deep blue eyes, except where he is tall and lithe, I am shorter and curvier. Something the media never ceases to point out.

"I have the new play opening this evening." I help myself to another cup of tea as I make my way over to the plush red loveseat. Everything in the palace is ornate and over the top.

"Good heavens, you're not wearing that, are you?" His look of disgust is palpable.

"No, I was not planning on it. You don't have to be so horrified at what I'm wearing. This is only for the luncheon today."

"Sorry, Ellie. Came out wrong."

"I get enough grief from the media and my own people. I don't need you criticising me."

He holds his hands up in defeat as he sits next to me. "Sorry, you're right. Wanker move. But I am hoping you'll join me for an evening out."

"Did you not just hear what I said? I have the play opening tonight."

He waves me off like this is a minor inconvenience. James acts as if his whole life is one big party. "That's early. You haven't been out with us in ages. I want to head to Club Mayfair tonight, and you can't say no to me."

"And why's that?" I raise my eyebrows in his direction. It's very easy to say no to my brother. Most people don't because he is so persistent, but not me.

"Charlotte is going to be coming out with us." Damn. I haven't seen my cousin in a few weeks, and she's one of my favourite people. Not many people know what it's like to grow up under a microscope, but she is one of them. "Besides, I won't get in as much trouble if you come with me."

"I'm not your keeper, James."

"Ooh, James. Now I know I'm in trouble." His voice is full of laughter. Nothing ever fazes him.

I stand and walk over to the windows. Even in the grey, dreary day, the Royal Mall still stands proud in all her glory. "Can you ever just be serious for once?"

"My dear sister. You need to loosen up. Even Grandmum has a more exciting life than you. You need a little excitement in your life. Besides, how do you plan on finding a partner if you aren't going out and searching?"

"Sleeping with half of London isn't the same as finding someone to take on this life. Besides, you know it isn't the same for me as it is for you. You're the playboy prince, and I would be labeled a slut if I so much as looked at a man."

I hate the double standard of being a royal. Instead of enjoying life as a twenty-eight-year-old woman, I have to attend charity events and state dinners almost daily. My life has never belonged to me. It's been out for public consumption since the time my parents stepped foot outside the hospital wing when we were born.

"You look awfully sullen over there." Jamie pours himself a cup of tea, sitting in the chair opposite mine. "You need a night out. Please come, Ellie." His pleading brown eyes stare into mine.

"Fine. I'll go with you. You're lucky Charlotte is coming, otherwise you'd be on your own."

"Thank goodness! Who knows? Maybe you'll find a grumpy prince to match your own attitude."

"And maybe you'll find someone who has more than two pence to rub together." My snarky attitude is unmatched today. My busy diary of events is weighing heavily on me, more so than usual.

"That's unfair. It's usually more like three."

Laughter bubbles out of me. My brother is one of the few people who knows how I truly feel about royal life. That on a good day, it's suffocating. That I can't take the pressure of being in the spotlight. Any weight gain or loss is scrutinized for days by the tabloids. It makes his criticism of me that much harder.

For leading such a privileged life, all I want are the simple things. Waking up, going to a job I love, and coming home to a small flat that I pay for. Instead, I'm shuffled between events, never alone, and coming home to an empty cottage that is more or less funded by taxpayer dollars.

There's a sharp knock on the door, followed by Alice entering. "Your Royal Highness, Princess Eleanor. In order to make it to the event on time to allow for a walkabout, we will need to leave promptly in ten minutes." Her voice is short and to the point. I stand, giving a sad smile to my brother.

"No rest for this royal. I'll see you later." He stands, giving me a quick hug.

"I promise, tonight you'll feel better. I'll make sure of it."

I follow Alice out the door. The history of the palace walls bears down on me as my Personal Protection Officers, my PPOs, follow behind me. Taking the wide stairs down, I find the black town car standing under the receiving entrance, ready to whisk me from event to event today. I sigh, settling in for an interminable day ahead.

"PRINCESS ELEANOR. It has been such a pleasure to have you join us this afternoon. We are honored that you could be with us for such a special occasion." The Australian ambassador shakes my hand whilst dipping into a low curtsy.

"The pleasure is all mine, madam." I give her a bright smile. "It's been quite some time since I've been to Australia. Hopefully I will get down there next year."

"I think I speak on behalf of all Australians, Your Highness, that we would welcome you with open arms."

"Australia is always a favourite of mine to visit." We're at the door, ready to leave, when I plaster on my press-ready smile.

"Thank you so much for visiting with us today."

I nod as I head out into the flashbulbs of the press. "Until we see each other again."

My PPOs are pushing the press back as we head towards the waiting car.

"Princess Eleanor! Why did you choose to visit with the Australian ambassador over Canada's?"

"Your Highness! Why did you go with such a scandalous outfit today?"

"Eleanor! Care to comment that you've gained a stone this last month?"

The door to the car swings open and I slide in. We're off in an instant as I try to drown out the comments from the press. Only one comment about my weight today. Usually, it's all they can focus on. The comments regarding what I wear are normally saved for after the evening event. Must be a slow news day.

"Your Highness. You'll have an hour for dinner and time to switch into your evening wear before we need to leave for the show tonight." Alice is focused on the tablet in front of her, not paying me any mind.

"Thank you, Alice." My eyes are on all the people waving as we leave the embassy behind us.

"And remember to wear the black dress this evening. It's more slimming and will hopefully ward off any unwanted comments from the paparazzi."

Just another day in the life of a princess.

Chapter Two

SEAN

"So for today's session, we're going to outline everything, and then once it heals, you'll come back in a few weeks for the colour."

"Sounds great, man. Let's get rolling." Looking down at the intricate pattern before me, it's hard to contain my excitement at my latest piece. The level of detail even blew me away. It's an old-time maritime scene, complete with wooden boats, pirates, and sailors. Once the colour gets added in, it's going to be fucking amazing.

My station prepped and ready, I get to work. The buzzing of the tattoo gun is a balm to anything going on in my life. It's been a stressful few weeks, but whenever I'm working on someone, the background noise fades away. I love watching the way the ink bleeds into the skin to create a masterpiece.

"So how long have you been doing this?" Wiping the excess ink off, I grab more and keep moving on the lines of the boat.

"'Bout ten years now."

"You been in Shoreditch for a while?" he asks. I don't

mind the idle chitchat that people make when getting tattoos. It usually helps distract them from the pain.

"Best spot in London."

"Oy, Sean! Call for you." Trevor's voice carries over the shop, distracting me from my work at hand.

"Sorry, mate. Be right back." Pulling the gloves off, I grab the phone from Trevor.

"Sean speaking."

"Hi, Sean. It's Melanie."

"Melanie. Where the hell are you?" It's the first time I've noticed she hasn't been in the shop all morning. She's usually the first one here out of all of us.

"Listen, I'm sorry to do this over the phone, but I can't work there anymore." Her voice is quiet as she drops the news on me.

"What do you mean you can't work here anymore?" I can't hide the irritation in my voice. Instead of working on the piece I've been looking forward to, I'm having to deal with this kind of shite.

"It just isn't going to work out. I'm so sorry." She ends the call, leaving me hanging.

Fucking hell.

"Pierce! What the hell happened?" I can't contain the annoyance in my voice when my brother appears in front of me.

"What happened about what, bro?" Crossing his arms, he leans against the wall, looking calm and collected, the exact opposite of how I feel.

"You know what. Why did I get a call that our receptionist quit on us?" This is the third one we've lost this month.

"It's probably because she asked out Trevor and he said no. You know how everyone is about him." He rolls his eyes. I do know, and it's a pain in my arse. Every person, man or woman, has fallen at his feet when they start working here. If he wasn't so damn good at his job, I'd think twice about keeping him on.

"We need a no fraternization policy amongst the staff. I can't keep hiring for this bloody job." Even though Trevor has been with his girlfriend for a number of years now, it doesn't stop anyone from asking him out.

Scrubbing my hands over my stubbled jaw, I know this day just got infinitely longer. Owning my own tattoo parlour, the responsibilities fall to me. I could pass them off to my brother, but sometimes his whining could do me in.

"Sean, relax. It's going to be fine. I've got a slow day if you need me to help out." I hate that word. Relax. Did anyone in the history of the world ever relax when someone told them to relax?

"I'm going to go get a jump on my day so you don't throttle me. Let me know if you need my help." Pierce leaves me be, whistling, just to irritate me further. Some days, I love working with my brother. Other days, like today, I could strangle him. I have enough on my plate to worry about other than to take walk-ins and calls about design work.

Thankfully, the rest of my day should be relatively easy. The piece I'm working on now should only take a few hours, and after that, my schedule is light.

Dropping the phone, I grab a new set of gloves and get back to work. "Sorry about that, mate."

"No worries. Can't imagine having to deal with people and their crap."

I just shake my head. "Tell me about it."

I love my job. I really do. I love seeing the pieces people dream up come to life. I started out like any other tattooist, doing butterflies and Chinese characters that people wished to mean hope and joy. But after graduating from uni with a degree in art and design, I started working my way up and opened my own shop. I love getting to mentor the people who are just starting out and nurture their talent. It makes me feel like a proud parent when their work is done.

It more than makes up for the annoyances I'll face in having to hire someone new. I was able to nab a prime piece of real estate on the high street here in Shoreditch. It usually equates to a lot of walk-ins for business, but also, a higher probability that I'll be able to fill Melanie's spot soon.

"Sorry about the last girl, mate." Trevor's voice is loud against the noise of the shop. "Hopefully we'll find someone soon."

"Maybe if you put a paper bag over your head while working, we might have a better time keeping someone around," I joke. Trevor and I have worked together since our apprenticeship, and we've become mates because of it.

"Or maybe I should tattoo my girlfriend's face on my arm." He cringes at the thought.

"You know the rules. No faces or names."

"Don't I know it." I did a cover-up for him a few months back on an old girlfriend's name. It's my shop rule —no names or faces of people that aren't permanent in your life. I could retire off the number of people who come back for cover-ups because they regret it later.

"Maybe just put a picture of you two up together to ward off the crazies."

"Yeah, I don't think that'll turn people off of you." The guy in the chair that he's working on pipes up with his two cents.

"Oy! Don't add to his already huge ego. He already has a hard enough time fitting it in the door."

"What can I say, Seany, people love a bad boy." As if to

prove his point, he flexes his arms. If he wasn't working on someone, I'd throw something at him.

"Feck off, and get back to work."

"Excuse me, hi. I was hoping to talk to someone about a new tattoo?" A quiet voice pulls my attention away from Trevor.

Pierce gives her his winningest smile, welcoming her in. "Sure, follow me."

THE NOISE of the pub is deafening. I couldn't handle a quiet night at home, so I dragged the boys out after work.

"You know it's a bad day when Seany is the one dragging us out." Pierce winks at me as he uses my childhood nickname.

"Feck off. It's been a bloody rotten few weeks, and now I have to deal with hiring someone new."

"Just hire Trevor's girlfriend. Then you won't have to worry about anyone hitting on him."

"Tough luck, mate. Ruby wouldn't leave her school for anything. Even for me." He glazes over at the mere mention of his girlfriend. What a sucker.

"Smart girl," Pierce quips.

"Look, I don't care who we hire, as long as we hire them quickly. Because we'll be rotating who takes the walk-ins now." Both of them groan before diving back into their pints.

"Quit your bloody whining." I shake my head as I go back into my own.

"You really need to get laid, bro." Not with this shit again.

"I don't need to get laid. I'm doing just fine," I say while flipping him off.

"I agree with Pierce. So you know it must be bad," Trevor agrees.

I brought the lads out tonight because I needed the distraction. I didn't want to be on the receiving end of their jabs.

"You think we could find him someone to take home?" Pierce's eyes are now roving around the bar.

"Fecking hell. There is no way I'm taking home some random woman tonight."

"Sheesh. We're just looking out for you. You really do need to lighten up."

"You two are buying the next round for all your talk." They both shrug their shoulders at me and go back to their perusal of the women at the bar.

While I know what they are saying is true, I don't want to worry about a girlfriend right now. After everything went south with the programme I wanted to start, I couldn't focus on anything but the shop.

And the shop is my life. It's what I've always wanted in my life. From tattooing myself, to my very first anchor tattoo that I inked on another person, I was hooked. So much so that I have that same tattoo on my bicep. It's a reminder of how far I've come, but also where I still want to go in life.

"As much fun as it is razzing you, Sean, I'd rather be home with my girl." Trevor has never been happier than when he is with Ruby. I can't fault him for wanting to be at home with her, rather than keeping us company.

"Piss off, mate." Pierce is oh so kind in his dismissal of him. Trevor flips him off as he drops a few pounds on the table.

"See you boys for Sunday lunch." They've become a

second family to us since we opened our own shop. It's what helps pass the days when I can only focus on keeping my shop above water.

"Of course we'll be there. We wouldn't want to get on Ruby's bad side." He claps me on the shoulder as he heads out of the pub.

"As much as you're content with your life over there, Sean, I'm going to go and find me a lady for the evening."

"Godspeed."

Chapter Three

ELLIE

I should've known better. Jamie said he would make my coming out tonight worth my while. We hadn't even gotten our drinks before he was distracted by a blonde, his "future queen" as he told me, and left me to my own devices. If only I had gone to Charlotte's beforehand, I wouldn't be sitting here by myself looking like a helpless little princess.

"Ooh, if it isn't the princess herself." I look up from where I'm sitting in the VIP section to see a tall, dark, and decidedly unhandsome man in front of me.

Looking around, I see my PPOs are stationed off to the side. Close enough in case there is a problem, but just far enough away to give me the illusion of freedom.

"Looking for your Prince Charming? He's right here." He waves his hands over himself before taking the seat right next to me. He smells of cheap cologne and bad vodka.

"I'll be sure to let you know if I find said Prince Charming." I slowly sip my drink, showing as little interest as possible. Usually, the whole princess thing is enough to scare any potential love interests off, but this man has a cocky air about him. He has no interest in me as a person. People like him only want to say they spent the night with the princess.

"Ouch. Right through the heart." His calculated gaze peruses my dark, form-fitting jeans and off-the-shoulder top. "Let me buy you a drink, then I can show you what a real Prince Charming I can be."

Who is this guy and where did he come from? I down the rest of my drink as the waiter brings over another. "Wow, they have great service here," he comments.

"It's been nice chatting with you, but I must ask you to leave now." It hasn't been nice chatting with him, and the longer he sits here, the more irritated I get.

"Oh, come off it. One drink, and if I can't show you a happily ever after, then I'll go."

A prince charming thinking he can show me a happily ever after? It's the most common pickup line I hear. And so dreadfully unoriginal.

"I'll pass." Looking around, I see Charlotte has finally arrived. Her timing couldn't be more impeccable.

"One more thing, Princess." I turn to look at him and he snaps a photo before I can even process what he's doing. As soon as the flash goes off, my PPOs are escorting him out of the VIP area as Charlotte squeezes her way in.

"Already getting into trouble, I see?" Charlotte asks, sitting next to me.

"Just someone who thought he was my Prince Charming."

Charlotte's face turns in disgust. "Ack, no thank you! Don't they know that is the most unoriginal thing we've ever heard?"

"Apparently every man thinks we'll fall at their feet at the mere mention of Prince Charming."

"I'd rather have a tattooed version of Jamie from Outlander." She wiggles her eyebrows at her latest obsession.

"You know, you could just call him up and have him at your disposal. A royal perk if you will."

"I like the way you think, Ellie." She looks around the club, as if trying to find someone. "Now, how did Jamie convince you to come out this evening?"

Being fifth in line to the throne, there is not as much pressure on her. Her schedule is lighter, and she handles the paparazzi with more grace than I do. Charlotte has always been a stunner. Curves she flaunts to the media, long dark hair that is expertly curled, and lips painted her signature dark red. She's a media darling.

I sip on my seltzer and vodka, the loud music in the club giving me a headache. "What can I say, Jamie made a good case tonight." My emotions are also on a trigger after a long day of events and comments about my appearance. "And it's been ages since I've seen you."

"We really don't see each other as often as we should. I'm pleased he managed to draw you out of the palace." Charlotte reaches over and squeezes my hand.

"Well, we're here tonight." Charlotte is one of my closest friends as she is one of the very few people who know what we go through. "Although, I will not be in charge of Jamie."

Jamie is a big fan of Club Mayfair and the attention of the women here. While I usually don't enjoy coming out, I needed it after my day. A lady can only brush off the comments of her appearance so often. Everyone tells me I should have a thicker skin, but it's hard. It's hard when everything you do is picked apart.

"No one should be in charge of James," Charlotte snickers over her own drink. He's currently dancing with a new woman. I can't keep track of the number of women he has had on his arm just tonight. It changes by the half hour. If I had a new man as often as he had a new woman, I would be labeled a slut by the paparazzi. Jamie is seen as the darling prince of the media who is only sowing his oats. The double standard is never-ending.

"Earth to Ellie. Are you even listening to me?" Charlotte pulls me out of my thoughts.

"Sorry, Lottie. Just been a long day for me." I sigh and gulp down the rest of my drink. Another appears before me. It's one perk of the VIP section—my hand is never devoid of a drink.

"The media is just terrible to you. You looked absolutely fab today, love." Switching my drinks, I give her a doubtful look.

"I thought so too. But apparently blue is not my colour."

"Well, I think you looked ravishing. If you don't want that dress anymore, I will gladly take it off your hands."

I give an unladylike snort into my drink. "And I'm sure you'll get rave reviews if you wear it. Might even find yourself a new man."

"I am not interested in finding another man. Not after Michael."

Charlotte's face still holds a sadness I wish I could wipe away. The press is awful to anyone we try to bring into our fold. Charlotte and Michael were together for two years before they broke up. Michael couldn't handle the scrutiny. Charlotte was devastated when their relationship ended. She thought he would be the one to finally stick.

Neither of us has ever had luck in the love department. As second in line to the throne, I know it will take a certain someone to fit into the fold. The few men I've dated were overgrown man boys and weren't worth my time. If only I could find someone who was worth it.

"Well, maybe you could have a little fun," I urge her. "Jamie can't be the only one out living his life."

"That's pretty rich coming from you." She gives me a knowing look. "When was the last time you did anything for yourself?"

"Maybe if my every move wasn't monitored, I would be able to. Thankfully my holiday is coming up, so maybe I'll be able to have some time for me."

Charlotte snorts into her drink. "A palace-approved holiday is the furthest thing from fun"

"I'll have you know I do love Kenya. It's always peaceful when I visit."

"Oh, please. You don't need to feed me that line. I know you'll be sucked into some sort of volunteer work while you're there."

I sigh, knowing it's true. There's no such thing as time off for a royal. "At least I won't have the media hounding me. That will be a nice break."

"A nice break would be a holiday from your life." It's a lovely idea, one that plants a small seed in my mind. Before I go wild with the idea, a sweaty Jamie plops down next to me, stealing what's left of my drink.

"And where is your flavour of the hour?" I give him a stern look.

"Lighten up, El. We're just having fun." As of late, I've been getting more and more irritated with my brother and his carefree attitude.

"Ah, yes. The playboy prince who can do no wrong."

"It's not my fault everyone loves me." Jamie flashes his most winning smile at me.

"Then maybe *you* should become king." Crossing my arms, I level him with a stare that is not to be messed with.

"Alright. I don't know why you have your knickers all twisted up about it. Power. Control. Women. It'll be bloody brilliant."

Of course he would think that of being second in line to the throne. Whereas I've spent my entire life learning from my granddad and mum, he's been allowed to do as he pleases. Go to the university of his choosing. Even do active military service in the Middle East.

"You are so not ready to be king, Jamie. You would fall flat on your arse!" Charlotte's voice carries over the noise of the club.

"But I would have a pretty woman at my side to help."

"Is that really all you think about?" Disgust is laced through my voice.

He gives me a dumbfounded look. "We're twenty-eight. What else would I be thinking about?"

"And on that note, I'm going to call it an evening."

"Come off it. You've barely been out with me in weeks. Don't you want to stay and hang out with your favourite brother?" Jamie gives me his best puppy dog eyes.

"So I can sit here and have a drink while you run off to find your next conquest?" Patting him on the cheek, I grab my purse and head over to Charlotte. "I'll see you later this week, Jamie. Charlotte, good luck with this one." I point behind my shoulder as I make my way through the noisy club. A few club-goers try to get my attention as I leave, but I make a quick getaway to the back exit.

My PPOs are ahead of me, ready to usher me out. "We've got a few paparazzi outside, Your Highness." Bloody hell. This was the reason I hated coming out. As the door is pushed open in front of me, I'm met with a wall of blinding light.

"Your Highness! Over here!"

"How are you responding to the reports about your recent weight gain?"

"Your Highness! Is it true you're seeing Tom Hiddleston?"

The door to the Range Rover is already open as I dive my way across the back seat. The slamming of the door cuts the noise to a dull roar in my head. The paparazzi are getting worse and worse as of late, commenting on the way I look, whom I'm dating, or any other scandal they deem worthy to drag me through the muck.

The worst is their comments on my appearance. No matter what good I do in the world, it will always be overshadowed by whether or not I've gained a stone in the last month. My head aches as all of their shouted words fight for control.

As the car starts to pull away, I shift back to Charlotte's earlier thoughts. I'm supposed to be going on holiday for a few weeks, but what if I changed my plans entirely? What if I decided to be...*not royal?*

I was born into this life, my entire future planned out for me before I even knew my name. I still remember my panic as a little girl when a camera was first thrust in my face.

I never wanted to be a princess. It sounds terrible to say when I don't have to worry about a thing in my life, but I'm not built to be a princess. The constant attention on me is too much to bear. And I'm not even first in line to the throne yet. It will only get worse as time goes on.

But what if I could escape life, just for a little while? Where there were no expectations placed on me? No diary of events demanding my attention day in and day out? Maybe this upcoming holiday to Kenya will help me find more balance in my life. Or it might just be the perfect chance for escape.

Chapter Four

ELLIE

"When you arrive in Kenya, you will have a luncheon with the British ambassador followed by dinner with the president. The following day we'll have a selection of volunteer opportunities from which you can choose."

Alice is reviewing my itinerary with me for my supposed holiday. Instead of a relaxing few weeks, I am now looking at a packed schedule.

"Alice, do I have any time to actually take a holiday?" My voice is curt.

"Yes, Your Highness. If you see on page five, you have three days at the end of the month there. There are a few locations we've preapproved for the remainder of your time in country."

Three days in what should have been a month-long holiday. Charlotte's words echo around my head. *I know you'll be sucked into some sort of volunteer work while you're there.* By giving me options, they think it'll soften the blow of not having a proper holiday. I was hoping for a few weeks at the beach with nothing but a sinfully steamy romance novel to read and some time to get a better perspective on royal life.

Other than a royal tour scheduled at the end of the year through Canada, this would be my only time away from the palace. The weight of my schedule settles heavy in my chest.

"Alice, can we please continue this tomorrow? I'm feeling dreadfully tired."

"But Your Highness, you leave the day after tomorrow. We must review everything."

"There will be plenty of time tomorrow then. Now, if you'll excuse me." I stand, not bothering to listen to her objections as I leave the office in my cottage and head to my private quarters.

The gaudiness of my own bedroom isn't a reprieve from my spiraling thoughts. Heavy, velvet curtains hang from the floor-to-ceiling windows that overlook the sunken gardens around the palace grounds.

Flowers are dancing in the light breeze of the early evening. The chaotic noise of London is softer in this part of the grounds. Trying to pull myself from my sour mood, I head into my bathroom to draw a bath. The lavender bath salts I drop in are a balm to my frayed nerves.

Stripping out of my clothes, my gaze is drawn to my reflection in the ornate mirror. The bright lights do nothing to soften the harsh thoughts as I appraise my own appearance. By normal standards, no one would pay the slightest attention to the way I look. But being in the royal spotlight, every curve, every dip, and every new pound gained is highlighted and dissected for public consumption. And I detest it with every fibre of my being.

I've always been curvier. Heaven forbid a lady have some curves. I have my grandmum to thank for that. No matter how well I eat or how much I exercise, my thighs will always touch and my stomach will never be flat.

Turning the water off, I step into the tub and let the hot water invade my senses. Goose pimples erupt over my skin, the cold air surrounding me a contrast to the warm heaven of the water. It reminds me of the ocean waters off the Kenyan coast where I was going to be spending my holiday.

There has to be another way to actually get a holiday. More than just three days spent surrounded by my Personal Protection Officers. I don't want to worry about the foreign press snapping an unflattering photo of me and it making world headlines. The one benefit to a royal holiday is that I'll have Alice and one other advisor with me. It wouldn't be hard to make a change of plans once I get to the country. It might take some convincing, but it's worth the fight.

I hate that I feel this way. I hate that I can't brush off the criticism of the press and put a happy face on for my country. But mostly, I hate that I can't step away from my life, for even a few weeks.

My thoughts are pulled away when there's a rustling of noise outside my door before Alice barges into my bathroom.

"Alice! What on earth are you doing in here? Please leave at once!" I try to cover myself as best I can, but others are standing just outside the door. There is no such thing as privacy when you're a princess.

"I'm sorry, Your Highness, but please get dressed and come outside to speak with me. It's imperative." She drops into a curtsy as she leaves the bathroom, closing the door behind her.

Bloody hell. I can only imagine what is going on right

now for her to interrupt me. I can't even go thirty minutes without something requiring my attention.

Stepping out of the warmth of my bath, I dry off and slip into my satin robe. Piling my hair on top of my head, I step into my bedroom. Alice, two of my advisors, and my PPOs are all wearing looks of horror. This can't be good.

"What's going on that has you all looking like the world is ending?" Apparently that was a poor choice of words, as all their faces drop.

"Your Highness. Do you recall going out with someone and not having them sign an NDA?" Alice's face is trying not to be accusatory, but it's written clear as day over her expression.

"You know I haven't been out with anyone for ages. What's the meaning of this?"

"We received word that there is going to be a story in the press tomorrow from a man detailing his night with the princess."

I rear back, as if I've been slapped. "That's ridiculous. You know I haven't seen anyone in months." Alice keeps track of these types of things better than anyone I know. It's embarrassing to have to worry about, but it comes with the territory.

"Well, apparently this man has intimate knowledge of a night you two spent together this past week."

I start to protest when Alice turns and shows me the photo Prince Charming snapped before he was shown out of the VIP section.

"I'm sorry, but how does this insinuate that we spent a night together?" Whereas before I was trying to calm down, I'm now boiling with anger. "How was this picture not deleted?" I turn to my officers, no doubt an accusatory look painted on my face.

"It must have been on the cloud, Your Highness. We apologize for the oversight."

"You apologize for the oversight," I huff. "Now on top of having to go on a 'non-holiday holiday'"—my tone is coming out laced with anger as I wave my fingers in air quotes—"we'll have to deal with fallout from someone lying about having an intimate relationship with me."

"This kind of stuff happens with Prince James all the time. It will all blow over," Alice says quietly.

"And do you know why it blows over, Alice?" My rage is exploding out of me. After the long week I've had, it's the final tipping point. "It blows over because he's a man and they think it's endearing that Prince James loves all the women of his kingdom. It will not, however, blow over for me because I'm a woman. And as such, I'm held to a higher standard. An impossible standard when you add in the crown!" I'm shouting now. Everyone has backed up a few paces from me, but I can't keep my voice down.

"Everyone leave! I'm sure you will handle this without me needing to be present, seeing as how I haven't spent more than a moment's time with this despicable man. Out! Now!" I rush to my door and hold it open until everyone vacates my room. Slamming it shut, I stalk over to my bed and throw myself on top of it.

With everything else piled on top of me, I now also have to deal with a potential sex scandal. I'm always careful how I present myself, and because of one careless mistake by my PPOs, my carefully constructed persona I present to the world could be shredded with one photo.

With that horrid thought in my head, my determination takes hold. Come hell or high water, I will be having a holiday. A true holiday where I have no appearances to make, and where no one will even know I'm a princess. And I can't bloody wait.

I CAN'T REMEMBER the last time that I was so happy to see the hustle and bustle of a busy London morning. By this time in the morning, I would usually be off to my first event of the day. But instead of leaving for my spring holiday, I made a break for it.

Charlotte planted the idea, and the events of the other night made my decision an easy one. A holiday is never a true holiday as a royal. I always have to be dressed just right in case the media happen to find where I'm staying.

But right now, not a soul has paid any attention to the girl with pink hair. I was able to convince my PPOs to take me to the corner market by the palace, where no one pays me any mind late at night, and get a few things I needed to make my escape with no one noticing. Not even the paparazzi noticed, which is a feat unto itself.

And so, during the morning switchover of guards surrounding the palace, I ran. I packed a bag, left a note, and made my escape. Wanting to get as far away from the palace as possible, I came to Shoreditch. It was on my mind from our canceled event earlier this week, and with my new pink hair, I blend in perfectly with the artsy neighbourhood.

This cute, corner coffee shop has been the perfect start to my morning. The sun breaks through the grey clouds for a brief moment, warming my pale, winter-weary skin.

"Another cuppa?" The waitress comes by and I give her a quick nod. She barely gives me a second glance as she's off to the next table. It feels like there is a flashing sign above my head shouting *Runaway Princess! Call the palace at once! Do not let her escape!* But a woman with pink hair and large, oversized sunglasses? No one would believe it's the princess escaping her royal duties.

Sitting here, in the noise of London's rush hour, is a freeing feeling. To not to have a single moment of my day planned. I could do anything I want. I could spend all day sitting here in the café. I could wander through the main road here and shop in any store I want. It truly feels like the world is at my fingertips. Or, at the very least, the best of London.

Thanking the waitress for the second cup of tea, I notice a small shop across the street. A flashing, neon tattoo sign hangs above the door, but it doesn't hide the large 'Help Wanted' advert in the window. Maybe this would be the perfect way to spend the next few weeks. After all, my holiday was supposed to last about a month. Maybe I could get a taste of the life I've always wanted.

Fishing out my wallet, thankful I had the foresight to bring the cash I had on hand, I drop a few pounds on the table and gather the courage to ask for what I want.

"SORRY, we're not open for another hour." A deep voice rings out over the tinkling of the bells as I enter the tattoo parlour. Old Edison bulbs gleam off black and white chequed floors. Large posters of art decorate the space over separate stations.

"I was hoping to inquire about the 'Help Wanted' sign." The man behind the voice comes out of a small office behind the desk. My heart squeezes in my chest as I stare into the deep, navy-blue eyes of the sexiest man I've ever laid eyes on.

A sleeve of tattoos decorates one arm, and the muscles

in his arms flex as he stares me down. Brown hair hangs over his eyes as his gaze moves over me, leaving zings of electricity in its wake.

"Do you have any experience with being a receptionist?" His face gives nothing away as he stares me down.

"Yes, I do. I am highly organized and can deal with all types of people." Not a lie. Even though Alice always manages my events, I can tell you what is on the diary for the next few weeks at any given point. And I've gotten very good at the princess smile. I can fake it with the best of them.

"Do you have your documents?"

Shite. This might be over before it even starts. "Look, I don't have them with me." Think, Ellie, think. "I left in quite a hurry and was only able to grab a few things. I could really use this job."

The mystery man in front of me scrubs a hand down his face as he takes me in. "Look, you have to have proper documents to work. I can't get around it. But if you need work for a few weeks, I can help you out until I find someone permanent." His gaze softens a bit.

"That's all I need." I reach forward, resting my hand on his arm. He jumps back, as if on fire. But I felt it. The spark that practically leapt between the two of us at the briefest of touches.

"Alright, welcome to Shoreditch Ink." He turns to go, but I stop him.

"Sorry, what's your name?"

"Sean. Sean Davies." He doesn't extend a hand, as if he's afraid I might burn him with a simple handshake. "And you are?"

Bollocks. I can't give him my real name. What if he puts two and two together? "Kat. It's Kat." Again, not a total lie. My middle name is Katherine after all.

"Alright, Kat. Let's get started."

"OKAY, so here is the reservation system. Bookings are over here, and inquiries are over here where you need to call them and get more information as to what they want." It's hard to focus with Sean leaning so close to me. His clean laundry smell invades my senses.

"Reservation system. Got it." It can't be that hard, can it?

"Are you paying attention?" He pulls back from where I'm sitting and crosses his arms. Thick, corded forearms flex under the tattoos inked along his skin on one arm. I have never felt so drawn to another person before. I thought earlier might have been an adrenaline high from absconding on my holiday. But it's not. It takes all my willpower to not reach out and trace the lines of his tattoos with my fingers.

Snapping fingers in front of my vision startle me out of my ogling. "If you can't pay attention, you can go." Sean's deep voice is annoyed. Not wanting to be let go, I turn back to the computer and show Sean exactly what he told me. I may be distracted, but I can still figure out a computer. It's one thing I've perfected over the years—drifting off while Alice goes over my diary in painful amounts of detail but still retaining everything she says.

"Fine. You were paying attention." His jaw ticks, as if it annoys him that I might be good at this job. "If you have any questions, let me know."

He stalks over towards his station, growling as he goes. My eyes are drawn to him as he walks away. The way the black T-shirt pulls taut over his back. The way his jeans hug his backside just right.

"See something you like?" I jump at the sound of a voice next to me. Sean's brother, Pierce, is grinning like a Cheshire cat. Sean begrudgingly introduced him to me earlier. My face heats at the thought of being caught staring at his brother.

Pierce looks nothing like his brother. Where Sean has lean muscles, Pierce is stocky. Pierce's dark brown hair has a slight wave to it, but Sean's light brown hair, whilst longer on top, makes me want to run my fingers through it.

"Just trying to get a lay of the land."

"I could always give you a better lay of the land, Pink." He gives me a wink as he leans over the reception stand. "Ever see Shoreditch in the evening?"

"Pierce, quit foolin' around and get back to work!" Sean barks from where he's bent over his table. Deep navy eyes cause fire to run through my veins. I couldn't look away from his heated gaze if I wanted to. I'm entranced.

"Looks like you've got him all riled up." He laughs to himself as he starts backing away. "If you need any assistance, Pink, just let me know."

"Much appreciated." The lie slips out easily. If I need anything, I know exactly which brother I'll be going to. And it's the one sending furious glances my way that light up my entire body. This holiday just got a whole lot more interesting.

Chapter Five

SEAN

Christ. I made the worst snap decision of my life. Hiring the first woman who walked into the shop was a mistake. Not because Kat won't be able to do the job.

No. She's a fucking pink-haired goddess hell-bent on destroying me. With one simple touch, I've felt more for this woman than I have with all my previous girlfriends combined.

I gave her a brief tour of the shop before showing her the reservations system. Any time I caught the sweet scent of her perfume, I'd have to think of tattooing old, burly men to not get hard.

I could feel her eyes on me all morning. Any time Trevor or Pierce went to talk to her, I was breathing fire. I wanted to go over and shove them out of the way. I'm acting like a child, wanting his favourite toy back.

"Earth to Sean. What's crawled up your arse today?" Trevor kicks my boots off the table in the back room. I came back here to give myself some space. Being between appointments, I needed to breathe Kat-free air.

"Long day. Started work on that back piece and it's going to take me longer than I thought." Pierce chooses that moment to walk in.

"What are we talking about?"

"Sean has a crush."

"Called that. Anyone can see you've got the hots for Pink." I hated that stupid nickname for her. Mainly because I hated him having a connection with her. I wanted that connection with her. No way in hell am I letting them in on that secret.

"Like hell I do." It's the most bald-faced lie ever.

Trevor pierces me with a withering stare. "Bullshit. You've been shooting us death glares all day."

"Remember my no fraternization policy?"

"Okay, keep telling yourself that, bro." Trevor and Pierce share a look.

"If you two chase her off, there will be hell to pay. Now, get your arses back to work."

"Yes, sir. We don't want to mess with the boss when he so obviously does *not* have a crush on the new girl." Trevor slaps me on the back as he leaves the back room.

Fecking hell. I know these two are going to make life miserable for me.

"YOUR NEXT APPOINTMENT is running a few minutes late." Kat's silky voice appears over the top of the dividers between our stations.

"Appreciate it." I try not to look up at her, but damn, if I'm not drawn to her. Her long, pink hair is draped over one shoulder, and the T-shirt she's wearing hugs her curves. Curves I want to feel under my hands as I thrust into her from behind.

Shite. I need to get a handle on these thoughts, otherwise I'm going to scare her away.

"So, what all is involved in the process of tattooing someone?" Her eager blue eyes are piercing as she bites down on her bottom lip.

"You really want to know?"

She nods her head in response. "Yes. I've never gotten a tattoo before, but I've always heard so many interesting stories behind them."

I hold my arm out in front of me as I study the ink on it. From wrist to shoulder, I'm deliberate in what I put on my body. Nothing that I would want removed in a few years' time, and always something that is meaningful.

"You always have to start off with a good design."

"Like this one?" Her fingers brush over the anchor of my bicep, and it takes everything in me not to flinch away from her touch. Heat travels through me straight to my groin at the smallest touch. My eyes are drawn to her fingers moving up and down the intricate patterns, and I never want to move from this spot.

"Yes. This was one of the very first tattoos I ever gave someone. I was an apprentice at the time and fucking loved the story behind it, so it was one of my first tattoos."

"Why don't you have any on your other arm?"

I flex my right arm, slightly showing off. I'm not above trying to impress this woman. The way Pierce is hanging around and calling her Pink is driving me crazy.

"Haven't found anything I like enough to put there yet."

Her lips curve into a small smile. "So, what do you do after you have a good design?"

"Then you create a pattern and size it to how you want

it on your body." I restrain myself from reaching out and touching her. "And after that, you make it permanent."

Her eyes are still focused on my arm as the chimes of the door sound, breaking her intense gaze. "Oh, sorry. Guess I better get back to it."

"If you have any more questions, just ask." Giving her a wink as she goes, I grin as her face turns the same shade as her hair. I shouldn't like how easy it is to be around her. Kat's the perfect distraction from the failure I faced with the art programme. She's only going to be here for a few weeks, and if I continue this flirting, it's going to make it even harder when she does leave.

Kat

AS THE LAST client leaves for the day, I lock the door behind him. Pierce and Trevor left a little while ago, and it's just me and Sean. I kept creeping over to watch him while he worked. I was fascinated by the way his arms flexed as he moved the tattoo gun easily over the skin he was working on. The designs he creates are beautiful. I can see the appeal in wanting to get a tattoo. I can only imagine having something he creates on me, his hands on my body as he works the ink into my skin.

"Are you heading home?" Sean asks, cutting off my wayward thoughts.

Right. A place to stay. I hadn't thought that far ahead. My main priority was leaving the palace without being caught, and I didn't think about where I'd be staying.

"Any chance you could direct me to a nearby hotel?"

Sean's brow furrows in confusion. "You don't have a place to stay?"

"It's okay. Just point me in the direction of where to go. I'll be fine."

He stares at me, his jaw grinding as if he's working me out. "Grab your bag and come with me." Spinning on his heel, he heads down the dark hallway towards the back of the shop. Not wanting to be left behind, I grab my bag that I stashed under the desk and hurry after him.

Next to the back door is a stairway that, it turns out, leads to a small flat. "It's not much, but you can stay here."

Trying not to make contact with Sean as he holds the door open, I take in the small space. There's a tiny kitchen to my right, a bathroom in the back, and a bed in front of the windows that can only look over the main street.

"Sean. This is too much." He's leaning against the doorframe. This entire flat could fit inside my bathroom at the palace, but I've never seen anything so wonderful.

"It's fine, Kat. Look, I don't want you wandering around the streets trying to find a place to stay." Sean is a virtual stranger, and yet I've never been shown such kindness.

I can't find the words, so standing on my tiptoes, I drop a kiss on his cheek. It's very unlike me. I'm usually much more composed as a princess, but Sean has been a true prince. My lips tingle from the contact. He hisses in response. Perhaps I'm not the only one feeling the connection between the two of us.

"Right. There are towels in the bathroom and the sheets are clean. We usually crash here after a long day, but it's been a while. You'll be safe here."

"Thank you, Sean. Truly."

He walks into the kitchen and pulls something out of the drawer. "If you need anything, here's my number." He scribbles it on a piece of paper. "And the key if you want to go out." He drops it on top of the note. He tips his head in my direction as he backs out of the room. "Have a good night, Kat."

"You too, Sean."

With the door softly closing behind him, I'm by myself for the first time. There are no advisors lurking in offices in a different part of the house. No PPOs standing guard around the building to ensure no one breaks in.

For the first time in my life, I'm well and truly alone.

Flopping onto the bed, the smile on my face is huge as it finally hits me that this is where I'll be staying the next few weeks. Instead of being on a plane to Kenya, I'm tucked away in a small room across the city. I'm doing exactly what I want to do for the first time in my life, with no one telling me I can't.

I can dance naked. I can sleep in. I can do whatever the hell I bloody please.

The buzzing in my bag pulls me out of the clouds. Seeing the familiar number, I know I have to answer.

"Hey, Jamie. What's going on?" My voice is chipper as I answer on the cheap mobile I bought at the store.

"What's going on?! Are you fucking kidding me right now? Christ, Ellie. Where the fuck are you?" Jamie's voice rings out loudly through the small studio. I have been expecting this call since I left a note for him with this number. I was rebelling, if you want to call it that, not trying to have the entire world on the lookout for me.

"Jamie, I'm fine. Really." Whenever someone asks how I am, it's always a lie. I'm fine, thanks. But for once, I am.

"You sound different. Have you been kidnapped by a cult? Alice is losing her bloody mind over here."

I can only imagine the reaction Alice had when I was supposed to be leaving for holiday and I wasn't there.

"Relax. Everything will be fine. I just needed a break."

"You were going on holiday. How is that not a break?" Jamie's voice is confused. This is the difference between being second in line for the throne and third in line. When I have children, they will inherit the throne, so James will never have to worry about appearances like I do.

"It was not a break and you know it!" I walk over to the windows overlooking the main street. Londoners are busy going about their night. Noise drifts down the street from the corner pub. Patrons are spilling out over the sidewalk with pints in their hands. What it must be like to go to a pub every night with friends without a care in the world.

"Jamie. Please. I need this." My voice cracks with desperation. I haven't even been gone twelve hours, but I already feel calmer. Settled. Like my body is finally at ease without the weight of the entire kingdom bearing down on me.

"You're lucky I can use my royal might to keep Alice at bay, sis."

I let out a deep breath I didn't realize I was holding. "You're the best brother, you know that?"

"I'm your only brother. I'm just trying to think of how I can use this to my advantage."

There's the brother I'm used to. "I'm rolling my eyes at you."

"Oh, come off it, Ellie. I always have your back. Now are you going to tell me where you are?" I can hear the curiosity in his voice. I know it will drive him mad by not telling him.

I look around the tiny studio, a smile brightening my face. "You wouldn't believe me if I told you."

Chapter Six

KAT

"Kat!" Sean's voice booms through the small shop. It's been a busy morning, with several walk-ins coming in. It's a rush, getting to talk to all these people when they come in wanting tattoos. Not a single person has recognized me. I love the feeling of being anonymous in my own city.

Sean's told me several times to move people through, but I love talking to them. They've opened up easily about the tattoos they've wanted and the stories behind them. I love it. And the more I talk to them, the more I want my own. I keep brainstorming ideas, but I don't know if I could ever do it.

"Where are the new supplies?"

"What supplies?"

Dark pools of anger turn to look at me. "The supplies I asked you to go pick up earlier for our afternoon appointments?"

Shuffling the papers around, I see the note I wrote down this morning. "Oh, Sean. I'm so sorry. We got slammed and I completely forgot."

"How the hell am I supposed to work without the specialty colours?"

I wince as his voice increases in volume. "Can you not use the ink you have here?"

"No. It was vegan ink. I don't keep it on hand, because I never have had the request. Bloody hell, I'm going to have to cancel. I doubt they'll be a return customer."

I jump out of my seat. "No! I'll go get it now. You can delay, right?"

"No, it's going to throw off the rest of the day. I thought you said you could do this job when I hired you." Sean shakes his head and stalks off.

A lead weight settles in my stomach. I can't believe I messed up so badly. If I hadn't spent the morning talking to everyone who came into the shop, I might've remembered. I should just quit now and go back to the palace.

"You alright, darling?" A tall, leggy brunette is standing before me. She's wearing a tight dress that displays tattoos on her arms and legs.

"Sorry." I focus on the woman, trying to push my screwup out of my head. "How can I help you?"

"Is Trevor around?"

"He ran out for lunch. Did you have an appointment with him?"

"Oh well. I was going to surprise him. I finished sooner than I thought today." She extends her hand to me. "Sorry, we haven't met. I'm Ruby, Trevor's girlfriend."

"Kat. I'm the new receptionist."

"Brilliant. So not one of the ones that have hit on Trev."

"Unless you want me to hit on him, I won't be." A growl from behind me causes me to spin in my chair. Sean is glaring at the two of us before going back to what he was working on.

"Don't mind Sean," Ruby whispered. "He's been a bit of a grump lately."

I turn my attention back to her. Sean has been nothing but a gentleman to me. "I only just started, but he's been wonderful to me." A knowing smile plays on Ruby's lips.

"Sean, can I take Kat here out for lunch?"

"Fine by me. Not like I'm busy right now."

I wince at the dig.

"Fab. Grab your bag and let's go."

Ruby is out the door before I have a chance to decline. "Sean. I can go pick up everything now. I'll call them and explain it was my fault."

Deep blue eyes hit me square in the chest. I hate that I'm having such a visceral reaction to this man. Anytime I'm anywhere near him, butterflies swarm my belly.

"Sure, fine."

His brisk reaction tells me it's anything but fine. I give him a small smile before heading outside to meet Ruby. I hate that I messed this up for him. But there's the small benefit that my mistake isn't plastered all over the morning headlines for the world to see.

"Kat. It is so lovely to meet you. Tell me all about yourself." Ruby links her arm with mine. I barely hit her shoulder with the thick, platformed shoes she's wearing.

"Not much to tell. Born and raised in London and looking for a change in my life, so figured why not start at a tattoo shop."

"And what do you think of our Sean?" I smile at the way she says *our Sean*.

"Not sure what you want to know. I've only known him a few days, but he's been quite nice to me. Especially for giving me the job." Even though I'm not very good at said job.

Ruby stops at a kebab cart on the corner of the street.

"The best kebabs in London," she states, ordering us each one. After we each get our lunch, I walk us in the direction of the tube. Even if I messed up Sean's appointment, I still want to get the supplies to show him I take this job seriously.

"Are you attracted to Sean?" Ruby breaks the silence as I bite into my kebab to delay my answer. Holy shite, this really is the best. Am I attracted to Sean? How could I not be? The instant spark when I met him was undeniable. But I have to fight this attraction. There is no possible way I can get involved with someone. I'm a princess. No matter what I'm leading myself to believe right now, the real world will come back up to meet me in no time.

"It doesn't matter," I say.

"Brilliant. That's all I need to know." That sly grin is back on her face.

"Why's that all you need to know?"

"Ruby! Kat! What are you doing over here?" Trevor jogs up to us from the opposite direction.

"I finished up early, so wanted to surprise you with lunch. But I met Kat here instead."

"And what do you think?" They exchange a glance that only years of trust and intimacy can establish.

"I think we should invite Kat to Sunday lunch."

"Hell, yes!" Trevor's voice echoes through the street.

"What about Sunday lunch?" My gaze darts between the two of them.

"You'll just have to come and find out."

THE REST of the week went by without issue, but I was treading lightly around Sean. There's nothing worse than getting on someone's bad side, and I didn't want to disappoint him. I wanted to prove to myself that I could do this. That I was more than just a pampered princess.

Trevor and Ruby host everyone for Sunday lunch since the shop is closed. Sundays are usually a light day for me, meaning only two events, followed by an evening off. We used to have family meals together growing up, but with our own royal duties, we stopped them altogether.

I find the small building where they live, and Ruby is opening the door before I have a chance to knock. Her outfit shines brighter than her personality. A cheetah print crop top accents her lime-green mini skirt. She's the most colourful person I've ever met. I look tame in my jeans and jumper by comparison.

"Kat, darling! I'm so happy you could make it." She pulls me in for a hug like we're old friends. We've chatted a few times this week, but it's hard not to be sucked into Ruby's bubble. "Come in, come in."

She sweeps me into their house. Bright purple paint is splashed across the walls. A set of stairs leads up to a bedroom that overlooks the living room. The kitchen in the back opens up to a backyard, a rarity in London. The laughter of three men filters in through the open door.

"This place is brilliant, Ruby."

"Perfect spot in Shoreditch. It's all we need."

Pierce comes through the door and sweeps me in for a hug. Pierce reminds me so much of Jamie. While Sean has an invisible weight holding him down, Pierce doesn't seem to have a care in the world. Maybe it's why I'm so drawn to Sean. I know what it's like to have the weight of expectations bearing down on you.

"Pink! I didn't think you would come. Want anything to drink?"

"A proper Sunday roast? I wouldn't turn that down for anything," I laugh.

"And here I thought I was finally getting a girlfriend." Ruby shakes her head in my direction as she hands me a cocktail. "Cheers to new friends." She gives me a wink as we all toast. "Now, Pierce. Head back outside with the men so we women can finish up in here."

I give her a look, but she shakes her head. Pierce just shrugs and walks back outside. Sean's laugh hits me and I feel it everywhere. Damn it, Ellie. You're not supposed to be feeling like this.

Trying to distract myself, I ask Ruby what I can help with.

"Oh, I didn't need help. Trevor does all of the cooking. I set the table, and that's already done. I just want to chat without the ears of those nosey Nellies outside listening in."

I snort over the drink in my hand. "You are quite the deceptive one, Ruby."

"And yet, none of the boys have figured it out." She shakes her head as she leads me over to their grey velvet couch. "How has your first week gone? Aside from the small mishap?"

My face still burns hot at the thought of messing up. It's been ingrained in me since I was a child that I should be someone the people can lean on. So whenever I make a mistake, it's hard to push past it.

"Uneventful. Which is what anyone would want, I guess."

"And Sean? Treating you well?" Her eyes glimmer with mischief.

"What's this all about?" I return her look with equal measure.

"I'm just calling it like I see it. There's something

between you two." I smile into my drink as I take a large gulp.

"How can you tell? We've hardly been around you."

"You have so much to learn. Those three men out there are the biggest gossips in London. Trevor came home last week raving about you. Said he's never seen Sean look at someone like he looks at you."

"That can't possibly be true."

She shakes her head at me. "And yet it is." The timer on the oven dings, and chaos descends upon the kitchen. Everyone comes inside, and plates are passed around as the roast, potatoes, pudding, and stuffing are all divvied up.

"We're eating outside, so go ahead." Ruby ushers us all outside as the delicious smells waft over me. Being the last out, the only remaining seat is next to Sean. Ruby and Trevor are grinning like fools at me. All part of their master plan.

Strands of colourful lights are hung across the top of their small garden, while a fountain trickles in the corner. It's the perfect oasis in the heart of London.

"Ever had a Sunday roast like this?" Sean's voice is quiet as he leans into me.

Sunday lunch at the palace usually consisted of four different types of meat, any type of pudding you could imagine, and every kind of potato you could make. But this? This is simple. And decadent. And bloody perfect.

"This would be a first." I cut off a large piece of meat and shovel it into my mouth. "Trevor, this is fecking incredible." I take another very unprincess-like bite. Sean laughs next to me as I savour the meal in front of me.

"You're welcome round any time, Kat." Trevor's leaning back, his arm thrown around Ruby.

"And I gladly accept." Shite, I don't know why I said

that. It's not a promise I can keep. I so desperately want to keep it, but my time here is fleeting.

"Sean also makes a crack roast if you want to try his." Ruby waggles her eyebrows in my direction. These two could not be more transparent. They are playing the role of matchmaker today. And if I wasn't a temporary person in their life, I would willingly give in.

"A man who can cook? I like the sound of that." I lean back in my chair, my arm resting against Sean's. I make no move to pull away. Heat radiates from the contact through my body.

"Breakfast is my specialty. I make a mean bangers and mash." Sean's deep blue eyes lock onto mine and don't move. Lust takes over my body, as need coils deep in my core. I'd love to have this man make me breakfast.

"I can't say anyone has ever made me bangers before." I swipe another bite of pudding, letting the fork linger on my lips. The blue of Sean's eyes disappears as they widen, focused solely on my mouth.

"I'll be sure to make it for you then, love." A swarm of butterflies takes up residence in my stomach when Sean's hand moves down to my thigh and gives it a squeeze. It's the smallest of touches, but I'm completely bewildered by this man. He leaves his hand where it is as he goes back to eating lunch.

My body is swirling with emotion and arousal. It's a bad idea to let these emotions run wild in me, but there's this connection with Sean. Every day I'm around him, it grows stronger. I'm distracted and unfocused when he's near.

"We're going to go inside and get dessert. C'mon, Pierce." Ruby taps him on the shoulder to follow them in.

"Why can't I stay out here?" Ruby rolls her eyes at him

as Trevor whispers in his ear. A huge grin spreads across his face.

"We'll be back." He winks at us, before following the other two inside.

"I doubt we'll be seeing those three anytime soon." Sean leans back in his chair, pushing his plate in front of him.

"They aren't exactly subtle." I take a sip of my drink, trying to look anywhere but at Sean.

"Kat." His voice is smooth like whisky. Goose pimples break out over my skin. My eyes are magnets to his. "You catch on quickly. No one has ever accused those three of being subtle."

"That's a nice way of saying they're a bunch of wankers. Who raised you to be such a proper gentleman?" My voice comes out on a laugh to break the tension.

"That would be my mum." He sips on his gin and tonic, the liquid sitting on his lips as his tongue darts out to lick it off. What I wouldn't give to be able to lean over and lick it off myself.

Shaking myself out of my thoughts, I go back to the conversation at hand. "Does your mum live in London?"

"They live outside of the city. Dad is a professor and travels a good portion of the year now, so Mum goes with him. They like being by themselves now. We see them enough, so can't complain. How 'bout you?"

His question catches me off guard. It seems no matter what I say, I would give them away. But it's my own insecurities. Sean has no idea who I am. There's no spark of recognition on his face.

"We see each other regularly. Sometimes more than I'd like."

He just gives me that playful smirk of his. "One of the perks of your parents not living close. You can still be close, without being physically close. Don't get me wrong, I love them. But sometimes Mum can be a little overbearing."

"As any good mum should be."

"I can only imagine your mum. Chasing after a little pink-haired toddler."

I throw my head back in laughter. "Do you really think I had pink hair as a little girl?"

"Fine. Purple?" His smile is playful, but no less sultry, as he pins me with a heated stare.

The spring day has nothing on the heat surrounding us. Sean's hand is still on my leg, drawing lazy circles. Each swipe of his thumb sends another jolt of desire through me. I could combust I'm so worked up. My mind is blank as I try to think of anything to break the heated moment between the two of us. I want this moment with Sean more than I've wanted anything in my life.

But our connected fates are temporary. It's written in the sand. Fleeting at best. Whatever this is, it won't last.

"You alright, love?" There's that nickname again. Sean's warm, calloused hand covers mine, and I instinctively turn my hand to hold his.

I give him my best princess smile. "I couldn't be better."

Chapter Seven

SEAN

I can't figure out Kat to save my life. And it's driving me up the bloody wall. That smile she gave me at Trevor's was fake. She's so tight-lipped on where she's from that I can't get a read on her. But everyone that comes into the shop immediately falls for her. She's a ray of fucking sunshine welcoming everyone into the shop. You can't help but be pulled under her spell.

Shaking off my wayward thoughts of Kat, I clean up my station for the night. It was an easy day. Steady, but not overly busy with walk-ins.

"So, how has everything been going?" Kat hasn't made a mistake since her first week here. I could see how much she hated doing it, and it made me feel like a wanker for making her feel bad about it.

"It's been great. I never thought I'd get to meet so many wonderful people."

I shake my head at her comment. "You watch too much TV. Not everyone who gets a tattoo is in a motorcycle club or gang."

A blush spreads across her pale skin, and it makes her even sexier. "That's not what I thought. I guess I thought they would be more gruff and surly. Not in biker gangs."

"Well, I'm glad they proved you wrong."

Kat's gaze lingers on me, as if she's studying me, trying to uncover something about me. "Want to have dinner with me? My treat for messing up last week."

"Kat. You don't need to buy me dinner. It was an honest mistake."

She's chewing on her bottom lip. I want to pull it out and suck on it myself.

"Fine. As a thank you for the job then."

She is not going to take no for an answer.

"Why are you so hell-bent on going to the pub tonight? It's just bad pub food and drunk arseholes watching the match." I give her a weary side-eye.

"Because I haven't had fish and chips in ages. I want greasy pub food and a pint." She clasps her hands under her chin, batting those big, blue eyes at me. I don't know what this thing going on between us is, but every time I'm around her, I want to stay in her world. Her sexy smile and unassuming laugh suck me in.

"Bloody hell. Let's go. But I'm buying." I point a finger at her as I go to close up the shop.

"As long as you're coming, I won't complain." She claps her hands in front of her as she turns off the harsh overhead lights. The old bulbs cast her in a heavenly glow. The way her hair is pulled up makes her look like an angel with a pink halo.

Fuck, if I don't get these feelings for her under control, I'm going to be sporting a semi all the way to dinner. And I don't want to scare her off.

"Ready?" she asks, a soft smile playing on her lips.

"Let's go." Kat walks down the back hall, and my eyes are drawn to the sway of her arse. Christ, it's a good one. And it's doing nothing to alleviate the pressure in my groin. There's going to be a permanent indent from my zipper on my dick if I'm not careful.

It's a cool spring night when we step out onto the main road. Being a weeknight, there aren't as many people out and about.

"I love London on nights like this." Kat's voice is quiet as she looks around the street. It's not busy. "It's almost quiet. Makes you feel like you're in a small town and not one of the world's biggest cities."

I study her as she speaks. There's that inkling again. The one I can't describe because she's keeping part of herself closed off from me. "I think you might be the only person that feels that way."

"So be it. Now, where's the best pub for fish and chips around here?"

"The Owl and Pussycat."

"Are you serious?" Kat asks on a laugh.

"Best pub around. You'll get your fish and chips, but they also have billiards if you care to try your hand."

"Well then, lead the way."

We make the short walk together, the setting sun lighting the sky on fire. Noise drifts out from the pub as lads are standing outside smoking with pints in their hands. We nudge past them into the crowded pub and thankfully find an empty booth in the corner. The table is still sticky from whoever was here last.

"What'll it be?" The waitress is abrupt as she appears at the end of the table.

"Two lagers and two fish and chips." She doesn't give us a second glance before she leaves the table. Not two minutes later, two pints are dropped off as she rushes off to the next table.

Kat's eyes are roving all around the pub. I've never seen someone so excited to be eating cheap food in a grubby bar.

"So is this living up to your pub dreams?" I clink my glass against hers. I watch her throat work as she takes a long drink. Fecking hell. I don't know how I got in so deep. Everything about her is mesmerizing, from the slope of her neck to the soft curve of her lips as she stares up at me. Her eyes give her away. Whether she's happy or upset, I know just by looking into her eyes.

"This is brilliant. Cheers." She taps her glass against mine again and finishes off half her beer in one swallow.

"Easy there, love. We've got all night."

"Sorry. Just happy to be out tonight."

"You haven't been staying at the flat every night, have you?"

She takes another longer gulp of her beer, as her cheeks flush. "And what if I have been?"

Foam lingers on her upper lip, and it takes everything I have not to lean over and lick it off.

"I figured you'd be out with Ruby every night. She really likes you."

"Ruby is wonderful. But I don't think she wants to be pulled away from Trevor."

I tap my finger to my temple. "Those two are connected at the hip. Bit disgusting, really."

Two baskets of fish and chips are set down in front of us. "Need anything else?"

"Few more beers, please," Kat responds before I can get a word in. She finishes off her drink before diving into the greasiest basket of food. I watch as it happens—Kat tears off a steaming bite, and regret is written across her face.

"Hot! Hot! Hot!" She reaches across the table and takes a swig of my beer.

"You alright there, love?" Covering her mouth with her hand, she gives me a shy look.

"Sorry. Just couldn't help myself. Even hot, that is delicious."

"Did you doubt me and think I would take you anywhere where they served crap?" I tuck into my own dinner with more care than Kat.

"I should know better." She winks at me. A wink I feel everywhere. Damn it. What the bloody hell is going on with me? I've never been so taken with a woman before. Kat's only temporary. She even told me as much when I gave her the position. I should be focusing on the shop and not getting distracted by Kat. But here I am, falling for her.

"YOU'RE QUITE PRETTY, you know that?" The hiccup tells me Kat has had one too many pints.

We didn't make it to billiards. Kat was sucking back beer like it was going to dry up tomorrow. As she takes another sip of her beer, I grab the glass from her hands.

"I think that's enough for you."

"Let's go take a boat ride!"

"I'm sorry, a boat ride?" I can't imagine what's gotten into her pretty little head.

"Yes. I've always wanted to sail around the Thames. It'd be a fab idea today." Her lazy eyes lock in on mine.

"Not tonight, Kat."

"You're no fun, Sean." She pouts those pretty lips at me.

"Sorry, love. But you'll thank me tomorrow when you don't feel like a train wreck." Calling the waitress over, I pay for our meal and pull Kat out of the booth. The sway of her body into mine is a dead giveaway on how many pints she had.

"Can I thank you with a kiss?"

This woman is going to be the death of me.

"You're drunk, Kat." Her arms wrap around my waist as I lead us through the crowd and out into the now cold night. She shivers against me. I pull her closer to me, trying to keep her warm. I love the feel of her tucked against me. No matter how much I keep trying to tell myself I shouldn't want her, she sucks me in.

"But you want to kiss me?" *More than I want my next breath.*

"I'm not going to kiss you tonight."

"Why don't you want to kiss me?" She stops and leans against the building, giving me her best pout.

"I'm not going to kiss you when you're bloody well pissed."

She turns her hazy, drunk eyes on me. "But you do want to kiss me?"

I lean into her, letting her feel my very obvious desire for her. Kat runs her hands through the scruff on my jaw, lighting up every cell in my body. Christ, this woman is going to kill me.

"Yes, Kat. But the first time I kiss you isn't going to be when you're drunk."

She's biting her bottom lip as she focuses in on me. I lean closer, cupping her face in my hands. It would be so easy to take what I want. "Because, Kat,"—I pull her lip out of the clutches of her teeth and a quiet gasp escapes her lips—"because when I kiss you, I want you to remember it. Because when I do kiss you, it will be the only kiss you'll ever want to remember. It will be the best kiss of your life."

"Cocky much?"

"Confident, not cocky."

Chapter Eight

KAT

Ugh. Between the pounding in my head and the sun streaming into the windows, I want to die.

Die of a wicked hangover and of embarrassment. I drank enough last night to feel terrible, but not enough to forget what I did. Or I should say, what I didn't do.

Why did I ask to kiss him? Pulling the pillow over my head, I curl back under the covers. It's safe under here. I don't have to go downstairs and face Sean if I stay here all day.

No such luck. The pounding in my head echoes on the door into the flat. "Go away."

"Kat. Open the door!" Ruby's voice carries through the small space. At least facing Ruby is less embarrassing than facing Sean.

Climbing out of bed, I notice I'm not in my own clothes. Not sure where I got them from, I open the door for Ruby and head right back over to bed.

"Looks like someone had a good night." She jumps onto the bed next to me, jostling my sensitive head.

"I wouldn't call it a good night."

Ruby looks around. "Well, no. Unless Sean ditched you this morning."

I sit up too fast and clutch my head. "He was the perfect gentleman. I threw myself at him like a cat in heat."

"Well, I do come bearing gifts." She hands over a cup of tea and pulls out pastries from the bag sitting between us.

"You are a queen." I want to take the words back as soon as I say them. I've been so careful, but I don't want anyone to guess who I am. No one would give a second glance to the girl with pink hair, but if you stopped and stared, one could put two and two together. "Wait, how'd you know I drank too much last night?"

"Sean may have called me to pop over on my way to school this morning."

"Why does he have to be so perfect?" I moan, breaking the croissant apart and shoving it in my mouth.

Ruby shakes her head at me. "Oh, he's so not perfect. He wouldn't do this for anyone else. Just you."

"Ruby! That makes it even worse. I can't face him today!" I shove my face into my hands, wearing embarrassment like a second skin.

"You can and you will. I only have so much time before school, and I'll go downstairs with you. It won't be weird unless you make it weird."

I give her the side-eye. "It's going to be weird. I called Sean pretty and pouted like a toddler when I didn't get my way."

"I'm sure he's seen worse with Pierce's women."

"And I'm not one of those women. I've never gotten so pissed in my life, and the first time was in front of Sean!" I throw myself back on the bed in a rather dramatic fashion. Being second in line to the throne, I'm always careful about how much I drink when I'm out. I never want to be overserved and cause the paparazzi to question if I have a drinking problem.

"I guess that means we need to have girls' night so you won't be so drunk next time." She says this like it's no big deal. But inside, my roiling stomach stills.

It's always been hard to make friends. Everyone always had an ulterior motive so I was wary. The few who stuck around long enough were like shooting stars. Bright for that time in my life, but then faded to the background because they hated the press.

But after meeting Ruby, I don't want to lose her. I have no idea what will happen, but she is one of the most genuine people I've met. She hides her tattoos when she goes to work, but her colourful personality still shines through with her bright wardrobe.

Whether it's the lingering effects of the alcohol from last night or this woman taking me under her wing, I pull her to me in a crushing hug.

"What's this all about?" She doesn't hesitate, wrapping her arms around me.

"It's always been hard for me to make girlfriends. So it's nice to actually have one."

"Kat, you are stuck with me. I am surrounded by too much male energy. Don't get me wrong, I love those boys, but a little feminine energy around would go a long way to bringing them down a peg or two."

I give her an extra squeeze before letting her go. "I guess I should get cleaned up and face the music."

"That's the spirit, love. Besides, if Sean didn't kick you out of here last night, I'm betting that's a good sign."

THE SHOP IS ALREADY BUSTLING with excitement when I get downstairs.

"It's still early. Why are there people here?"

"Oh, shite. You don't know. It's their flash day. Once every few months, they'll do set designs for people for a flat fee. In and out. Cheap and easy. All the guys do it for the day. Busy, but it's fun."

"Why didn't you start with that?" I slap her on the arm, heading over to the desk where there's a line of people.

"You wouldn't let me get a word in edgewise, love." She gives me a wink as she heads over to Trevor before leaving.

Summoning what courage I have, I walk over to where Sean is inking a tattoo onto someone's arm. It's beautiful, like everything he does.

"Morning, Kat. How you feeling?" Sean's smile only increases the tension in my body. It's coiling so tight that I could snap like a rubber band.

"Good. How can I help?"

"Just start taking names as they come in. We get to them in the order they arrive as soon as we're done."

"How long does this go on?" There's a line out the door.

"We take people until three, but we stay until everyone is done. So buckle up, love."

There isn't time to be embarrassed about how I acted last night. Sean is too busy tattooing as many people as are coming in the door.

"Hi there, ladies. Names and designs, please."

"Doll, that is some fab pink hair! How did you get it done?"

I pat my hair down, self-conscious of these two women

staring at me. I can't tell them I started out with brown hair and bleached it before adding the color, or they may figure out who I am. "I just got a box from the store. You really like it?"

"It's brilliant! You think I could pull this off?" She turns to her friend. "I don't care. I want to try it anyway. You look fab."

"Thank you." My smile is shy, as I've never had someone praise my appearance. It's a contrast to what I'm used to hearing. My wayward thoughts stray to the man who is now standing behind me. It's crazy after such a short time that I can feel his presence behind me without having to look.

"Pink looks good on her." Heat radiates from his palm at my waist. "Sorry, need this for the next appointment." He's looking over my shoulder at the waiting list. I can't focus on anything but his overwhelming presence. The clean scent that is all Sean threatens to overtake me. "Ladies, we'll be with you soon."

Sean gives me a gentle squeeze before going back to work. I sway into the warmth he left behind. I crave this man with a desire I've never felt. The closeness I felt to him last night was something I want to experience now. Without the blur of alcohol.

"Bloody hell, he is sex on a stick." My gaze swings from Sean's retreating form to the two women in front of me. "Are you screwing him?"

My mouth opens and closes. She grins and continues, "Sorry, that was rude. Sometimes I have no filter. But you're one lucky woman."

"Thanks. We'll be with you soon." There's not much I can say after that. I make my way through the line, my thoughts and gaze drifting to Sean as the guys work through the long list of customers. I've never seen such an operation before. I'm in awe of how the guys are working through the crowds today.

The shop has never been busier, and I love it. Finally having a moment to breathe as the line dwindles down, I catch bits and pieces of the conversations happening in line.

"Did you see the latest royal scandal?" My ears perk up at that. Latest royal scandal? What in the bloody hell is going on now?

Looking around, I ensure that no one is paying any attention to me. There's too much going on today. Sneaking away to a quiet spot, I pull up the news and I start fuming. I wouldn't be surprised if steam was coming out of my ears.

Prince James caught in a scandalous position with mystery woman. Might our playboy prince have finally found his princess?

A RED HEAD, not his usual type, is glued to Jamie, with her hand down his pants. If I were caught in this position, I would be set on fire by the press. But Jamie? It's only the prince looking for his princess. I keep scrolling, the headlines causing an anger I've never felt before to take over.

A night with Princess Eleanor! Get an exclusive with a man who has shared the Princess's bed. Is she really ready to lead our nation?

Royal Reckoning

YOU HAVE GOT to be fucking kidding me. Jamie finds his princess, and they are questioning if I am ready to lead the nation? I've only been learning to be queen my entire life.

"You hiding from me?" I jump out of my skin at Sean's sneaky presence behind me. Rage is making my brain fuzzy.

"Why would you say that?" I slide my phone in my back pocket, not wanting him to see what I was looking at.

"You've been twitchy all day. Are you stressing about last night?" Sean rests his hand just above my head, leaning over. He's all-consuming. I can barely think straight.

"I was earlier," I whisper, "but not anymore." No. Now, my embarrassment has been quickly replaced with anger. Anger at the press. Anger at my brother. Anger at being told to be the perfect princess at all times, yet still no one believes I can be queen.

"I want a tattoo," I blurt out. Sean pulls back, his face staying even.

"And what's bringing this on?" His hand drops lower, hovering by my face.

"Because I want one! Because we work in a tattoo parlour. Because I trust you." I shove Sean out of the way, pacing the small space at the back of the shop.

My skin is tight as I'm buzzing with energy. It's the final straw. Every single thing I've done in my life is in service to others. For the first time in my life, I'm living for me. And getting this reminder, while I'm here, is a slap in the face. To the press. To the crown. To my entire life that I am no longer happy with. To the fact that no matter what I do, I will never be held to an equal standard as my brother.

"Kat. You need to breathe." Sean stills me, his arms on my biceps. "You don't need to get a tattoo."

"But I want one!" I shout.

"I'll give her a tattoo if you won't." Pierce squeezes past Sean as he grabs more supplies.

Fire lights Sean's eyes. "Piss off, Pierce."

He smirks at Sean as he leaves us be. It helps to dissipate some of my anger.

"Do you even have a design in mind?"

"Wildflowers." It's the first thing that comes to mind, but I know it's right.

"And where would you put it?"

"What's with the twenty questions?" I flex my hands at my sides, trying to push past the surge of anger coursing through me.

His fingers brush a stray lock of hair behind my ear. It's a caring touch, one I lean into. "I don't want you to make a decision you regret. You can't just wipe it off."

"I won't regret it, Sean." I'm toying with the hem of his shirt, not able to look him in the eye. "It's you or no one else."

"Has anyone ever told you no before?"

The laughter in his voice pushes out the final flares of anger that have a hold over me.

"You'd be surprised." I pierce him with a stare he won't be able to refuse.

"I'm going to do this, aren't I?"

Yes, yes, he is.

Chapter Nine

SEAN

"Are you absolutely sure? These are permanent." I give her another stare. She's only been here a short time, and she made a snap decision. Being in the business, you get a sense of when people will regret their decisions. I'm not getting that from Kat, but I have to be sure.

"Positive." The gleam in her eye tells me not to ask again. Message received.

"Alright. Let me get it on transfer paper and we can get started." The design turned out even better than I imagined. Sometimes, it's so hard bringing a client's vision to life. Sometimes, things don't turn out exactly how they want. But when it does? I fucking love it when they see it and are blown away.

Kat's reaction when she saw her design? The smile lit up her entire face. It was practically glowing when she saw her idea come to life. It's why I love doing what I do.

It's eerily quiet in here tonight. We're doing it after hours. Coming back around to my station, the overhead lights are dim, lighting Kat up like an angel. She has the look. The look all people have before they get their first tattoo. The excitement and nerves battling it out in her eyes.

"Don't worry, love. It'll be great." She's chewing on that bottom lip. The one I've wanted to suck between my lips since she told me she wanted to kiss me the other night at the pub. Damn her and those kissable lips.

"I wouldn't want anyone else's hands on me for this." That simmering look in her eyes causes a stirring deep in my chest. I don't know what it is about Kat, but every time I'm near her, I have the same visceral reaction. Heat like nothing I've ever felt before courses through my veins whenever she is near. I know she feels the same way. Her throat clearing breaks me out of my thoughts.

"Right. You're going to need to lose the shirt, and I'll get this put on and you tell me what you think. Placement, size. If you want to change it, speak now or forever hold your peace."

"Clever. How often do you say that?" Her eyes are bright as she pulls the T-shirt over her head. I look away, even though I know my hands will be on her for the next few hours.

"Only to the pretty girls." She shakes her head at me as she drops her shirt on the chair next to my stand. "Now, come stand over here so I can get this on you."

The sweet floral scent of her perfume wafts over me as she stands between my legs. The gentle curve of her waist is soft beneath my fingers as I go about applying the stencil. Once I'm happy with where it is, I smooth it over her pale skin, peeling it back. It took me a few days to get the design just right, but Kat's reaction is why I love what I do.

She had tears in her eyes when she first saw it. Blues, pinks, and purples mixed together, creating a wildness that's hard to capture. It matches the woman I'm tattooing. This bright, whirlwind of a woman.

"Alright, go see how it looks." Walking over to the full-length mirror, she lifts her arm to see the final product. Her breath catches in her throat.

"Sean. It's amazing. Truly." Her delicate fingers trace the pattern over and over. The vines, the flowers, the leaves, everything. "It's better than I ever could have dreamed of." The awe in her voice has me wanting to puff out my chest and sing my own praises. But I don't. Instead, I call her back over to the chair and help her lie down at the right angle.

"Okay, just relax for a few minutes while I get everything sorted, then we'll get started."

She looks at me, a knowing look in her eyes. "You're really good at this."

"What?" I look up at her from where I'm getting my station ready. I love this part—making sure everything is perfect before I get started. The colours, the right needles. It's always been calming to me, especially with the chaos of the last few months of my programme tanking.

"Putting people at ease. I always thought tattoo artists were these big gruff people without a lot of feelings."

"Tell me how you really feel."

"Oh, shut it. I'm serious. It takes a certain kind of person to make people feel okay when getting a tattoo. I notice it every time someone comes in."

There's a twinge in my chest, and I like it. I like that she pays attention to how I treat my clients. I have worked hard to get where I am today. I try to play off how much it affects me that she notices. "Well, I don't want people crying and screaming in the shop. People might think it's a torture chamber."

The small laugh that escapes her further lights me up. Damn it, why is she affecting me so much?

Having set the last of my tools up, I buzz the gun a few times to find the right setting. "Ready?"

"As I'll ever be." She swings her arm over her head as I dip the gun into the coloured ink.

"If you want me to stop at any time, just say so. As long as you're comfortable, we can go as long as you like."

"I'm sure you'd like to prove how long you can go." Her smirk tells me she didn't miss the innuendo behind my comment.

Setting my hand on her side, I apply a decent amount of pressure to hold her down. The first pass of the gun can be jarring for some. I notice the small goose pimples that break out over her skin at my touch. I shouldn't like it as much as I do, but damn, do I ever.

Stepping on the pedal, I make my first pass as I start tracing the stalks of the flowers.

"Shite, is it going to hurt that much?" She tries to peek over her shoulder at me, but she's at too awkward of an angle on the table.

"Sorry, love, but probably more. It's not bad starting out but hurts more as we go."

"Damn. Alright, keep going." She squeezes her eyes closed as I start again. The sound of the gun is hypnotic. Every time I do this, I get lost in my thoughts. It makes it easier for me to forget it's Kat on the table. That my hands are gingerly moving up and down her side as I permanently alter her body. I can't wait to see the finished product on her side.

"So why is this one special, Kat?"

"What?" Her voice is pained as it squeaks out.

"Do you need a break?" I haven't done much, but for newbies, it can hurt.

"No. No, I'm okay. It feels like my skin is on fire, but

shite, no stopping." Her skin is turning a fiery red, but I won't tell her that.

"Okay, concentrate on me then. Tell me why this tattoo is special."

She blows out a breath, trying to calm her nerves as I keep moving the gun over her skin, wiping excess ink off as I go.

"It reminds me of my grandfather. He's a very important person in my life."

"How so?" The more I can keep her talking, the less she'll want to focus on the pain.

"He was always around when I was growing up. He has a house in Scotland where we would spend summer holidays, and I loved the wildflowers there. He'd take me on long walks after supper. Just me and him. It was our special time together. He calls me Wildflower."

"He sounds like a nice guy." It reminds me of my own granddad, even though I don't get to see him all that often.

"Everyone loves him. It will be quite hard to live up to his memory," she whispers, almost as if I'm not meant to hear.

I pull the gun back and stare at her face, scrunched up, as if this memory is causing her pain. "Why would you need to live up to his memory?"

"Don't you want to live up to your granddad's legacy? Or even your dad's?"

"My dad is a university professor. Quite renowned, if you will, in the world of physics," I laugh. I would never be able to live up to his reputation.

"How did he take you wanting to be a tattoo artist then? Did he want you to follow in his footsteps?"

"Christ, no. I would've been a terrible professor. I hated school growing up. I did enough to get by but went to school for art instead." I dip the gun into the green ink again and continue making progress on the base of the flowers.

"But he wasn't upset with you that you didn't like academia growing up?"

"Mum supported us in everything we do, still does, and he is crazy about her, so it wouldn't have mattered."

"Must be nice." Her voice is wistful. It's driving me mad that I can't figure Kat out. She's so quiet about her past and where she came from that I have no idea what to make of it.

"Do you not get a lot of choices?"

"My future was determined from the day I was born. It must be nice to have such a supportive mum."

"She's the best. She's American, you know."

"How ghastly!" She laughs. "How'd she end up across the pond?"

"Uni. She loved England so much she convinced my granddad to send her to school here. I think he was hoping it would cure her of her love of everything British. A week into school, she met my dad, and they've been together ever since."

"That's so sweet. You said they don't live in London, right?"

My plan of distracting her is working. The muscles under my hands feel more relaxed than they did when I started. It's always easier to tattoo someone who isn't tense with pain.

"They live out in the country now. My dad took a job at a smaller university but travels more and does speeches across the continent. Mum goes with him. They are blissfully happy."

"I wish I could be blissfully happy like that." She sighs, her curves moving under my hands. I linger longer than necessary when wiping the ink off, savouring how she feels under my fingers. Wondering what it would feel like to be on top of her. Shite, I shouldn't be having these thoughts right now. I need to be professional.

"And why aren't you blissfully happy, Kat?"

"I'm not exactly doing what I really want to in life."

"And why can't you make a change?"

I rest the gun on the table as she turns to face me.

"It's not that simple for me. I can't change what I want to do like some people."

"Could you learn to be happy? I mean, are you happy right now?" I hate the feeling that Kat isn't happy. It's rare when Kat doesn't have a smile on her face. She's never seemed unhappy here.

"I'm the happiest I've been in a long time, Sean."

I can't hide the grin that comes over me when she says this. "Well hopefully, wherever you land, you'll continue to be happy."

She's quiet now as I finish the last of the stems. This part is easy. The shading is going to take some time to go back and fill in after.

"Why don't you take a break, and I'll get the next batch of colours ready to go?"

"Can I take a peek?" she asks.

"If you want. It's going to be all red right now. I promise, the flowers won't look bloody when it's done."

She laughs at me as she walks over to the mirror, wincing only slightly. Her eyes widen as she sees the progress I've made.

"We're only a quarter of the way there?" Her voice is a little high.

"More or less. I still have shading to do once I fill in the colours."

Her face pales as she looks back at the mirror, taking in the work I've done.

"We don't have to finish in one session. Lots of people come back to finish."

"No!" she shouts, turning to face me. "I mean, no. It needs to be done tonight. I'll be okay. Just give me a few minutes to rest."

"Take all the time you need, love." I pat her knee as she sits down on the table. Her hair is a tangled mess from lying on it. She couldn't look sexier if she tried.

"Do you ever get tired while doing this?"

"I've got good stamina," I say, winking as I finish pouring the colours into the tiny caps on my tray.

"I'll be sure to leave that in my review then."

She lies back on the table, getting situated again. "Alright, let's get this over with."

"Just what every man wants to hear."

"YOU READY TO LOOK NOW?" I wipe the rest of the ink off and put more cream on her skin. Angry red blotches and dots of blood mar her now tattooed side.

"I've only been waiting for hours."

"It's been three hours. Some people have pieces that take over ten."

She sways slightly as she sits up. "You alright, love?" I ask.

Kat nods slowly, tilting her face up to look at me. "Just a little woozy, that's all."

"Let me give you a hand." Grabbing her elbow, I help her off the table and steer her towards the mirror to show her the finished product.

She's quiet. Her eyes move over the pattern as she takes it all in. "Sean. I…" she starts but can't finish. When her eyes meet mine in the mirror, they're glassy. Shit, does she not like it?

Before I know what's happening, her arms are around my neck and her lips are crashing against mine. It takes me point-two seconds to get my wits about me. Mindful of the likely screaming pain her side is in, I settle one hand low on her hip and slip the other into her hair, easily taking control. Christ, I've wanted to kiss this woman since she walked into my shop.

I slide my tongue along the seam of her lips, and she easily grants me entrance. Kat tastes like the cup of tea she had before we started, and it's intoxicating. The velvet of her tongue tangles with mine as she meets me stroke for stroke. The soft gasp that escapes tells me she can feel how hard I am for her. Tipping her head to the side, I trail kisses down her jaw to her ear.

The moan that escapes her has me shifting and pressing her against the mirror as I nibble down her neck. Shite, her skin is perfect. I want to bite and mark her as mine so no man will ever look at her.

Trying to be aware of her aching skin, I pull back ever so slightly, pressing my forehead to hers. Her eyes are half-closed, lips swollen from our heady kiss.

"So, I take it you like your tattoo then?" A smirk plays on my lips. Looking up at me, she stares into my eyes, a few pink hairs ghosting across her face.

"Sean, it is the most beautiful thing I've ever seen in my life. I can't believe it's on me. Forever now. A piece of you will always be with me."

Christ, now I'm ready to tattoo these bloody flowers on my skin so I can carry her with me. How the hell did I get in so deep with this woman, and what in the fecking hell am I going to do about it?

Chapter Ten

KAT

The pinch in my side pulls me awake. Getting out of the small bed, I head into the bathroom to look at the new tattoo on my side. The skin is an angry red. But underneath it is the most beautiful and intricate pattern. I can see why people love getting them. The flowers are a perfect match to the ones at the castle we would visit in the summer. It brings a smile to my face to have them here.

I loved those summers more than anything. There was no pressure to be the perfect princess or to look and act a certain way. Behind those castle walls, it was just family. Those days spent with Granddad there were some of my favourites. They were few and far between. And now, as a delayed act of teenage rebellion, I'll carry those memories with me in a more permanent way.

I trace the still tender skin, where Sean's hands inked me. My body was buzzing with need the entire time. I can still feel the pressure of his hand on my hip as the needle moved over my skin. I couldn't help my reaction. His lips were so soft and firm, I can't help but want more of them. I want to feel his lips and hands all over my body.

Stepping out of my pyjamas, I take a quick shower before I have to head downstairs, taking extra care with my new tattoo. Nerves are igniting my body as I think of seeing Sean this morning. Need is snaking down my spine in anticipation.

I wanted—no, needed—an escape from my life. The pressure to be perfect is too much. But with Sean? There is no pressure. I don't have to be the perfect princess. I can show my true self without having to worry if I'll be judged too harshly.

Not paying attention as I leave the flat, I run smack into a hard body at the end of the stairs.

"Mmm, morning, love." Sean's steadying hands grip my elbows so I don't fall backwards. A smile brightens his handsome face. It makes me weak in the knees.

"Good morning." There's a connection between us that we didn't have before last night. I had never given a second thought to getting a tattoo, even if the decision was made out of an angry reaction, but there's an intimacy involved in it. One that I feel wholeheartedly with Sean.

"How are you feeling this morning?" Sean tucks a loose strand of hair behind my ear. Even the casual touch sets me on fire.

"Happy." I return the smile.

"I'm glad to hear that, but I was asking about the tattoo. Any pain?"

My face burns with embarrassment. I can't be the only one feeling things after last night, can I? He was equally greedy in that kiss. Before my mind spins out of control, Sean gives me a lingering, chaste kiss. I lean into him as his lips leave mine.

"I should've led with that." Sean's eyes are alight with amusement. "But c'mon, I do want to see how your tattoo is doing." Taking me by the hand, he pulls me down the hall towards his office. I feel like a giddy schoolgirl with a crush.

Sean shuts the door behind me before taking a seat in his leather chair. Stepping between his legs, I sweep my pink hair to the side and lift my shirt. His warm hands hold me still on either side of the new artwork. The air crackles with electricity. A storm of emotion brews in my belly. I never want to forget the feel of his touch. It's more consuming than I've ever felt in my life. It should scare me how quickly this is happening, but the man who is holding me at his side is one of the most real people I've ever met.

"Why don't I put a little more cream on it for you? It's looking great." His thumb is rubbing slow circles just under my breast. Peering down at him, my eyes catch his and they are ablaze with heat. Dropping the side of my shirt, I push him back in the chair and straddle him.

"Can I get a proper good morning kiss first?" I'm loving this newfound courage that I seem to have found. Maybe it's the pink hair. Maybe it's that no one knows who I am. But Kat takes what she wants. And right now? I want Sean.

Sean answers by sealing his lips over mine, gentle at first, but then his tongue demands entrance. I feel powerful being over him, at feeling how turned on he is. His hands on my backside pull me closer into him. We barely fit on the chair, but there is no way I want to break this kiss.

The electricity sparks around us as we lose ourselves in each other. His hands in my hair, my hands running down his chest. His lips at my neck, nibbling along the sensitive flesh. My greedy moans give away just how much I want this kiss.

"Fuck, Kat. If we're not careful, I could take you right here. And that's not how I want to do things." His swollen lips and hooded eyes tell me how much he wants me. I know he felt the connection last night too.

"And how do you want to do things, Sean?" His hands move tenderly over me, like he wants to treat me with care.

"I want to take you out on a date tonight."

"I'll have to check my diary." A giggle slips out.

"Oh yeah?" He squeezes my backside, and I fight the groan as pleasure snakes through me.

"I might have another hot date tonight." I love the cheeky side that comes out when I'm with Sean.

"Need I remind you whose lap you're sitting on right now?" He squeezes me closer to him, and I hold him to my chest, resting my cheek on top of his head.

"A very handsome man."

I let the quiet wash over me for a moment. I never get to have moments like this with a man. It's usually a date at a restaurant and dodging the paparazzi. I have no idea what our date will consist of tonight, but I already know it will be the best one yet.

"Kat?" Sean's hot breath ghosts over me as my thoughts come back to where we are. I pull back, cupping his strong jaw in my hands. I don't know if I'll ever get my fix of this man.

"Tonight. But you have to pick me up after work. I need time to get ready."

"Love, I'll give you all the time you need." He gives me another kiss before moving me off of him. "Now, let me take care of your tattoo and then we've got a shop to run."

"SHOREDITCH INK. Kat speaking. How may I help you?" It's been a busy morning, but I love it. I've been sneaking peeks at Sean all morning. The other boys keep making kissing faces at us, but I couldn't care less.

"Hi, Kat. Is one of those precious Bond boys there?"

"Bond boys? I'm not sure who you want to speak with." The voice on the other end has a slight American accent, as if years of living in England has watered it down.

"Sean or Pierce? I was hoping to catch them before their dad and I leave for Amsterdam." Wheels start turning in my head as the voice on the other end of the line keeps talking.

"I'm sorry, but I'm new here. You're their mum? Sean and Pierce?"

"On the days they claim me. Are either of them around? They weren't picking up their phones."

"They're back in Sean's office. But back to this Bond boys business." My voice is dripping with excitement.

"Darling, you're British. You know who James Bond is."

"Absolutely I do. But why are they your Bond boys?"

"Oh, fuck." Sean's loud voice is behind me as I swivel to see him coming out of his office. "Kat, give me the phone."

"Oh, he sounds mad. Yes, dear. I named them both after James Bond actors. Growing up in America, I was in love with everything British and Bond. Who can help but swoon at those accents?"

"You are so right. Swoon-worthy indeed." The grin I'm giving Sean as he hovers over me is sparkling. "You have absolutely made my day. May I ask your name?"

"Jacquelyn. It's lovely to meet you, Kat."

I'm smirking at Sean and Pierce, not quite ready to hand the phone over. "It's lovely to meet you. Now, seeing as how I'm getting death glares from these Bond boys of yours, I'll hand the phone over."

Pierce grabs the phone from my hand as Sean hovers over me. Fisting his shirt, I pull him down closer. "James Bond, huh?"

He drops his head to my shoulder. "I really need to change the landline number."

"Oh no, you don't, Bond. I want your mum to ring here all the time." I can't keep the laughter out of my voice. "I love knowing that my sexy tattooist is named after the actor who portrayed one of the most iconic characters ever created."

"You don't have to be so excited." His lips at my ear send tingles rushing over my body.

"Oh, I am very excited. My very own James Bond. Will you take me somewhere tonight so we can have martinis?"

"Date is over before it even began." He pulls away and heads back over to his station.

"Hopefully it was good while it lasted, Bond."

He shakes his head. "Mum."

"See you at seven, Bond."

EVEN THOUGH IT was a busy afternoon at the shop, Sean let me leave early so I could pick up a few things for tonight. Not knowing what I would be doing while on my "holiday," I didn't pack date-appropriate clothing. Thankfully, I was able to pop into a local shop and find a simple dress.

Butterflies have taken up residence in my stomach as I apply the finishing touches on my hair and makeup. It's simple. I didn't want to overdo it. Finishing the braids in my hair, I twist them around my head and secure them in place. The black dress I found stands out against my pink hair. I've gotten so used to looking in the mirror and seeing pink. It's fun. It's bright. It's so far out of my comfort zone that I love it. I'll never get to have this again, so I'm enjoying it while I can.

A soft knock at the door quells all thoughts in my head. I've never been more excited for a first date before. And with Sean? The nerves are fighting for control. I want everything to be perfect. Taking a deep breath, I walk over to the door and open it. The sexiest man I've ever seen is awaiting me, in dark jeans hugging his thighs and a white shirt with the sleeves rolled up, exposing his tattoos. He's droolworthy. How did I get so lucky to find this man?

"Wow, Kat. Just wow." Grabbing my hand, he holds me at arm's length, his gaze lazily taking me in. I give him a quick spin, the skirt of my simple T-shirt dress floating around my legs.

"Stunning. Absolutely stunning."

"I can say the same about you." I drink in the man in front of me. The tattoos, the rolled sleeves…it all adds up to a man I am undoubtedly falling for. "So where are you taking me, Bond?"

Sean just shakes his head at me. "You think you're so funny, don't you?"

Wrapping my arms around his waist, I pull him closer to me, a grin plastered over my face. "I'm hilarious, and you love it."

"Whatever you say, Kat. Now, let's get going because otherwise, we won't make it out tonight."

SEAN

Christ. I've never seen such a beautiful woman in my entire life. I wasn't prepared for Kat when she opened the door, standing there in that dress.

Legs for days.

Curves I want to feel under my hands.

Hair in an elaborate updo.

And those lips. I can't wait to taste them again.

"You're staring." Kat's voice breaks me out of my obvious perusal.

"It's hard not to when you're so damn sexy." A blush creeps up her neck at my words as she pushes me out the door.

There is a low hum of activity on the street as we head out the back door. It's a rare, perfect spring night in London. Just what I wanted for tonight.

"So, where are you taking me?" Kat asks again, lacing her fingers through mine. It's an instant shock to the system. I felt it the day she walked into my shop and it's only gotten stronger.

"You are not one for surprises, are you?" I look down at her. Her light blue eyes are happy as they gaze up at me.

"Let's just say my life is usually very well planned. I know where I'll be every day for months on end. So it's hard not to know."

I give her a curious stare. She is tight-lipped, revealing very little to me. "Maybe it'll do you some good, love, to not know."

"As long as you're my guide this evening, I'll be very happy." She rests her head on my shoulder as we quietly wander in the direction I've planned for us this evening. It's a comfortable silence as we enjoy the street art on our walk. I always want to fill the silence, but with Kat, it's different. I can feel her head moving as she takes in the street art that surrounds us.

"Is this why you decided to open a shop in Shoreditch?" Her eyes are trained on the intricate roses painted on the front of a building ahead of us. They are on fire in the evening sun.

"Because of all the art?"

She nods her head. "Maybe you could paint these roses on me next." She drops my hand and moves to the building, tracing the outline of the flowers on the wall.

"Why don't you let the first one heal and then we'll talk seconds." Let's be honest, there's no way I would deny this woman anything. She's taken a firm hold of me and hasn't let go.

"I think I'm healing quite nicely. Maybe in a few weeks, I can have something on my other side."

"Whatever you want, love." I wrap my arms around her waist and turn her to me. She looks like an angel in the sunlight. I catch her lips with mine. They move gently beneath mine, as we stand in the spotlight of the sun on a crowded London street.

We stay like this, wrapped up in each other for who knows how long. It isn't until someone bumps into me from behind that we pull away from each other. Kat's eyes are closed as she holds on to me, her lips swollen from our kiss.

"I think we should head to dinner." Brushing my knuckles over her cheek, I drop a kiss to her forehead before we continue down the pavement. Kat's hands wrap around my arm as we walk. Her fingers move up and down my exposed forearm.

"You know, I might have a few ideas for this arm." Her voice is filled with amusement as she continues tracing the veins on my forearm. Her touch lights me up from the inside out. I can't get enough of it.

"Oh yeah?"

She nods her head gently against me. "Maybe you could have a pink-haired woman on your arm."

I bark out a laugh. "Sorry, love. You know the rules."

"I know. No faces or names."

"You're a fast learner. Here we are." I swing her attention to the old brick building in front of us. She stops and gives me a skeptical look.

"A pub? Really?"

"Don't give me that look." Her hands are on her hips as she pierces me with her most withering stare. "It's not just a pub. C'mon. You'll love it."

She shakes her head at me as I take her hand in mine, leading her inside the old building. There's restaurants and event space all around us, but the real highlight is out back.

"Wow. This is incredible." Kat's voice is full of awe as I push open the old metal door. The large outdoor space has picnic tables set up all around. Food trucks and bars line the space. Strands of old lights cross the patio, glittering back at me in Kat's wide eyes. She looks fecking gorgeous.

"Told you it's not just a pub." Wrapping my hands around her waist, I guide her in front of me towards the food area. Asian, Caribbean, burgers. You name it, this place has it.

"What'll it be, love?" I whisper in her ear.

She turns back to look up at me, her face bright with excitement. "How about a little of everything?"

"Coming right up."

"THIS MIGHT BE some of the most delicious food I've ever had." Tucked into a quiet corner in the back, Kat's leaning against me ever so slightly. Empty trays of food are scattered in front of us.

"Truman's is one of my favourites." I take a long drink of my beer, setting it down and facing Kat. "It always changes, so you never know what you're going to get."

"Maybe you'll have to bring me back then to see what else they have."

"Pretty cocky there thinking this is going well, love." I love that she's already thinking about a second date. I'm thinking well beyond that.

"I didn't scare you off that first night at the pub." Her cheeks redden at the memory. "And I'm pretty sure I'm going to get a goodnight kiss tonight. So yes, I'm planning ahead."

"Plan away."

Soft, slow music starts to drift around us, and Kat's face lights up. I look around and see that couples are starting to make their way to a makeshift dance floor. I don't even need her to ask to know what she wants.

"Dance with me." She's biting down on her bottom lip in anticipation of my answer. I'm not sure there's anything I could deny her. It should scare me, the intensity of my feelings for her, but it doesn't.

Standing, I drop my hand to pull her up from the table. Her eyes beam with happiness as we walk over to the dance floor. Couples are moving quietly around us as I take Kat in my arms.

The air is thick with heat as I gently move us to the rhythm. I don't recognize the song, but it doesn't matter. The feel of Kat's curves under my hands, her arms wrapped around me as she hums along to the song, is indescribable. I'm trying to stay cool, but my heart could beat out of my chest right now. There's no keeping it cool with Kat.

Running my hands up her back, I cup her head in my hands and turn her to look at me. Pools of blue are swimming with emotion as I take her lips with mine.

It's the most sensual kiss of my life. I don't care that we're surrounded by people. I lick the seam of her lips, and she immediately opens to me. Her hands are bruising on my back as I deepen the kiss. I swallow the moans as I pull her closer to me.

I can't get enough of this woman. She came storming into my shop, and now it's hard to imagine my life without this pink-haired goddess. Christ, I'm well and truly fucked, aren't I?

Chapter Eleven

KAT

For a Friday night, it's slow. There's usually more walk-ins at this time, or so I'm told. Trevor has been working on someone for the last hour or so, but other than that, it's been quiet. Pierce and Sean disappeared into his office a little bit ago, leaving me out here on my own.

I try distracting myself by reading my book, but my brain keeps going back to Sean and our date last night. It was like nothing I'd ever experienced in my life. It was simple, but perfect. Instead of trying to impress me with the latest Michelin-starred restaurant, Sean had known exactly what I needed. He took me to a local spot he knew I would like. And that soul-searching kiss at the end? It kept me up most of the night. My face gets hot still thinking about it.

"Oy! Princess, are you listening to me?" Fingers snapping in front of my face cause a panic to spread through me. A larger man is standing in front of the desk with two friends behind him. His glassy eyes and pungent smell mean he must have staggered in from the pub down the street.

"I'm sorry. May I help you?" I try to keep my voice even. There's no way this man knows who I am, but it's rattled me. Whatever this thing Sean and I have, it's new. Too fresh for a secret of this size to come to light right now.

"Yeah, I want a tattoo." Years of training to deal with the press keeps my face unchanged at this mess of a man in front of me. My eyes shift to Trevor, who is now watching the exchange closely.

"Do you have something in mind?" There is no way anyone will give this man a tattoo tonight. He's bloody pissed from one too many at the pub.

His eyes move over my chest in a lecherous way. "Maybe I can get you to give me this tattoo."

"Well, that's impossible. That's not something I do."

"That's a shame. I'd pay good money to have your hands on me." He licks his lips, as if that would entice me. I'm done with this creep of a man. His friends are snickering behind him. Men…if you can even call these boys that.

"Sorry, but no one is going to be tattooing you tonight. Come back tomorrow when you're sober."

"That's no way to treat a paying customer, princess."

"Seeing as how you're not a paying customer, I can treat you any way I want. Now you need to leave. Right now." He staggers back slightly, as if he can't believe he's being told off by a woman. Trevor is now standing, his arms crossed in a menacing manner.

His eyes drift behind me as he asks, "Are you going to let her treat me like this?"

"Damn straight. Now get the hell out of my shop and don't come back." Sean's voice as he steps out of his office is deep and growly. Turning to face him, I'm shocked I don't see smoke coming out of his ears. The jingle of the bell tells me the three idiots have left.

"My office." Sean turns and stalks off. Trevor whistles as I go to follow.

"Damn. I don't think I've ever seen him so pissed." I give him a quick look before following after Sean.

I don't know what that man was hoping to get out of here tonight, but clearly that wasn't what he wanted.

I'm not the meek little princess anymore. No, I'm standing up for myself like I've always wanted to. And that makes me feel like a badass.

Sean is on me before I even close the door. His hands fist in my hair and his lips crash down on mine. His tongue demands entry into my mouth, and I grant him access.

This kiss is hot. It's possessive. It's everything a kiss should be. Fisting my hands in his shirt, I pull him into my chest, feeling his hard muscles under my hand. And, oh God, I can feel his erection digging into me.

"Sean." My voice is lust-filled as he kisses down my neck.

"Kat. That was the fecking hottest thing I've ever witnessed in my life."

Sean nibbles on my bottom lip, tugging it between his teeth. I've never been more turned on in my life.

"What, me putting him in his place?" My hips move on their own, seeking out the heat from the growing bulge in his pants.

"Yes. I heard them come in, but clearly you don't need anyone's help taking care of things."

The confidence he has in me surges through my veins. It feels good to not be the compliant little princess. I'm not doing exactly what is told of me. No. I'm standing up for myself and telling people off. And it feels fucking amazing.

Pushing up on my tiptoes, I seek out Sean's mouth. My hand moves to his backside, squeezing him closer to me.

"We need to take this upstairs, love. I don't want our first time to be on my desk."

"Mmm, maybe we can save the desk for next time," I whisper in his ear.

"I like the way you think. Now, upstairs." He spins me around to face the door, slapping my backside as we go to the flat.

The moment the door closes behind me, my earlier confidence starts to fade. Every rude whisper and snarky comment about my body battles for dominance in my head. I want to stay in the moment with Sean, but it's hard when I'm battling my own inner turmoil.

Sean pins me against the door as he flicks the light switch on. His lips never leave my neck.

I flick the light switch off before Sean turns it back on. "Off," I whisper against his lips. He pulls back, his face drawn in confusion.

"I want to see you. I want to see your face when you come. When you're turned on to the point you might explode."

My skin feels tight as I walk over to the window. It's embarrassing to have to tell someone you want to sleep with that you hate how you look. Everyone always says to have a thick skin, but when the media rips apart your appearance every chance they get, it's hard.

"What's wrong, love?" That heat from his body is a welcome distraction behind me.

"I just..." I sigh, turning to face him. I know my own cheeks are probably red with embarrassment. "It's just...I don't want you to see me, you know, naked."

He rears back, as if I slapped him. "You know that's hard to do when you're having sex, right?"

Fisting my hands in his shirt, I keep him at a distance. "When your appearance is judged, and judged harshly, it starts to seep in that you are not worthy based on how you look." My voice is quiet as I stare at my hands. His fingers tilt my chin up to meet his gaze. Anger and lust swirl in the depths of his icy blue eyes.

"Who is telling you this?"

I shrug. "People."

"These people are arseholes. Shitheads. You are the sexiest woman I have ever laid eyes on, and I can't wait to feel these curves without clothes in the way." As if to prove his point, his hands slide around my back, dipping under my shirt. "I'll let you have no lights tonight. But I am going to devour you. I am going to kiss every inch of your skin and tell you why I love it. And when we're done, you'll have no doubts as to who is the sexiest woman in the universe."

His lips crash down on mine and I can only hold on for dear life. As his hands move around to my backside to lift me up, I don't think about how everyone says it's oversized peaches. All I can think about is how good his tongue feels against mine. About how good him squeezing said backside feels. And, oh God, how good his erection feels against my core.

Sean sets me down on the bed in front of him, the glow of the streetlamps making him look devastatingly handsome. I grab the hem of his shirt and pull him down over me, while tugging the shirt over his head. The ink on his skin dances in front of me. I've never been with anyone before who has tattoos. But the contrast of colours against his skin is sinfully sexy. For once, I don't have to hide my perusal of his body. My fingers lightly trace the patterns that are intricately decorating his chest.

Sean grabs my fingers and brings them to his lips. "If

you keep doing that, love, this is going to be over real fast. Embarrassingly fast." I can't hide the smile that brightens my face as I lay back on the bed. Heat and nerves fight for control over my body, as Sean's gaze travels from head to toe.

"Get out of your head, Kat." His hot breath ghosts over my lips as he kisses his way down my jaw to my ear. His heavy weight settles over me, keeping me in the moment.

"Want to know what I like about your neck?"

"What?" My voice is full of lust as it escapes in a long breath.

"I like how you stretch it when you've had a long day. All this exposed flesh just begging for my teeth." He nibbles his way down my neck, licking the sting away as he goes. Heat coils tight in my core as Sean's hands push my shirt farther and farther up.

"Tell me more."

Sean's face is directly over mine as he tugs my shirt up and over my head.

"I like the sound of your voice." His lips are back on my neck. "I like how breathy it is. I like how happy it is when you're at the shop." His lips are at the top of my breasts. I suck in a deep breath as he pulls one of the cups down, exposing a taut nipple, ripe for the taking.

"I like that I cause this reaction in you." Sean's mouth covers my nipple, taking it between his teeth and giving it a hearty pull.

"Oh my God!" My back arches off the bed, wanting to be closer to Sean.

"Do you even know how bloody gorgeous you look in those shirts you wear?" Sean kisses his way to my other breast, giving it the same treatment. "These tits. Fuck, I've wanted to have my hands on them every day." Sean sits up, taking my full breasts into his hands, rubbing his thumbs over my nipples.

Reaching behind me, I unsnap my bra and fling it off. Sean's hands move farther down my stomach, resting on my waist. Biting down on my lip, I close my eyes. I'm not ready to hear his reaction to my fuller sides. Or not hear any reaction at all.

"Eyes on me, Kat." My eyes open to see his are on mine. They are full of lust and passion. I couldn't look away if I tried.

"Sean, I—" He cuts me off with a searing kiss, his tongue tangling with mine. He pulls back ever so slightly and my lips chase his.

"No. These curves. You're one of the sexiest women I've ever seen. Do you know what I felt when I had them under my hands when I was inking you?"

I shake my head in response.

"I thought I was the luckiest bastard in the world to get to see you so vulnerable. To hear your story of why this tattoo means something to you." His fingers trace the still sensitive flowers on my side. "I love what I do, but getting to do it for you was a privilege."

My heart starts to flutter. Sean's hands move over my curves with a reverence I've never felt. Those lips I love so much move over my curves, curves that normally cause me so much pain. But right now? I feel like a sex goddess pulling my man in with my siren song.

My core is aching for relief. Sean's hands deftly undo the button and zipper of my jeans and he slowly works them over my hips and thighs. "And fuck...these thighs, Kat. I can't wait to have them wrapped around my head as I make you come all over my tongue."

"Yes! Sean, I need your mouth on me now." My voice comes out on a moan, as I'm now laid out in just my thong before him. His hands are rubbing up and down my legs, like he can't get enough of my curves.

"I haven't had my fill of you yet. Of just how beautiful you are." Goose pimples break out all over my skin as his warm hands move up and down my legs. The bulge in his jeans shows just how much I affect him. And I love it.

This time, when his hands skate over my legs, they continue to the apex of my thighs. His thumbs brush ever so lightly over my dripping core as he slides my thong down my legs and off. It's an explosion of heat and fire as I try to quell the storm of emotions racing through me. Sean's lips come down on my hip bone, gently tugging the skin between his teeth.

"I'm going to mark every inch of your skin as my own. You're mine, Kat." God, it's sexy to have him want to brand me like this. Coming from anyone else, it would grate on me. But from Sean? It makes me feel treasured. Worshipped.

I push that errant thought out of my head. It's too early to be feeling these emotions. But when Sean's lips finally land where I want them, every thought is pushed from my mind. His tongue is pure magic as it traces up and down my slit.

"You're so ready for me, Kat."

"Uh-huh." My fingers thread through his hair as I clutch him to me. I don't want his mouth to move from my pussy. As he slides one finger into my heated channel, his lips suck down on my clit, and he teases it with his tongue.

"Sean! Oh, yes! Right there!" My legs close tighter around his head as he drives me closer and closer to orgasm. Sean adds a second finger as he starts pumping faster and faster. The orgasm barrels through me as I come on a shout. Technicolour stars burst behind my eyes as I ride Sean's face through an earth-shattering orgasm. Pleasure courses through my entire body, from the top of my head to the tips of my toes.

Sean's hands on my legs bring me out of my post-orgasm bliss. His lips are wet with my release as I pull him up to me. Capturing his lips with mine, I moan in delight as I taste myself on him. Distracting him with a soul-searing kiss, I flip us over so I'm on top of him.

"It's my turn to worship your body."

"Mmm, worship away, love." I kiss my way down his body, mirroring the attention he was giving to me only moments ago. But when I come to the tattoos on his chest, I lick the intricate patterns. I smile against his skin as I feel his hard cock beneath me. "Christ, Kat. That feels amazing."

My fingers and lips move lower as the ink disappears into the waistband of his jeans. Making quick work of his belt, I lower his jeans, leaving him in just his boxer briefs. Sean kicks his jeans to the side as I take his cock out. It's the perfect size. Giving it a few pumps, I move my lips over the head, swiping the bead of precum from the slit. Sean's hips move on their own, thrusting into my mouth. I moan and hum as I start pulling him deeper. I savor the taste of him as I move over the velvet iron of his cock.

"Kat. I need to be inside you. Now." His voice is growly as he pulls me up and over him. "Rubbers are in the pocket of my jeans."

"Really?"

"Figured I'd stock up. Just in case."

"Such an optimist." I drop a chaste kiss on his lips as I lean over to grab a rubber while he pulls the boxer briefs the rest of the way off. Ripping it open, I deftly roll it down his erection. He tries to pull me back under him, but I push him down. Any lingering doubts about my body were blasted out with the orgasm to end all orgasms.

With each pass of his tongue and lips over mine, he tore down my walls. I don't want to hide my body. Not from him. I want to put it on display where he can worship it. Settling over him, I line myself up and sink down onto him.

"Fuck." Sean's voice slips out on a hiss as I still over him. My nails drag down his chest as I adjust to his size filling me. Sean's calloused hands rub up and down my thighs. A slight squeeze brings my gaze down to his.

Locking eyes with him, I start to move. Every roll and grind amps my pleasure to new heights. Heights that I am already looking back on after my previous orgasm. Sean's hands move higher, brushing over my clit as heat swirls between the two of us.

I've never felt so powerful and in control as I do now. Heat and desire are etched on his face as he leans up to take a nipple in his mouth. The long locks of my hair caress my backside as my head is thrown back in pleasure.

"I'm going to come again. Oh my God!" I shout as I tumble over the edge. Sean holds me tight to his chest as he continues thrusting into me. The world could be imploding around us, but as Sean comes on a final thrust, everything fades into the background. It's just him and me in this small flat, tucked away in London. There's no pressure to look or act a certain way. Just the two of us, holding onto one another like we never want to let go.

His breath is hot on my neck as we cling to one another, not moving, our skin slick. My body is liquid. I never want to move from this spot, with Sean underneath me and his arms holding me tight.

"Christ, Kat. That was fecking amazing."

"Eh, I give it a seven." Sean flips us over, his cock already growing hard inside me.

"Seven, eh? Are you just trying to get another round in?" His eyes are playful.

"I don't know. You'll just have to prove your worth, Bond."

Chapter Twelve

KAT

The early morning sun streaming in the room stirs me awake. My body aches in the best possible way. I've never had a night like I did last night. The men I'd been with were mediocre at best. When with a royal, one must sign a non-disclosure agreement before taking one's clothes off. But last night there wasn't even the thought of an NDA. It was all passion and lust. Only teeth and tongues and lips and our bodies moving together.

The lazy smile on my face is happy, despite the bed being cold beside me, and I finally get the energy to sit up. Sean's in the kitchen, wearing nothing but sweatpants that hang low on his hips, exposing the sexy ink covering his back. Finding his shirt, I slip it on and walk over to him in the small flat.

"Morning." My voice is gravelly as I wrap my arms around his waist and drop a kiss to his back.

"Mmm, morning, love." Sean's hands cover mine before he turns and pulls me into his chest. "I hope you're hungry. I'm making bangers and mash."

"I'm one lucky girl. No one has ever made me such a spread before."

"Then no one has been deserving of you." He drops a soft kiss on my lips before pulling back. On instinct, I wrap my hand around his head and pull him back down. I don't want to lose contact just yet. He tastes like mint and tea, the perfect morning combination.

"This is all very James Bond of you. Wooing your girl with breakfast." Hopping up on the counter, I grab his tea and take my own sip. My ogling is obvious as he continues making breakfast. Is there anything sexier than a man cooking? The way his bicep flexes as he mixes everything is droolworthy. Very unbecoming of a princess.

"If making you breakfast woos you, I'll happily make it for you every day of the week." The cheeky smile on his face sends sparks straight to my toes. I hide my own smile behind the cup of tea as Sean plates our breakfast.

Instead of going to the small table, we stay where we are. The smell is divine. Usually, breakfast consists of yogurt or oatmeal before I'm off to another event. But the sausage and mash is the perfect morning pick-me-up.

"Stop your staring, love. I still have to open the shop, and if you're lucky, you might get to join me in the shower."

"Well then, this sounds like the perfect morning."

"DO we really need to go to work?" I'm wrapped in a towel as Sean finishes getting dressed. "Don't you want to stay in bed with me all day?"

"Love, there is nothing I want more than to stay right here with you. But just think. It will make tonight even better." He comes over to me, his hands diving under the towel. The warmth of his hands at my waist heats my entire body. His lips ghost over mine.

"Now, get dressed and come downstairs. Maybe I'll take you out for a long lunch."

"Tease."

"Don't be late. Hate to dock your pay." Sean turns and leaves, a playful smile on his face. He just gave me another amazing orgasm in the shower, and watching him leave causes a burning need to wash through me. I don't know how I'll ever get my fill of this man.

I grab the first thing I can find in the dresser. Sean still had clothes here for late nights at work, and I throw on one of his shirts and tie it at the waist. It will drive him wild today, and I want to torment him as much as he was tormenting me earlier.

Throwing my hair into a messy bun, I head downstairs. It's quiet, still not opening time. But as I turn the corner, three sets of eyes stare me down.

"Well, well, well. Look who's finally here." Ruby's face sparkles with excitement, while Trevor and Pierce stare back at her.

"It's ten in the morning, Ruby."

"And I expected you to stay upstairs much longer."

"What in the world are you talking about?" Pierce and Trevor share a confused look.

"Guys. We open in thirty minutes. Let's get rolling." Sean's eyes land on me as everyone leaves the back area. His eyes are black with desire as they scan my attire.

"What in the world are you wearing?" I love the way his hands wrap around me, holding me close to him.

"Well, you wouldn't let us stay in bed today, so I had to have a part of you with me." I give him the most innocent of looks.

"You don't play fair." His lips suck down on the spot behind my ear. I'm purring with delight.

"And neither do you. Now, I do believe you said it's time to go to work." Giving his backside a firm squeeze, I leave him hanging.

"You're going to pay for that, Kat."

I turn back and give him my sultriest look. "Looking forward to it."

"SO, HOW WAS LAST NIGHT?" Ruby brought lunch for everyone but told the men to stay up front. "We need girl time," she said.

"Just your standard night at the shop. Why do you ask?" Sipping my drink, I give her a coy look.

"Trevor said Sean was ready to murder those blokes who came in the shop. But then he never saw either of you again."

My face heats at the memory. There was a hunger between the two of us that I've never felt before. The raw need was palpable.

"If you saw us, it would've been quite the scandal."

"Is he as good in bed as he looks? Christ, don't tell Trevor I asked that. But the men in this store are their own specimen of fine."

"Truer words have never been spoken, Ruby. It was fantastic." The way he worshipped me, kissed me, laved attention on me…it was out of this world.

"Best shag of your life?"

"Without a doubt," I answer without pause. "But you are not to tell him that!"

She throws her hands up. "Girl code. Whatever you say stays between the two of us."

I blush at her words. I've never had a good friend like her. It was always hard to make friends growing up. You never knew if someone wanted genuine friendship or something from you because of your position.

But Ruby is one of the most genuine people I've met. I was welcomed into her world after knowing her for all of five minutes. My mind keeps drifting to when I'll be back at the palace in just a short time. I can't imagine my life without these people in it.

"Now, enough talk about these boys. I want you to help me design my new tattoo."

Chapter Thirteen

KAT

It's a perfect day. It's been gloomier than usual lately, with no sun in sight. But on this rare, sunny day, I dragged Sean with me to the park. It's packed with families and small children, no doubt needing to get out and enjoy the day.

And what an enjoyable day it is. Sean's head is resting in my lap while I read. I can't remember the last time I've read for fun. Usually after a long day of scheduled events, I'm too tired to do anything but fall into bed. But sitting here in the park with Sean, it couldn't get any better than this.

It's the kind of perfect day that might not be in my future. It's getting closer and closer to when my holiday is supposed to end. An ache I've never known settles over me every time I think about leaving this place. About leaving Sean. I can't imagine going back to the palace and having every minute of my life scheduled. Having every move, every look picked apart. It's panic-inducing.

"Where'd you go, love?" Sean's voice brings me back to

the present. My fingers have been stroking his hair, loving the silky feel.

"Just thinking about you." It isn't an outright lie, but I don't really want to get into the truth now. How does one go about telling someone they are falling for that they aren't who they say they are?

"Hopefully good things," he says, leaning up and capturing my lips with his. The taste of the beer he had with lunch lingers on his lips.

"Like how I have my very own James Bond and all the wicked things I want to do to him."

"Oh, I do like these things. I don't know why we're lazing around here when we could be going at it in bed." His eyes are telling. He's ready to bolt and make good on his word. And while it wouldn't be the worst way to spend the afternoon, I shove him right back down.

"Cool it, Bond. We're taking advantage of this day. I could use some sunshine." Usually getting sunshine means tucking myself away in a corner of my garden where I can't be seen. But being out here in the park where no one knows who I am is the most incredible feeling in the world. "I want to get back to reading, so you hush."

"And what are you reading, love?" His eyes are closed again as my hand drifts under the V of his T-shirt. I've memorized the patterns of ink that mark his skin.

"A romance book." It was too tempting to pass up at the corner market when I was getting my escape items. I never get to read for pleasure, and the half-naked man on the front was very enticing.

"And what kind of romance book?" His hand comes down on top of mine, stilling my motion. The beat of his heart under my palm keeps me settled.

"Historical. A lady is betrothed to a duke whom she

does not love. She is secretly in love with a duke from a neighboring village, and their villages are feuding."

"Sounds very British."

"Very much so. And the sex scenes are rather good."

"Oh yeah?"

"Yes."

"Tell me about them." His voice is deep, full of desire. It shouldn't be such a turn-on to tell him about my book, but it sends shockwaves through my body.

"Well, the lady runs away in defiance of her parents. She doesn't want to be forced into a loveless marriage. It causes a big to-do in her tiny village, but she stays with her duke. The one she loves."

"She's quite feisty, this lady. Like someone else I know." He squeezes my hand but doesn't let go.

"Quite. She ends up marrying the duke she loves, and it causes a fight to break out. But they can't help the passion they feel for one another. Their desire and love are all-consuming."

His eyes are now on me, his lips parted, as if I could read him the entire story and he would be enraptured.

"Their lovemaking is incredibly sensual."

"Describe it to me."

His heart is racing under my hand as his gaze stays fixed on mine. I couldn't look away if I wanted to.

"She sneaks into his room—"

He cuts me off. "Why aren't they sleeping together?"

"The men and women slept in separate rooms back then."

"I'm glad we changed with the times. I don't want you sleeping anywhere but next to me." Thank God I'm sitting, because this man is absolutely swoon-worthy.

"Yes, times have indeed changed. The lady is only in her dressing gown when she finds her love. He is still awake, drinking whisky, sitting in front of the fire. She is terribly in love with him. She has never been with another man before, but she cannot wait to be with him." I know the feeling. Being around Sean, my body is always in tune with where he is. It's as if there's an invisible thread locking the two of us together.

"Instead of her dropping her clothes, the duke removes his pants, standing in just his riding shirt. He's already hard in anticipation." Just saying this out loud to Sean feels indecent, as we're surrounded by families in the park. But I can't seem to stop myself from continuing. Heat and fire are coursing through my veins. It's as if Sean and I are the duke and the new duchess.

"She goes to him, ready to give herself over. They've barely shared a kiss before now, but she's ready to be his in every sense of the word."

Sean sits up in a flash, pulling my chest to his. My nipples are hard beneath the fabric of my thin T-shirt. His hand goes to my hair as his mouth whispers next to my ear.

"What happens next?"

"He shoves her dressing gown up and slowly, oh so slowly, slides into her." His voice is a growl as he starts nibbling on my neck. Never have I been a part of something so erotic.

"He doesn't rip it off of her? I wouldn't be able to wait to see her naked beneath me."

"He is still a gentleman. They make mad, passionate love. She gives him something precious to her, and he vows to protect her with whatever comes next."

Sean's lips crash down on mine in a fervent kiss, filled with desire and passion. His tongue slides against mine in a fight for control. I've never been more turned on in my life. I can't keep my hands off of him as we sit in the park and kiss like our lives depend on it. The heat swirling between the two of us is palpable. The sounds of London drift off into the background as Sean starts working his way down my neck. I'm about to tell him we need to stop when the first drop hits me square in the face.

Opening my eyes, I realize that the sun is gone and storm clouds have moved in. We were so distracted that the entire world was fuzzy around us. Everyone else has run for shelter as we're the last ones in the park.

"Shit!" Sean yells as the skies open up. We barely have time to pack everything up before we're dashing through the park, trying to make it to safety. Finding a tree, we grab what little cover we can while trying to get things organised before leaving.

"Hey." Sean grabs me and pulls me towards him, causing me to drop the few things I have in my hands. His T-shirt sticks to his muscles, showing off his powerful chest. I pull his head down to me, not wanting to leave this spot. Our kiss is just as heated as it was before the heavens opened up. I pull his bottom lip between my teeth, loving the growl that hits my ear.

"Don't think just because it started raining, I'm done with you." He leans closer to me, whispering in my ear. His hands pull me in closer so I can feel the heat of his hard body. "Don't think that duke has anything on what I plan on doing to you when we get home."

THE HALLWAY IS quiet as we rush into the back of the shop to get out of the rain. The buzz of the tattoo guns is softer back here. Instead of going upstairs to the studio, Sean is crowding me from behind.

"Do you realize how sexy you look wet?" He brushes the tangle of my hair to the side as his lips find my neck. Oh God, I love it when he sucks where my shoulder and neck meet.

"I have a feeling you'll tell me." I love Sean's hands. They are all over me as he works my shirt up and over my head. The groan that slips out is needy and full of desire. A slap to the ass brings me out of my thoughts. I don't think I've ever been more aroused in my entire life.

"You're a fucking wet dream, and I've been dying to take you all afternoon. Much like the duke." His breath ghosts my ear. "Now, we need to be quiet. Otherwise, someone out front will hear us, and I'll have to punish you."

I turn to peek at him. "Promise?"

He growls, ever so softly, and attacks my lips again. The snick of the zipper echoes loudly in the hallway as Sean tugs my pants down my legs.

"Fuck, are you not wearing underwear, love?" I turn, wiggling my arse in his direction as he trails hot, open-mouthed kisses down my back.

"Trying something new." The sting of a bite on my backside causes a rush of heat to gather in my core.

"You drive me wild." His tongue licks my slit as I hold myself up for dear life. The movement of his tongue and those nimble hands of his squeezing my arse is lighting me up from the inside out. I cover my mouth, moaning into my hand as he drives me closer and closer to bliss. Just when I think he's going to let me come, he's gone. I can't hide my whimpers of displeasure as I rub my legs together, needing some friction.

"Uh-uh. That's my job." Before I know it, I hear the sound of a foil packet opening, and then he slides his cock between my legs.

"Oh, God." I throw my head back, meeting his hard chest. He fists my hair, pulling my head to the side. Soft kisses on the slope of my neck have me rocking my hips over his cock. "I could come just like this." My voice is a breathy whisper. The thought that anyone could come back here and find us has me rocketing back towards the edge.

"As much as I would like to try that, I want you coming all over my cock." Slowly, too slowly, he slides inside me until I'm so full I couldn't possibly take anymore. Sean places my hands on the wall before he slides out, finding a rhythm that has me convulsing with need.

I bite my lip to keep my moans to myself. Every time with Sean is better than the last. My senses are overwhelmed—the feel of him as he slides in and out of my slick channel, the sound of his belt clanking in the empty hallway, the taste of him on my lips. I need more.

Pulling a hand off the wall, I find his hair and tug him towards me, capturing his lips with mine. It's a fight for power as our tongues tangle. His free hand dips low on my body, finding my clit. I grab ahold, our fingers working me over together. Sean knows just how to play me to drive my pleasure to new heights.

"Close. So close," I whisper against his lips. He sucks my bottom lip into his mouth and he picks up the pace of his thrusts.

"Was it like this in your book?" Thrust. "The duke and his lady fucking in hidden corners?" Thrust. Thrust. "I don't know how much longer I can hold back, love." Thrust. "I'm going to need you to come."

And I do. I explode around him in a cacophony of colours and lights and stars. Fireworks as bright as the New Year's sky light me up from the inside out. I don't know how loud I'm being, but my entire body is awash in new feelings as Sean's own orgasm starts to sweep over him.

His hands are digging into my sides, keeping us both upright as we come down from the best high I've ever known. Sean's lips kiss up my neck, working over my jaw before lightly kissing my lips, gentle and easy compared to the fast and furious pace of what we just did in the hallway.

This isn't something a princess should be caught doing. Ever. It would devastate the monarchy in the worst way. But right now? I couldn't care less. I just had the best sex of my life with the best man I've ever met, and I'm in heaven.

He slowly pulls out, and I lament the loss of him. He ties off the condom before pulling his jeans, and then mine, back up. I turn to face him, standing in only my bra and jeans. His eyes are heavy in his post-orgasmic state. He's never looked sexier.

Lifting me into his arms, he presses me against the wall by the stairs. "I guess I'll need to punish you now."

"I was quiet." I didn't know if I was quiet. The world could have ended, and I would have been none the wiser.

"I'm surprised no one came back here. The whole of London probably heard you after that orgasm."

"Well, if you rock my world again like that, then by all means, take me to the tower and punish away."

The hungry gleam in his eyes tells me that's exactly what we'll be doing for the rest of the day.

Chapter Fourteen

SEAN

"Wake up, Kat." She barely stirs next to me. I shouldn't be all that surprised considering how late we stayed up. We're insatiable. I can't remember the last time I've had so much fun with a woman. I'm doing things I never thought I'd be doing with Kat. Her wide-eyed innocence makes me want to run off and leave all responsibilities behind.

"It's too early to get up." Her voice is muffled by the pillow. Her pink hair is practically glowing in the late morning sun. She looks like a dirty angel, lying here with her back exposed. Her side is no longer an angry red from her tattoo. It's healed nicely. I'm ready for the next tattoo. Ready to move my hands over her skin, inking her. It makes my dick stir. But we don't have time for that.

"It's almost noon." My voice is a whisper behind her ear as I gently run my fingertips up and down her spine.

"Noon?" She shoots up onto her elbows. Creases mar the side of her beautiful face. Fuck, this woman has burrowed her way into my heart.

"We were up late, love." I brush the silky locks of her

hair behind her ear and draw her lips into mine, morning breath be damned.

"Mmm, I do remember." She stretches before flipping onto her back, the sheet falling to expose those gorgeous tits I love.

"Kat. You really do need to get up. I have a fun day for us planned."

"We could have a fun day here instead." Her voice is still sleepy as she tries to pull me on top of her. As much as I don't want to resist her, I know she'll enjoy what I have planned.

"If it was up to you, we'd never leave this bed."

"And that's a problem because?" Her fingers trace the tattoos on my arm. She does this to distract me, but I'm on a mission to enjoy this day with her.

"As much as I would love to stay here with you in bed, I think you'll enjoy this too."

"Spoilsport." She throws the sheet off and stalks off, naked as the day she was born. I'm starting to question my own sanity by not staying in bed with her.

"Christ, Kat. Way to tease a man." She shakes her ass at me as she makes her way over to the bathroom.

"Maybe you could make it a quickie before we go?" She disappears behind the door, and I'm out of the bed and dropping my joggers before she can even turn the water on.

"ARE you going to tell me where we're going?" We got a later start than I had planned, but it was worth it for the mind-blowing sex in the shower. No man will ever complain about that.

"You'll see once we get there. I hope I'm not overselling it." Ever since we went to the pub, she wanted to go back and try others. I didn't quite see the appeal, but something about her enthusiasm made me want to bring her here.

"Sean." She stops and pulls me back to her. "As long as you and I are spending the day together, everything else is a bonus." She tilts her chin up to me, awaiting a kiss. What the lady wants, the lady gets. Dropping a quick kiss on her pretty pink lips, that sweet floral scent of hers does me in. I can't get enough of it.

"Well then, I hope you enjoy, because we're here." I spin her around to see the main gate of the Maltby Street Market.

"A street market?" Her eyes are hidden behind her sunglasses in the afternoon sun, so I can't get a read on her.

"I know it might seem simple, but you were so happy that night at the pub. I figure you'd enjoy something like this. Wandering around, eating and drinking whatever you wanted." Her face wasn't giving anything away. Shite, I completely blew this. "Christ, now this sounds totally lame, and you were probably wanting something—"

She cuts me off by throwing her arms around my neck and planting a long, hard kiss on my lips. My arms hold her close to me as she deepens the kiss for just a moment.

"Sean. This is absolutely perfect. Just spending the day together. It's bloody brilliant. Any day with you is." Her blue eyes are sparkling with excitement as she moves one hand over my cheek. I don't think anyone has ever looked so happy to go to a street market.

"Well then, let's go. I hate to keep the market waiting." She is beside herself with excitement as she grabs my hand and pulls me ahead.

"Ooh, cocktails! Let's get one as we wander around." Her smile as she turns back to me hits me square in the chest. I don't know where Kat came from or much about her past, but fecking hell, if I'm not falling in love with this pink-haired goddess of a woman.

"Afternoon, there. What'll ya have?" Kat orders both of us a smoked gin and tonic without second thought. She passes over a few pounds, and the bartender hands Kat the two elaborate drinks.

"Cheers, mate." He nods at us as we make our way over to a high-top table.

"This is so good," Kat moans, her eyes closed as she takes a large drink. I lean down and pull her lips into mine. The gin cuts through her sweet taste, but damn, if this kiss isn't delicious.

"Tastes pretty great to me, love." I wink at her as a blush creeps over her pretty face. Whatever is in this drink is bloody amazing.

"I am so glad you decided to bring us here." She cuddles up into my side as we watch people come and go into the market.

"Well, if you enjoy this, there's a great wide world of markets out there for you." The joy coming off of her is palpable. The idea came to me this morning while I was watching her sleep. She was too beautiful to wake up.

Kat rests her hand on my chest, her face relaxed and happy. "As long as you are my guide, I will follow you anywhere."

"I like the sound of that."

"Plus, I get a pretty killer view." She squeezes my arse as she barks out a laugh.

"You had to ruin it with an arse grab." Reaching behind her, I return the favour, pulling her square into me, but I let my hand linger there. The feel of Kat in my arms is unlike anything else. I've never been around a woman who affected me this badly. Just the sound of her voice while we're working makes me happy. It makes me want to plan a million little things like this to keep that smile on her face.

"Sorry, it's a nice arse. I'm pretty sure you didn't mind it last night."

"You might not want to bring that up right now. It would be rather inappropriate for me to be sporting a semi walking around the market." I know she feels it because she's now biting on that blessed bottom lip I want to suck into my mouth.

"Just slightly inappropriate. Now, let's finish these cocktails because I see some baked goods that are calling my name."

Kat slams back her drink, grinning at me as she puts her glass back on the table. She was timid when she first came to the shop, but now, her happiness is contagious. I can't imagine her not being in the shop every day. She puts everyone at ease when they walk in, whether it's their first tattoo or their fiftieth.

I don't know how Kat is feeling, but I'd love to make this thing between us more permanent. She's tight-lipped about where she came from, giving me no details. I don't know if she's running from something, or Christ, someone, but I want her to be a set fixture in my life. Hell, my parents would love her. Pierce loves her. She's so easy to love.

"Sean, which do you want?" I point at the first thing I see, still lost in my thoughts. I can't seem to keep my hands off of her as she waits for the spoils of her hunt. Wrapping my arms around her waist, I pull her back into me. She looks up at me, pulling me further under her spell.

"Hi, love." My voice is barely above a whisper.

"Hello." Her hand grazes my arm, tracing the outlines of the tattoos there. It's a habit I've noticed, and I don't think she even realises she's doing it. Whether we're lying in bed or eating next to one another, she absently traces the patterns inked on my skin. And it's fucking amazing.

"Listen, Kat—"

"Here you go, ma'am." The baker hands us the pastries, effectively ending my train of thought. I have no idea how to go about asking Kat if she wants to continue doing what we're doing. I have no idea what the future holds, but all I know is I want her with me. But what if she doesn't want the same thing? What if she's just having fun? Taking a break from wherever she came from? Christ, even thinking of her going back to wherever she came from makes my heart twinge inside my chest. I'm way deeper in this than I thought.

"Sean, you coming?" Kat is twisting out of my arms, ready to go explore the market. She tears off a bite of the pastry, and I grab her wrist and bring it to my mouth.

"Cheeky bastard." She is smiling as she says it. Wrapping my arm around her waist, I bring her in for a kiss. I tease her lips with my tongue and she willingly opens for me. I don't care that we're surrounded by people in the middle of the crammed alley. All I care about is her.

It's not until someone bumps into us that I pull away from her.

"We really need to stop doing that in the middle of crowded streets." Her voice is playful as she gazes up at me.

"Love, I never want to stop doing that. Ever."

"Promise?"

"With every fibre of my being."

Chapter Fifteen

SEAN

"Pierce, I'm heading upstairs. I'm done."

"We still have two hours until close." He's working on someone as I pack up for the night.

"Perks of being the owner. I'm wiped after that last piece. And to be perfectly honest, I miss Kat." For the first time in a long time, I'm not thinking about my failed art programme, or worrying about the shop. The only thing I'm worrying about is getting to Kat.

"Must be nice to be a kept man." He flips me off as I leave the noise of the parlour behind me for the day. The faint sounds of music drift down to me as I head up the stairs.

"Mmm, something smells good in here, love." Kat is a dream, standing in the kitchen, singing softly to some pop song I've never heard. I let her leave work early tonight because I had a client with a large piece on his back and knew I wouldn't want to take any walk-ins after that. There was no point in her waiting downstairs when she could have been relaxing up here.

"Hey, you. You're done sooner than I thought."

Turning to face me, her face is red from the heat of the stove. "I was going to surprise you and have supper ready, but you'll have to wait."

"No one has ever made me supper before." I wrap my arms around her waist, peeking at what she's cooking. "Curry?"

"It's the one thing I'm good at making."

"I can't wait to try it." I drop a kiss on her neck and she tilts her head, giving me better access. "But I'm hungry for something else." It was a busy day, with lots of new walk-ins and designing pieces for new clients. I've gotten used to sneaking away for lunch with Kat. Instead, I ate in the office between clients while finishing off some pre-made designs. It should scare me how much I've gotten used to her being in my life, but fuck, I love it.

"Alright, you. Go sit, and dinner will be ready soon. I'm not wasting this meal because you can't keep it in your pants."

Dropping my head to her shoulder, I could stand here while she cooks and be perfectly content. But she shoos me away. I grab a beer and sit and watch while she cooks. I'm the luckiest bastard in the world, having this pink-haired goddess fall for me.

"How'd it go this afternoon?" Soft wisps of pink hair fall over her shoulder as she turns to look at me.

"Brilliant. Bloody fucking brilliant. He absolutely loved it, and it was hard, but some of my best work." One of my regulars had an old tattoo on his back that he wanted to cover up. Instead of doing something small, he wanted an intricate pattern of a lion erupting out of Trafalgar Square. The level of detail on the background was incredible, and he was ecstatic with how it turned out.

"I'm sure he loved it. But I'm biased because I love everything you do." She gives me a cheeky wink as she turns the heat off and plates our dinner. Passing my plate to me, she grabs a beer and comes to sit next to me, her knees between mine.

"Christ, this is just what I needed tonight." Inhaling deeply, I shovel a large bite in my mouth. Fuck, if that's not the best curry I've ever had. "Damn, Kat. This is delicious."

"Told you I wouldn't waste this meal." She leans over for a quick kiss before devouring hers. "Because I can't make much, but I can make this well," she says around a huge bite.

"I guess you'll need your energy for later then. I've got big plans for you tonight."

"KAT, I'M STUFFED." We moved over to the bed, leaving the dishes for later. She's curled up into my side, both of us content to stay just like this the rest of the night.

"You didn't have to have seconds. Or thirds. It keeps just fine." Her warm hand drifts lazily across my stomach. Her touch lights me up within seconds. I grab her hand, not quite ready for what she wants.

"You're going to have to hold off on that, love. I can't move." I bring her hand up to my lips, kissing each fingertip on her dainty hand. I can feel her shifting next to me until a waterfall of pink hovers over me.

"You better hurry, Sean, because I'm quite ready for you." She drops her lips to mine in an easy kiss. Easily opening to her, I try to take control, but she pushes for domination. For control. And I give it to her.

Grabbing her hips, I pull her on top of me. Food coma be damned. Her hips have a mind of their own, moving over my rock-hard dick. She breaks the kiss and trails her lips down my scruffy jaw to my ear. "I thought you couldn't move," she whispers, nibbling on my earlobe.

Pulling her to me, I flip us over so she's now under me, a smirk lighting up her face.

"Fuck that, Kat." I waste no time pulling her shirt over her head before losing my own. Seeing the ink I marked on her skin makes me feel possessive. I love that I was the first to tattoo her. The first to mark her beautiful skin. Christ, I feel like a caveman that I know her like this. I never want another person's hands inking her sexy as sin body.

I trace the still bright ink. I can't keep my hands off her. "Fuck, I love seeing my work on you, Kat." She guides my head back down to hers, eager to kiss me.

It's a fight for control as Kat tries to flip us again. Her nails digging into my back just forces me to push her deeper into the bed. "Not so fast. You took care of me tonight. Let me take care of you." Her blue eyes are hazy as she throws her arms over her head.

"I'm at your will, Sean."

"Best words I've heard all night."

Leaning down, I shove the cups of her bra down and pull a hard nipple into my mouth. Her moans are the sexiest sounds I've ever heard. Lavishing the most beautiful set of tits with all the attention, I ignore the rolling of her hips.

"More. I need more, Sean." Her eyes are closed as I kiss my way down her stomach. Ever since that first night, she's let me see her. All of her. She's the most beautiful creature I've ever known. Every time with her is better than the last.

Unbuttoning her jeans, I slowly pull them down her legs, taking her thong with them. Her pussy glistens with anticipation as I take in this woman spread out before me like a feast. Pulling her legs apart, I settle my face between them, giving her a long lick that I know drives her wild.

"Yes!" She's up on her elbows now, looking down at me as I delve my tongue inside of her. Her blue eyes are dark as they stay locked on mine. Spreading her lips apart with one hand, I find her clit with the other. Her pussy clenches around my tongue.

"Someone is enjoying themselves." I pull away ever so slightly, biting the inside of her thigh. I lick the sting away before making my way back to my own personal heaven. Her moans are driving me wild. Everything about Kat drives me wild.

"I'm so close. Please don't stop!" she says on a moan, her voice breathy. Inserting a finger into her tight channel, I pull her clit into my mouth. Between my tongue and my fingers, she explodes around me, shouting my name on her release. My name has never sounded so sweet.

When she finally comes down, her body is limp as I stand next to the bed, fully naked now, stroking my dick as I watch the beauty in front of me.

"Are you just going to stand there? I can think of much better things to do."

"I don't mind the view from where I am." I tweak her nipple between my fingers as I roll my hand over the head of my cock, spreading precum down the hard length.

"I have a better view in mind."

"Yeah?"

Kat pushes off the bed, getting on her knees.

"Kat, no. I want—" But the words are lost as her lips close over the head of my cock. Bliss. Her mouth is pure, unadulterated bliss. Those small hands of hers close around the base, working me from both ends. Just as I grab her hair, I hit the back of her throat.

"Fucking hell." Her warm mouth is working me closer

and closer to blowing my load. The tension coiling at the base of my spine needs a release, but I don't want to come down her throat. Fisting my hand tighter in her hair, my dick glistens as I pull her off me. "I'm coming inside you tonight."

She doesn't say a word, just reaches over to the nightstand and grabs a rubber and rolls it on, giving me a squeeze as she releases me. "Get up here." I pull her up into my arms and wrap her legs around my waist, leaning her against the wall. There's no finesse. No easy pace. It's an all-consuming need as I slide easily into her slick pussy.

I bury my face in her neck to try and stave off an instant orgasm. But it's hard. So damn hard when the smell of her surrounds me. When her pussy is clamping down around me. With a subtle move of her hips, I start moving. I set a punishing pace as I bite down on the tender flesh of her skin. Kat's hands are everywhere, clutching me to her as my movements become more hurried.

"Oh, God! I'm coming!" My back is going to be scratched to hell tomorrow, but damn, if it doesn't feel amazing as she shatters around me. She clutches me to her chest as I take a nipple into my mouth and tease her through her own release. I'm close, but I want another orgasm out of my pink-haired goddess.

Pulling out of her, I drop her legs from my waist and turn her to face the wall. "Don't think that's all for you tonight," I whisper in her ear.

"I don't think I can take it." She's breathing heavily, but when I reach around to find her clit again, she leans into my touch.

"You sure about that?" I'm rubbing my dick in the cleft of her ass as she rocks into me.

"Please don't stop."

"Your wish is my command, love." And I don't stop.

My fingers work her clit, driving her crazy. We're chest to back, not a breath of air between us, our skin sweat-slicked from the intensity of our passion. The air crackles around us.

"Sean. I need you inside me. Now." Her hand is on mine, our fingers now working her as I easily slide home into her pussy, chasing my own release. Fire speeds down my spine as Kat comes again, pulling my orgasm out of me. Fuck, if I'm not having the best sex of my life with Kat.

Kat is limp beneath me, completely sated. Moving my hand up to her stomach, I hold her up against me. I'm not ready to leave her warmth. There's something about this woman that settles me. That quiets the voice of failure in my head that I couldn't make my art programme work.

"Sean. I need to lie down. I don't know how much longer I can stand. You've turned me into jelly." Pride surges through me.

Using my weight to keep her up, I pull out and tie off the rubber. Pulling her into my arms, I carry her over to the bed and lie down next to her, keeping her close to my side. I'm absolutely spent, and the feel of her breathing at my side lulls me to sleep, but not before I hear her whispered words, "How in the world am I going to keep you, Sean?"

Chapter Sixteen

KAT

"Shite. That's all wrong." Sean's annoyed voice carries through the store. He's been on edge all day for some reason, and I can't pinpoint why. His brow is furrowed in annoyance as he continues working on the design in front of him.

"What's bothering you?" I wrap my arms around his shoulder, trying to stifle his annoyance.

"It's nothing." Well, if that isn't a lie.

"Something is bothering you. Just tell me so I can help."

He puffs out a breath, dropping the pen in his hand. "I can't get this design right, and it bothers me. I'm supposed to have it done by now, and I don't."

I can feel the tension coursing through him. "Why don't you take a break?"

"Because I can't. He's going to be here tomorrow, and I need to have this done." He rips the page out of the notebook, and throws it in the trash. I can only squeeze my arms tighter around him. Sean is a level-headed person, never one to get overly emotional. But right now, he's wound so tight. Tighter than I've seen him these last few weeks.

"Let's get out of here. We can come back later and work on this."

"I need to get it done tonight, Kat." His voice is short, something I've never heard from him before. It further strengthens my resolve.

"You need a break. Let's get out of here for dinner."

"I need to finish."

I grab the notebook from the desk and pull it out of his reach. I've never seen Sean so wrapped up in a design before. I admire his dedication to his job, but it isn't going to help anyone when he is wound so tight.

"Let's go."

"Go where?" he asks.

"Somewhere that's not here. You need a break." As I smooth my hands over his hair, he finally looks like he is relaxing. His face is contemplative as he looks at me.

"Can I show you something?" he asks.

"Anything." Sean stands up as he pulls me into an embrace. There is no place I'd rather be than there in his arms.

"Boys, watch the shop. I'll be back later."

He doesn't wait for an answer. Sean laces his fingers through my hands as he pulls me out the door.

"SEAN, WHERE ARE WE GOING?" We've been walking for an interminable time, with no end in sight.

"You really don't like surprises, do you?" His arm is around my shoulders as he pulls me to a stop. "Here we are." We're standing in front of an old brick building with

Royal Reckoning

brown paper covering the windows. "I know it's not much to look at, but let me show you."

"This place is yours?" Sean holds the door open as I walk inside. My eyes are immediately drawn to strands of lights hanging from the ceiling. Desks are lined up with a few chairs, but not much else.

"What is this place?"

Sean's hands are tucked into his pockets, as he shyly looks around the space. "This is what has been taking up so much of my time these last few months. I've been trying to get an art programme off the ground."

"An art programme?" My head is spinning as I try to piece together what he is saying.

"Mum worked when we were little, so Pierce and I always had to have somewhere to go after school. It wasn't until we found a small art school that I realized what I wanted to do with my life. There's nothing like it around here, so I wanted to start my own programme for kids in this area."

His voice is quiet as he takes me in his arms, burying his head in my neck.

"And why isn't it up and running yet?"

His breath is heavy as he lets out a lingering sigh. "I had a few people who were going to back me, but they pulled out at the last minute. I sank all of my savings into leasing this place, and I had nothing left."

I'm at a loss for words when realization strikes like a hammer. The event that Granddad and I were supposed to go to. We were coming here, I know it. My breath leaves in a whoosh. Would Sean and I have been fated to meet? Would we have had the same connection if we met that day as a princess and one of her citizens?

"Sean. This is absolutely brilliant. Is there anything I can do to help?" My mind starts working as I think of who

I could contact to be a donor for such an incredible programme.

"I love that you're willing to help, but I've pulled back on it. I still have the space, but I'm wary of asking for help now."

"Is this why you've been so tense? Why you were so upset about losing that job?"

He nods his head. "I thought I did a pretty good job hiding it. I just feel like such a failure because I couldn't make it work."

"No." My voice is hard. I want him to know that he is anything but a failure. He could never be a failure in my eyes. "It's just delayed."

I turn in his arms and cup his cheeks, my fingers dancing over his lips. I was in deep before with him, but hearing what he wants to do? I've fallen even harder for this man. This kind, thoughtful, wonderful man. It should scare me at how quickly I'm developing these feelings for him, but it doesn't.

"I love your confidence in me, Kat." Sean's eyes are soft as they skim over my face.

"Whatever help you need, I'm here." I brush my lips over his as my fingers tangle in the soft strands at the nape of his neck. If there's one thing I can do, it's help Sean get this programme started. I have no idea what is going to happen in my life in these next few weeks, but I know I can help him with this wherever I end up.

"Okay, enough depressing talk." He tries to laugh it off and walks across the room to peer out a window, but I can see just how upset he is that this stalled. It makes my chest ache that he wasn't able to get this started.

Not one single person I've dated would have ever thought to do something like this. The men I have dated—if you want to call them that—only wanted to further their station in life with a princess. But not Sean. No. I have never met a more selfless man. He has the biggest heart.

"Not depressing. This is incredible." My voice is full of awe as I take in the rest of the space around me. I make a vow that no matter what happens, I will make this dream of his a reality. I don't want him to forget about this amazing place even after I leave.

"I'm glad you think so." There's a bitterness to his voice I'm not used to, and it breaks my heart for him.

I walk to him, wrapping my arms around his waist and looking into his sad eyes. His eyes are anything but hopeful. I can see that it's been a long day for him, but I have faith in him.

He cups my cheeks, his deep blue eyes reflecting emotions that I don't want to name. Lust. Desire. Passion. Love. That last one is what scares me most of all. Because how in the world am I supposed to keep this man?

"Where in the world did you come from?" His voice is quiet in the small space as his lips come down on mine. He wants to deepen the kiss, but I don't let him. This place is a sacred space to him, and I don't want it tarnished when I have to leave him.

"Sean." I pull back from him, taking in his soft, sad features. "Make no mistake. Come hell or high water, I will do whatever it takes to make this dream of yours a reality. You deserve this."

"What did I do to deserve you?" His voice is quiet as he gazes at me.

"You took me in. When I needed a place to land, you caught me."

His eyes are heavy with emotion. There is nothing I want more in this world than Sean. He's made it easy to fall for him. "Love, you make it easy to catch you. I'd walk through fire to rescue you from the clutches of the world."

My knees go weak at his words. I've never believed a man's words more than his. It's the hardest fall of my life, but it's also the best one of my life. "I only want to stop falling if it's with you."

"I'm waiting, love. I'm right here, waiting to catch you."

Chapter Seventeen

KAT

"We're getting off early tonight, love. I've got plans for you." Sean's voice is a whisper in my ear. His hot breath sends tingles down my spine. We don't even have to be in the same space and my body lights up just being aware of him. The stolen glances while he's prepping his station, the casual touches when he's passing by me while I'm on the phone. My body seeks him out wherever he is.

After last night, the connection to Sean is even stronger. Sean fell asleep early, but I stayed awake, staring at the man I'm falling in love with. Would we have met if his programme had been funded? Could we still have ended up together?

All I know is, it's getting harder and harder to hide who I really am. My royal holiday is almost up, and I don't want to lose what we have. I don't want to go back to the palace and know Sean is over here and not be able to have him in my life.

"Something you had in mind?" It's been a slower than normal day at the shop without a lot of walk-ins. I like staying busy. It keeps my mind from wondering what will happen when my supposed holiday is over.

"I have a surprise for you tonight." He brushes the long strands of my hair away from my shoulder and drops a kiss on my neck. How I love his lips there.

"I guess I can be pulled away for a few hours." Looking up at him, I watch a smile brighten his face. I can never get my fill of his handsome features. I joke about it quite often, but he really is my own James Bond. This strong, devilishly handsome man who swept me off my feet. He may not be saving the world, but he's certainly changing mine.

"Dress warmly then. Might be a cool evening." Sean pulls my lips into a sweet kiss before heading back to his office. He walks backwards, facing me the entire time, giving me a wink before he goes through the door. A blush creeps up over my neck and face. This man.

I never thought I would meet someone when I decided to break away from my everyday life. I'm feeling things for this man that I've never felt before. That I never thought I would feel for someone. But here I am, falling for the most perfect man I may never get to call my own.

Saved from my own wayward thoughts, I turn my attention back to the woman who just entered the shop. "Excuse me, miss?"

"WHERE ARE YOU TAKING ME?" We're strolling along the Thames, the late evening sun casting deep pinks and oranges that give way to purples and blues across the London skyline. It's the perfect evening. There's a bite in the air, but it's not cold enough to stay curled up at home.

"I'm surprised you haven't figured it out yet." Being in the Westminster area of London has my nerves pulling tighter than they have been these last few weeks. Even the mere proximity to the palace has me unnerved. Sean's warm hand laced through mine keeps me here in the moment with him.

"All I see is Big Ben and The Eye. Are we going for a ride?" I pull him in closer to me, resting my chin on his bicep.

"Different kind of ride, love." He points to a dock just before the famous Ferris wheel. A large boat lined with seats and an awning awaits the passengers in line.

I stop, causing people to swerve around us. "A boat ride?"

I can't hide the awe in my voice. I can't believe he remembered that I wanted to do this. I mentioned it in passing at the pub that night. The fact that he didn't chalk it up to my drunken ramblings that night causes tears to blur my vision.

"Are you not happy?" Worry mars his handsome face as he pulls us out of the main walkway.

"Sean, this is…" I can't seem to find the words. Never has anyone done something so thoughtful for me without wanting anything in return. So instead of telling him, I show him. Cupping his face in my hands, I pull him down for a kiss. His hands fist through the pink strands of my hair as he tucks me in close to him. Gently caressing the seam of his lips, he opens to me, my tongue desperately seeking his. Languid, massaging strokes as we stand here in each other's arms surrounded by some of the most recognizable of London's landmarks, the most famous of which starts tolling her famed bells.

"Saved by the bell, I guess." Sean tucks a loose strand of hair behind my ear. His eyes are hazy, staring down at me, and I'm wishing we could continue this kiss, but only in more private quarters.

"C'mon. I don't want to be late." Lacing our hands together again, Sean leads us over to the boat that will guide us through the city tonight.

"AND ON YOUR left is the famous Tower of London." Tourists are oohing and ahhing as the famous building comes into sight. Being a royal, I've gone there more times than I can count. But sitting here, on this boat with Sean, pints in our hands, I couldn't be enjoying the view more.

"So, is this everything you hoped it would be?" Sean and I are tucked in the back of the boat, away from the rest of the people. The Tower Bridge looms large ahead of us. Beer lingers on his lips after he takes a long pull.

Reaching up to wipe it away, I give him what can only be described as a million-watt smile. "This is the most wonderful thing anyone has ever done for me." I stay close to him, my face pressed against his neck. The smell of fresh laundry mixes with the cold spring air. It's a simple thing, what Sean did for me. But considering the schedule of my daily life, I never get to see my city like this, as if we're tourists ourselves.

"I would give you many more nights like this. Just say the word." Sean's gaze never wavers from mine. The sights surrounding us blur into the background. It's just the two of us. It makes my heart ache. I want every night to be like this with Sean. I don't care where we are, as long as it's just the two of us.

But I don't know how I can make that happen. Sean is so focused on the shop and his failed programme that I don't know how we could ever begin to make this work in the real world. In the royal world.

As if he can sense my thoughts pulling away from the now, his voice is a calming reassurance. "Look." One word and he's turning my thoughts to the bridge ahead of us. We're treading water where we are as the bridge starts to rise.

"What a treat we have for you tonight!" The tour guide's excited voice booms over the speakers as everyone rushes to the front of the boat to see the opening of the bridge. Sean and I stay where we are, content in one another's arms. The sting of the wind isn't felt with the warmth swirling between the two of us.

"Legend has it that it's good luck to see the bridge open." The guide drops facts about the bridge as it's raised to allow for the passing of another ship.

"I'll take all the luck I can get." I can feel his lips at my temple. My pulse starts racing as I take in the meaning of his words. It can't mean what I think it means, can it? I start to turn, but Sean keeps his arm firmly around my shoulders.

"I love you, Kat." There's a tug in my chest when he says my name. Not my real name, but one of my names nevertheless. "I don't know where you came from, or where you're going, but I have fallen hopelessly in love with you."

This time, when I go to face him, he doesn't stop me. Setting my drink down, I wrap my arms around him and bury my face in his neck. The words spill from my lips before I have a hope of stopping them. "I love you, Sean." There's more I want to say, but I can't. What is there to say? Come back with me to the palace? Give up your entire life and watch me get torn to bits by the media?

Instead, I squeeze him to me as he pulls me into his

lap. No one is paying us any attention. We're still stationary in the water as the larger vessel drifts slowly by us. No more words are said as we stay like this. This is the only place I want to be.

The gunning of the boat engine breaks our moment. Sean's smile is soft as my fingers drift lazily over the stubble on his jaw. He catches my hand and brings it over his heart. The beat is rapid, matching my own. No doubt he can feel it where his fingers graze my wrist.

My heart continues to beat quickly as a feeling of loss takes over. I can't explain it, but in this moment, I feel like I'm losing Sean. There's still time before I have to be back at the palace. But how do I go about explaining to this man who I really am? Will he be able to move past the fact that I'm a princess, never mind that I've been lying to him these last few weeks?

Tomorrow. I'll tell Sean tomorrow. I don't know what is going to happen, but I can't lose this man. He's too important to me.

"Let's go home. Make love to me, Sean." My voice comes out broken, filled with lust and a sense of overwhelming urgency.

"There is nothing I want more in the world."

Chapter Eighteen

SEAN

Kat's mood has been up and down all night. I don't know what is going on with her, but she seems happy again. It's almost as if my confession of loving her threw her for a loop. I couldn't contain the words as they spilled out. But as soon as I said them, I knew it was right. I don't know what is going to happen with the two of us, but right now it doesn't matter. Because only Kat matters. And loving my pink-haired goddess of a woman.

We leave the boat tour quickly. I had planned to go for dinner and drinks, but we just need to be with one another. Because as soon as we make it back to the studio, clothes are shed as we race up the stairs. She wastes no time unclasping her bra and dropping it at my feet.

"Fuck, Kat. You are fecking gorgeous. The things I want to do to you." My voice is a growl as I lean down to take a pert nipple into my mouth. Her hands in my hair guide my motions. I know she's enjoying it when her grip tightens, causing the slightest bit of pain to turn into pleasure. I'm hard as a rock, my zipper no doubt carving permanent marks into my dick.

Grabbing Kat around the waist, I carry her to our bed. This used to be a place I crashed when I stayed too late at the shop. It's crazy how quickly I've come to think of it as our place. Letting this stranger stay here turned out to be one of the best things I've ever done.

Laying her in the center of the bed, I pull back and can't help but cast my gaze over her. Kneeling between her legs, my fingers ghost up and down her sides. Goose pimples break out in my trail. Placing my hands on each side of her head, I lean over her, locking those blue eyes with mine. Words aren't said, but emotion is heavy in the air.

Sure, I've had my fair share of women before, but never love. Never like this. "Fuck, Kat. I love you." Her hands join around my neck and pull me down to her, our lips crashing together in a want I've never felt. It's almost like she's memorizing my lips and the lingering taste of our earlier drinks. The touch, the feel of my lips against hers makes her cry out in delight. I kiss a trail along her jaw to the spot on her neck that she loves so much.

I suck down hard, then lick the sting away. I don't think I've given someone a hickey since high school, but there's an overwhelming sense to mark her as mine. To let other men know they need to back off. The rocking of her hips against mine tells me she liked it. So I do it again, this time moving lower.

"God, Sean. That feels so damn good." Her nails cut into my back, pulling me in closer to her. Her nipples are hard against my chest as her powerful thighs squeeze around my waist.

I move down her chest, kissing and sucking as I go. She is a writhing mess beneath me as I kiss my way over her soft stomach. I've learned the feel of each and every one of her curves these last few weeks and I cannot get enough of them.

Pulling her legs off of me, I slowly undo her jeans. More slowly than I usually do, because I love to drive her wild. I kiss just above her thong as I pull them down her legs, not quite relieving her of her need.

"Stop teasing me!" she shouts. Kat's hands are in her hair, desperate need wafting off of her.

"Just for that, I think I'll take my time." I kiss her through the lace fabric, loving the smell of her need. I palm my dick through my jeans to keep my own pleasure at bay. It's not important right now. Right now, making Kat feel incredible is the only thing in the world that matters.

Running a finger slowly over the wet fabric, I grin down at her. She's biting down on her bottom lip, head thrown back in pleasure. "Seems like you need some relief." Playfulness laces my voice. I love worshipping every bit of this woman, but seeing her outright frustration at her need for me is the best kind of turn-on.

"Please, Sean. Please, please, please." She is muttering incoherent words as I slide my finger beneath the small swath of fabric, not bothering to move it. Just as I can see she's about to yell at me again, I dive two fingers into her tight channel. Her back bows off the bed as I start pumping my fingers in and out of her. The time for games is over.

Bending over, I rip the fabric away from her body as I take her clit in my mouth. "Mmm, that feels so damn good." Her fingers pull my hair taut as she guides my movements. A smile plays at my lips while my tongue works. Even when I'm in control, she has all the power. I would move heaven and earth to make this woman happy in the smallest of ways.

Kat is close. Her pussy is clenching around my fingers

as I continue driving into her. The breathy sounds she makes get louder the closer she gets.

"Sean. Sean, oh yes! Oh God, yes!" She spasms around me as she comes. She rocks into my mouth as she rides out her orgasm, those thighs I love so much squeezing tight around my head.

As she comes down, I pull back, releasing my dick from his denim prison. Kat's a blissed-out goddess, laid out like a feast before a god returning from battle.

Pushing herself up, she gets down before me on her knees. And when she draws my cock into her hot mouth? I feel like a god. She takes me as far as she can, her other hand working my balls over. Those delicate, feminine fingers know just how to drive me into a frenzy.

Lightning pleasure courses through my body, settling at the base of my back. My balls get tighter as she continues laving me with attention. I'll never get enough of her mouth on me. This perfect goddess of a woman is my dream. Nothing else matters but her. And as much as I would love to come in that pretty mouth of hers, I don't want to. I want to be balls deep in my woman when I explode.

Grabbing her by the chin, I pull out of her mouth, a small trail of saliva creating a tiny thread between us. Wiping her swollen lips clean, I lift her back up onto the bed. Being the cheeky woman she is, she gets on all fours, shaking her ass at me. I can't resist. Grabbing a rubber, I roll it over my hard length as I sink my teeth into her luscious arse.

"You ready for me, love?" I rub the head of my dick through her crack, to her wet pussy.

"Always."

I waste no time, driving balls deep into her. I have to think of everything I do to prep my station so I don't come too early. Being inside of Kat is a heaven I've never experienced before I met her. I never want to forget this feeling.

Once I'm sure I won't lose it, I set a punishing pace. Her body responds to every touch as my hands caress the expanse of her back. They glide over the intricate lines now inked on her side. Her once virgin skin that is now permanently altered at my hand.

"Fuck, Kat." My thrusts are driving her farther up the bed, her head now pushed into the sheets, as she holds on for dear life. An epic orgasm is building. Leaning over her, I use the wall for leverage, rolling my hips every time I hit that sweet spot inside of her.

"Oh God, I'm coming!" Her voice is muffled as I feel her clenching around me. It would be enough to draw an orgasm from a lesser mortal. But I want another orgasm out of her before I come. Her pleasure is the only thing that matters right now.

Not letting her catch her breath, I cover her back with my chest. Moving one hand down, I grab her hand and tangle it with mine, bringing it to her clit. I slow my punishing pace ever so slightly as our fingers dance over her clit.

Kat's head turns underneath me, flushed pink from her orgasm. "Kiss me."

Her head turns to capture my lips as we both move closer and closer to release. Our lips barely touch as our hot breaths mingle.

"Sean, I'm almost there. Please don't stop. Don't ever stop." I capture her pleas with my lips as her hand moves in a frenzied pace on her clit. I remove my hand and grip her hips, resuming the pace I set earlier. I'm gripping so tight, it'll leave bruises, but that only heightens my need for her.

As she starts to come, I can feel myself ready for

release. Pulling out of her, I rip the rubber off and work my dick as thick spurts of cum paint her back. My head is thrown back in pleasure and I can't keep the groan inside at the picture before me. I haven't seen anything so sexy in my life.

My body is spent after the best orgasm of my life. I know I should clean us up, but I collapse next to Kat on the bed. Her beautiful blue eyes are staring at me with nothing but love. Tucking a pink strand of hair behind her ear, I grab my boxers from the end of the bed to wipe her off. She doesn't move. Her arms are tucked under her chin as her eyes drift shut.

"Sean?" I spoon into her side, not wanting an ounce of air between us.

"Kat?"

"Promise we'll never stop doing that?" I'm losing her to sleep, so I can only whisper to her as sleep pulls me under.

"Every day, love. I'll worship you every day."

THE PIERCING SOUND of the phone cuts through my sleep. Who the fuck is calling me this late? The clock shows three in the morning. Bloody hell. It's quiet again before the shrill piercing cuts in again. Reaching for the nightstand next to me, I grab the phone and answer quietly, trying not to wake Kat. Her chest rises and falls with her soft breaths. The sheet has slipped low, exposing her sexy tits.

"Hello?" My voice is scratchy when I answer.

"Who the fuck is this?" the voice on the other end shouts.

"You're calling me. You tell me." Nothing like being awakened to a wrong number in the middle of the night.

"What are you doing with Ellie's phone?" My brain is tired. Exhausted from making love to Kat all night. I'm not in the mood to dick around with this guy.

"You've got the wrong number, buddy. No Ellie here." I go to hang up, but a soft hand on my bicep pulls me away. Kat's face is strained.

"Give me the phone, Sean." Confused, I hand her the phone, seeing the name on the screen. Jamie. Who the bloody hell is Jamie?

"Jamie? Why are you calling so late?" The voice on the other end is muffled, but the colour drains from Kat's face. Standing, I grab the sweats next to the bed and quickly pull them on. Her hand covers her face, tears now glistening in her eyes.

"It can't be true, Jamie. It can't be." I can only look on in confusion. Who is this Ellie person, and why does Kat have her phone?

My confusion only grows as she mutters her next words, "God Save the King."

Chapter Nineteen

ELLIE

Pulling the sheet up over my bare chest, I look Sean in the eye. Confusion mars his beautiful features. Pain laces my heart that this might be one of the last times I see him. I was supposed to tell him tomorrow. He wasn't supposed to find out like this.

Jamie's words echo in my head. The king had a stroke and isn't expected to make it to morning. I need to come back to the palace now. I have to leave behind this life that I have no right to.

"I'll call my PPOs and get to the palace as soon as I can. Are you there now?" I'm staring into Sean's eyes. The confusion gives way to anger as I can see him looking more closely at me, studying my features in a way he never did before. I shake my head, hoping to tell him I'll explain everything as soon as I end this call. This life-changing call I never wanted to receive.

"They are there now. Do you really think I wouldn't have found you and kept you safe on this little adventure?" His voice is sharp, hard. So unlike my playful brother.

"What in the world are you talking about?" Hurt laces my tone.

"You really think the heir to the throne could go off and fuck around with some tattoo artist and we wouldn't have eyes on you?" The hurtful words stun me.

"Fuck off, James. I'll see you when I see you." I end the call and throw the phone down on the bed. Pressing the heels of my hands into my eyes, I need to keep it together. My sweet granddad is going to die. The lively man who used to sled with us during the holidays. Who would tell us the sordid history of our family when no one else would. The strongest leader our country has ever seen.

"Kat. What in the world is going on?" Sean's voice is quiet. This can't be it. This can't be the end with the only man I've loved. "Or is Kat even your name?"

I wince. Of course he would have heard Jamie calling me Ellie. "Kat is my middle name."

"And why is it you go by your middle name?" He starts pacing, an anxious energy rippling off of him.

"Because I didn't want you to know who I really was."

The look he gives me could cut glass. The pain I feel will be nothing when I deliver this blow. Worse than a sword penetrating armour.

"Because you have a husband at home? Wanted to play around?"

I stand, the sheet falling away from me. Looking for my bag and clothes, I have to start packing up what little I have here. Sweeping it all away like this piece of me never existed.

"Because my real name is Eleanor. Princess Eleanor Katherine Jane."

Sean stares back at me as if he's never met me. I sweep by him, trying to quickly dress when he grabs my arm and pulls me back to him. My still naked chest hits his bare one. My hand lands on his pec and the tattoos there that have become so familiar to me.

"What the hell do you mean, princess?" His voice is acid. I look down, our toes touching. My breath hitches, pain and sadness threatening to pull me under.

"Just what I said. I'm second in line to the throne. Technically, first now." I wince at that thought.

"First?"

"That was my brother on the phone. Jamie, or Prince James as you know him. My grandfather, the king, had a stroke. He isn't expected to make it through the night. I have to go home. Now."

I take advantage of his stunned silence to break free of his hold. Grabbing the first clothes I can find, I dress quickly and throw everything else in my bag.

"So what the fuck has this been these last few weeks then? Just some game to you?" Only years of training for dealing with the press and public events keeps my features even. The hurt in his voice is devastating.

"Of course it wasn't, Sean. I know this sounds terrible to say, but I hate my life in the palace. The overbearing eyes that watch what I do at all times of the day. The tabloids monitoring how I look and what I wear. The stuffiness. All I want is a quiet life, so I ran. And I ran into you."

He shakes his head, going back to the pacing. I step into my shoes, knowing the PPOs will be up here in the next five minutes if I'm not in the waiting car, speeding back to the palace.

"How lucky for me then." He's muttering to himself as I watch him. My bag slung is over my shoulder, but I don't want to leave him like this.

"Please, Sean. I just wanted time away from my life. From the structure and never-ending events. It's not me. I hate it. All I want is to have my own flat and a job I love. I was going to tell you tomorrow."

"You were going to tell me? Easy to say now that the secret is out."

One bloody phone call ripped away any chance for a future the two of us might have had. If only I could have explained it to him myself. If only Jamie didn't have to call with the worst news imaginable. This wasn't supposed to happen.

"Sean. Please, I can't explain right now. Just, believe me. Believe me that this was real. That everything I feel for you is real." Shite, there isn't enough time. "I have to—" The loud banging on the stairs pulls our attention to the door, seconds before my PPOs burst in.

"And I guess now we'll never know." He sits on the bed, his back to me. The air in the room is rife with nervous energy—mine at having to leave Sean and my PPOs at getting me back to the palace. But I can't leave him like this. He has to know that everything I felt for him was real. You can't fake those kinds of emotions.

I wrap my hand around his neck, dropping my head to his.

"I love you, Sean. And no matter what you think, this wasn't a game. It was real for me. And I will *always* love you." I kiss his head and walk towards my security officers.

THE MOOD at the palace is somber. Staff loiter around the halls. Rumours are undoubtedly being passed as to what is happening. The security detail takes me straight to the private quarters. Looks and whispers linger in my wake at my disheveled appearance. I ignore them all. The only person I want to see may not even realize I am there.

"Ellie!" A familiar voice bellows behind me. Jamie comes running up to me, in his own state of disarray. He slows to a stop in front of me, taking in my appearance. "What did you do to yourself?" He plays with a piece of my pink hair. I stare down, now realizing I'm standing in joggers and Sean's old grey shirt I loved so much. His familiar scent is the only thing keeping me grounded right now. Even though he probably hates me. I'll never forget the look on his face when he found out who I am.

"Had to make myself harder to recognize." I glance up into his red-rimmed eyes. "We can talk about it later. I want to see Granddad."

"You're in no state to see him right now."

"Well, I really don't give a shite what you think. I'd rather see him like this than be presentable and not have the chance. So shove off, James." He rears back. I knew the blow would land the second I used his full name. In a right fit, I stomp off towards my granddad's bedroom where his own security officers stand guard outside.

"May I see him, please?" They give me a once-over, before nodding and opening the door.

The beep of the heart rate monitor is the only thing heard in the large room. The soft glow of lamps creates an ominous mood. My grandmum is sitting in a chair at my granddad's bedside. My mum and dad stand behind her with my aunt and uncle. I move farther into the room, my presence still not known until Jamie comes up beside me, clearing his throat. All eyes turn to him. Then me. I can feel the reproachful glares.

"Eleanor. What have you done with yourself?" My mother's voice is full of consternation. The pink hair must be a shock. I can only imagine what they would think if they saw the tattoo underneath. I move closer to my granddad's bed. The once formidable king is small, already starting to fade away. I set my hand down on my grandmum's shoulder, giving it a brief squeeze. Her wrinkly hand clutches mine. Her glassy eyes turn to me.

"You were always your grandfather's favourite." Her voice is solemn. Quiet. "Take a moment with him." She stands, giving me a peck on the cheek as she ushers everyone out to the sitting room. As the door closes, the dam on my emotions starts to break. Tears well in my eyes. All the emotion from the last hour is simmering, waiting to break free. I go to sit on the edge of the bed and take his still warm hand in mine, giving it a brief squeeze.

"I'm sorry I wasn't here, Granddad. But I hope you know how much I love you. Now that Mum is taking over, I really don't know what to do." I look down at our clasped hands. The ring of our family crest sits loose on his thin finger.

"These last few weeks with Sean have been the best of my life. I wish you could have met him. You would've liked him. Kind. Caring. Funny. Everything I've always wanted. I know I was born into this, but you know it's never what I wanted. A quiet, simple life. The kind of love you and Grandmum had. But I think I've lost it. I wish you could tell me what to do, but it's not possible. I'm going to miss you and your guidance so much. I love you." I kiss the back of his hand, not wanting him to leave this world.

It gets harder to breathe the farther away from him I get. The only person I want right now hates me. Leaving Granddad's room behind, I'm adrift. I don't know where to go when a steadying hand comes down on my shoulder.

"Come, my darling. Let's get you straightened out." My mum's voice is clear. I hate that my granddad will be gone from this world in a few hours' time. My mom's arm wraps around my waist, guiding me towards her room. Her stylists are there, ready to fix me up.

"We'll talk about this later." She waves her hand over my appearance. "But right now, we have other things to tend to. James will be waiting outside for you once you're finished. I'm going back to sit with Mum."

"I don't need a babysitter." My voice is scratchy and harsher than I intended it to be.

"That remains to be seen, young lady. Now, we'll get you taken care of and get you appropriate attire for what will no doubt be a terrible moment. I'm sorry you had to come home like this."

She is out of the room, and the stylists descend on me. Before they start yanking my clothes off, I grab the robe that's being held in front of me.

"Stop. Please. Just let me have a moment."

Heading into the loo, I take stock of my appearance. My eyes are dull and my cheeks sunken as I strip out of Sean's shirt and cover myself up with the robe. The lingering smell is the final straw. Tears rush from my eyes as the dam finally breaks and the overwhelming emotions crash into me. The loss of my granddad, the larger-than-life man who has always been in my life and the loss of Sean, my new love, and the life that could have been.

"Your Highness." Alice is at my side, squeezing me into her. "Everything will be alright." Her voice is oddly comforting as my heart is breaking.

With not even a moment to reflect, I'm being pulled out of the loo. The stylists are attacking my pink hair. I don't pay attention to the whispers around me as I'm plucked and prodded to within a centimetre of my life. I close my eyes, blocking out the world around me and wishing with every fibre of my being that I could take back these last few hours.

Chapter Twenty

ELLIE

Breaking News

British News Network is reporting that King Edward has suffered a stroke and passed away early this morning. The Queen, his two children, and their families were by his side. Princess Katherine will now be the reigning monarch of our beloved nation. More to come on this developing story.

The last few hours have been a whirlwind of the worst kind, blending from one after the other into the next. The whole family was here as our beloved granddad slowly slipped away. We were given a few short hours before we had to make ourselves presentable.

I'm in a simple black cape dress, with my hair now restored to its natural colour and pulled back into a low bun. Our pictures are being snapped as we leave the palace. Crowds are gathering at the gates and calling for our attention. A sea of flowers stretches as far as the eye can see.

My face is devoid of any emotion as Jamie and I slip into the car to take us back to Clarence House with the rest of the family. I'm trying to keep it together as best I can. My heart shattered hours ago, and I'm not sure if it will ever be fully put back together. The death of my beloved grandfather. The loss of Sean. My future changed before my eyes, as I'm now the first in line for the throne.

"Are you going to speak to me? Or are you going to wallow all day over there?" Jamie's voice is cold. Staring out the dark tinted windows, I don't bother with looking at him. Anger is firing through my body at his earlier words, still ringing in my head.

"No, I don't think I will." We drive through a wall of noise as we leave the palace to make our way to Mum's. It's then a paralyzing thought hits me. It will no longer be Mum's house. It's the residence of the heir apparent. A sickness washes over me at the thought.

"You look like you're going to be sick. Are you okay?" Jamie's hand comes down on my arm as I try to take in deep breaths.

"No, I'm not okay, you daft idiot!" I shove his hand off of me, as my voice carries in the small space. All eyes are on me. "The world is changing before our eyes, and you have the audacity to ask me if I'm okay!"

"You need to pull it together, Ellie." His voice is harsh this time.

"Don't you think I know that?" I hiss. I don't have the luxury of losing it in public. While the nation gets to mourn their king, we have to hide our grief. Keep calm and carry on. "Now, in the interest of 'pulling it together,' leave me be."

The short drive to Clarence House feels endless. The

crowds around the palace are enormous and growing by the minute. Mum and Dad are waiting for us with Uncle Albert and Aunt Helena. Grandmum is still at the palace. There are protocols in place when the king or queen dies. But right now, everyone looks out of sorts.

"Ellie. Come with me." Charlotte is at my side, pulling me into the house. Leading me to a small sitting room upstairs, she keeps her hands in mine.

"What has been going on? Where have you been? And why did you show up to the palace with pink hair?" She's firing off questions faster than I can think. My emotions, on a hair trigger now, explode out of me on a sob.

"Oh, darling." She wraps her arms around me as I let the tears flow. I cling to her for dear life, as her hands move over me in a soothing manner.

"Charlotte. I don't know what to do." My voice is shaky. I've lost one of the most important people in my life and will likely never see the other again.

"Ellie. Talk to me. What happened?" Wiping the tears from my face, I tell her everything. From heeding her advice to meeting Sean along the way.

"I fell in love, Charlotte. I love him and I have no idea what to do."

She wipes away the tears still streaking down my face. "Can you talk to him? See how he feels?"

"I lied to him, Charlotte!" I move away from her and start pacing the room. "He was devastated. How will he ever get past that?"

"Eleanor. You need to take a breath. You aren't going to do anyone any good by having a nervous breakdown."

I turn and face her, pinning her with an unwavering gaze. "Have you ever thought that maybe I'm tired of living for everyone else? For once in my life, I was living for myself. And it was incredible. No one was telling me where to be or what to do. And the press wasn't watching my every move. I've never felt more like myself, Charlotte. It was incredible."

"Was it because of Sean?"

The sound of his name causes pain to flash through me. "Yes. No. I made the decision to run away, but meeting him? It gave me a confidence I never knew I had."

"Maybe he feels the same way. Maybe he'll want to stay with you too."

I look around the grand sitting room we're in. It's one of the less formal sitting rooms, yet still older than most of London. "Why would anyone want to take on this world? Sean has his own life. He's building something wonderful that he wouldn't be able to leave."

"Ellie." She walks over to me and wraps me in a hug. I push her away, unable to take her sympathy.

"No. I—" Having kept a lid on my emotions my entire life, it's hard to tamp them back down. "I'm sorry, Charlotte. But I can't discuss this anymore. I have to go."

Rushing out of the sitting room, I follow the hallway to my own room. It's nothing like the small studio apartment I've been staying in for the last few weeks. The entire apartment could fit in my bedroom alone. It's cold and too glamourous for what I need.

All I want, *all I need*, is to feel Sean's arms around me. There's an emptiness in my chest that feels endless. Falling to the bed, I let the tears continue, hoping sleep will eventually take me.

"ELEANOR. ARE YOU READY?" Mum's voice is calm. She's been nothing but a beacon of hope in the last week since being proclaimed the reigning monarch. Granddad has been moved to lie in state at Westminster before his service at the end of the week. Mum insisted on one final, private family viewing before the public visitation.

"As I'll ever be."

"My sweet girl. I'm worried about you." I wish her voice had the same calming effect from when I was young, but I'm stuck in my own head.

"There's not much to do about it now. Just need to make it through these next few days, and I'll be okay."

"Will you, though? Every time I look at you, your pain just gets worse and worse. It breaks my heart."

"I'm sorry. I'll try to pull myself together." Easier said than done.

She shakes her head before pulling me in for a hug. "No stiff upper lip with me today, Eleanor. It's going to be a hard day. You're allowed to feel your feelings. I'll be by your side today."

"Mum. That's impossible. You're the queen now." I let out a shaky laugh, the first time in days.

"Bollocks. I'm the queen. If I want to be by my daughter's side today, I will be by her side."

A smile breaks through. A rarity these last few days. I can't imagine the pressure she is under right now. No one wants to become king or queen when it's at the sacrifice of another life.

"Let's go get this day over with." I grab her hand and give it a squeeze. The days have been endless as we get closer to the funeral. It's a day I never want to experience, but it is a part of life.

I only wish I had more time with my grandfather. It never feels like enough time. There is so much wisdom I still could have learned from him. But now, life is looking clearer than ever before. The last few weeks with Sean proved how I am not cut out for this royal life. For being in the spotlight and having my every move watched. Having my every day planned down to the minute.

It took running away for me to realize what I truly want out of life. I want to be able to wake up, go to a job I enjoy, and come home to the person I love. It's simple. It's easy. And there's no easy way to go about getting it. The royal family is in a state of distress, and I don't know how I can further add to it.

Stirring myself away from my thoughts, I follow Mum to the cars that will take us to Westminster. The closer we get to the abbey, the more distraught I become. For the first time in my life, I'm not keeping my emotions in check. As mum said, no stiff upper lip today. People and press line the roads as we make the short drive from the palace. Flowers are flung onto the road as we pass. It only adds to the heaviness of my own emotions today.

There's already a line of people waiting to start the visitation. In all my years of being a royal, I've never felt so on display before. All I want is to go back to that studio apartment and stay curled up until these days are over. But I'm not granted that ability.

Charlotte appears at my side and we walk in behind our parents. The smoky smell of incense lingers through the abbey as we make the long walk to where the king is lying in state. My chest constricts the closer we get to him. And when we finally arrive? I'm inconsolable.

One of the most important people in my life is gone and there is nothing I can do about it. No matter how I try to comfort myself or tell myself it will be better, I'm at an utter loss. Furiously wiping the tears from my face, I try to pull myself together. Jamie comes to my other side, offering me support that I would have rejected any other day. I'm too tired to rebuff him today.

"I'm here, Ellie. It'll be okay. I promise." I can only nod at his words. His strong arm around my shoulders gives me the strength I need to soldier on through the day. Grandmum is here and the epitome of grace and strength. Not a tear falls from her stoic face as she says her goodbyes to the man she loves. Eighty is too young for a larger-than-life personality to be gone from this world.

But seeing the love my grandparents shared brings a sense of calm over me. It's as if the heavens have finally opened up and the rains have finally cleared. I've experienced the love they had. They were never an arranged marriage. It was love. And I had that with Sean. And that's what I want. It won't be easy, but for the second time in my life, I'm going to do what I want. The rest of the country be damned.

Chapter Twenty-One

SEAN

The buzz of the tattoo gun is the only thing that cuts through the mindless chatter swirling around the tattoo shop. The vibrations keep me from continuing my spiral. The last few weeks have been endless. The day after Kat left, or Eleanor as I should call her, the news was announced that the king had died. It rocked the entire country.

Me? I could only focus on the images of the king's granddaughter as she stood outside the palace. She was no longer my pink-haired goddess. She was the princess that belonged to the nation. And seeing her there with her dull brown hair, not being able to reach out to her, was a hell I don't wish on my worst enemy.

Her eyes are pure torture. The pain flickering in them is more than I can handle. Everywhere in London is a reminder of her. We were never destined to be together. As upset as I was with her, I could see her struggling. I wanted to wrap her in my arms and not let the world touch her.

But I couldn't. So I buried myself in my work. I can't remember the last time I'd done so many tattoos. I'd been busting my arse so I wouldn't think about Kat. Damn…Eleanor.

Finishing up with the client on my table, I send him on his way. Thankfully, I don't have any more appointments for the day. The rain-soaked London day matches my mood. Pierce side-eyes me as I head back to my office. The bastard won't stop pestering me about my attitude.

Sitting in my office, I distract myself with paperwork. For once, I wasn't thinking about the programme I wanted to start or about making more money for the shop. Eleanor pulled my head out of my arse. She fit so perfectly into my life. Never once did I suspect she was a princess. Sure, she was more proper than most of the women I dated, but she slipped seamlessly into my life.

"What in the bloody hell are you still moping about?" Pierce bursts into my office without invitation.

"I'm fine. I'm just trying to get work done." The stare he gives me tells me he doesn't believe me.

"You've been a sad sack ever since Kat left." I wince when he calls her Kat. "Are you really that upset that you're no longer getting any pussy?"

I'm up and out of my chair before I can even think twice. Slamming him against the wall, anger is firing through my veins. "Don't ever talk about her that way."

"Christ, you really are distraught over losing her. Just go talk to her. Whatever you did can't be that bad."

I shove off of him before I do something I know I'll regret. I thought burying myself in my work would help rid her from my mind, but everywhere I turn, memories of Kat overwhelm me.

"What makes you think I did something?" Pierce really can be a wanker.

"It's usually always the man's fault. Hasn't Dad taught you anything?" He laughs to himself. Our dad always told us that if you ever upset a woman, to apologize. I don't know why, because he could do no wrong in Mum's eyes.

"In this case, it's definitely not my fault. I can't go get her back. It's not that simple."

"Why does it have to be that hard? It's not like she's bloody royalty."

I stop dead in my tracks at his comment. There's no way he knows who she actually is. But shit, did I just give it away? The look on his face tells me I did.

"Fuck, are you serious?" His face is a mix of shock and excitement. "Kat is the princess? What? I mean, how?"

"Hell if I know. Kat didn't exactly hand me her CV when she got here. Fuck, Eleanor!" I push my hands through my hair with more force than necessary. My brain is a fucking mess. Hell, I couldn't even go out back without thinking about our day in the park and fucking in the back. Kat wanted to learn everything about running the shop. Just her presence made everyone here happier. I'm well and truly fucked.

"Are you going to be okay?" Pierce now looks at me with concern.

"I'll be fine."

"Bullshit. There is no way you'll be fine. You were about ready to punch me in the face."

"That's because you were being an arsehole."

"Had I known how you felt about her, I wouldn't have said anything."

I give him a skeptical look. "Oh yeah? And how do I feel about her?"

"You're in love, you wanker. Anyone with eyes can see it."

I couldn't argue with him on that point. I'd gone and fallen irrevocably in love with my pink-haired goddess. And now what the hell was I supposed to do?

"I can't be here anymore. I need to get out of town."

"You going to Mum and Dad's? Mum would be very disappointed if you tell her you fell in love with the princess and didn't realize it."

Shit, he was right. She'd never forgive me if she found out I fell in love with her. Damn her and her love of everything royal. The perfect place hits me.

"You think you can cover me for a few weeks?" A last-minute ticket to the states is more than I want to pay, but I can't be anywhere in London. Hell, anywhere in Europe where the recent changes to the British royal family is front and center news.

"Between Trevor and me, I think we can cover. Where are you going to go?"

"The one place in the world that won't be concerned with the royal family."

THE MOUNTAINS in the distance are a familiar sight. It's been too long since I've been to Dixon, Idaho. Walking out of the airport, the familiar voice calling my name tugs my attention to him.

"Hey, Pops." My granddad stands almost a head taller than me.

"Seany. I'm so happy you're here." He pulls me in for a hug. We always came to visit him over the summers growing up, and I never appreciated him as much as I do now.

"Thanks for letting me come on such short notice." He pulls me towards his old, beat-up truck. The same truck that he has had since I was in high school. "Still have ol' Betty?"

"You can't get rid of perfection. Now, you gonna tell me why you're here?"

"Can't I just want to come visit my family?" He gives me the side-eye as he pulls out of the airport. Nothing gets by him. I forgot how much I love coming here. We're immediately in the middle of nowhere as we head towards the ranch.

"If you wanted to come visit, you would've planned ahead. Besides, your mom called me and said she was worried."

Fucking Pierce. Couldn't trust him with anything sometimes. If he told Mum about Kat, I'm going to strangle him the next time I see him.

"It's about a girl."

"It always is. Care to explain?" The sun is sinking below the mountains. It looks like everything is on fire. It doesn't hold a candle to London.

"I fell in love with the wrong woman."

Chapter Twenty-Two

ELLIE

"As for the last item of business. The king has a few letters for each of you." The solicitor hands each of us an envelope. The thick stationery with my grandfather's crest and initials is another painful reminder that he is gone.

"I believe that concludes everything for today. You may reach me at the office should you require anything further." The old man snaps his briefcase shut. He bows to each of us before departing. I stare at my name written in my grandfather's tidy handwriting. Jamie has opened his letter and is frowning. My mum across the table is smiling reading hers. Clutching mine to my chest, I stand. I don't want to read this here. Instead, I leave everyone, finding a footman standing at the doors.

"Please call my PPOs. Tell them I wish to leave the palace immediately." I head towards my room. We've been staying here at the palace with everything going on. It's been somewhat easier being all together. Changing into joggers and a jumper, I throw on my rain jacket and head towards our private entrance, my grandfather's letter in my pocket.

"Your Highness. Where are we going today?" my security officer asks.

"Peter Pan statue. Please." I slide into the car. "No entourage. Just you two, please." She nods, closing the door behind me. It's easier for them to grant these requests when I'm not running around London on my own.

I rest my head against the seat of the car. The rain is quiet as we make our way through the city. The drive is quick, as London is not busy in the early Sunday evening. Hitting the entrance to the park, my security officers walk behind me as I follow the path I've known so well throughout the years. The small bronze statue has always spoken to me. Wanting to remain young. Not wanting to become an adult and step in as the reigning monarch of the United Kingdom.

A tree sits behind the bushes across from the statue. My own protected cove to hide away and just sit. To not be seen. Tilting the umbrella that my PPO gave me, I take the letter from my grandfather out of my pocket and begin to read.

My darling granddaughter,

If you are reading this, then my unfortunate end has come. Hopefully I went out, as our friends across the pond say, guns blazing. But likely, it was old age. And in old age comes wisdom. Wisdom I now wish to impart on you.

Don't be beholden to the path that is laid out

before you. My dear, you have so much fire and spirit inside of you, that I would hate to see that squeezed out of you. Sometimes, we are born into a certain lot in life. You were afforded one many only dream of. Yet, you dream of a different kind of life.

I will always cherish my time spent with you. Teaching you what I knew about the throne. You teaching me about things only a little girl would know. And in these precious moments with you, I learned the most valuable lesson. That sometimes, you must set free the thing you love the most in the world.

And so, my darling Eleanor, go. Go live your life as you see fit. Maybe I have completely misjudged you, as an old man may not always be of sound mind, but if you want the throne, then lead with all the fire and passion you possess. But, and I think this old man may be spot on, find the life you want to live. There is no shame in not wanting the life you've been given. There may be some pushback, but tell them this old man said you could. No one can fight with the dead king.

My greatest wish for you is to find someone to walk through this life with you. Your grandmother was the love of my life. I hope you experience this kind of great love in your life. You have so much to offer the world, and I hope you find someone who treats you well and can help you navigate this new chapter in your life.

Do not be sad that I am gone, for I will always be with you. I have cherished our time together and cannot wait to see what you do with your life.

Love,
Your favourite Grandfather

A TEN-POUND NOTE slips out from the envelope. Our own private joke over the years. Tears are now flowing freely, splattering on the letter my grandfather left me, knowing exactly the words I needed to hear. Never did I think my distaste for the life I was born into was shown to those around me. I wipe at the tears. The vise that has been squeezing my heart all these years loosens its hold on me. I carefully fold the letter and tuck it inside my jacket. I let the umbrella fall, letting the raindrops hit my face, mixing with my tears.

"Thought I'd find you here." I open my eyes, seeing Jamie standing in front of me. That same look from earlier furrows his brow. I give him a smile as he sits down on the wet ground next to me.

"So, what are you going to do?" His voice is quiet. So unlike the vibrant brother I'm used to. These last weeks have been strained between us.

"I think if you're asking, you already know." I reach

over and take his hand, giving it a squeeze. He lets out a heavy breath.

"Grandfather is quite sneaky. Training both of us to take over the throne, knowing you would eventually renounce your seat." His voice is shaky. "Am I really prepared to take over the throne? Who in their right mind would give me the keys to the nation?"

I turn, crossing my legs and facing him.

"I believe in you. It's not like you're going to take the throne tomorrow. It'll be years. You can learn from Mum. We've been in this family for years. It's not like you won't know what to do. You'll always have me in your court." I look down at our joined hands.

"Ellie. I'm sorry for how I acted when you came home. I was upset and hurt that you left. Even though I said to go, I was jealous that you wanted something badly enough to go after it."

I look up at his tear-filled eyes and pull him in for a big hug.

"I'm sorry too. For dropping an entire kingdom on you. For not being able to handle this life. For wanting something different. No matter where I go, I'll always love you and always be in your corner." We're both crying, sitting on the wet ground in the quickly darkening London sky. Not a prince and princess. But two siblings lamenting their loss and accepting what the future will hold.

"C'mon. I'm cold and need a drink. And you need to tell me all about this Sean. I can't have you running off for just any old guy. I need to approve."

I give him a wet smile before standing and helping him up, and we walk back to the cars. The Peter Pan statue is no longer a symbol of an impending adulthood I don't want but something that I have to fight for. With everything I have.

"WHAT DO YOU MEAN, you are renouncing your place in line?" My mother's voice is even, but her face betrays her confusion. "Please, give us the room." With a wave of her hand, she dismisses her staff.

"I'm sure I didn't hear you correctly. You cannot give up your place in succession of the throne." The tight line of her lips tells me she heard me perfectly.

"I meant exactly what I said. These last few weeks have shown me that I am not capable of ruling this country the way Granddad did."

"No one expects you to run the country like Dad. He was one of a kind. You have to make your own mark on the throne. It takes time to learn."

"I've been learning this my whole damn life!" The sharp snap of my voice shocks even me. "I am not cut out for this life."

"You are born into this life. It will be the great privilege of your life to be able to lead this country with dignity and grace."

"But I don't want to!" Rising from the chair, I start pacing the room. It's warm in here for a spring day. It makes it harder to breathe. The heavy sweater I put on earlier is doing nothing to help.

"You are acting like a petulant child. I do not have time for this." She starts shuffling the papers on her desk in an attempt to dismiss me. I will not take this lying down.

"Make time. I'm your daughter, not some staff member you can easily dismiss."

"Eleanor, I've heard enough. Show me some respect and stop this conversation right now."

"I'm showing you respect by telling you of my plans. I don't plan on changing my mind."

"You should not make snap decisions at a time during great upheaval in your life. I promise you will feel better in a few weeks once things have settled down." She has gone back to the papers on her desk. My temper is boiling because she is not taking me seriously.

"This isn't some snap decision, Mum!" The room starts to spin, but I keep talking. "My entire adult life has been spent being picked apart by the media. One hair out of place, one word out of line, and I'm dragged through the mud. I cannot handle the pres—" Black spots mark my vision as I start to sway, catching the velvet couch before the world goes dark.

"ELEANOR. THANK HEAVENS, ARE YOU ALRIGHT?" Mum's face is above mine as the world starts to come back into focus.

"What happened?" I try to sit up, but a hand to my shoulder keeps me horizontal.

"You fainted. You were ranting and then you went ghostly white and fainted. Thankfully you didn't hurt yourself." Her face is full of concern, as her hand strokes my hair in a soothing manner.

"I'm sorry to worry you." This time I sit up, turning my head in shame that I fainted while trying to show my mum that I want to live a normal life. If I can't even take care of myself, why would she ever see me having the strength to make such a life-altering decision?

"Oh Ellie, my darling girl. It is I who should be sorry. I

have never truly seen the pressure you are under. Or maybe I just didn't want to see it."

Her hands are warm on my face as she keeps my gaze on her. Mum has always made time for Jamie and me. Being raised in the royal light was not normal. We were being paraded in front of people for as long as I can remember. But if we needed her for a scraped knee or a cut, she was there. Just like she is now.

"I can no longer take my role." My voice is quiet. I try to hold back the tears, but they start leaking out. "These last few weeks have shown me what I truly desire in life. To wake up with someone I love. Work at a job I love. And at the end of the day, come home to a family I love. Without the media tearing me down at every turn."

"Is this truly what you want?" She swipes my tears away as I look at her. Instead of confusion, her face is full of concern. "This isn't something you can come back from."

I think of Sean. Of the short time we spent together that meant everything to me. I don't know where he is or what he is doing. I don't even know if he would want me back in his life after lying about who I am. But even if he won't take me back, I know this is what I want.

"This is what I want. Truly. I know you may not understand it, but I want a simple life."

"I don't know why anyone would give this up, but she has my support." Jamie's voice echoes throughout the quiet room as he joins us on the couch, pulling me in for a hug.

"She's discussed this with you, Jamie?" She's looking at both of us with glassy eyes.

"She has. I admit, I haven't always been the best support for her, but I'm ready to step up." His voice is steady. He gives me a squeeze before turning to our mother and addressing her. "I know I haven't taken my position seriously. But I will try. I know you will be under a microscope this year before the coronation, and I promise I will change."

"James. While I don't agree with you on some things, your lively personality will be a great strength for you. I want you to stay true to yourself because the country will be lucky to have you."

A very unprincess-like snort escapes. "You might want to tone down the visits to the clubs."

"There are some things I don't need to know about my children. It's why I don't read the news, but I'm afraid it's made me short-sighted where you two are concerned. I'm sorry if I haven't been there for you."

"If you're there for us, I can't claim I have mummy-issues when I'm trying to find a woman to take all this on." Jamie waves his hand around to indicate the reality of our life.

"Jamie! For fuck's sake, Mum does not need to know about how you spend your free time!" I shove Jamie away from me. But his antics have brought a much-needed smile to my face.

"She just said she wanted to be more involved in our lives. Someone has to keep her updated since you'll be running away."

"James. Keep me updated to a point. I do not need to know everything, darling. And as for you, Eleanor," she starts, her voice back to being quiet as she pulls me towards her, "I expect you at family dinners and holidays."

"Oh Mum," I say, as a sob escapes. She wraps her arms around me as a weight lifts from my chest. I don't know what the future holds, but right now, support radiates from both my mum and Jamie. It will be a hard few months, with transitioning out and becoming a private citizen, but I know it's a decision I won't regret. No matter what happens next, I'm finally ready and open to taking whatever the future may bring.

Chapter Twenty-Three

ELLIE - FOUR WEEKS LATER

Breaking News from British News Network

In a stunning turn of events, Buckingham Palace has released a statement that Princess Eleanor will be renouncing her place in the royal line. With the passing of King Edward earlier this spring, she was set to be first in line once Princess Katherine is formally crowned early next year. We will follow this breaking story and talk to royal insiders about the preparedness of Prince James for his new role in the royal line.

"Are you going to stand out here all day?" Pierce's voice jolts me from my morose thoughts. I've been watching people come and go all morning, working up the courage to talk to Sean.

It's been a long couple of weeks, untangling myself from the threads of royal life. Figuring out what would happen with my patronages, funds, and housing was all more confusing than I care to admit. But I finally found my own place, on a gated street, that I can call my own.

"You going to come inside?" Pierce's voice is hard, harder than I've ever heard it. Iciness spreads through me at the thought of how angry his brother is.

"If it's okay."

"Of course it is, Kat. Wait, can I even call you that?"

"Ellie. You can call me Ellie." The buzzing of tattoo guns brings a smile to my face. My eyes search out Sean, but he's nowhere to be seen.

"Well, well, well. What do we have here?" Trevor stands, crossing his arms. I didn't expect anything less, but it's hard. My heart is ready to beat out of my chest. My skin is tight with anxiety.

I throw my hands up. "I come in peace. I…" I start, my voice breaking. "I was hoping to talk to Sean."

"He's not here." Trevor goes back to what he's doing, as Pierce motions for me to follow him back to the office.

"Hey, Kat." I turn to face Trevor. "Ruby misses you. Now that you're a commoner like us, come by for Sunday lunch."

I fight the tears that threaten.

"She's the next person I'll see." After everything that happened, I thought I would have lost these people. The kindness they're showing me, even though they're upset with me, reinforces the decision I made, no matter how painful it's been.

"So, any big news to share?" I close the door behind me, as Pierce takes the seat that Sean usually occupied. It doesn't fit him.

"Oh, nothing too much. Just giving up the crown, no big deal."

"And why'd you give up the throne, Ellie?" He emphasizes my name. He's not used to calling me that.

"Because I was miserable. Because up until a few months ago, I was merely existing, not living. And then I ran away. I came here and discovered everything that was missing from my life. A purpose. Friendship." I swallow back the tears that blur my vision as I make my case. "I found love."

"It's about damn time!" Pierce sweeps me into a huge hug. "He's been a miserable old sod without you."

"He has?" All the air leaves my lungs as I tighten my grip on Pierce. I never thought I'd be so welcomed back by him after what I did to his brother. But that person isn't here.

"Where is he?" I pull back, my gaze swinging around the empty office. As if by sheer force of my will, Sean might materialize in front of my eyes. "May I speak with him?"

Pierce just laughs. "We're all bloody idiots. How none of us realized you were the princess with your formal tone, I'll never know. But Sean's not here, Pink."

The nickname is exactly what I needed to hear to calm my raging nerves. "Where is he?"

"He might've had a nervous breakdown."

"He what?!" I shout, not meaning to. "I'm sorry, but is he okay? I need to see him at once."

"You know you're not a princess anymore, right? This 'at once' business has to go," he says on a laugh.

"Pierce. Where is Sean?" Any patience I have is wearing thin.

"He left. He couldn't take being here and seeing how sad you were, so he went to stay with our granddad."

My heart pangs at the mention of their granddad. Sean mentioned him a few times and held him in such regard. He still has his, while I lost mine. It still hurts.

"Sorry, Ellie. I didn't think. But Sean's been stateside the last few weeks."

Grabbing his arms, I pull Pierce in front of me. "This is very important. I need to see him. This can't be done over the phone."

"You'd fly to Idaho to see him?"

I smack him upside the head. "Of course I would! I fell in love with him, and I have to see if we have a chance. I have no idea if he'll take me back, but I have to try. He's it for me, Pierce. So yes, I have to go see him. Please."

He pulls out a sheet of paper and starts writing something down, before handing me an address. He pulls back before it's in my grasp. "I only ask for one thing in return."

Of course he wants something. "And what might that be?"

"That I'm there when you meet Mum. She's going to lose her shit when she finds out Sean fell in love with the princess."

I'M TAKING PERHAPS the biggest risk of my life. Well, perhaps the second biggest after giving up my claim to the crown. I was prepared to work much harder to win Pierce over. He was an easy target. After promising to bring Sean home, I booked the first ticket out of Heathrow.

The cool, summer air hits me as I exit the car in front of the large ranch home. After spending the last eighteen hours traveling, it feels good to be outside, stretching my legs. In all my travels, I can't remember the last time I came somewhere so remote. Dixon, Idaho is a small town that took countless hours to get to. The family farm was even farther outside the small town.

Gulping in lungfuls of clean air, I'm hit with the stark contrast of the open skies versus the congestion of London. I wouldn't trade the busy metropolis for anything, but it's calm and peaceful here. I can see why Sean loved coming here growing up.

"Ma'am, can I help you?" A deep, booming voice comes from the front porch, thick with a country accent. The two-story house behind him looms large. It looks like a vintage log cabin, straight out of a magazine with a wrap-around porch and deep green shutters. The view of the mountains in the distance makes it look postcard ready. It's breathtaking.

"Hello, hi. I'm looking for Sean." My voice is scratchy after flying.

"You sound like you've come a long way. Come on inside. I'll see if I can track him down." His voice is warm, like hot chocolate on a cold day. It instantly puts me at ease.

"Thank you, I appreciate it. Are you Sean's grand-dad?" He holds the door open for me, nodding as I'm hit with the smell of pine. The large lobby has an empty fireplace and a bar with a few lingering guests.

"Can I get you something to drink?" The moustache tickling his upper lip makes him look even more kind with his glittering blue eyes. Eyes that mirror Sean's.

"If you have a glass of white wine, I'd love one. I'm Ellie, by the way." I extend my hand to him.

"Thomas. You're Seany's girl?" The calluses on his hands give away years of hard work. A shy smile flirts across my lips.

"I hope, but I don't know. It's been a difficult few weeks." I take the glass of wine he passes to me, taking a large gulp. To say the last few weeks have been difficult is a gross understatement. The blowback from renouncing my title was swift and cutting. I didn't leave my place for days because of the media. But thankfully, Mum and Dad had an overseas tour scheduled and took the heat off me.

"Sean keeps it close to the vest. He filled me in somewhat. So, what are you doing here, princess?" His voice is full of mirth.

"No longer a princess. For once, my future is mine. And I'm here to see if maybe there's a place for Sean in it." It is still weird to say I'm no longer a princess. Maybe the more I say it, the easier it will get.

"I am sorry to hear about your grandfather. It's never easy losing a loved one." My hand instinctively goes to the flower necklace he once gave me. It still hurts to think about him. Losing him wasn't easy, but I'll always carry him with me.

"Thank you. It's been hard, but I'm carrying on."

He smacks his lips, taking a large gulp of beer. "How very British of you."

"Stiff upper lip, if you will." I give him a wink as we continue our conversation. Thomas puts me at ease. The entire flight over here, my stomach was a ball of nerves. I still have no idea what I'm doing, but I'm hoping Sean will be happy to see me.

SEAN

"GEMMA, I'm telling you. This car is shot. It'll break down on you again. You need a new one."

"Just fix it. I'll deal with it later." My cousin huffs, turning on her heel and stalking off to the main house.

Royal Reckoning

My mum's family all stayed close, living on the large property here in Dixon. Each grandkid has a cottage on the property, but some live in town. It's been the perfect escape these last few weeks. I haven't seen them in a long time, so getting to see all of them at once was just what I needed.

The place is quiet this time of day. Most guests are still coming back from the parks or taking in the sunset. Being here, in the shadow of the mountains, I feel calm. The hustle of London did nothing to help ease the ache in my heart. But when I stepped foot off the plane and saw my grandpa standing there waiting for me, I knew I had made the right decision.

His stern face cracked me within seconds and I told him everything. We had a glass of scotch at the main house, and I slept for ages, waking the following afternoon, feeling more relaxed and calmer than I had in ages.

I throw down the rag, giving up on Gemma's car for the day. My grandpa taught me car repair when I spent my summers here. I always loved spending the time with him. I appreciate it even more now knowing what Kat is going through. Or Eleanor. Or whatever she is calling herself these days.

Stretching to put the tools away, my hand idly traces the new tattoo on my bicep. Normally a piece this big would be done in stages, but I had Pierce go straight through, needing the pain as a distraction from the pain in my chest.

All I want is to grab a cold beer and then go relax in the small house my grandpa had ready for me. As I push open the door to the main house, the open windows pull in the evening breeze. It never feels this good in London. Gemma's back behind the counter, her eyes wide. I look at her, confused, until I look past her to the bar. Sitting there, with my grandpa, is Kat. Her hair is back to that vibrant pink I loved so much.

I still have a visceral reaction to seeing Kat. Everything about her turns me on, yet I don't understand what she's doing here. Why she's not off learning the ropes to become the future monarch.

"Hi, Sean." Her voice is soft. Quiet. She looks tired, like she hasn't slept in weeks.

"What the hell are you doing here?" The question bursts out of me before I can stop it. My grandpa leaves the bar, slapping me on the back of the head as he goes.

"That's no way to talk to a lady, son. Now go talk to her and hear what she has to say." He gives me a small shove in Kat's direction.

"Is there somewhere more private we can talk?" Kat asks, looking over my shoulder. Gemma is openly staring at the two of us. No doubt she is enthralled that Kat is here.

"Follow me." I head back out the door I had entered, holding it for her. She brushes past me, and I suck in a breath. That familiar floral scent tugs at my heart. This woman burrowed her way deep into my heart and didn't let go. Even when shit hit the fan.

We walk the short distance to my place, and I allow her to go inside. Her gaze sweeps over the tiny kitchen and living room. It's small, but cozy.

"Sean—" she starts, but I cut her off.

"I don't even know what to call you. Kat? Eleanor?" After everything that went down, I couldn't help the hurt at not knowing who she really was. I took that pain out with the tattoo that was the very essence of this woman in front of me.

"Eleanor. Ellie Ainsworth. Former Princess of the United Kingdom. It's a pleasure to make your acquaintance."

Damn, if she still doesn't have a regal air about her. I take her extended hand, and a spark of electricity shoots up my arm. Christ, the effect this woman still has on me. Even running away, I can't escape it. Maybe I don't want to escape it.

It takes a minute for my brain to grab on to what she said.

"Wait, former princess?" I try not to think about how good she looks standing here with me. She may sound regal, but right now, she's every bit my pink-haired goddess.

"You haven't been watching the news?"

"Why would I be watching the news?"

She shakes her head at me. "Well, something kind of big happened. I only assumed you'd hear about it. I gave up the throne."

Holy shit. She gave up the throne? A shock like I've never known rolls through me. Was she even allowed to give up the crown? Was she running away again? My head was spinning. "Are you even allowed to do that?"

"I can. And I did." She's smiling. A smile that I know is only for me.

"Is this a joke?" Her face falls. She crosses her arms in front of her.

"It's not a joke. After my granddad passed away, we each got a letter from him. Mine told me to follow my heart. That it was okay if I didn't want the throne. I suspect he always knew. So I gave up my claim to the crown and am now a private citizen."

"Wow." No words come to mind. I try to speak, but just open and close my mouth, gaping like a fish. I can't wrap my head around this revelation.

"I came here because I want to see if we still have a chance. I know I hurt you when I didn't tell you who I was, but I love you, Sean. It was never a game. Never a bored princess wanting to play a part. You gave me a safe place when I ran, and I fell in love with you." She takes a few tentative steps towards me.

"I know it may take some time to get back to where we were, but I want you. I want to live a quiet life with you. Wake up next to you. Find a job where I can make a difference. And come home to our own place. To you. Make love every night."

I try to hide the smile, but I can't. Her version of our life sounds pretty damn good. I take a few steps forward. My hands rest on her hips, turning her so I can lift her onto the counter. I want her more than I want my next breath. I crave her with a bone deep ache in my soul. The love I have for her is a once-in-a-lifetime feeling. Ellie is it for me.

"We'll have a lot to figure out. I can't imagine they'd just let you go quietly." I rest my forehead against hers. Her hands tentatively rest on my chest, not knowing where to go. It's so unlike my feisty girl from a few weeks back.

"Security will be an issue, but we'll have that for some time until we can figure out a better plan. I'm hoping you still might need a receptionist because I'm kind of unemployed now." She lets out a small laugh. God, all I want is to kiss those lips of hers. Having her here reminds me of how much I missed her these last few weeks.

I wrap my arms around her waist, pulling her closer to me. "Ellie. I won't lie. It hurt when you didn't tell me who you really were, but I get it. You're the fucking princess. Or were, I should say. But being here, talking with my grandpa, made me realize I do love you. And it killed me because I thought I was going to have to let you go. I mean, what right does a half-British, half-American tattoo artist have to the princess?"

Ellie's hands cup my cheeks. Firm. This time, knowing exactly where they belong. "You are the only person who ever saw me for me. The only man I've ever loved. You have every right to me. To my body. To my heart. No one else."

Passion and love blaze in those deep eyes. Eyes I've missed. Lips I've missed kissing. My lips crush hers. Tasting her. Claiming her. She opens immediately, and I sweep my tongue in and groan at the taste of her I've missed so much. Her hands scrape the nape of my neck. I pull her closer to me. Not a breath of air between our bodies. Our tongues clash, fighting for control, neither one of us ready to relinquish to the other. She pulls back first, her lips swollen.

"So, what do you say, Sean? Want to take on a jobless, ex-princess with no idea what she wants to do with her life?"

"Are you ready to take on a tattoo artist who will do nothing but support you and love you and walk next to you while you figure out your life?"

"Oh Sean." Her voice breaks as she pulls me back into her. Soft gasps escape as she clutches me tightly to her, no doubt releasing all the pent-up emotions from the last few weeks.

All I can do is hold her. Hold on and never let go.

"How are you doing, Ellie?" The name rolls out easier than I thought.

She gives me a watery smile. "You know what the worst part is?" I shake my head. "The money is changing."

"The money is changing?" I'm confused. She must read that confusion, because she continues.

"Growing up, Granddad would always sneak us a ten-pound note. 'So you don't forget my face.' And now, they are already changing the money. And I'm so worried I'll forget his face."

Tears stream down her cheeks as I pull her back into my chest. Her hands wrap around my arms. My shirt sleeve rides up, exposing my new ink.

"Sean." Her fingers cover her lips as she takes in the matching tattoo on my bicep. It's the same wildflowers she has on her side, just more to cover the space. She doesn't touch it, but stares. "You got this for me?"

"I was angry and upset. But I never stopped loving you." I drop my forehead to hers. "I always said I needed to find something I wanted enough to put there. Turns out, it was you."

"It's beautiful. I can't believe after all this time, this is what you got tattooed here." Her eyes watch her fingers as she traces the pattern. I pull her hand away, kissing each finger.

"I love it, Sean." Her lips are on mine again. A deep, soul-affirming kiss. My hands go to pull her shirt and bra off. The bright ink on her side is a reminder that our time in London was real and beautiful. I have to have her right now.

"Just so you know, no one is ever allowed to ink you." I trace the pattern on her side, brushing the underside of her breasts. "Only me. No one else gets to touch you."

"Only you," she whispers. I lift her off the counter and carry her to the bed, lying down with her on top of me. Her lips are a hot brand as they move over my skin. My hands move to the button and zipper on her jeans, before moving to cup her ass, rocking her into me. The need and friction grow between us. Before I can make a move, she's off me. She's biting her bottom lip, eyes roving over my body. My dick tents my pants. She slowly wiggles out of her jeans and underwear. This woman I love with everything I have is here. I can't believe it. I stand and wrap my arms around her, leaning her against the wall and biting down on her shoulder. My fingers skate down her skin, her bare pussy slick and ready for me. She gasps as I easily slide a finger in. Her hand flies to my neck, holding on for dear life.

"God, I've missed this. How you know me so well." Her voice is husky, dripping with need. I lick back up to her ear, sucking her earlobe into my mouth, nibbling down.

"No one knows you like I do. And no one ever will." I continue working my finger in and out of her. Adding another, then a third. Her pussy is a vise every time I drive back in.

"Oh, God! I'm…" She doesn't finish her statement as her body shakes with pleasure. Her orgasm races through her. Her inner walls pulse on my fingers, my hand now sticky with her release. Ellie's body is limp in mine. I forgot how much I love when she's blissed out like this.

Not wasting any time, I shuck my jeans and boxer briefs off. Using her wetness to stroke my dick, her beautiful naked body makes me painfully hard.

"Are you ready for me?" I carry us back over to the bed. With all the care in the world, I set her in the middle of the comforter. My hands brush the pink hair from her face.

"Sean. I need you now." Her fingers are caressing my face as she pulls my lips down to hers. A moment passes between us. There's no need for protection as I slide through her slick folds, finding heaven once again.

"Fuck, Ellie." Her slick pussy engulfing my dick is almost too much. Her warmth surrounds me in the best way. Looking down at where our bodies meet, I start to move, thrusting in and out of her in a devastating pace.

"God, I've missed this." The muffled sound of her voice rings out as I thrust in and out of her. My own orgasm is building. My balls screw up tight, ready for release. My spine tingles as I feel her start to lose it. Her pussy suffocates my dick as she screams. "Yes!" The shout pushes me over the edge.

"Ellie. Fuck, Ellie. Yes!" I say her name over and over. I can't get enough of her. I never want to leave this perfect heaven we're in.

"That was the best fucking thing in my life." I feel her smile against me.

Falling to her side, I wrap my body around hers. I've missed her curves. Missed falling asleep with her and waking up with her by my side.

"I still can't believe you're here." I brush a few stray hairs from her forehead. "And you went back to pink."

She smiles. Her face fills with love for me. The best fucking thing in the world. "Don't they say pinks have more fun?" The touch of her fingers on my tattoos is a balm I didn't know I needed. "It took me too long to get here, but there was a lot to sort out."

"How did everyone react? How's your brother doing with all this?"

Her eyes briefly close, filled with guilt. "It wasn't as much of a shock to him as I would've thought. We've both been doing this our entire lives, and now his timeline just got moved up. I worry about him handling it, but my granddad gave me the courage to do it."

"I wish I could've met him. Not the king, but the man. He sounds wonderful." Those deep blue eyes get glassy. I pull her tighter into my arms, dropping a kiss onto the top of her head.

"He would've loved you. It's been a rough few weeks,

but I'm hoping now it'll be easier." Her breath ghosts my chest.

"What's the plan?"

"Stay here in bed with you. Make up for lost orgasms." She kisses my pec, tracing her fingers up and down the ridges of my abs.

"As wonderful as that sounds, and I'm not disagreeing, seems like we still have a lot to figure out." I run my hand up and down her arm, hoping the answer will come to us. She sits up, swinging her leg over me to straddle me. Her hands land on my chest, absently tracing the tattoos there.

"We could stay here for a little while. Let the chaos in London die down a bit. I don't really know what the future holds now, but I just want to be with you. Have a family. I don't care where."

"Jumping pretty far ahead there, aren't we?" I smirk at her, but she just beams down at me. My heart stops in my chest at how much I love this woman.

"I realized how much I wanted a family, kids, with you. I was always so opposed to the idea because it was forced upon me. All that 'heir and the spare' business. But having your kids? Give me a dozen."

I sit up. Our naked chests brush together, her arms wrapping around my shoulders. "You really want to have kids?"

She nods her head, biting on her lip. Fuck if that doesn't make my dick twitch. She feels it because she grinds herself on my lap. I flip us over, settling back on top of her.

"Better get started then."

Epilogue

SEAN - NINE MONTHS LATER

"Ellie! Car's here. We need to get going." Fiddling with the cuffs on my shirt, I glance at the clock to see we need to leave now if we're to be on time. All week, the stress of today has been coming off Ellie in waves. I know she doesn't want to be in the spotlight, especially now, but it's a big day. Coronation Day.

"Coming, love. I forgot how long it takes to get royal ready." Her sweet voice carries down the stairs as I wait for her. I never thought we'd get to live this life together. When I found out who she was, I thought we were over, that there was no future for a princess and a tattoo artist. But she gave it all up for her own future. For me. And now, our life was going to be even better.

"What do you think?" Her voice draws me out of my own head. She always steals my breath with her beauty, but damn if she isn't gorgeous in the most elaborate dress I've ever seen.

"You look fecking incredible." I pull her to me, capturing her lips with mine in a sweet kiss.

"They did some good work. You can't see a thing." She

steps out of my hold, turning to her side. Whoever made this dress did a damn good job at hiding our secret.

"I'm glad we get to keep the little one to ourselves for just a little while longer." I rub my hands over her stomach. She's got the barest hint of a bump, but with all the material of this dress, you'd have no idea.

"It would cause quite the scandal if the press could see me now." Ellie's voice is quiet, and she tucks her hands over mine.

"I don't give a shite about any of them. It's you and me, love. Always us." I turn her head and capture her lips in a deeper kiss. Her little remark tells me just how nervous she is about today. Thankfully she isn't hounded by the media like she used to be. For a few weeks when we returned to London, she was hounded daily. There's still some paparazzi, but it's not as bad as it could be. Thank God.

A sharp rap on the door breaks us apart. "Just a few hours and then we'll be home."

"Promise?" she asks quietly.

"Promise."

ELLIE

"YOU THINK this will actually start on time?" Sean's warm hand on mine is the only thing keeping me grounded. The amount of material on my dress floating down in layers is astounding. While it hides the small bump I have, it's extremely warm in the packed abbey.

"We can only hope." At that precise moment, horns

start trumpeting outside. "Looks like you must be good luck."

The sound of thousands of people rising echoes throughout the grand hall. "Here we go," Sean mumbles beside me. Taking a deep breath, we rise with the rest of the crowd, awaiting my mum's grand entrance.

What seems like hours later, she finally makes her appearance. The Coronation Robes are held by my father, brother, Charlotte, and my uncle. The jewels on her crown gleam brighter than I've ever seen them. My mother is the perfect queen. There is no one more fit to lead our country than she.

As she takes her place front and center, Jamie takes his place beside me.

"Doing alright, Ellie?"

My voice gets caught in my throat, so I can only manage a nod. He pulls me into a quick side hug, my other hand holding onto Sean. As the Archbishop calls for us to sit, the long ceremony begins.

Imagining myself in my mother's shoes causes my chest to tighten. The weight of the crown. The weight of the robes. It all presses down on me thinking this could have been my future. If this would have been me today, I don't know how I would be feeling. I wouldn't be ready. But my mother is the epitome of regal. Having also been taught by my grandfather, she will lead the country with all the grace and confidence I could never muster.

"Madam, is your Majesty willing to take the Oath?"

"I am willing." Her voice is strong as she accepts her oath to the crown.

"HOW ARE YOU FEELING, YOUR MAJESTY?" Mum comes over to our small group at the celebratory ball. She's changed into a new gown, a beautiful off-the-shoulder gown with intricate gold threads woven throughout the flowers on the dress to represent the entirety of the Commonwealth.

"Queen-like."

"Congratulations, Your Majesty." Sean leans over to greet her as our family mingles with the guests.

"Thank you. And how is everything going with the foundation?"

Sean's smile is bright. "It's going very well. I couldn't have done it without Ellie." He pulls me into his side.

"She was always good at fundraising for her charities," Mum says, laughter in her voice.

"You're both too kind. If it weren't for Sean, there would be no programme to start with. I'm just lucky I get to help out."

When we got back to London, helping Sean get the funds for his art programme was at the top of my to-do list. As a former princess, I wasn't above throwing my name around to get Sean the funds he needed. And now I split my time between the shop and the school. There's nothing I love more than being covered in paint by the time I head home for the day. And seeing Sean work with the students and share his love of art? I didn't think I could love him any more.

It's a far cry from where we are now. Being surrounded by all this pomp and circumstance makes me grateful this isn't my life anymore.

"Mind if I steal Eleanor away for a few minutes?" Mum's voice pulls me from my thoughts.

"You're the queen." Sean kisses me on the cheek before

Mum loops her arm through mine and guides me down an empty hall.

"How are you doing today, Eleanor?" The long hall is quiet as we leave the noise of the ball behind us.

"Shouldn't I be asking you that?" I turn to look at her, but her concern is only for me.

"This was something I've been preparing for my entire life. I learned from the best." She goes quiet as she remembers her beloved father. "I was ready."

"You did beautifully. I couldn't be prouder." I squeeze her to me. I thought when I left the royal folds, I would feel a disconnect from my family. But instead, it's only brought us closer together.

"Thank you, my darling. Now, would you like to fill me in on your little secret?" Her knowing eyes turn to me.

"What are you talking about?" I keep my voice steady, not wanting to give anything away.

"I might be the queen, but I'm still your mum, Eleanor. I know you're pregnant."

My hands instinctively go to my stomach. "How can you tell?"

Her hands cup my face and bring my eyes to hers. They are glassy with emotion. "You are practically glowing. And Sean has barely let you out of his sight all morning," she says on a laugh.

"I can't get him to give me breathing room. He thinks I'm going to break," I say with an eye roll.

"Did I ever tell you how your dad treated me when I was pregnant with you and James?" I shake my head in response. "God love him, he followed me around everywhere. Had water or different shoes or a change of clothes if I was hot or cold. Couldn't breathe without him being on top of me."

"I can't even imagine. That will probably be Sean the

entire time." My eyes drift down to my hand, which is rubbing my stomach.

"I'm sure he'll calm down once things progress further. Or until you put him in his place."

"Yes, that will happen. I'm pregnant, not fragile." I give her a quick glance, before looking back down. "You're not mad I didn't tell you?"

"Oh darling, no. I know the worry of not telling people until you're past a certain point. I can't believe that I get to be a grandmum." Her smile is so bright, it's infectious.

"I can't wait to be a mum. I'm so happy, and I love the life I have. The life Sean and I created. There's nothing I wanted more in life, and I finally have it."

"I know I didn't always understand why you wanted to leave, but you have carved out a beautiful life for yourself, Eleanor, and I couldn't be prouder."

My vision blurs as tears cloud my eyes. On a day that is supposed to be all about the queen, she's being my mum first and foremost. Wrapping my arms around her as best I can with the large gowns we're wearing, I squeeze her tight to me. Mother and daughter. Not the queen and a former princess. I won't remember the pageantry when I think back on this day. I will cherish this moment between the two of us.

"Mum! Ellie! Where are you two?" Jamie's voice carries down the hall, breaking apart our moment.

"Right here, James." Mum takes my hand as we walk over to meet him.

"You're not supposed to disappear. You're the woman of the hour," Jamie says, swinging his arm over Mum's shoulders.

"I'm the queen. I can do what I please."

"Can I use that excuse? That sounds bloody brilliant."

"You're not the king." Mum's stern gaze turns to him.

"Thank God. I'm not ready for you to be our king yet," I say on a laugh.

As we return to the ballroom, Sean is standing on the outside, looking in at all the dignitaries still partying the night away. Butterflies still flutter in my stomach every time I see him. Just a short year ago, I never thought I would find my happily ever after. The path my mother is so eloquently following in today was my destiny.

Sean's eyes swing in my direction, and it pulls me into his orbit. God, I love this man and the life we've created together.

"Ready to go home, love?"

"Yes."

As for this princess? She finally got her happily ever after.

The End

Want to find out more about Sean and Ellie's life in London? Signup for my newsletter for an exclusive bonus scene!

And join my Facebook reader group to stay up to date on all the news!

Author Note

I have had this book written for months, and it just so happened to release with the passing of Prince Philip. As a lover of everything royal, I was so sad to hear of his passing. He was such a stoic leader for the United Kingdom, and his love story with Elizabeth is one for the ages. I hope we should all be so lucky to get to experience the love these two had.

To all the amazing authors out there that have supported me on this journey…YOU ARE THE BEST!! I never dreamed of the support I would receive from the romance community when I started this author dream, but romance is really where it's at! And to my Accountability Tribe… Norma and AK…you two are amazing and keep me going on the days I want to throw in the towel!

To the best beta readers…Tara, Audrey, Norma and Nicole…thank you for helping me make this book amazing! To my ARC team…you guys rock and I love having you on this journey with me!

And to all the amazing readers out there…you all have made this one hell of a journey so far, and shown me so much love that it brings me to tears some days! I can't wait to see where this year takes us together!

xo, Emily

Reckless Royal

AN AINSWORTH ROYALS STORY

Reckless ROYAL

EMILY SILVER

TRAVELIN' HOOSIER BOOKS

Chapter One

JAMES

"Can you think with anything besides your prick, James?" Bloody hell, I'm in for it now. I can't help it if the paparazzi are leaking old photos of me. Even if this one is awful. I'm getting sucked off in a club. You can't see anything inappropriate, but anyone with half a brain knows what's going on.

"The Queen will be over to have a word with you shortly. This is out of my hands." For fuck's sake. It's never good when the Queen has to get involved.

"I'll be sure to let her know it won't happen again."

My advisor, Charles, gives me an appraising look. His bushy white eyebrows are furrowed. I'm sure I've given him wrinkles early in life. I can't help it if I like to have fun.

"Will it, though? This isn't the first time we've seen this happen, and I doubt it will be the last. You're first in line to the throne now. This behaviour is unbecoming of the future King."

"You don't need to remind me of my position in life." My voice is harsh as I snap back at him. Ever since my twin renounced her spot in the royal line, all eyes have been on me. Before, my behaviour was considered cute. That of a playboy prince sowing his oats. Now, everyone has turned on me.

"Someone needs to." That voice sends people scurrying to stand and bow. It's still strange seeing Mum as the Queen. I stand, buttoning my blazer as I do. "You all can leave. I'd like a moment with my son."

My advisor and his staff exit on a bow. Cowards. Leaving me here to fend for myself. Heading to the tea cart, I pour us each a cuppa.

"Thank you, darling."

I take a sip, eyeing her with suspicion. "To what do I owe the pleasure of this visit, Mum?"

"As if you don't already know." She sits on the velvet loveseat in my office. Everything here is velvet. Quite annoying really, considering I'm the future King and it's decorated for an old grandmum.

"Why don't you enlighten me?" I can't help the cheekiness in my voice.

Mum sets her cup down on the coffee table in a huff. "James, this has to stop. You are almost thirty now. You can't keep expecting people to excuse this behaviour."

"It's amazing how quickly they turned on me."

She pinches the bridge of her nose. Mum's hair was always a dark brown like mine, but now there's more grey peppered in. It gives her a regal air. But today, it's just pissing me off.

"If you don't start making some changes, and soon, I'll be forced to take action."

"You'll be forced to take action? What the bloody hell does that even mean?" My voice carries as I push off the loveseat. "I don't need you controlling my life." Shoving my hands through my hair, I try to take a calming breath.

"You have yet to prove to me that you are capable of

taking on even the smallest of duties that I was doing for your grandfather when I was your age. You are just not ready to be King." Her voice becomes quiet as she mentions him. He died almost a year ago, but it still hurts to think about him. He was one of the best Kings England has ever seen, and I know Mum is doing everything in her power to live up to his standard.

"Maybe if you'd actually give me those duties to do, I could try. Have you ever thought of that?" My hands on my hips, I stare Mum down. I hate being questioned like this. "I'm already being held to an impossible standard."

I know I've hit a sore spot when Mum rolls her eyes. "An impossible standard? You were allowed to run around with no regard to the crown and get away with it. Your sister was held to an impossible standard and look where that got us."

"That was below the belt." Ellie hated everything about royal life. The media. The people commenting on her every move and appearance. She's much happier living as a private citizen, but damn, if that doesn't hurt.

"It's true. You need to be held accountable, James. And it's going to start right now." She pushes off of her seat and goes to leave.

"What do you mean 'it's going to start right now'?"

"I am not getting any younger, James. This position has a way of aging you before you're ready. Dad did everything he could to prepare Eleanor for the crown, but now, I'm afraid I must do the same for you."

"Mum. I'll do better. I promise."

She opens the door to leave. "Until you show me that, then I'll continue with my own plans."

Fucking hell.

THE MUSIC IS TOO loud tonight. Club Mayfair has always been my favourite. I get special treatment here. All the free drinks, sexy women fawning all over me, and no press allowed inside. The scotch is doing little to quell my nerves. A blonde is sitting by my side, her dangerously long nails trailing up and down my thigh. It's doing little to arouse me tonight.

I'd be all for a quick romp in the sack with her, but right now, Mum's words keep playing on a loop in my head.

Not ready to be King.

How does one even prepare to be King? It's not like I haven't been paying attention all these years. Sure, I've been more concerned with women, but I still know what it takes to run a country. Or at least I think I do.

"You want to get out of here, Prince James?" Any attraction I might have had to this woman goes down the toilet at those last two words. I know most women are with me because of who I am, but I can't handle it tonight.

"Sorry…" Bloody hell, I can't even remember her name. "I'm just not feeling it tonight."

I nod to my Personal Protection Officers, my PPOs, that I'm ready to leave. It's still early, so hopefully I can pop over and see the one person who might actually be able to talk some sense into me.

"Are we heading home, Your Highness?" my security officer asks, as I dodge the questions of the paparazzi that are awaiting my exit before getting in the idling car.

"Head to Ellie's, please." I throw my blazer over the backseat and close my eyes. Why is this shite bothering me even more today? Maybe because it's coming from Mum.

It's my advisors who are the ones to condemn me for my behaviour. Never has Mum gotten involved before.

"Shall I call ahead and let her know that we are coming?"

"Please do. Otherwise, she may be irritated."

The car lurches into the street as the noise of the club fades away. I'm hoping my sister will be a voice of reason. For being this early in the evening, it's a quick drive through the city. When we pass through the gated entry of Ellie's neighbourhood, I release a breath.

"Thanks, guys. I won't be long." I hop out of the car, seeing Ellie at the front door. Her once brown hair is now pink, a stark contrast to mine.

"Why the hell are you coming over to my place at nine at night when you could be out at the clubs?" She waves me in as I kiss her cheek.

"No Sean tonight?" My sister's face softens at the mention of her partner, Sean. If she hadn't stumbled into his tattoo parlour when she ran away from the palace, I don't know where I'd be right now. That's a slippery slope to go down.

"He had a session run late. What's brought you over here?"

I flop down on her couch, rubbing my eyes. "Mum. The palace. You name it."

She messes around in the kitchen before returning to the living room. "I'm guessing it has to do with that picture that is spread all over the news?" She hands me a scotch before sitting in a chair next to me.

"You saw it too?" Christ, I didn't think she'd be looking at tabloids once she left the royal life behind.

"It's hard not to hear it from the parents when they're whispering about me at the school." Ellie took the reins of Sean's after school art programme and helped build it into what it is today. She keeps it running on the days that Sean is at his tattoo parlour. I don't know how they manage both, but they love it.

"Hopefully you didn't see it." I shiver, taking a long pull of the scotch.

"Absolutely not! I wouldn't go out looking for that. But it serves you right for getting caught. It's not like you were ever discreet with your women."

"Thanks, Ellie. Just what I needed tonight." My eyes roll on their own.

"Why are you so morose tonight? Couldn't find anyone to take home at the club?"

"Is that really all people think I do?" Shite, maybe Mum does have a point.

"Jamie. It's all you lead people to believe. There're no photos of you going to galas or art show openings or state dinners because you're always going out with women. It takes precedence over anything else you might do."

"Fecking hell. You sound just like Mum." I shake my head. "But you may have a solid point."

"Is the world ending?" she asks on a gasp. "I don't think I've ever heard you say those words to me before."

"Alright, alright. Quit being a smart arse."

The front door opens with a bang as Sean races in. "Is everything okay in here?" He looks haggard. "Oh, hey, James. What are you doing here? I thought something happened."

"Other than me being a prick, nothing going on."

Sean walks over and drops a kiss on Ellie's head. I can't be bitter towards my sister. She was not cut out for royal life. Seeing her this happy, starting her own family, makes me realize I do need to step up and take responsibility for myself.

I gulp down the rest of my scotch and drop it on the table behind me. "Thanks, Ellie. You've been a big help."

She looks confused. "You don't have to leave now that Sean is home. Are you going to be okay?" Her voice sounds concerned. She worries about me more than she should.

"I'll be fine. You just helped me see a few things more clearly."

Ellie gives me a wary look. "If you're sure." She walks over to give me a hug as I head out.

"See you later, Sean."

"Always a pleasure, James." He waves me off as I jog down the stairs.

I just need a plan to present to Mum. Maybe she'll see reason if I start to take control of my life. As much as it pains me to admit, even cutting the club visits in half would be a good start. I may be the prince, but I'm by no means a saint.

Chapter Two

QUEEN KATHERINE

"Lord Kendall. Thank you so much for meeting with me today."

"Your Majesty. It's such a pleasure to meet you. Please, call me Xavier." The duke bows, his bald head shining bright towards me. One of the perks of being the Queen. If I need to take action, people are at my beck and call.

"Please, have a seat. Would you care for some tea?"

"That sounds delightful, Ma'am." I ring the bell next to me, my indication to the wait staff to bring it in.

"Please, call me Katherine."

"Katherine, then. What summons me to the palace today?"

As the tea is prepared, I drop my hands in my lap, a position that has been engrained in my head since I was a girl.

"Here you are, Your Majesty." I take the cup, giving my butler a grateful nod.

"Xavier, I was hoping that you and I could come to an arrangement of sorts."

"An arrangement? What kind of arrangement are you thinking of?" His brows furrow in confusion.

"I know finances have been a bit hard for you lately."

"I'm sorry, but how is that any of your business?" He sets his cup down, as if he's about ready to walk out. No one walks out on the Queen.

"My apologies, Xavier. But I'm merely stating facts that are public record as a duke. We are both in a position where we can help each other out."

"And how is that, Your Majesty?" I don't miss the extra emphasis on my title.

"My son needs stability. You need money. I believe your daughter is around my James's age, yes?"

He gives a sharp nod. "What are you getting at?"

"An arranged marriage." I hold his gaze. There's a slight tick in his jaw.

"With your son? The 'playboy prince'?" He winces this time, giving me an apologetic look. "Sorry. I'm sure he's a fine young man, but with everything the press runs with, all I see is his long line of women."

"I agree. He's had little direction in his life until this point. He was always going to be second in line for the throne, so he was never held to any sort of standard. And I'm afraid much of that is my fault. But now, he needs to get serious about his position. And I don't see that happening."

"Unless he has a woman on his arm."

"Precisely. And your Zara is unattached."

Xavier gives me a firm look. I can see he's fighting himself. He doesn't want to agree to this plan, but he also can't say no to the Queen. The latter part is what I'm hoping for.

"It will ensure your financial future." The perk of being a royal is that we have deep pockets. And I'm not above using personal funds at this moment to benefit the entire kingdom. "James has it in him to be one of the best Kings this country has ever seen, but he needs a steady hand at his side."

"And you think my Zara is that steady hand?" Xavier sips his tea.

"Yes, I do. There is no mention of her in the press, she teaches at a good school, and comes from a respectable, steady line."

"I didn't know our family line would be called into question," Xavier states firmly, setting his cup down.

"No one is calling your family line into question. You come from a good background, and we would be lucky to have someone of Zara's calibre in our family to carry on the Ainsworth line."

"Ahh, yes. The heir and the spare."

I bristle at his remark. "We don't call our children that."

"Isn't it what will be required of them?" He raises an eyebrow at me in challenge.

"While there are certain expectations to carry on the line, they are not simply the heir and the spare."

"And what will the expectations of Zara be?" He leans back, crossing his arms.

"While we cannot guarantee they will be scandal free —because the paparazzi publish what they want—I don't want to see Zara plastered over the news falling out of a nightclub or being caught in any compromising positions."

"My Zara is better than that."

I give him a slight nod of my head. "She seems like a fine young woman. Someone who will be an asset to our country. She'll also be required to be a patron of some of our more established royal charities but can also establish one of her choosing."

"And of course, the royal offspring."

"Yes, bearing children will also be required."

"When will you need an answer?" He stands, awaiting my dismissal.

"I'm sure I'll hear from you soon. Lord Kendall, it was a pleasure having you here this afternoon." I extend my hand. He takes my hand willingly, even if he might not agree with what I'm proposing today.

"Your Majesty. I'll be in touch." He bows before leaving the room.

"Your Majesty, can we expect to set up the tea for next weekend as originally planned?" My advisor is at my shoulder the moment he leaves.

"Please do. I am positive he will say yes."

"And Prince James?"

"Cancel anything he has planned and make sure his advisors are aware he is not to be late. Best set the appointment for an hour earlier for him to ensure he's here on time."

I love my son more than words can describe, but it's time I take his future into my own hands. For his own good, and the future of this country.

Chapter Three

ZARA

"Everyone's practised, yes?" Looking around, I see nervous faces staring back at me. Never a good sign.

"Okay then. Ready." I raise my baton and instruments are readied. I move my hands on memory alone as the students start playing. Notes are missed, strings aren't tuned, and the beauty of the song is lost. It takes everything I have not to stop the song immediately and dole out criticism. Their lack of practise is evident.

As the song ends, I take a deep breath, steeling my face. "Sounds like we could use some work on that song."

"It was bloody awful, Miss Cross," one of the students pipes up from the back.

I fight to keep my face straight as murmurs of agreement break out. "Not your best work, no. But since it's a Friday, let's see if we can clean it up a bit and then we'll break out the pop songs."

"Yes!" A chorus of cheers go up around me. Nothing like pop music over the classics to motivate a group of secondary students.

"Alright, alright. Still need to make it through Beethoven." This time, when they start playing, it actually sounds like the famous overture.

As I'm passing out the sheet music for the new song, the final bell of the day rings.

"Okay, since we didn't get to this today, practise over the next two days, and we'll play it Monday. Have a lovely weekend."

Students gather their bags as they head out for the weekend. "Bye, Miss Cross. See you Monday," is called out by many as they leave, and I wave in return. Planning next week's music for our end-of-term concert can wait until Monday.

What I've really wanted to do all day is work on my own piece. Music has been a part of me for as long as I can remember. As much as I love it, teaching was a more stable career choice. And as the daughter of a duke, I was expected to have a stable career.

Picking up my own prized violin, I tune the well-loved instrument. It's my most cherished possession. The one my mum used to play daily. I get my love of music from her. If only she could see me now.

Pulling out the sheet music, I start playing the song I've been writing over the past few months. The beginning is fine, the middle okay, and the end terrible. I've been stuck and can't seem to find a breakthrough.

"This is all wrong!" I mutter to myself, dropping my bow. The melody is there, in my head, but I can't seem to grasp onto the fading notes. It's been this way for weeks. I've always been able to write my own music, but lately, there's a block. One that I haven't been able to push past.

"How did I know I could find you in here?" My best friend's voice rings throughout the quiet studio that is my classroom. Students are long gone.

"Because I'm driving myself crazy trying to get this piece out?" Marnie's at my side, pulling my violin from my hands.

"You do realize it's not going to come by forcing it out, right?" She has a point, but it doesn't mean I'll listen.

"I thought it was coming today." I blow out a breath, looking at the messy pages in front of me. "It's no use. It's never going to come." I crumple the sheets up in anger and toss them in the bin behind me.

"Not with that negative attitude."

"Then I'm *positive* that it will never come." I give her my cheekiest smile.

"Okay. We're leaving and hitting the pub tonight."

"Do we have to?" I love Marnie to bits. We met my first day at the conservatory where we teach and have been friends ever since. She loves the London nightlife, while I'd prefer a night in with friends.

"Don't pout those lips at me, Zara. You owe me a night out since you bailed on quiz night." Damn. I forgot about that. I was sulking over this piece, yet again, that I can't seem to write.

"First round is on you."

She beams back at me. "If it means you're coming out, I'll gladly buy."

"SO HAVE you found any good matches yet?" Marnie's words are hard to hear over the loud noise of the bar. It seems half of London is out tonight.

"If I get one more dick pic, I might scream." Marnie was in a low point after her most recent boyfriend dumped her. After too much wine one night, she somehow convinced me to sign up for an online dating site with her. Safety in numbers, right?

"Nothing worth taking for a ride?" She waggles her eyebrows in my direction.

"I've seen better." She tips her drink in my direction, as I sip on my gin and tonic, not hiding my grin. "Honestly, is this really the best London has to offer?"

"We should move to Sweden. All broad-shouldered hunks of men. I think you'd be hard-pressed to find an unattractive Swede."

"You cannot move to Sweden and ditch me here!" I slap her arm. "Who would rescue me from these endless dates I keep going on because of you?"

She lets out a sigh. "If only Prince James could just fall into my lap, I'd be set for life."

"You and every other eligible woman in London." I roll my eyes. "I'm surprised you'd want the 'playboy prince.' Last I saw, some poor woman had her hands down his pants."

"I wonder how big it is. You think he's overcompensating?" Marnie wiggles her pinkie in front of me, and a snort of laughter escapes.

"Of course he is!" I cry. "Women are only with him because he's the prince."

"You do have to admit he is attractive. Probably knows how to please a woman too."

"Only because he's been with so many. Honestly, Marnie, I thought you had better taste in men," I chuckle. "The prince is so not your type."

She nods her head at me. "I need someone girthier. He'd snap like a twig under me." Marnie has curves and knows how to flaunt them. She can bring down any man she chooses, if only she could find the right one.

"I'd settle for anyone who can go more than two seconds without looking straight past me." I'm tall and straight as a board, so there's not much to look at.

"If it makes you feel better, I don't stare at your chest when I'm talking to you." She winks at me.

"So much better." I finish the rest of my drink. "As much fun as it is bemoaning our nonexistent dating life, I need to get going. I have an appointment with my dad tomorrow afternoon."

"What are you helping your dad with?" Marnie gives me a questioning look.

"Not sure. He rang me up this week and told me he'd be picking me up early, as we would need to spend the day together."

She tips her head at me. "That sounds rather ominous."

I shrug my shoulders. "Nothing out of the norm."

She drops a few pounds on the table as we walk outside. "I'm glad I got you out for a night. See you Monday?"

"See you Monday." I drop a kiss on her cheek and head into the warm, spring night. London in the springtime is my favourite. The city comes alive after being cooped up during the winter.

It's a short walk home to my townhouse. It's been in our family for generations, seeing as how my father is one of the handful of remaining dukes in the country.

Walking into my house, waves of exhaustion roll over me. Teaching is no easy profession. I love my students, and I love my music, but this week has taken its toll. Between students not wanting to learn and fighting this block I have, I'm ready for the weekend.

"ZARA? WHERE ARE YOU?" I hear my dad puttering around downstairs as I put the finishing touches on my makeup. He was rather vague as to where we'd be going today, so I went with a plain black dress. Nothing fancy, but easy enough to fit in with any crowd.

"Coming, Dad," I shout down the stairs, before spritzing on perfume and joining him.

"Morning, darling." Dad gives me a peck on the cheek. "Sorry for being so secretive about where we're headed today."

"And where might we be going?" I grab my jacket and purse as we head out the door.

"Buckingham Palace. We have a meeting with the Queen." His brow pulls tight as he says this.

"The Queen? Why would you not tell me we're meeting the Queen? I look like I'm going to a convent!"

Dad waves me off. "You look fine. I don't think anyone will pay any mind to what you're wearing."

"But I will."

"Too late now. We best be going. I don't want to keep the Queen waiting." Disdain laces his tone.

"Why do you sound upset about meeting the Queen? Isn't it an honour to meet her?"

He rolls his eyes before opening my door to his car. "Some things aren't all they're cracked up to be. Now, let's get this over with."

"What aren't you telling me?" He starts the car and pulls out into early London traffic.

"Just know, I love you very much, darling."

"Why do I feel like I'm off to the dungeons instead of a meeting with the Queen?"

"Don't be dramatic. You'll be fine."

Easy for him to say. He knows why we're going to the palace. Between his cagey looks and his tense posture, it feels like I'm being led straight to the dungeons with no warning as to what is to come.

Chapter Four

JAMES

"Again, why are we having tea today?" Lounging on the loveseat, I lament being at the palace today. My diary was all set for the day before this unplanned event with Mum. I had a visit to a new hospital wing on my calendar but was told that it was going to be rescheduled. What the Queen wants, the Queen gets. And my new plan of action is going to have to wait another day.

"James. Might you appear more proper? You look like you're hanging out in a club."

"I can't help it if you're keeping me in the dark about what we're doing." It's hard to keep the contempt from my voice. After the other day, this must be part of Mum's plan.

I stand, pacing the small space in her sitting room. "I'm taking your words to heart, Mum. I have a plan to do better."

She's staring out the window to the back gardens. It's a grey, rainy day. "And what is your plan, my dear?" She turns a stern eye on me.

Shite. I should've known she would ask me this. After

our little chat, I knew I needed to do better. But I hadn't gotten that far.

"More charity work. Fewer clubs."

"That's your plan? We're far worse off than I thought."

"Your Majesty. Your guests have arrived." The announcement draws my attention away from Mum. Anger is boiling just below the surface like a volcano. I'm ready to erupt when a portly man with a bushy moustache enters the room. Behind him is a willowy brunette, long hair flowing around a simple black dress.

"Lord Kendall. Lady Zara. I'm quite pleased you could join us today." She tips her head in his direction, as he bows before her. Mum addresses Zara with the appropriate title of a duke's daughter. I'm wary of what this means.

"Your Majesty. The honour is all mine."

"James, this is Lord Xavier Cross, Duke of Kendall." Mum extends her hand in his direction.

The man bows to me, the woman following. "Your Royal Highness. It's always a pleasure to be in your presence. May I present my daughter, Miss Zara Cross." He motions to the woman behind him.

"Zara. I'm thrilled you could join us today."

"Your Majesty. The pleasure is all mine." As she curtsies to Mum, this poor woman's face is equally as confused as mine. Hers does hold less contempt than mine, however.

"Zara, it's nice to meet you." I try to grab her attention, but her eyes keep flitting around the room. If you've never been to the palace, it's easy to be distracted by the glamour of it all.

"Please, come have some tea." Mum motions to the small table set up in the sitting room. An unsettled feeling starts to come over me. I don't know what's going on today, but I can't imagine it will be in my favour.

"Thank you, Ma'am." This delicate woman accepts a

cup and sits. I take the empty seat next to her. Stretching out my legs, I lean back in the chair, drinking my own cup. The harsh look from Mum tells me she isn't pleased. That makes two of us. She straightens, setting her tea down.

"I'm sure you two are wondering why we've brought you here today." Zara gives me a look, only a small one. "The duke and I have entered into an arrangement."

Oh feck. This can't be good. "And what sort of arrangement is that?"

"An arranged marriage for the two of you." Her voice is curt as she drops the bomb.

"Are you fecking kidding me?" Outrage drips from my voice as I explode out of my seat.

"James! Where are your manners?"

"Oh yes, I'm sorry. Where are my manners when you've just told me I'm to marry a complete stranger!" I throw my hands up in the air. There's no beating around the bush with Mum. She came right out with why she brought me here today. Zara's staring up at me, shock written all over her face. "One typically doesn't hear of arranged marriages in this modern age."

"Zara, I apologize for my son."

"Your Majesty, may I ask the reason for such an arrangement?" At least Zara has better manners than I.

"Yes, my dear." Mum is so composed; it just further angers me. "James, can you please sit?"

I have half a mind to refuse, but it will only drive home Mum's point that I'm not ready to be King.

"James needs a wife. One that is fit to be Queen." Zara's eyes go wide, mirroring my own. "You will be the perfect match for James."

"And do I not get a say in my own life? In finding my own wife?" My words are harsh.

"Are you able to make sound decisions with the kingdom in mind?"

It would not do well to get into a pissing match with the Queen, but every fibre of my being is itching with disdain right now. An arranged marriage? "We're not in the nineteenth century anymore. I think we're both perfectly capable of making our own decisions." Anger drips from my voice.

"But why me? I'm sure there are hundreds of eligible women." Zara's voice carries the shock that I feel, but I can't help turning my anger on her.

"I'm sorry, eligible women? What is this, an eighteenth-century courtship ball?"

"Sorry to offend you, but this is rather sudden." She pins me with a glare. At least she's not falling at my feet. I'd be more concerned if she were. "I'm trying to wrap my head around all of this."

"Rather sudden? Do you know anyone whose parents have found them their future partner?" I'm not doing well to keep my annoyance to myself, as evidenced by the glare from my mother. It's hard to be concerned with her right now.

"Your Highness. There is no reason to raise your voice to my daughter." Lord Kendall turns his grey eyes on me. What kind of person promises his daughter to someone in this day and age? Only someone who isn't in the position to refuse the Queen.

"I'm sorry, but I can't be here." I move to leave, ignoring the voices calling me back. This day has taken a turn for the worse. Does Mum really think an arranged marriage will make me fall in line?

Zara

"ZARA, dear. I'm very sorry for my son. He hasn't been himself lately." The Queen is stunned at the departure of her son. I can't say I blame him. An arranged marriage? I was supposed to be teaching lessons today, but instead, my entire future has been decided for me. Shock and anger are fighting for control in my head. Why on earth would Dad do something like this?

"It's quite alright. Not the sort of news any person expects to hear, I'm guessing." I sip my tea, not making eye contact with either the Queen or my dad. When Dad said we were meeting with the Queen, I didn't know what to make of it. I certainly didn't think it'd be an arranged marriage.

"Xavier, all of the arrangements will be made. I think a spring wedding would be ideal. That would give the country time to get to know Zara."

The country? Getting to know me? Even though my father is a duke, I've never been one to enjoy the spotlight. I like staying behind the scenes while my students shine.

"Don't you think this fall will be better? Make the press think they've been together longer than just meeting now." Dad runs his hands over his moustache. "I think that would be better."

"Fall it is then. I shall have my advisors meet with you, and Zara, you too, to make plans."

"A fall wedding? Can a royal wedding be planned in only six months?"

A fall wedding. To the future King. An arranged marriage. My head is spinning.

"What about my students? What about my job? Will I have to move into the palace?" Questions burst out of me before I can grab onto them. I don't think I've ever been so overwhelmed in my life.

"There will be plenty of time to sort that out, darling." The Queen is cavalier in her response. Easy for her to say. Her whole life wasn't changed in a matter of mere minutes.

"Will you please excuse me? I need some fresh air. This is all quite a bit to take in." I stand, giving the Queen her curtsy, as required.

"The gardens are at your disposal. Take a left, and at the bottom of the stairs, go straight until you see the garden doors." The Queen is polite in her response. "Don't worry, Zara. Everything will work out."

"Thank you, Ma'am."

Once I'm out of the sitting room, I follow her directions to the formal gardens in back of the palace. The rain has died down a bit since we arrived. Spotting a gazebo, I run in that direction, but not before slamming into a solid mass.

"Oof. I'm so sorry." My hands are on the most solid chest I've ever felt.

"Zara. Did they send you out to find me?" James's disgust is now aimed at me.

"Your Highness, please. I am just as shocked by this as you are."

"Call me James. I am to be your husband after all." I wince at that. Husband. I'm going to have a husband. A husband that I met a mere thirty minutes ago. Sure, I've known my whole life who James is. It's hard not to when you grow up with the royals surrounding you at every turn. But to marry this man? He was just plastered all over the news with his latest woman. What makes Dad and the Queen think he'll actually settle down?

"They did not send me out here to find you. I needed

some air. I can assure you, this came as just as much of a surprise to me as it did to you." My voice is quiet as the rain falls softly around us.

"Christ, come on." His warm hand slides down my arm, pulling me in the direction I was heading. The patter of rain on the roof is a welcome distraction. "I'm sorry for going off back there. It's just a shock for me." James's hands are pulling on his hair. Objectively, he's quite handsome. Thick, dark hair. Bright, blue eyes. He's tall—taller even than I am in my heels, which is not the norm. And from what I felt earlier, he must work out quite regularly to have such a strong physique.

"Is this all because of the photos that leaked?"

He pierces me with a punishing stare. I can see how this stubborn man always gets his way. It doesn't faze me. I'm used to these pleading looks from my students.

"Yes. My mother doesn't seem to think I'm fit to be King." He leans against the railing, crossing his thick arms over his chest.

"And how is one determined to be fit to be King? Is there an exam?"

A smile cracks his full lips. "You haven't heard? One must play polo, learn how to smile and wave the proper way, and know the waltz to dance at the ball. All boxes that must be checked before one is proclaimed King."

"It's the polo playing you're having trouble with?"

I don't try to hide my smile as he barks out a laugh. "Quite cheeky, aren't you?"

"Just trying to wrap my head around everything that's going on today. It's a bit much." My eyes grow wide at what I just said. "I'm so sorry. I don't mean that you're too much. It's just, I've never been promised to someone before." That sounds terrible. Are we promised to one another? "I'm mucking this all up."

"It's alright." James walks over, rubbing his arms up and down mine. It's meant to be soothing, but it just grates on me. I'm supposed to convince the world I'm in love with the prince? "I mean, if I can prove to them I can do this, they won't actually make us get married next year, right?"

Even he doesn't believe that. "Hate to burst your bubble, but they're talking about a fall wedding."

"A fall wedding?" The words explode out of him. "You're fecking with me, aren't you?"

I shake my head. "Somehow Dad seems to think that it would be more believable, like we've known each other longer than a few months."

"Bloody hell. How in the world did it come to this?" The words are whispered, meant for just himself.

Nerves are rolling off him in waves. It's setting me on edge. I don't want to be here any more than he does, but this is the unfortunate situation we're now in. I have no idea what possessed my dad to agree to such a thing, but just the thought has me fuming.

"I know you don't want to be in this situation any more than I do, but this is going to be our new reality. We might as well try and make the best of it."

James turns his blue eyes on me. They're heated. I shouldn't like the intensity I see there, but I do.

"And how do you suggest we make the best of it?" Sarcasm hangs on every word.

"I'm sorry if this wasn't your idea. It wasn't mine either!" I snap at him. "You're acting like a petulant child. No wonder your mummy had to come up with such a drastic plan."

His shoulders sag with regret. "I'm sorry, Zara. I'm really not handling this well." That's an understatement. He drags his hand down his face, jaw stubbled with scruff.

"I had this grand plan of what I was going to do to show Mum I was ready to take over the throne."

"That's just it, though. Why are you showing her you're ready now? It's not like you'll be taking over the reins tomorrow. You're thinking too big. You need to pull back."

This time, James gives me a pensive look. "How would I do that? Think smaller?"

"Based on the fact that they are marrying you off, instead of trying to rewrite your entire personality, show people you can do the work. Focus on the charities that you have. No one's expecting you to take over tomorrow."

James walks over to me. Even though I'm eye level with his chin, his presence looms large. Like any good future King should.

"Zara, I believe this is the start of a beautiful relationship."

Chapter Five

ZARA

"I'm sorry, you're what?" Thank God, Marnie hadn't taken a sip of her wine, otherwise she would've spit it all over me.

"Promised to the Prince of the United Kingdom." I sip my own wine.

"To Prince James. The Playboy Prince."

I wince. "Can we please not call him that?"

"Is the future Mr. Zara Cross better?"

I throw my head in my hands. "Of course it isn't! I am betrothed to the prince!"

"Technically betrothed to be betrothed."

I pierce Marnie with my most menacing stare. "You are not helping this situation."

"How would you like my assistance then? Tell you he's a one-woman kind of man and will fall madly in love with you and have lots and lots of babies?"

A sickening thought hits me. "Oh God. I'll have to have two at least. Isn't it the whole thing with the spare and the heir?"

Marnie spins her finger at me. "Other way around, love."

"Marnie! I'm being serious. My children will rule this country one day." I slam my head down on the table.

"But at least you'll have very cute children." Marnie gives me a shove in the shoulder.

"I'll be in the spotlight for the rest of my natural born life. I'm going to be sick."

Marnie gulps down the rest of the wine she's drinking. "Are you even supposed to be telling me this? This seems like something that the palace would forbid."

"I told them you were nonnegotiable. I can't have this big secret and not tell you. I'd go crazy."

I turn my head to see Marnie staring at me. "I'm glad I'm included in the need-to-know people."

"I just can't believe my dad did this to me! I mean, what was he thinking?" Maybe if I picked up any of his numerous phone calls this last week, I'd know. But I'm too angry with him to think straight.

"Why didn't you say no then?"

"Could you say no to the Queen? She has this air about her." I wave my hands around me. "She's the Queen. You can't say no to her. It was a done deal before I even walked into the room."

"While I know I should be mad on your behalf, can I also be excited?"

As much as this whole situation is wearing on me, Marnie's reaction makes it a little lighter. "I guess. You'll get to attend all the events for the wedding too."

Marnie's eyes sparkle at this news. "I'll have to be sure I get the best fascinator in town. No one can upstage the best friend."

"I'm glad you're thinking big picture here."

"They said fall wedding?" I nod in response to her

question. "It'll be absolutely gorgeous. Your dark hair, with a fur wrap walking into Westminster Abbey? I can practically see it now."

I've lost her. Details were fuzzy at best, but the royal wedding was to happen within the next six months. I'd get some say, but most details were to be left to the royal staff. I was never a little girl who dreamed of her own wedding. My mum passed when I was little, so I hardly remember her. I was so passionate about music, having that connection to her, that nothing else mattered.

But now? The thought of not getting to plan my own wedding or have my mum by my side has me itching to plan the entire thing myself.

"What kind of dress will you get? Just think, everything you wear now will be sold out in minutes."

"You've officially lost maid of honour duties."

"I'm going to be your maid of honour?" She looks shocked.

"Right up until that comment about the dress."

"Bugger off, you. You're no fun." Marnie smirks at me.

"Okay, Marnie. I love you, but time to go." I wave my hands towards the door. Trying to absorb everything that will happen in the next few months is not easing my nerves.

"Zara, for real." Marnie grabs my hands, pulling me up and into a hug. "Everything will work out. You have more grace and poise than anyone I've ever met. If there's anyone who would be a worthy Queen, it'd be you."

The annoyance I felt just moments ago fades. "Fine. Maid of honour status reinstated."

"Yes!" She pumps her fist. "Trust me, Zara. Things always work out the way they should. I mean, how many people can say they were talking about bedding the prince and then he just falls in their lap."

"Pretty sure that was you saying that." I shake my head as she makes her way to the door.

"Well, at least now we'll know for sure."

I let out a sigh. My patience is nonexistent right now. "Know what?"

Marnie winks as she shouts over her shoulder, "If he's really overcompensating."

Chapter Six

JAMES

This is already going to be a nightmare. I'm twelve years old again, my mum setting me up on play dates. Except this time, it's with the woman who is going to be my future bride. But not that I have any say in it. I mean, if I become the prince Mum wants me to be, she won't make me go through with this, right? I'll just play by their rules until I can come up with a plan to end this whole charade. Which means playing nice with Zara.

I'm meeting her at a posh club for dinner and drinks. I offered to pick her up, but she insisted on meeting me here, no doubt to cut out early if she wants. Fine by me. I can head to the club after. Shite. I'm not supposed to be doing that. I need to prove to Mum that I am fit to be King. And hopefully not be tied down to this woman. Based on her first impression, I can't imagine she wants me.

Arriving at the club, I notice a few paparazzi lingering about. That should help get the buzz out about Zara and me being together. The more believable this is, the better.

Flashbulbs pop as I enter the dark club. Cherry wood walls make it darker. Old gas lamps on the walls give it a sexy feel. Adjusting to the change in light, I spot Zara at a cosy booth in the back. Zara, with her long brown hair, big doe eyes, and deep red lips, has an understated sexiness to her. She's quiet but has quite a bit of cheek to her.

"Zara. Lovely to see you this evening."

She stays where she is. "Nice to see you too."

I unbutton my blazer and take a seat. This is going to be much harder than I thought. She fidgets in her seat. It's clear to anyone passing by she doesn't want to be here.

"Your Highness. It's lovely to have you here tonight. Can I get you your usual?" our waitress asks as Zara's eyes are perusing the menu.

"How about a bottle of the house red?" I give her a wink as she struts away, a little sway in her hips. Swinging my gaze back to Zara, I'm busted.

"I know you like your women, but if we're to make this work, you'll need to at least appear to be interested in only me." She goes right back to the menu. Damn, if this woman isn't going to keep me on my toes.

"My apologies." The waitress chooses this moment to drop off our wine. As she pours our glasses, she bends over, trying to get me to look down her shirt. Instead, Zara's gaze locks with mine. A smirk plays on her lips as our waitress walks away.

"Cheers." I clink my glass with Zara's, drinking more than is considered polite.

"So, James. Have you thought anymore about the predicament we find ourselves in?"

Zara is quite the lady. Her lips close around the glass of wine, taking a demure sip. The image of her on her knees, sucking my dick, pops into my head. Bloody hell, I need to get my head in the game. I can't be attracted to the woman that is supposed to be my fiancée.

"Like you said, maybe if I start small, I can convince

Mum that I'm fit to be King. Maybe then they'll put an end to all of this nonsense. I mean really, an arranged marriage?" I try to keep my voice quiet, but I'm annoyed. I've been annoyed since the moment I left that blasted tea last week.

Zara nods along. "And how do you think they'll take not planning a royal wedding?"

"We'll convince them we want a long courtship and a long engagement. People do that these days, right?"

"I hate to point out the obvious, but seeing as how I've never been married, I can't comment." She smirks at me behind her wine glass.

"Otherwise you wouldn't be here. It's considered blasphemous if a royal marries someone who's been divorced."

"Probably because they aren't a virgin."

I choke on the sip of wine I just took, thankful I didn't spew it everywhere. Where in the world did this woman come from?

"Your Highness. What will it be for dinner?" The waitress bats her eyes at me, completely ignoring Zara.

"Zara?" I tip my head in her direction. She gives her order to the waitress, a knowing smile on her face. I give her mine and dismiss her.

"Will this be my new normal? My very existence being ignored?" She waves a hand in the direction our waitress went in.

"For now? Yes."

"Way to sugar-coat it." Zara rolls her eyes, taking a sip of wine.

"Zara." I cover her hand on the table with mine. "It's a hard life. But once they realize who you are to me, you'll wish for anonymity."

"I guess I should be thankful then." Her voice is quiet now.

"Enough about that. Tell me about yourself, oh future bride of mine."

She rests her chin in her hand. Her brown eyes cut into me, flecks of gold sparkling at me. "Let's see. I'm twenty-nine, teach music at a local conservatory, and am newly betrothed." She wiggles her eyebrows.

"Are you always this cheeky?"

"Apparently you bring it out in me."

I give her my most winning smile. "That's not what I usually bring out in people."

"I'm well aware." Zara's eyes are anywhere but on me.

"Something wrong?" Her eyes zip to mine. She looks nervous now.

"Sorry. I just feel like all eyes are on us in here."

The room is relatively dark. The club is meant for privacy inside, but wandering eyes are always glancing around to see who is here.

"It comes with the territory. You'll get used to it." I take a long draw on my scotch.

"Will I though? I haven't the first clue as to what I'm supposed to do in this role."

Zara's fingers are playing with the napkin on the table. She's nervous. Of me or what she's gotten herself into, I don't know. Reaching over, I still her hand with mine. Zara's tall, but her delicate hands fit perfectly under mine. It's a bit jarring how perfectly my hand holds hers.

"It's not as if you'll be thrown into the role of Queen tomorrow. I won't hang you out to dry all on your own." I give her hand a squeeze.

"That's oddly reassuring."

"Well, I have been doing this my whole life."

"Seems like your mum might think otherwise." Zara gives me a soft smile behind her wine glass.

"Coming out with the big guns, I see." Our food gets

dropped off, and I notice Zara once again being ignored by the waitstaff.

"So, what's the best part of being royal?" she asks, cutting into her food.

"The best part of being royal?" I don't think anyone has ever asked me that. Sure, people always assume it's being in the spotlight, but to be honest, I've never thought about it.

"There are some days where I feel like I'm helping people. Not just doing it in name only, but really helping them."

"And here I thought you were going to say the women."

"My reputation precedes me." Even Zara thinks I'm a ladies' man. Can't say I blame her. If the only thing she knows about me is what's written in the press, then that's all she'd know.

"I know people don't take me seriously, but I want to do a good job. I want to find something that I can put my name behind and believe in. We have this event next week, at one of the national museums—"

"We do?" Zara cuts me off.

"Best get used to your life being planned out to the minute."

"Sounds lovely." She rolls her eyes at me, going back to her dinner.

"You get used to it. This event next week is for the British Arts. It was something Ellie always supported, and it's now fallen on me. I'm fine supporting the arts, but it's not my calling."

Zara studies me, her eyes penetrating my own protection shields. "You're different than I thought you'd be."

"I'm hoping good different."

"I like that you don't want to just take what is given to

you. You are striving to be better. To make a name for yourself. I can't imagine how difficult that must be in your position. Especially considering why I'm here."

"Where in the world did you come from?" I ask on a laugh, trying to diffuse the tension coiling inside my chest.

"I'm serious, James. It must be so hard being raised in the spotlight and everyone thinking you're one person, and then having to be someone completely different."

"I'm glad you see it that way." I give her a soft smile. This conversation got much heavier than first date conversations should get. But I guess that's what happens when you're dating your future wife.

Chapter Seven

ZARA

"Miss Cross, are you dating the prince?" one of my students pipes up in the back. We're working on a new piece today, but they've been badgering me all day after seeing the pictures of James and me leaving the restaurant the other night.

"If you keep asking, I won't give you our new song to play today."

Their moaning isn't held back.

"I don't want to play more Vivaldi!"

"Ugh, dead music is so boring!"

"Alright, alright. If you give me your very best for the next thirty minutes, we can switch back to the newer pieces next week."

Cheers go up around me. I tap my baton and twenty students straighten, readying their instruments. Waving my hands, the music swells around me. As much as my students whine, they are brilliant performers. The music takes over, and I'm swept away. My eyes close as I lean into the motion. It's familiar. Soothing. It doesn't matter what is going on outside this room. Music is in my soul.

As we hit the crescendo, and then the music quiets, I come back to the room. Focused faces are drawn tight as the piece ends.

"That was absolutely brilliant. Well done. I'll have the new music ready for tomorrow. You've earned it!" I clap my hands, signalling to them they can put away their instruments.

"Can it be Beyoncé? I really want it to be Beyoncé!"

"I'll make a note of that, Eugenie. Now get going. Have a nice evening, everyone."

Cases shutting and chatter from the students are the last sounds for the day. It's been an exhausting few days, and I can't wait to get home. This weekend is another planned outing with James. The few paparazzi that were outside the club ate up our appearance together. James said with a few more outings like that, we'll be established as a couple. I try not to let the thought make me sick.

I hate the limelight. James loves it. I guess you have to be comfortable in the spotlight when you grow up with cameras being shoved in your face. James has a natural rapport with them. I hope I develop a thick skin. They won't be easy to deal with.

Packing up, I lock up my room and make the short walk to my house. I love Hammersmith. It's quiet. You don't feel like you're in the hustle and bustle of London. Slinging my violin higher on my shoulder, I turn onto my street. There's a commotion down the street. Getting closer, my nerves start tingling. They can't be in front of my house, can they?

"Zara! Zara! Over here!"

My worst fears are confirmed as cameras are shoved in my face. One paparazzo turns into five, which turns into ten. Where in the world are they coming from?

They're surrounding me on all sides.

"Zara, are you sleeping with the prince?"

"What's James like in bed?"

"Will you be the future Queen?"

I'm being pushed from side to side. A violent shove from behind sends my bag skidding across the sidewalk. Everything is flying out. Bending over, I try to scoop it all up when it happens in quick succession. A camera gets shoved right in my face, throwing me to the side. I can't focus on the jolt of pain, because my violin is next to hit the ground. The crunching sound of the bag over the crowd is crushing.

"No!" The initial shock has worn off as I start to push my way through. "Back up, you vultures!" Grabbing the case, the tinkle of wood stings my heart. My most prized possession is likely damaged beyond repair. Shoving everything in my purse, I hurry to the security of my house. Thank God for the gate.

The chaos behind me fades away as my trembling hands unlock the door and I rush inside. Tears prick my eyes. Setting my violin down with all the care in the world, I grab my phone and dial James.

He answers on the first ring. "Hey there, fiancée."

"J-James?" I stutter, not hiding the panic in my voice.

"Zara. Are you alright?" All lightness in his tone is gone. "Is everything okay?"

"No. There were paparazzi waiting for me at my house."

"I'll be right there." He hangs up before I can get another word in.

Looking in the mirror, an angry red cut mars my cheek. What in the world will the students think tomorrow?

Hot tears stream down my face. It's a struggle to catch my breath as I collapse into the safety of my sofa. How in the world did they find me? The house isn't listed in my name. Will I have to fight my way through them every day now? Will I have any privacy anymore? Panicked thoughts race through my head as the commotion outside hits a new high.

A pounding on my door has me hiding behind the wall. Are they able to get on private property? Aren't there laws against this?

"Zara? Open up. It's James." Rushing to the door, I confirm it's him and pull the door open, hiding behind it.

"Are you alright?" He pulls me into his arms, but not before I see his security officers escorting the paparazzi away.

I only shake my head, my throat clogged with emotions. I squeeze him tighter to me. The spicy scent of his cologne soothes my frazzled nerves. If I could burrow into his arms, I'd stay here.

His hands smoothing my hair back is calming. The stubble on his neck is scratchy, grounding me.

"What happened, Zara?" He pulls back, cupping my face. Anger churns in his eyes.

I walk away, seeing my violin case. My heart is in a vise as I open the case. "I was walking home from school, and they were there. I don't know how there were so many of them on me all at once, but I couldn't get away. They were shoving me, and then they knocked my purse and violin out of my hands."

My stomach drops to my feet as I see the damage done. My most prized possession is broken. My mum's violin. One of the few memories I have of my mum is her playing for me on this violin. And now it's shards of wood and string tangled together. James's warm hand is on my shoulder.

"Can we fix it?"

I slam the lid shut. "No! We cannot fix it!" Rage is

coursing through my veins. "It is a custom-made violin from California. You cannot fix it! It was a wedding gift from my dad to my mum. I don't know if they even make these anymore." The tears won't stop. Forget the ache in my face. The ache in my heart is splitting me in two.

"I'll make this right. I don't know how, but please, Zara, let me help."

I stalk away from him, heading through the short hallway into the dining area. I need a drink. Pulling off the stopper, I take a swig of scotch, wincing as it goes down. I have it for when Dad comes to visit. But tonight? Tonight, it's needed.

"I thought I'd have more time." I'm staring down into the crystal bottle. Did my life just become public fodder for the entire world to see? Sure, my students knowing is one thing. But I'm not quite prepared for billions of people to know my name.

"I'm so sorry, Zara." The heat of James's body is behind me as I take another hit of the scotch. "Okay, if you don't slow down, I'll be carrying you to bed." James grabs the bottle from my hand, setting it down behind me. "I usually like a woman to be sober when I take her to bed for the first time."

He tries to break the tension settling over me. It does little to quell the racing thoughts in my head.

"How am I going to navigate my life? Will they be out there all the time now?" I wave towards the window.

"I've already called Mum and made the request for you to have security officers with you at all times." He brings his hand up, stopping me before I can interrupt. "I know you won't like them, but I can't have anything happening to you."

"Right, because it'd be terrible if your fiancée were to be hurt." I roll my eyes.

"Stop it, Zara." His voice is firm. The hands on his hips tell me now is not the time to argue, but feck it, I'm in a fighting mood.

"This isn't a love match. We're not in love. Why are you so upset by the truth?"

"Just because we're not a love match doesn't mean I want to see you get hurt! I'd have to be pretty cruel to leave you to the wolves." His voice rises with anger.

"They are terrible, aren't they?" James's anger on my behalf takes the fight out of me. "Will it always be this bad?"

"The press can be great when things are going well. But when there is a scandal? Forget about it."

"So, every day of your life then?" I give him a playful smile. My nerves are settling. I can't think about my violin, or the anger will return.

"Ouch. I like this cheeky side of you, Z." My cheeks pink at the nickname. I've never let anyone call me Z before. But when James does it? I quite like it.

"What can I say? I guess I'm feisty when I'm tossed around." That takes the laughter right out of him.

"Can I take a look at your face?" He touches my cheek where it stings.

"Sure." I'm tired. A headache is forming, and the adrenaline from the day is fading.

James's hands are gentle on my face. "Got a plaster? You're bleeding a bit."

"Really?" I rush to the mirror, and sure enough, blood is caked on the small cut under my eye. Grabbing James by the elbow, I direct him to the half bath at the end of the hall.

"Pop up." He pats the counter and I do as he says. He's focused on the task at hand, digging out the plasters from the first aid kit.

I wince from the pain as he dabs antiseptic on the cut. "Ouch! Is that really necessary?" He takes my face in his hands, blowing gently on the cut. I'm starting to like the feel of his hands on me.

"You don't want an infection." His eyes bore into mine. He's ready to fight me on this. I give a subtle nod, allowing him to continue.

"Besides, maybe this will give you some street cred with your students."

I grab his hand, dodging his touch. "Have you ever met a music student before? I think I would get more street cred if I met the conductor of the London Symphony Orchestra."

"And here I thought I was one of the cool kids," James says on a laugh.

"I'm pretty sure everyone tells you you're one of the cool kids just so they don't hurt your feelings. That or they want to meet the Queen."

"Wow. So much for progress." His touch is light as he puts the plaster on my cheek. I hate to admit it, but it really does feel better now. James drops his hands on either side of me on the counter. We're at eye level.

James has some of the most expressive eyes I've ever seen. They really are the windows to his soul. Whatever he's feeling, you can see it in his eyes. His blue eyes are dark now, fighting a storm of emotions.

"Zara. I know this wasn't in your plan. I'm dragging you through the weeds, just to change the world's view of the 'playboy prince.' If it's too much, you have to tell me now. Fuck whatever agreement our parents have. If you can't handle this, say the word."

The kindness in his eyes settles me. I made a promise to him. I hate going back on my promises. Aside from that disastrous first meeting at the palace, James has shown me nothing but compassion.

"Whatever your decision, I'll respect it. If you want to walk away, I'll respect that. I know this isn't what you signed up for," he says as he cups my cheeks.

The heat from his touch is new. Not like the other times he touched me tonight. No.

This feeling is new.

The butterflies are new.

The need to taste his lips is new.

And it's frightening. James is a womanizer. He didn't get the nickname Playboy Prince because he's a saint. More like a sinner. I can't have feelings for this man. Feelings are dangerous.

His breath ghosts my cheek, heightening the sensations coursing through me. "But if we do this, I will do everything in my power to keep you safe. I know what the world thinks of me, but I promise, I'll do everything I can to shield you from the paparazzi." The sincerity and vulnerability in his voice solidifies my decision.

Taking a deep breath, I clasp his wrists. His pulse is racing. Could he be just as affected by me as I am by him?

"We're in this together, James. There's no going back now."

Chapter Eight

JAMES

Our date last week went better than I thought it would. Zara couldn't be more different than the woman I first met with at the palace. The woman at the palace was hesitant, uncertain. But the Zara I'm meeting now is lively. Maybe it had to do with the fact that she got herself tied to the "playboy prince" and is responsible for helping clean up my image.

"So, have you bedded your future wife?" Oliver's voice breaks me from my thoughts.

"Are you serious with this shite right now?" I look over at my oldest friend who has his long blond hair pulled back into a bun. He's always trying to impress the ladies and appear more rocker than his Cambridge upbringing would care to suggest.

"I'm just messing with you. Christ, this woman has already got your knickers in a twist."

I flip him off, taking a long pull of my drink. "The whole point of this is to prove to everyone that I'm ready to be King. If I bed her, as you say, that would be the exact opposite of what I'm trying to prove."

"And how long do you plan to keep this up?"

"What do you mean how long? It's a done deal."

He gives me a cheeky look. "Come off it. You mean there's no way that you can get out of an arranged marriage?"

"Would you want to cross my mum?" I give him a knowing look. Even when we were little, one cutting look from her and we'd fall in line.

"Fair point. So, you're just going to marry some woman you don't even know?"

"Ahh, that's where you're wrong. They were trying to rush us, but now they're giving us until the fall to date and get to know one another before they announce the engagement. I'll know everything there is to know about my future wife by then."

"I've seen you take longer to decide where you want to eat dinner. There's no way you'll know enough about this woman by the fall." Even in the dark club, I can see anger tighten his face. "I can't believe you're going along with this."

"It's not like I have any choice." Bitterness laces my voice. "This is the last thing I wanted. But there's no other option since Ellie fled."

"How is she doing, by the way?"

"Pregnant." As unexpected as it was, I'm quite looking forward to being an uncle.

"No shite. Missed the train on that one."

"Oy! She's quite happy as she is, so you can feck off." Oliver wasn't the only one of my friends I had to fend off Ellie. It seemed all my friends wanted to date her when we were growing up. One of the downsides to having a twin sister.

"Alright, alright." He throws his hands up in defeat. "I wasn't serious. But good to know she's doing well."

"Part of why Mum wants me to settle down. No one is going to take me seriously as the King if I can't keep it in my pants."

He snorts over the drink he just took. "Did she actually say that to you?"

I shake my head. "She didn't, but my advisors did. Talk about an awkward conversation."

"Shouldn't you be used to everyone talking about your dick?"

"And on that happy note, I need to get going. I have to pick Zara up for another event this evening."

"Wow, they're not wasting any time." Oliver stands, clapping me on the back.

"What can I say? True love waits for no man."

Zara

IT'S ONLY BEEN a few days since our first date, and my weeks are already planned out for the next three months. There are no fewer than three events each week to ensure maximum exposure for the two of us. It's exhausting to even think about.

After dinner the other night, James and I walked out together. While there were only a few paparazzi around, it was enough. They've been following me every day since to and from school. Thank God for the security officers, or I don't know what I would do.

Tonight, they'll be swarming. It makes me uncomfortable to think about that many people snapping my picture because of whom I'm with.

Because of the early hour of the event, James is picking me up straight from school. I did a quick change in the bathroom and am trying to calm my nerves before he gets here. I'm glad the students have already left, otherwise it would be even more of a spectacle. The press has been stationed outside the school since they found me.

Nerves surge through me as James's motorcade rolls to a stop in front of the school. I was fine with meeting him at the event, but he wouldn't have it.

"My future Queen." James's deep voice washes over me as he steps out of the car. If I wasn't so upset about this situation my dad had pulled me into, I could appreciate what a gorgeous man James is. I'm not noticing how good James looks in his suit, or how his irises disappear as he gazes at me. I changed into a simple grey cocktail dress with a lace overlay, hitting me at my knees. I'm trying not to notice how goose pimples break out as his eyes blaze a hot trail over my body.

"My future King." I accept the double-cheek kiss as he waves me into the awaiting car. "And what does tonight's event entail? You were rather secretive."

"Tonight's benefit is for the national museum to raise funds for a new exhibit on British history. People tend to be fast and loose with their money if you feed them more alcohol."

"I'll have to add that to the list of things I need to remember."

He shrugs, giving me a playful smile. "That's why we're not in charge of the planning. There are people much smarter than us who know these things and plan accordingly. We're not much more than pretty faces."

"And is this one of your new charities that you're taking on?"

Reckless Royal

James does a good job of hiding his nerves about his new place in the royal line. But underneath all the bravado of this man lies someone who really doesn't want to mess up in his new role. I can't imagine the kind of pressure he's under.

"It's one Mum reassigned to me. Not my favourite by any means. Ellie was much more into the arts than I have ever been."

"Are you able to find something that you're passionate about?" I don't have the first clue about how royals come by their patronages, so I can't really offer much in the way of support.

"Sometimes yes, sometimes no. There are the charities that, historically, we've always supported that we will continue to do so. But sometimes there are new ones that we can get behind as long as it's a sound investment."

"And what will my charities be once I'm in the fold?" I observe the long line of press as we get to the museum.

"We'll worry about that later. Are you ready to wine and dine everyone tonight?" James waggles his eyebrows at me.

"As ready as I'll ever be." I didn't expect to be thrown into the deep end so soon. I thought there would be more of a learning curve, but here we are.

The flashbulbs are bright as the car door opens and James steps out. Taking a deep breath, I slide out behind him and take his awaiting hand, holding on for dear life.

"James! James! Over here!" James gives the person yelling his name a big smile. I'm not sure how he can distinguish him from the rest of them. "How did you and Zara meet?"

I shouldn't be surprised that they already know who I am. I can only force a smile as James tells them our fake story about us meeting through mutual friends. They eat up his every word. James is a natural at this. He has an easy grace that makes him perfect for the role he was born into.

"Zara. How does it feel to be dating the prince?"

James pulls me closer to his side as I try to formulate an answer. I knew there would be press here tonight, I just didn't think we'd be stopping to chat with them. But I guess it's all part of the palace's plan to rehab James's public persona.

"James really is a prince." *Really is a prince?* I want to die on the spot. James squeezes me closer as a playful look lights up his face.

"You certainly seem to have charmed him."

"That she has. Now, if you'll excuse us. Have a nice evening, everyone." James is polite in his dismissal as he pulls me towards the museum entrance.

"Glad to know I really am a prince." His hot breath ghosts my ear, sending butterflies through my stomach.

"Shut it. I completely blanked on anything even remotely normal to say." I give him a hard shove in the stomach, but he doesn't move an inch.

"I guess we'll just have to work on that then." The jest in his eyes gives way to something else. Something almost like lust and longing. But that can't be possible, right? We were thrust into the most unlikely of situations and have only known each other a short time.

"Prince James. Lady Zara. How lovely of the two of you to join us this evening."

An older man wearing a pinstripe suit and an oversized moustache greets us at the door.

"Dr. Sharpe. It's a pleasure to see you again. May I introduce you to Lady Zara Cross?"

"It's a pleasure. I am so happy the two of you could

join us this evening." Excitement is dripping from every pore as he leads us into the crowded museum. "All of the exhibits are open. Wine and cocktails are being served, so if you have any questions, please do not hesitate to let me know." He bows as he backs away from us.

A server walks by with a tray of champagne, and James grabs two, one for each of us. "To a night of fun." He winks at me before clinking his glass against mine.

"Cheers."

"So, care to work the room with me?" James gives me his arm as we mingle amongst the guests.

"How many of these people do you actually know?" Being the daughter of a duke, I recognise certain faces, but everyone's face tonight is a blur. It's the first official event the two of us are attending together. Trying to put my best foot forward is even more nerve-wracking than I thought it would be. One false move, and we'll both be making headlines tomorrow.

"I know a lot of them, but a lot are new. Take that guy." James points in the direction of a tall, older man with a young woman on his arm. "That's his third wife, I believe. Could be number four. He's always a good person to chat up. Likes people to know he has money and will spend it."

It's hard to hear a word of what James is saying because "—you can't get past her tits, right?" James finishes my thought for me.

"I mean, would you look at those?" My voice is a loud whisper as I take in the woman's appearance. "They can't be real. They're like two water balloons!"

"Shh, you don't want anyone to hear you. We can't be judging the people we're trying to schmooze." His voice is filled with laughter as he takes me in that direction.

"Prince James! Who is this gorgeous woman on your

arm?" asks the gentleman as we approach. The woman with him shoots me a menacing glare.

"Lord Paxton. This is Zara Cross. You may know her father, the Duke of Kendall?" Lord Paxton gives me an appraising look.

"Ahh, yes. How is the duke doing these days?"

"He's quite well, thank you." I tip my head in his direction.

"Splendid to hear. It's nice to see you young folks supporting such a marvellous cause. One can never get enough of our own history."

"The National Museum has always been a cause near and dear to my heart." James is so full of shit, yet this portly man is hanging on his every word. James's eyes are sparkling with amusement as they carry on their conversation. The young woman pays me no mind. It's just as well. I should get used to being invisible.

"Yes, well, I'll be sure to match my donation from last year. I don't want to keep you. I'm sure everyone wants to meet this beauty on your arm." Lord Paxton bows low in our direction, as an uneasy feeling washes over me.

"Do they always make you feel so slimy?" I whisper to James as we walk away.

"Those old men? Yes. I don't see him often, so at least there's that."

"Thank goodness for that."

James stops and pulls me into a small alcove, hidden from the eyes of onlookers.

"Are you uncomfortable being here?" His eyes hold mine captive.

"Not uncomfortable. It is just different than I thought it would be." It's hard to explain. "That man seemed to look right through me, yet was also looking at me like he wanted to make me his next wife."

"Well rest assured, you're no one's wife but mine." His smile is dazzling, bright white teeth standing out in the dark corner, as he moves in closer to me, caging me in.

"Doesn't that sound medieval?" I poke him in his hard chest.

"Your dad and my mum arranging our marriage is medieval. I can't help it if that means that no one else gets to look at you like that."

This protectiveness shouldn't be as captivating as it is. And yet, I'm finding myself completely taken with this man.

"Well, it could be worse." I shrug my shoulder. "You could be with Miss Tits back there and suffocate anytime she tried to cuddle with you."

Laughter bursts out of James, and I muffle my own in the crook of his neck. That spicy scent of his is intoxicating.

"God, I can't even imagine. He probably bought them for her."

"I'm telling you right now." I grab him by the chin, looking into his bright blue eyes. Eyes that I can get lost in. "I am never getting anything like that. I may not be well-endowed, but I would topple over if I had those."

The air is sucked dry around us as James goes quiet. His gaze is so focused on my face, as if he's trying to ignore the area of my body I just pointed out. His tongue darts out, licking that full bottom lip of his. I bet it would taste like the champagne we've been sipping on. What I wouldn't give to suck that bottom lip into my mouth and taste him.

"We should probably get back out there. We don't want people to think we've already ditched the party." His voice is rough, filled with a need I feel down to my toes.

I take a settling breath, trying to recalibrate after this

heated moment with James. "Right, fundraiser. A prince's work is never done."

Chapter Nine

JAMES

I'm all over the place. For the last two weeks, I've been fighting all of my emotions for Zara. I was raging at Mum for setting us up. It's the twenty-first century. Why are arranged marriages still a thing?

Then I was annoyed at Mum for finding Zara. She could have found someone that I didn't like to make it easier to stay mad at her. But no. The woman I'm coming to know now is full of zest. Full of life.

And fecking hell, if that isn't making me crazy. When she called me after the paparazzi attacked her outside her house, it took everything in me not to wring their necks. Instead of running, she doubled down on this crazy life with me, even if it means having a camera constantly shoved in her face.

It's a fact of life. The paparazzi will do anything to get a shot of us. Especially if it's in a compromising position. But when they hurt someone who's been out with me one time? Rage. White-hot rage that I've never felt before. It meant that I couldn't keep my hands off Zara at the fundraiser last night. It was like if I wasn't touching her, she would disappear. I liked having her by my side. She was winning people over like I could only hope to.

I shouldn't want more from her. I can't want any more from her. I can't destroy her life any more than I already have. Sure, she says she's all in. But in this life? The paparazzi already following her every move? Already attacking her once? I hate to think of what else could happen to her.

My sweet, music-loving fiancée.

She doesn't even know how sexy she is. How sensual. Fecking hell, I'm getting hard again just thinking about her. It's been a struggle to push thoughts of her out of my head, but after a long day, I give in.

Taking my dick in my hand, I free him from his cotton prison. Just the thought of Zara has me ready to explode. Imagining it's Zara's nimble fingers and hot mouth on me, I give a few hard strokes and am close to coming. Those pouty lips of hers would know exactly how to suck me off. It'd be better than some nobody doing it in the back of a club, just for the need to get off. She'd look up at me with those big doe eyes, and bloody hell, I'm coming harder than I have in a long time. *Faster* than I have in a long time.

Feck. I'm covered in cum. Stripping off my shirt, I clean myself up before finding a new pair of boxers. I shouldn't be jacking off to thoughts of Zara, but damn, this woman is crawling under my skin no matter how hard I try to fight it. I'm just going to have to try harder.

IT'S the day of the Royal Flower Show, and it's going to be teeming with press. The Royal Flower Show was always

Ellie's event. But now, it has been passed off to me. Another duty I have to show that I'm fit to handle.

Standing at Zara's door, I smooth my hands over the lapels of my jacket and ring the bell. I'm nervous. I can't remember the last time I was nervous to take a woman out. But when Zara opens the door and ushers me in, all thoughts flee my brain.

Feck. What did I say about trying harder to not be attracted to her? She's wearing a white jumpsuit that shows off all her curves, and her hair curls around her shoulders. She's beautiful.

"Zara. You look incredible." I kiss each cheek, breathing in her sweet scent. She's radiant, and I can't seem to stop staring at her.

"You look quite dashing yourself, James." My khaki trousers and navy blazer are an easy outfit for an official, yet casual, event. Everyone always tries harder to make the flower show a fancier event than it really is.

"Are you ready to woo your citizens?" Shite, why am I acting like Granddad? No one says woo these days. What is it about this woman that drives me mad?

"As I'll ever be." She takes my proffered arm, and I lead her out of the house. Her hand on my arm tenses as we make our way to the car. The paparazzi are now confined to the other side of the street, thankfully, which means we can get in and out of her house without being swarmed. Sure, this moment will be splashed across headlines tomorrow, but at least I don't have to worry about a camera being shoved right in Zara's face.

"You're doing beautifully, Z."

She gives me a shy smile as my PPO opens the door for us. "So, is there anything I need to know about today?" she asks once we're settled in the car.

"Other than oohing and aahing over a lot of flowers,

no. Since I took over the patronage midseason, we didn't do a stall. That will come next year."

"Fawning over flowers, I can do that." She nods her head, twisting her hands in her lap.

"I promise, you'll do great." I grab her hands, and they still under my touch. Her gaze is fixed on them. Running my thumb over her knuckles, I try to be as reassuring as possible.

"You're a caring person, Zara. This will be easy for you. You connect with people without even trying." Her eyes flit to mine.

"How could you possibly know that?"

"Because I pay attention. Because after you came with me to the museum fundraiser, you had everyone eating out of the palm of your hand. They couldn't get enough of you." She blushes. The same blush I imagine on her cheeks when I'm making her come. Christ, these are not the thoughts I need to be having right now.

"Thank you, James. That means a lot coming from you."

"What can I say? There's a lot more to me than just the 'playboy prince.'"

PRESS ARE CRAWLING at the arrivals gate. We've slowed to a stop as it's time to get out.

"You've got this, Z. I promise." I give her hands a reassuring squeeze as the door is opened. Everyone is immediately calling for our attention. Zara has a death grip on my hand. I pull her closer to me. I want to wrap her in a bubble and not let the outside world touch this beautiful woman attached to my arm.

"Your Royal Highness. Lady Zara. It's a pleasure to have you both here today. I'm Olivia and I'll be your host for the day." Olivia bows before me, then takes Zara's extended hand. Flashbulbs continue to pop as we meet our guide for the day. I'm used to the press being at every event, but it seems like lately there are more than usual. Maybe because Zara is a novelty, and they want to catch every moment of our budding relationship.

"It's a pleasure to meet you, Olivia. I've never had the opportunity to come to the Royal Flower Show." Zara is kind to everyone she meets, regardless of how nervous she is right now.

"Well, I'm thrilled I'll be showing you around." She takes us deep into the hall, skylights overhead bright with the spring sun. Any nerves Zara had seem to have faded with Olivia's welcome. She drops my hand, and I can only follow. It's rare when my presence is overlooked. It's a new feeling, something I'm not quite used to.

"So, Olivia. What's your favourite part of the show this year?" The perfume of the flowers should be overwhelming, but it's not.

"The orchid farm. You'll have to visit. It's stunning. We also have a beautiful set of instruments made entirely from plants that I think you'll enjoy, Zara." Olivia is paying me no mind. She is absolutely taken with Zara.

Zara grabs her arm as excited eyes find mine. "You must take us there. It sounds wonderful."

"Please, this way." Olivia extends her hand, and Zara follows her, a little extra pep in her step. It's nice to see after the stressful few weeks she's had. I find my thoughts drifting to her more and more during the day. She didn't mind the security officers I assigned to her, but trying to get her to take a car to work proved more difficult. She's quite stubborn.

Zara stops suddenly, her eyes wide. The music installation is directly in front of us.

"Olivia, please excuse us," I say to our host. She bows to me and scurries away.

"I have no words." Zara's voice is quiet. Her eyes are everywhere, observing the life-size instruments in this part of the grounds. Violins and pianos made of greenery have flowers flowing out of them. It's something straight out of a fantasy novel. Zara is walking around, touching everything in sight. Her chocolate-brown eyes are unblinking.

"You like these, then?"

She hooks her arm in mine, pulling me close, her head resting on my shoulder. "This really is incredible. I know you have to do these kinds of events all the time, but the beauty and creativity these artists put into their work? I love being able to witness it firsthand."

"You've never been here before?" Her fingers are dancing over the pieces. Her head shakes on my shoulder.

"Dad never brought me. I was usually too involved with my music and couldn't be pulled away. But seeing these, I wish I had come."

My chest swells with Zara on my arm. Where did this woman come from? "Will you play for me sometime? I'd love to hear you play."

She pulls back, surprise on her face. "You want to hear me play?"

"Why wouldn't I?"

"I would love to. Of course, I'll have to find another violin." Hurt laces her tone. I know she's still upset about her violin.

I point to the life-size violin in front of me, covered in flowers. "Think you can play on this? I can probably get them to let me take it home."

Her laughter ringing out is music to my ears. "Yes, I'm

sure this would make the same sounds as I'm used to." She's grinning as she pulls away from me, dancing through the flowers. Bloody hell, how can I be in so deep with someone so fast?

"Maybe I could even play the piano for you." Zara's eyes are twinkling. She's glowing with the sun reflecting off her. She looks happier than I've seen her this last week. Instead of fear underlying her every mood, she's alight with happiness. I know she didn't want to be thrust into this position, but right now, I'm glad it was her.

"You're looking awfully thoughtful there, Your Highness."

"Just thinking about how good you look there." The blush that creeps over her skin stirs something inside me. Women fall at my feet, but it's been a while since one has appeared indifferent. And that's exactly how Zara was acting towards me. But after our event the other night, I'm seeing a new side to her. And damn, I can't help but be drawn to her.

"Excuse me, Your Highness. Lady Zara." Olivia is back at my side. "Are you ready to move on to the next exhibit?" Zara tucks a loose strand of hair behind her ear, coming to stand by my side.

"This was beautiful." Her eyes are still roaming over the instruments. Running my hand down Zara's arm, a shock of electricity hits me.

Shite, that's new. Zara's eyes swing to mine, and her eyes look so brown they're black. Did she feel that too?

"Are you ready?" Olivia's voice brings me back to the present.

"Yes, let's go." Zara breaks the staredown we're having. The soft sway of her hips as she walks away from me has my dick stirring in my pants. This is bad. This is very, very bad.

Chapter Ten

ZARA

"So was the Royal Flower Show everything you'd hoped it would be?" James's presence is a calming weight behind me. It had been an interesting afternoon with him. I've felt the growing desire with him this past week, but today, it was like he felt it too.

"It was brilliant." Pushing open the black door to my house, James lingers in the doorway. "Would you like to come in for dinner?" I ask suddenly. A few flashbulbs are popping across the street. James's smile is bright as he follows me inside.

"Are we ordering takeaway?" He toes off his shoes as I kick off my wedges. James follows me into the kitchen. It feels intimate, him in his bare feet padding across my house. Never in a million years did I think I'd have the future King in my house.

"If you're okay waiting, I can whip something up."

He's rolling up the sleeves of his shirt. The fine dusting of dark hair on his arms is drool worthy. James is at ease here, helping himself to a drink.

"I'm happy waiting. Can I be your sous-chef?" He's

swirling the drink, leaning against the counter. He looks so at home. I like having him here with me.

"Make me a gin and tonic, and then you can help."

"You've got this bossing people around thing down. You're fit to be Queen," he chuckles, winking at me.

"Well, I guess it's a good thing I'm marrying a prince."

He winces at that comment, as I get everything out of the fridge. Maybe he's a bit more sensitive to this arranged marriage than I thought.

"Is salmon okay?"

"Perfect." He hands me my drink, our fingers brushing. Lingering. I'm not supposed to fall for this man. It makes it that much harder to hold on to my anger towards my father if whatever this is between James and me is real. He has a kingdom to lead. I have students to teach. There's no way this can be real.

I take a large sip of my drink, needing to cool off.

"Alright, what do I get to do?" James claps his hands, rubbing them together.

I place a bag of carrots and a knife in front of him. "You're making the veggies. Just need to peel them and cut them."

"Peel and cut. Can't be too hard, can it?" He gives me a smirk, before opening the carrots. The salmon's already prepared, so I turn the knobs to start the oven, but my focus is on James.

The delicate way his fingers move the knife is hypnotizing. He's butchering the carrots, but he's doing it with such pride, I can't stop him.

"What?" He holds his hands out, like he can't understand why I'm staring at him.

Laughter bubbles out of me. "It's just, you're not doing it properly. You need to peel them, then cut."

He looks down at the mess he's made. "Shite. I'm not doing a very good job impressing you, am I?"

"That would mean I want to be impressed." I hip check him, moving in beside him.

"Ouch. You sure do know how to make a man feel special."

"Here, let me show you." I grab his hand with mine, the carrot with the other. My hands are dainty compared to his. I slowly move my hand, guiding his movements. Heat is radiating off him.

"I'm not a very good sous-chef if you're doing most of the work." His breath is hot on my cheek.

"Everyone has to learn somehow." Tilting my chin upward, his lips are right there. It would be so easy to lean up and capture his lips. To feel the stubble under my fingers as I take what I want.

"Zara." James's free hand wraps around my neck, his thumb on my pulse. No doubt he can feel the rapid beat. The heat of his hand settles in my core. Butterflies are dancing in my belly as he moves closer, his lips only an inch away from mine.

The ding of the oven breaks through the fog of lust clouding my brain. "Guess you better get that in the oven." James pulls away. I lament the loss of him.

I set the salmon on a pan, putting it in the oven before helping James finish the carrots. The tension from earlier is gone. It's for the best, right? Falling for this man is a bad idea.

"Put the carrots in the pan, and then I'll top off our drinks. Shouldn't take long for them to cook," I instruct.

"Look at me. Making dinner like a pro."

I can't help the laugh that bubbles out of me. "I'll give you an A for effort."

"Guess I'll stick to leading the country, eh?"

I shrug my shoulders. "How about another A for effort?"

"Is this what I have to look forward to for the next fifty years? Cheeky little bugger, you are." The smile plastered on James's face matches my own. I like this side of him. He never shows it to the press, but I like that I get to see it. It goes beyond the charming façade. He's fun, but also has a vulnerable side.

James and I continue our easy conversation while dinner cooks. I didn't think it would be like this. I thought it would be hard to be around the future King. But it's anything but. It's easy and carefree.

The buzzer sounds, pulling me away from the man holding my attention. "Grab some plates and we'll be ready to eat." I point in the direction of the correct cabinet, and he grabs what we need.

Plating dinner, we move to my small table that overlooks the back courtyard.

"Cheers." James clinks his glass against mine, extending his long legs across the small space.

"Cheers."

My eyes are drawn to him as he takes a bite, years of royal protocol obvious in the way he eats. "Zara, love. This is delicious. Better than any Michelin-starred meal that I've had." He dives right back in, taking another hearty bite.

"You flatter me. It's not that good."

"I'll be the judge of that." The wink causes those butterflies to stir again. This is why he's the "playboy prince." This charm he has always makes everyone fall at his feet. I hate that I'm one of them.

"So, how are you doing with everything?" I ask, digging into my own meal.

"Everything?" He looks up, midchew.

"With the whole reason why we're here. With you now

first in line for the throne." He puts down his fork, giving me a pensive stare, his brow furrowing slightly.

"At first, I wanted to be mad at Ellie. But then I could see how miserable she was, and I couldn't really blame her." He swirls his drink before taking a sip. "And now, the pressure is on. I can no longer run around and ignore the duties of what I was born to do."

James's shoulders are tense as he leans over the table.

"The press is no longer eating out of the palm of your hand?"

He grins as he goes back to eating. "No, I wish. They were much easier to please when I could just flash a smile and continue on my way. Now, I actually have to do more than just shake hands."

"Have you given any more thought to which charities are going to be your new patronages?"

"They've already been hand-selected for me, so just a matter of deciding. Not that I'll get much choice there either."

"And you really won't get a say in what you want to do?"

James's deep blue eyes stare into mine. It's so easy to get lost in them. "They are handpicked by the Queen."

Ahh. "So not things you're really interested in." James is very easy to read. He is not happy about this.

"Charities have been dropped in my lap since I was old enough to be a patron. But I want to find something I'm passionate about. I don't want to just go through the motions."

"And what are you passionate about?" I push my empty plate out of the way, resting my chin in my hand.

"What are *you* passionate about?" He gives me that smile that is known to drop panties of women everywhere.

I hate that I feel it all over. That liquid fire spreads through my body at the sight of it.

"I'm not the one that needs to get my life together, James. I believe that's you."

"Why can't I just use your passion? You love music?" I give him a small nod. "I'll go with music then."

"You can't just take my passion, James," I say on a laugh.

"Damn. And here I thought it was going to be that easy."

I stand, grabbing our plates and taking them to the sink. "Maybe I can help you narrow down the list."

"You don't have to do that." James is behind me, refilling his drink.

"If we're going to be married, I might as well be a sounding board for you."

"What a good fiancée you are." I can't quell the butterflies that start fluttering in my stomach again. I hate how he affects me like this.

"You have to keep me around for a reason. Now, start talking."

James finishes refilling his drink before hopping onto the counter. "So bossy." He takes a hearty sip of his drink before he does what he's told. "Maybe I could just make Sean's art school my charity."

"Would your sister like that?" I give him a stern eye.

"No, probably not." He's staring into his drink, the weight of the world heavy on his shoulders. "Do we really have to do this?"

I walk over to where he is, resisting the urge to put my hands on his strong thighs. "James. I'm not trying to make this into a big thing. Maybe just start thinking about it. You might find that if you do, some inspiration might strike you. Remember what I said? Start small. You're not becoming King tomorrow."

James pulls me between his legs, his fingers dancing up and down my arm. Goose pimples break out in their path. "You'll make a very good Queen, you know that?"

A shy smile breaks out across my face. "What makes you say that?"

"You see past my bullshit and put me in my place. Not to mention, you had Olivia wrapped around your finger. She loved you."

Laughter escapes my lips. "I passed my Queen lessons then?"

"With flying colours." James's eyes keep drifting to my lips. Heat is radiating off him, pulling me into his orbit. His gaze is soft as he leans forward, ever so slowly, and captures my lips with his.

My mind goes blank. My body leans into his, wanting to bottle the electricity shooting through me.

All thought leaves my mind as James's lips meet mine. They're warm and soft and taste like scotch. Butterflies are swarming in my stomach as I lean into the kiss and James pulls me closer into him. Big, warm hands are a hot brand on my body. Everywhere they touch, I'm singed with a deep desire for more contact.

I've never had such a visceral reaction to a kiss. Fire is sweeping through my body. A moan escapes, causing James to sweep his tongue into my mouth. My hands fist in his shirt, tugging him closer to me, deepening the kiss.

Keeping him close to me with one hand, I thread my fingers through the waves at the nape of his neck. The strands are like silk under my fingers, as I twist my hand through the curls. A deep groan reverberates through him.

James is off the counter and backing me into the wall.

His lips blaze a hot trail down my neck as he grinds his erection into me. I'm shameless in my need to get closer to him as I rock my hips into him. Desire snakes down my spine to my core. An ache so deep settles within me. I want more. More of his touch. More of his lips on mine. More of James.

"Fuck, Z." James pulls back, his breath hot on my cheek. Squeezing my eyes shut, I try to tamp down the need inside me. James's fingers brush over my neck, up to my jaw before tracing my lips. Fireworks are exploding inside my body at the slightest touch.

I skate my hands around his waist, not wanting to lose his touch. His strong muscles flex under my fingertips. "As much as I would love to continue this tonight, I've got a packed schedule tomorrow, and you have school."

"But you do plan on continuing this?" Hunger laces my husky voice. I want more.

James takes another kiss. Another deep, soul-stirring kiss. Say what you will about him being a playboy, but he knows how to kiss a woman.

"Does that answer your question?"

Chapter Eleven

JAMES

I've never been brought to my knees like that. Bloody hell, I've been distracted all day. That kiss last night rocked me to my core. Zara has wormed her way under my skin, and I have no idea what to do about it. It's unsettling, this feeling of wanting more with a woman. Women can always count on me for a good time. A quick romp before said woman signs an NDA and is on her way.

But with Zara? I want more.

"Your Highness?" Shite, I've been spacing off again. "Would you like to visit the new children's wing of the hospital?"

I give the hospital director my winningest smile. "Absolutely."

She walks me back, giving me a rundown of the new ward, sponsored in part by one of the royal patronages. "And what are all of these children in the hospital for?"

As we enter the area, I'm assaulted with bright colours and happy voices. The walls are painted with murals of the jungle and ocean, and the waiting area has books and toys of all kinds strewn about.

"These children are short term patients. Broken bones, minor surgeries. We have a play area for families while they're waiting," she says, gesturing to the area behind me, "and the nurses' station is set up in the middle, so they can keep an eye on all the children."

"This is a wonderful setup you have here." It's nice to see good work being done with the royal patronages.

"Are you really the prince?" A small boy in a wheelchair stops in front of me. A large cast overtakes one of his legs.

"Do you think I am?" I squat down so I'm on his level.

"I thought princes wore crowns." He gives me a puzzled look.

"No, stupid. Only princesses wear crowns!" A girl appears at his side, looking remarkably like him.

"I'm not stupid!" the boy cries. Oh dear, what have I gotten myself into here?

"Victoria. George. That's enough." A haggard looking woman runs up behind them. "I'm so sorry, Your Highness." She dips into a low curtsy. "We've been cooped up in the hospital a few days longer than we'd like."

"It's quite alright. What brings you in here?"

"Obviously it's him." The little girl rolls her eyes at me, before wandering back to the play area. Her mother looks like she wants the ground to swallow her whole. Ouch. Guess I don't have a fan.

"I'm so sorry about my daughter. She's ready to head home." She gives me a soft look.

"I can't imagine being cooped up in here. I bet you're ready to get home. And how'd you break your leg, George?" I'm down on his level again.

"I broke my leg playing football."

"And who's your favourite football team?"

"Chelsea. They're the best! My room is blue to match the team!" He's so excited about his football team.

"Chelsea just happens to be my favourite too, but don't tell anyone. Maybe I can get you some tickets once you're healed up."

His eyes widen in delight. "I've never been to a match before!"

I nod at Charles behind me, indicating for him to make it happen. "Well, you get better, and then you'll be able to go."

"You're the best prince we have!" He gives me a high five as the mother bows and heaps praise on me.

The director is beaming at me as we finish our tour. "You were quite the hit today, Your Highness."

"It's always a pleasure to visit here. Thank you for all you do." I shake her hand as the car is brought around.

"Thank you. It's been wonderful to have you here." She bows as I make my way into the car.

"That was quite the showing you had, James." Charles climbs in behind me as we speed off towards the palace. "The press was eating it up."

"I wasn't doing it for them." Although, it's an added benefit that the press was here today. Between Charles and my mum, I'm being told to watch every move right now, as I can't take any more bad press.

"Either way, it was a good day. We'll get that family set up with a day they'll never forget with Chelsea. Nothing like a special outing from the prince."

A special outing. There's someone else who could do with a special outing.

"Charles. Any chance you could make a special outing happen tonight?"

"Sir?"

Giving him my idea, he immediately goes to work as I

pull up my phone and dial the number to the one woman whom I can't seem to resist.

"Hi, James." Her voice is smooth as she picks up on the first ring. I love that there is no pretence in letting me wait.

"Zara, love. Any chance you're free tonight?" I look over at Charles, and he's nodding to me. Being the prince, I can make things happen. "Say, seven?"

"What do you have planned?" I love the playfulness in her voice.

"Is you saying yes contingent on what the plans are?"

"I don't know. I might have a hot date tonight already."

A hot spike of jealousy rages through me. "A hot date?"

"Yes. He's quite old, actually. Ancient, really. Known for composing a number of symphonies."

I huff out a sigh. "Way to give a man a heart attack. Is it Beethoven or Mozart tonight?"

Her laughter on the other end of the line is soothing. Since when does a woman's laugh settle me? "It was going to be Mozart. But I suppose he'll still be around tomorrow."

"Perfect. I'll pick you up at seven. Wear something fancy."

"Fancy? Where are you taking me, James?"

"You'll just have to wait and see."

***

"ZARA, YOU LOOK ABSOLUTELY STUNNING." The long red dress with flowers decorating it hugs her lithe frame. Her long brown waves curl past her shoulders. She's breathtaking.

"You don't look so bad yourself." She smooths her hands over the lapels of my tux. I waste no time capturing those plump lips of hers. She opens to me immediately. The softness of her tongue is a match striking the fire within me. I don't know how I'll ever get enough of this woman. If I didn't have this special night planned, I'd toss her over my shoulder and take her upstairs right this second.

"As much as I would love to stay here with you all night," she whispers, pulling back, "I do want to see what this surprise is that has us dressed to the nines."

"Well then,"—I tuck a strand of hair behind her ear—"let's get going, shall we?"

I give her my arm as I lead us outside. Flashes are bright in the spring evening. Zara stiffens at my side but doesn't waver. We ignore the questions shouted at us as we approach the waiting car.

"A limo? Where are you taking me tonight?" The door is opened and she slides into the limo. A bottle of champagne is chilling in the ice bucket.

"I promise you, you'll like it." I pop the cork and hand her a glass as the limo pulls away from the curb. "To surprises." I clink my glass against hers and take a sip.

Zara gulps half of hers down before turning her eyes on me. "You might just be the biggest surprise of all, James." Her eyes are dark as she takes my hand in hers. Her delicate fingers trace the veins on the back of my hand. It's intoxicating. What this woman does to me is unlike anything I've ever felt.

"And why is that?"

"Because I expected the Playboy Prince, and instead, I got Prince Charming."

"Maybe I'm a little of both." I turn my hand in hers, linking our hands together.

"You've got more charm in your pinkie finger than most people could ever hope to have." She turns a radiant smile on me, one that hits me directly in the centre of my chest. Fecking hell. I really am falling for this woman, aren't I?

"Your Highness. We've arrived."

Zara's gaze is pulled from mine as we come to the side door of the building. "You don't plan on killing me, do you?"

"Now why would I make you dress up if I was planning to off you?" I chuckle as I take her hand.

"Stranger things have happened, I'm sure." The door opens, and we're led through a long hall before we enter the lobby. Red velvet lines the wall, and two grand staircases circle their way upstairs. A crystal chandelier reflects soft light throughout the room.

"James. What are we doing here at the symphony?" The pressure on my arm causes me to stop.

"You are a music fan, aren't you?"

"Yes, but why are we the only people here?" Her voice is quiet as she surveys the empty room.

"There are some perks of being a prince." I pull her forward as her mouth drops open in awe. The doors to the concert hall open, and we're led to the best seats in the house. A bottle of champagne and a tray of chocolate-covered strawberries await us. Just like I planned.

Zara is glued to her spot, standing and staring at the stage as the orchestra starts to make their way to their seats. Her eyes are glassy as she glances around the empty room, before turning to face me.

"You rented out the orchestra for me?"

I can only shrug. "Well, technically I paid for an extra performance tonight. They only perform on the weekends, so this is our own personal show." I spin her around and rest my hands on her slim waist. "I want to experience this with you." I drop a kiss on her exposed neck. "I want to experience what you feel when you listen to music."

"James." Her voice catches in her throat, stopping me in my tracks. "This is one of the most thoughtful things anyone has ever done for me."

The look on her face hits me square in the chest. Pure happiness radiates from her. I would buy the entire orchestra and have them perform for her every night if it meant I could keep this look on her face.

"Your Highness." The attendant hands us each a glass of champagne as noise from the stage has Zara moving to her seat. I'm helpless to follow. A tune I'm not familiar with has Zara clutching my arm. "I don't think I've ever heard the music this loud in here."

The sheer awe on her face is striking. I've never seen someone so passionate about anything before. She's in a trance as the music continues to rise and lower around us.

As a new piece starts, Zara gasps, turning to look at me. "This is my favourite piece. It's so beautiful and so romantic."

"And why is it so romantic?" I lean in, whispering in her ear.

"It's the dance of two lovers. It's the will they, won't they. It's the excitement of a new relationship when you find one another. It crescendos with them finally acting on their love for one another."

Bloody hell, I've never been a big fan of classical music, but this might be my new favourite piece. The passion in Zara's eyes as she describes her love of this piece is unmatched. It's not hard to feel her love of music when she describes it like a real-life, breathing thing.

"Have you ever felt something like this before?" I ask, as she turns to me, her eyes sparkling in the dark auditorium.

"Not before, no." Zara sips her champagne, before taking a small bite of a strawberry. Before she sets it down, I grab her wrist and finish it off. Her eyes are hungry as she licks her lips.

"And now?" I drop a kiss on the inside of her delicate wrist.

"Now it's as if I'm living this song."

I don't waste another minute. I pull Zara to me and she's as needy as I am. The music peaks around us as we ignite. I can't remember the last time a kiss has ever felt so good. The need. The passion.

We're moving in sync with the beat of the music. The space between us is too much. Thank God we're the only people here, because I pull Zara into my lap.

"Oh God, James." Her voice is a whisper as I suck and nibble on her neck. Her throaty moans do something to me. I feel it down to my bones. The ache in my groin needs a release that only she can give me.

"Zara, love," I purr, tugging her earlobe. "I have to have you tonight. I can't wait any longer."

Zara pulls back, lust clouding her beautiful eyes.

"I want nothing more." Her fingers trail down my neck, leaving a trail of fire in their wake. Shite, I don't want to waste another minute here, but I want to give her a night she'll remember. "But we have to stay until the end. This piece really is my favourite."

She gives me a happy smile as she curls up into my side. Zara is humming along, the vibrations against my neck going straight to my dick. I've spent many a night wrapped around different women. It was always the perfect no-strings-attached situation. It wasn't easy having Mum shove this whole idea of an arranged marriage at me.

But right now? Nothing beats this. Sitting with Zara in

my lap, doing the thing she loves most in the world. What I wouldn't give to spend all my nights like this.

I want this woman. I want her with every ounce of my being. To make her mine in every sense of the word. And tonight? Tonight, Zara will be mine.

Chapter Twelve

ZARA

It's been a magical night. One of the best in my life, in fact. No one has ever done anything like this for me before. Most men I've dated don't understand my love of music, something that I cherish because my mum loved music the same way. It's the way I carry her with me. It's a part of my soul.

But James understands. He planned the perfect evening for just the two of us. Away from the prying eyes of the paparazzi.

"Are you ready to go?" James's voice is quiet as the music stops. It's dark as the lights on the stage dim. Tears prick the back of my eyes as I let this moment wash over me. I'm not ready to leave. I want to stay here in this empty auditorium, with James in my arms.

"Z? Are you still with me?"

I love when he calls me that. I pull back, staring into his dark eyes. Butterflies erupt in my stomach. His eyes are searching mine. I lean in, taking a kiss. His hands roam over my back, hot skin on skin. I cup his face, deepening the kiss. I know it's not good form to be sitting here like this, but I don't care. A need like I've never known is coursing through my veins. I need James.

"Your Highness." James's security officers break the moment. His eyes are heavy and his lips swollen. I love that I bring this out in him. "The car is ready if you are."

"Thank you. We'll be right there." He doesn't break eye contact. He starts to stand, forcing me off his lap. Before he starts to make his way out, I grab him and pull him back.

"James." My voice is raspy with lust. My eyes are on the departing orchestra. "Thank you. I will never forget this night."

The smile he gives me causes my heart to flutter. He really is the sexiest man I've ever met. And not just because of that smile. There's so much more underneath all that sex appeal that he doesn't let the world see.

"You're worth it, Zara. Don't you ever forget that." His breath ghosts my lips as he holds me close to him. "Now, are you ready to continue our evening elsewhere?" His eyes hold a knowing glint.

"My place then?"

His lips barely make contact with mine. "Your place. Let's go." James turns and pulls me along behind him, the same way we came in. The limo is at the door, ready to whisk us off. Sliding in, James wastes no time pulling me across him again. This time, his hands find their way up my dress.

"I've been dreaming of this."

His lips make their way down my neck, nibbling and sucking as they go.

"Oh God," I groan. His lips cause heat to gather in my core.

"You drive me wild, Zara." James pulls back, staring into my eyes.

Lust. Passion. Desire. It's all reflected in his eyes. I move closer to him, needing his lips on mine. His hands move to my arse, grinding me over his hard length. It feels amazing.

"See how you make me feel?" he whispers. I drop my forehead to his, rocking into him. "I bet if I slipped my finger inside you, you'd be wet."

I bite down on my lip to keep the needy moans inside as his finger trails over my hot core. There's no hiding my desire for him.

"Fuck, Z. Have you been like this all night?"

I trail kisses along his jaw back to his ear, tugging it between my teeth. I can feel him get harder underneath me. "Yes. When a man does something like you did for a woman, it's a huge turn-on."

"Duly noted, love." James turns, tugging my bottom lip between his teeth. A shot of lust moves through me as the car comes to a stop.

"We've arrived, sir." The driver's voice crackles through the small space.

"Still okay if I come inside?" James trails his fingers lightly over my cheeks.

"I might combust if you don't."

"I can't stay the night. It's bad form if they see me leave in the morning, but Christ, Zara. I need to be with you tonight."

"Then what are we waiting for?" I slide off him, moving to the door as it opens. I add a little sway to my hips as we make our way inside the house.

I barely have the door unlocked and open when James is at my back. As soon as he kicks the door closed, his lips brush my neck with hot, wet kisses and then move down my back. Thank God for the open back on this dress.

James's hands slide under the material at my hips as I throw my head back, guiding us to my room.

"James. If you don't stop, we'll be doing this in the entryway." I spin in his arms.

"I'm not seeing the problem." His eyes are playful as they rake over me.

"Bedroom. Now." I walk backwards, keeping my eyes on him as he loosens his tie. I can't wait to feel those hands all over my bare skin. Inside me. Driving me towards pleasure.

Sweeping my skirt in one hand, I race up the stairs, James hot on my trail. His hands grab me as I push open my door.

"I can't wait to get you out of this dress." James's voice burns with need. I tug the zipper down as he stalks towards me, like a cheetah on the hunt for his prey.

He holds the material at my shoulders, before sliding it down. The heavy material falls down around me, leaving me in only my thong and heels.

"Fecking hell. You are beautiful." His voice is dripping with need as his hands light an inferno inside me.

His thumbs skate over my nipples, turning them into diamonds. I arch into his touch.

"You're wearing far too many clothes." I fist my hands in his shirt, wanting to feel his muscles under my fingers.

My knees hit the bed and I fall back, my body aching with need as I watch him. James starts unbuttoning his shirt, painstakingly slow. Finally throwing off his shirt, his abs are on full display. A smattering of hair coats his chest, and a dark trail of hair disappears below his pants.

I try to quell the ache coiling in my centre, but James grabs my legs, throwing them apart.

"Your pleasure is mine tonight." Pulling me to the edge of the bed, he sinks to his knees. James plants searing kisses as he moves up my leg, getting closer to where I really want him. "I've dreamed about this pussy." His finger ghosting over the sheer fabric is enough to make me come.

"Damn it, James! I need your mouth—" I'm cut off as he finally sweeps his tongue over my slit. Ripping the tiny shred of fabric off me, he sucks my clit into his mouth. He moves his tongue with expert precision as he sinks two fingers inside me. My heels dig deep into his back, wanting to keep him where he is.

I'm riding his tongue and fingers without shame. I've never felt so wanton, so sexy, as I do with this skilled man who is driving me closer and closer to orgasm.

"You taste like a dream, Zara. I can't wait until you explode on my tongue," he whispers to me between licking and sucking. A few more strokes and I'm coming undone. Stars explode around me as the most intense orgasm sweeps through me. The only thing keeping me grounded is James's hand on my stomach. I'm a writhing mess beneath him.

James pulls off me slowly, his lips glistening with my release. I pull him over me, his weight settling on top of me, and claim his lips with mine.

It's hard.

It's raw.

It's sinful.

It's everything.

My hands are shaky from my orgasm as I undo his belt buckle. Reaching into his boxers, I pull his hard cock out. He's big, but not overwhelming. Velvet steel in my hand.

"Fuuuck, Zara." James's voice is drawn tight as I work my hand over his shaft, a bead of precum leaking from the tip. He's rocking into my hand as I move faster. James grabs my hand, pulling it out.

"If you keep doing that, I'm going to blow in your

hand. What would that say about me?" He rocks back, his hands holding my arms above my head.

"That I turn you on?"

"That you do." He sucks the tight bud of my nipple into his mouth.

"The feeling is mutual." My voice is breathy as he moves to my other breast, lavishing it with attention. It's a line of fire straight to my pulsing core, driving me closer and closer to another orgasm.

"If you don't get inside me right now, I'm going to combust."

James pops off me with a grin and stands. "We can't have that, now, can we?" He grabs his wallet as he kicks off his pants. Fully naked now, he is a fine specimen of a man. Abs for days, powerful lines, and that cock. Lord, am I ready to have it inside me.

"You're drooling."

Pushing up on my elbows, I scoot back on the bed. "Can you blame me when you look like that?" I wave my hand in his direction as he rolls a condom down his thick cock.

"You apparently don't know how sexy you look lying there in your heels. I want to do very dirty, very bad things to you, Zara."

"Then please come do very bad things to me." I spread my legs, touching my already sensitive clit. His eyes narrow in on where I'm rubbing myself. I'm slick with need as James strokes himself.

"This is the hottest thing I've ever seen, Zara." He crawls over me, settling back on top of me.

"It might get hotter." Looping my legs around him, I flip us over. There's a hunger in James's eyes unlike anything I've ever seen. Sliding my slick pussy up and down his hard shaft, I draw closer and closer to another orgasm. Right before I tip over the edge, I sink down on top of him.

"James. Oh God, James!" It's good. So good. Better than anything I've ever experienced in my life. The stretch of him filling me gives way to pure pleasure. It takes everything I have not to come immediately.

Clutching his hard pecs, I start moving, rocking my hips over him. Lifting up and sinking back down. "Yes, Zara. Keep going." James's hands move up my sides, cupping my breasts in his hands. Kneading, tweaking my nipples to the point of pain.

Drawing my nails down his chest, I play with myself again. James must like it if his quickening thrusts are anything to go by.

"You need to come now, Zara. Bloody hell, take it." He thrusts harder as his hands are bruising on my hips.

Another thrust and I'm crashing over the edge. I'm boneless as I fall on top of James. Electricity shoots through me at the strength of my orgasm. He holds me to him as he comes, pulsing deep inside me.

"Holy shit." My voice is muffled as my face is buried in James's neck. His spicy smell mixed with the heavy scent of sex is potent. I can't remember the last time I've come so hard. Twice.

But I also can't remember the last time I've ever felt so safe and secure in someone's arms. Never in a million years did I think it would happen with the prince.

"I wish I didn't have to leave tonight. I want to stay here with you all night." His fingers trail a path down my back. I love his need to touch me.

"If only the press wouldn't track our every move. There's nothing I want more than to wake up with you beside me."

"I'm glad you don't want to kick me out the first chance you get."

I push off him, staring into his eyes, and I see the insecurity lingering there. "Why in the world would you think that?" I brush my hands over his chest, the smattering of hair coarse under my fingertips.

"It's what usually happens when I'm with a woman. Once they get their fill of the 'playboy prince,' I'm useless."

"Well, now I might kick you out. Do you know nothing about women?" Incredulity laces my voice as I smack his chest.

"Sorry. Not to bring it up, but I just don't want to leave. There's nothing I want more than to stay here with you tonight. I've never had that feeling before."

My eyes soften, raking over his handsome face. "It's not just you. I hate that they're probably out there wondering what we're doing in here. I just want to stay wrapped up in you."

I hate that he can't stay. I hate that the paparazzi are sitting outside my house, waiting for a picture of him leaving at an indecent hour.

I nuzzle back into him, kissing his neck. His scruff is scratchy against my lips. "I wish our every move wasn't watched."

"I promise, it won't always be like this. We're new. A hot commodity."

"I find that hard to believe." I sit up, pulling off him. I lament the loss of him immediately.

James flips us around, throwing his leg over me. "Zara. I promise, I won't let anything happen to you."

"You can't make that promise." My fingers move on their own, tracing over the beautiful features of his face.

"Well, hopefully they'll back off. In case you haven't heard, they are eating up my recent appearances."

"They'll be forgetting all about the playboy, and only want this prince I get."

He looks down between us. "Well, maybe not *this* prince. This would certainly undo all the good work I've been doing."

I give him a playful smile. My hands glide down his chest, his cock already hardening at my touch. "Well then, if we're going to undo all that good work, might as well get our money's worth."

Chapter Thirteen

ZARA

"You little minx." Marnie's voice startles me from the quiet of my classroom. I've taken to eating lunch in my classroom to avoid the stares and whispers from other teachers. It feels like I'm back in secondary school and I'm left outside the clique.

"What on earth are you talking about?" I pierce her with a look. I have no idea what she's referring to.

"The photos of James leaving your house last night. I want all of the juicy details." She plops herself down in a chair next to my desk, her eyes dancing with intrigue.

"The paparazzi will be the end of me. Why is everyone so interested in me? I'm a nobody." I look down at my lunch, no longer hungry.

"Honey." Marnie's hand is warm on my forearm, pulling my eyes up to meet hers. "You are no longer a nobody. You are dating the first in line to the British throne. Of course they are going to be interested in you."

"I just wish that we could date like two normal people. Stay over at one another's houses and not have to worry about appearances if he sneaks out in the middle of the night."

Marnie's smile turns positively gleeful. "And just why would he be sneaking out in the middle of the night?"

My smile mirrors hers as I glance around the room, ensuring we're alone. "Because we slept together," I whisper.

"Tell me everything!" Marnie shouts, clapping her hands. "I want all the details. How was he? Does his dick live up to all the hype?"

"Shh. We're still in school!" I wave her down, trying to keep her quiet, but it's no use. "Of course it was amazing. I don't think it's ever been so good."

"I can tell by the way you're blushing." She wags her finger over my face. "You're like a schoolgirl who got kissed by the cute boy for the first time."

"I can't help it. He was so good. Amazing. Fantastic." I hated that James had to leave. Even the few hours we spent together last night weren't enough. I want more than just these stolen moments together.

"Best shag of your life?"

I nod.

"I knew it. There's no way he'd get into that many panties if he didn't know how to use what God gave him."

"He is more than just what's in his pants." I hate that even my closest friend only sees what the press puts out there. There's so much more to James than just his colourful past with women.

James's presence in my life has rocked me to the core. When we were told this arranged marriage would need to work, my walls went up. How did anyone expect me to fall in love with the "playboy prince"? The one who was more concerned with the women he slept with than the work he did? But now, I'm seeing a different side to James than the one that's splashed all across the media. He wants to do good work. He wants the respect of his citizens.

And now, he's slipped his way past my carefully constructed walls.

"I'll have to meet him then. Just because he has you falling in lust with him, doesn't mean he'll pass the best friend test." It's possible I'm falling more than just in lust with him, but she doesn't need to know that. Not yet anyway.

"How about Friday? There's no palace-approved event, so I could convince him to come over."

"Can't we go to the palace? I've never been before." Marnie gives me her best sad face to try and convince me.

"You know he doesn't actually live at Buckingham, right?"

"Fine. Kensington. I guess I'll have to rough it." She rolls her eyes at me. "I've already been to your house countless times. Why would we go there?"

"James likes coming over to my place."

"Oh, and why is that?" She waggles her eyebrows at me.

"Stop it, Marnie. Not everything has to do with sex."

"But with that man, it should."

I stand, pulling her up with me. "Marnie, I love you, but time to go. I need to finish my lunch before the students come back."

"Spoilsport." She sticks her tongue out at me as she waltzes out the door. Is this what my life is going to come to? Every person I know asking about the prince? Dad has remained relatively quiet on that front. Probably because he knows how angry I was at first. It's the twenty-first century. Arranged marriages aren't common here. But now? The thought isn't nearly as unsettling as it once was.

"I CAN'T BELIEVE I'm meeting the prince!" Marnie's voice is a loud squeal in my ear.

"You have to calm down. He's just a regular person." The car is pulling up to the palace gates, and my nerves are starting to get the better of me. Marnie is one of the most important people in my life. What if she doesn't like James? What if she only sees his past and not the person he's becoming with me? Shite, I'm a lot deeper into this relationship than I thought.

"He's going to rule the country, Zara. Of course I'm going to freak out." We pull up outside his door in the courtyard and Marnie flies out the door, not even bothering to wait for the driver to open it. James is standing there, casual as ever in jeans and a dress shirt, laughing as Marnie curtsies to him. She's going to ruin this for me before it ever gets started.

"I'm so sorry about her," I whisper, taking James's hand, who is now helping me out of the car. Ever the gentleman.

"Not the first time that's happened." He gives me a wink that has butterflies swarming my stomach. No wonder women fall at his feet. "Now, since this is Zara's first time here, would you both like a tour?"

"Not necessary."

"Absolutely." Marnie and I answer at the same time, and I give her a hard look.

"What? This will be your home soon, might as well learn the ropes." She winks at me as James takes my hand.

"She has a point, you know."

"Okay, Prince Charming. Lead the way." I sweep my hand in front of me, as James gives me a soft stare.

Those butterflies in my stomach? They're ready to take flight.

James gives us a tour of the main part of the apartment. Twenty rooms spread over several floors would be too much tonight. To be honest, it's a little overwhelming the deeper into the apartment we get. He's leading us around one of the upstairs rooms, but I can't focus on it.

I've always loved the quiet of my little house, tucked away in a nice London neighbourhood. But seeing where James lives reiterates the fast-approaching future and what my life is going to be.

"Hey, Marnie, why don't you wait for us in the living room. My friend Oliver should be here soon."

"Fab." She waggles her fingers in our direction, as James nods to one of his advisors who is close by and shows Marnie out of the hall we're in.

"What's on your mind, love?" James is leaning against the window, haloed by the setting sun over the palace gardens.

"This is all just a bit overwhelming."

"What's overwhelming? A twenty-room 'apartment' on palace grounds that will soon be your home before eventually moving into another palace? Being trailed everywhere by security, for every minute of every day?"

"When you put it like that..." I trail off. Ornate gilding lines the high ceilings. Velvet lines every wall here. Nothing about this place is simple. And soon, it's going to be the everyday reality of my life.

A worried look washes over James's face. It's rare that he's anything but happy, which is something I'm finding so hard to comprehend when faced with the press now on a daily basis.

"What are you worried about?" His warm hand envelops mine, pulling me between his legs.

My free hand plays with the buttons on his shirt. "I'm a schoolteacher, James. How am I supposed to come to terms with this life?"

James tilts my chin up to face him. His brow is furrowed as pain pools in his blue eyes. "It's a learning process, love. No one expects you to know everything on day one."

"But what if I call a foreign dignitary the wrong title? Or trip and flash everyone?"

"I called the King of Sweden the Prince of Sweden if it makes you feel better. And have you seen the paparazzi's coverage of me?"

"Way to quell my worries by bringing up your dick hanging out for all the world to see."

"Sorry, bad example."

His big hands wrap around my back, pulling me into his chest, tucking my head under his chin. "Did you really call the King of Sweden the Prince?"

Laughter vibrates through him. "In my defense, he looked really young. I mean, what seventy-year-old man doesn't have grey hair?"

"That's your basis for insulting the king of another country?"

"I know this might surprise you, but I'm not perfect."

A smile plays on my lips. "Hate to burst your bubble, but the mere fact that I'm here confirms that statement."

"Ouch." He pinches my side. "Gloves are coming off now."

Standing here in James's arms is settling. His presence soothes me in a way that once set my teeth on edge. "So, is this what our life will be like? Each of us having our own charities and events? Coming home to this big apartment together by ourselves?"

"You know we'll be moving into Clarence House soon after we're married, right?"

A sigh escapes my lips. "One more thing to adjust to."

James drops his forehead to mine. "I've seen you these last few weeks. After a few minor mishaps, you've adapted well. You have people eating out of the palm of your hand. Besides, I think it sounds pretty nice."

"What, eating out of my hand?"

"No, you loon. Coming home to you every night."

If I saw butterflies flying out of me right now, I wouldn't be surprised. James continues to shock me. When we were first told that we were to be wed, I thought it would be a loveless marriage. One where we could learn to live with one another in a shared space and fulfil marital obligations and move on.

But no. James has sunk his way deep inside me. Into my heart. Into my soul. It turns out I was wrong. I don't just want to fulfil my obligation when it comes to James. I want to give him everything. I want him to know every part of me. Every wrongdoing, every lie I've ever told, everything. I've never wanted that with anyone else.

But with James? I want it all.

James

"HE WAS RUNNING naked across the commons!" Oliver is shrieking with delight while telling Marnie an old story from university.

"What I wouldn't have given to see that." She's

dabbing tears from her eyes as these two regale each other with stories about the both of us.

"They are too chummy," Zara whispers over her wine glass.

"Need I remind you, this was your doing." I throw an arm over her shoulder, bringing her closer to me.

"It's not my fault you're somewhat of a novelty and my friends want to meet you."

"Best friend," Marnie chimes in from across the table. "And yes, I have to make sure you're right for my best girl."

"And do I pass muster?" I take a sip of my scotch, leaning across the table. I don't back down from her intense gaze.

"That depends."

"On?" Would she stop beating around the bush and get to the point?

"On how you'll treat Zara. Do you plan on going back to your womanizing ways?"

I peer over at Zara, and a smile stretches across her lips. "Did you know about this?"

"Oh no. But knowing Marnie, it doesn't surprise me." She tips her wine glass in her direction, before leaning into me. "But if I were you, I'd answer her questions. You don't want to get on her bad side."

I swing my gaze from Zara to Marnie, and she presses again. "Well? You going to answer, pretty boy?"

"Of course I'm not going back to my womanizing ways." The accusation cuts deep. I'll be the first to admit that I wasn't a big fan of relationships. The less I knew about the women I slept with, the better. But not Zara. The thought of hurting her makes my chest physically ache.

"And how will you protect her from the paparazzi?" Marnie takes another sip of her drink. Oliver's eyes are bouncing back and forth between the two of us like he's watching a tennis match.

"He's already done that. Next question." Zara's warm hand lands on mine. I flip it over, clutching her hand to me. I don't have to look at her to know that she feels safe now whenever she leaves the safety of her house or school.

"Fine. Do you plan to cook for her?"

Bollocks.

"You do not want James in the kitchen. He burned spaghetti at uni."

"How in the world do you burn spaghetti?" This time, Zara forces my eyes to hers. Laughter fills her eyes. I love seeing how happy she is. It fills me with a sense of calm that I didn't know I wanted.

"I didn't put enough water in." My voice is quiet as I take a sip.

"You nearly burned down the house, mate!"

"Oy, shut it with the stories already!" I throw my napkin at Oliver. "I'm supposed to be winning over Marnie here."

"Oh darling, you won me over the second I heard all about the night at the symphony."

A blush creeps up Zara's face as I look at her. "You told her?" I grab her by the waist, hauling her into my lap.

"Not everything."

"Good. Because otherwise there might not be a repeat performance." I nibble on her earlobe, not caring about the company we're in.

"And on that note, I think you and I should head to the pub and get some more drinks." Oliver stands, pulling out Marnie's chair for her.

"That is a fab idea, Ollie."

"Cheers then, mates. Zara, you'll do just fine keeping

this wanker in line." Oliver winks at me as he guides Marnie out of the room.

"Piss off!" I shout behind his retreating back, then turn to Zara and vow, "I blame you for any stories that get leaked to the press tonight."

She nuzzles her face into my neck. "And why would that be my fault?"

"Because now they're friends, and Oliver is like a high-speed train anywhere he goes. Best to hold on and see what happens."

"At least you know we can all hang out and it won't be boring."

I squeeze Zara closer to me. The space between us at dinner was far too much. Shite, now I'm sounding like a bloody romantic arsehole.

"You should know by now, Zara, that it will never be boring with me."

Chapter Fourteen

JAMES

"I promise, they'll love you." My voice is soft as I kiss along the shell of Zara's ear. I can't get enough of this woman. I've always been a one and done kind of man. Not something I'm proud of, but given my role in life, women only want one thing. And I was fine with that—until Zara came along. Now, all I want is her with me all the time.

"The last time I saw your mum I didn't exactly make the best first impression." She tilts her head just so, giving me better access. Her perfume lingers on the graceful slope of her neck. Christ, if we weren't on our way to lunch with my family, I'd take her right here. She's intoxicating.

"It wasn't the best day for either of us. This will be a much better meeting. Besides, they'll be so worked up over Ellie that they won't even pay us any attention." I drop a hot kiss where her shoulder meets her neck. The moan it elicits is downright dirty.

"Stop it. I don't want to look like two sex-starved people when we get there." Zara pushes me off of her, and I grumble a few choice words for her. "I want your family to like me."

"You've tamed me. How could they not like you?" I pull Zara into my arms as we inch closer to the palace. Being with her is the only place I want to be lately.

"Taming you and them liking me to be the future Queen of England are two very different things."

"And I assure you, they'll love you for both of those things." Almost as much as I do.

Bloody hell, where did that thought come from? It's too soon. I can't possibly be falling for the woman my mum set me up with, can I? But looking at this woman, curled into my side as we enter the palace gates, I know I'm falling hopelessly in love with her.

"Your Highness. Lady Zara. We're here." The driver pulls up and our door is opened, breaking the moment.

"Thank you." Zara's waiting for me as she steps out of the car. She looks absolutely stunning in the black trousers and jumper she chose to wear today. I can't wait to tear them off her later. Anything to distract myself from thoughts of falling in love with her.

"Shall we?" I give her my arm as I guide her into the palace.

Her eyes are everywhere as I lead her up a side staircase to the family quarters. The last time she was here, she came as a guest through the main corridor. This time, I'm taking her along a different route, but it's no less extravagant. The opulence on display here sometimes blows even me away.

"What's on your mind, love?" I squeeze her closer to me as we reach the top of the stairs. Family portraits from the centuries of rule stare down at us.

"Feels much different coming here this time than it did last time."

I turn, wrapping my arms around her. "There's

nothing to worry about. My sister will adore you in a heartbeat. Probably more than she does me."

Zara pulls me in close, resting her head on my shoulder. I love how perfectly she fits in my arms. Like she was made for me and only me.

"Let's get moving. The sooner we get this over with, the sooner I can take you back to my house and we can have our own fun." Her body shakes with laughter as she turns to look at me. Zara's eyes are happy. I love that I put that there.

"Alright, Prince Charming. Let's get going." She tugs my hand, as I'm helpless to follow her. I'd follow this woman anywhere, even if she's leading us in the wrong direction.

"This way, love." I tug her hand down the opposite hall, and she gives me a sheepish smile.

"There's too many halls here."

"I'll be sure to draw you a map when we move in."

Zara

LOUD VOICES from the end of the hall cause butterflies to erupt in my stomach. I don't know why I'm so nervous. I've already met the Queen once. It didn't turn out so well, but I'm still nervous to meet the rest of James's family. Can one pass out from nerves?

James tugs me through the open door, and I'm met with happy, smiling faces.

"The prodigal son returns." A woman with bright pink hair and a noticeable baby bump crushes James in a hug.

"What can I say, someone has to pick up the reins since you ditched us." She punches him in the stomach before fixing her gaze on me. "And you must be the famous Zara we've heard so much about. I'm this one's sister, Ellie."

"It's nice to meet you." I stick my hand out, but she brushes it aside, sweeping me in for a hug.

"I've heard so much about you. I can't believe you've managed to tame my brother." Her face is bright with playfulness.

"I don't think I like you talking to her." James appears behind Ellie's back.

"Nonsense. Go talk to Sean. I don't want Grandmum telling him anything inappropriate about birthing children."

His eyes go wide at that statement. "And you think I'd want to go join in on that conversation?"

Ellie gives him another hearty elbow to the ribs. "I want to talk to Zara. Off you go." She waves her hand to him as he sulks over to where Sean and their grandmum are. The Queen isn't here yet, so my nerves settle a bit.

"So Zara, how are things with James? From what I've been told, everyone seems to be loving the two of you together." We sit on the sofa in the sitting room. My entire house could fit in this room. Heavy drapes line the windows that open up to the back gardens and London's cloudy, lifeless skies. Newer photos of the family dot the furniture around the room.

"And what have you been told?" I give her a coy look.

"Only that everywhere the two of you go, you look like a couple in love."

"Gin and tonic?" James has a drink at the ready in front of me. It's like he knew I'd need one.

"Thank you." I give him a shy smile, not wanting to give any more ammunition to the rumours his sister is telling me about. He walks back over to Sean and his grandmum as I gulp down the drink.

"I believe that answers my question." Ellie leans back, rubbing her baby bump.

"How did that answer your question?" I'm confused as she just continues staring at me. It's unnerving. Ellie and James are mirror images of one another. Her bright pink hair is a contrast to James's dark waves, but they have the same bright blue eyes.

"He knew what you needed. There's this invisible thread connecting the two of you. Whether you choose to acknowledge it or not."

"It's still too early for that." I don't want to acknowledge my deepening feelings for James. It's scary, the world he lives in. I was hoping there wouldn't be any chemistry between the two of us and we could each continue living our lives. But the deeper I move into his world, the harder it is to reel in my emotions.

"Zara, it's never too early. I knew Sean was it for me within an hour of meeting him."

"An hour? You knew that soon he was the love of your life?"

Ellie nods her head. "Do you really think I'd give up my entire life for anything less than true love?" Her eyes get hazy as she drifts them to look at Sean. Their connection is palpable to anyone in the room as his eyes are drawn to hers.

"I'd say the feeling is mutual." I take another sip, trying to hide my smile.

"Just don't dismiss him because of this life. There's more than meets the eye with him. He's a good one."

"I know he is." She doesn't have to tell me twice. The persona that James shows the public is vastly different than who he is with me. He's flirty and fun with the press. They eat him up. But in the quiet moments I get with him, he opens up to me. I see the real James. And I am easily falling for him.

"Zara, it's so wonderful to see you today." The Queen's voice pulls me away from Ellie, a smile painting her face.

"Your Majesty." I stand, dipping into a low curtsy.

"Please. It's Katherine. We're all family here." She gives me a quick peck on the cheek before turning her warm gaze on Ellie.

"And how's the little one?"

"Doing just fine." Ellie's hands rub her growing belly as her mum sits between us.

"Still not going to find out what it is?"

"Mum. I've told you several times, no. We want to be surprised."

The Queen turns her stern gaze at me. "I've even tried telling her—as her Queen—that she should find out, but it's no use. And don't you get any ideas about not finding out." She wags her finger in my direction.

I hide my chuckle behind my hand. "Of course. You'll be the first to know. But that's still down the road."

"And I thought it would be a few years away for me but here we are, my first grandbaby is on the way." Her excitement is palpable.

"Darling, stop bugging them for grandchildren." Prince Frederick approaches his wife, pulling her towards the door. "Lunch is ready if you would like to head to the dining room."

Katherine gives her husband a tender look as she follows him. I can't help but wonder if these two were a love match or an arranged marriage like James and me.

"Ladies, shall we escort you into the dining room?" James and Sean appear before us. Sean helps Ellie, pulling her into his arms and dropping a chaste kiss on her lips.

Reckless Royal

"Can you two not do that in front of me?" James turns into me, burying his face in my neck.

"I think we've all seen enough of you plastered all over the tabloids, so get over it." Ellie doesn't turn to face him. She links her arm through Sean's, and they head off in front of us.

"She might have a point, you know." James's scent overwhelms me, as he drapes his arm across my shoulder, tugging me close.

"You're supposed to be on my side." His voice is a low growl.

I give him a smug look. "Well, you're all mine now. I don't want anyone else seeing any bits of you."

"I like the sound of that." Before he can kiss me, James's grandmother is walking up to us.

"Come sit by me, dear. I'd love to get to know you better." James's grandmother pulls me from his side. He gives me a consoling look before moving to sit by his sister and Sean.

The table is lined with several dishes, at least three different kinds of roasts, pudding, vegetables, and sides. They know how to do Sunday roast at the palace.

"Don't look so worried. I don't bite. At least not in a few years."

James's grandmother is a tiny human, but her reputation precedes her. The images of her at her husband's funeral showed a stoic woman without a tear in her eye.

"Would you get me another gin before you sit down, darling?" She hands me her glass, and I top her off before sitting beside her.

"What's a Sunday lunch without a little pick me up?" She smacks her lips after taking a hearty gulp.

"So right, ma'am." God, could I sound any more foolish calling James's grandmother ma'am?

"Zara, dear. Please do not call me ma'am. It's Minerva. Ma'am makes me sound old and fussy." Her wrinkly hand settles on my forearm as meals are distributed to everyone. "I've got a few years before I'm old and fussy."

"Sorry, Minerva."

"Now, how are things going with my grandson? Still have his head up his arse about this whole image thing?" She takes a bite of the roast and pierces me with a withering stare. I don't know what I expected from her, but it was definitely not this.

"I think he's been doing much better."

"Don't spin things for this old bat. I want the details." Shock must be written all over my face, because James is looking at me like he's ready to jump to my rescue. I give him a small smile before turning back to his grandmother.

"If it makes you feel better, I don't think there's been a single mention about his playboy ways in a few weeks."

She rolls her eyes at me. "Well, that's not exciting, now is it?"

"Isn't that the whole purpose of the two of us being together? To rehab his image?"

Minerva waves me off. "Where's the fun in that? My Edward and I used to get into all sorts of trouble together."

"Why don't I remember hearing about any of that?"

"Because we didn't have to worry about the paps like you do now. If you ever want to know about any of the hidden spots in palaces around the world, I'm your woman."

I almost choke around the bite I took. "I'll have to keep that in mind." The thought of getting sex advice from James's grandmum? I can't think of anything more mortifying.

"You probably won't, but that's alright. I can see how happy you're making my grandson."

A flush creeps over my cheeks. "He makes me happy too."

Minerva pops another bite into her mouth. "From the pictures I've seen, you're quite the couple."

"You keep track of us in the tabloids?" I take a cooling sip of my own drink.

"A way to pass the time. I'm old, and most of my friends are gone. No one cares about me at this point, so why not see what's going on with others?" She shrugs her shoulders as if this is no big deal.

"I wish we didn't have to worry about them." The press lingering outside my house still makes me anxious.

"Comes with the territory. I have no doubt that you'll be able to handle them with all the dignity and grace that my grandson does." She squeezes my forearm before going back to her meal.

It's been an eye-opening afternoon. Being surrounded by all these people who love and adore James makes me fall that much harder. He's kind and caring. He makes me laugh, and I've never felt sexier or more desired than when I'm with him.

I never thought I'd fall in love with my fiancé, but here I am. Doing it just the same.

Chapter Fifteen

JAMES

"My grandmother didn't scare you off?" I follow Zara into her house. We spend more time here than we do at my apartment, but this feels like home. I know we won't be able to stay here once the engagement is official, but damn, if I don't love the feeling of being in her space.

"Apparently she was disappointed we don't have better stories for her." She shakes her head as she sinks down onto her sofa. I sit, pulling her feet into my lap.

"Better stories?" I take off her heels and dig my fingers into her soles of her feet.

"Oh God, that feels amazing." Her groan goes straight to my dick. As much as I'd love to take her right here, right now, I'm buttering her up.

"You didn't answer my question."

Zara drops her head back onto the couch. "She said that she and the King used to get into all sorts of trouble, but we never heard about it because it was never in the press."

"Goes to show you how times have changed. Also, let's not talk about that."

"You mean your grandmum and granddad doing dirty things to one another?" Her head pops up on a laugh. "If you ever want to know good spots for doing dirty things in palaces around the world, Minerva knows."

I cringe, pulling Zara closer to me. "Never say those words again. No one wants to know about that."

"She's your grandmum!" she says on a laugh, snuggling closer to me.

I wrap my arms around her, tilting my head to whisper in her ear, "Play for me, Z."

She pulls back, a blush crawling up her beautiful face. "Now?"

"No, in ten years." I roll my eyes. "Yes, now. I've never heard you play before."

"But my violin is in pieces." She looks down, toying with the hem of my jumper.

"I know you have another." I lift her chin up, forcing her eyes to meet mine. "Why don't you want to play for me?"

"Because I'm nervous. What if you don't like how I sound?"

I drop my forehead to hers. Christ, this woman is doing me in. "Zara, love. I will love anything you play for me. I just want to hear you play."

"You promise?" Her breath ghosts over my lips, and it almost distracts me from the issue at hand. Almost.

"Yes. Now, play for me. I don't care what."

Her lips capture mine. They taste like her drink from lunch earlier. When her tongue glides along the seam of my lips, I open for her. There's nothing I wouldn't give this woman. But just as fast as she kisses me, she pulls away.

She leaves the living room before coming back with her violin.

"Just don't be disappointed if it doesn't sound amazing. I haven't played with Henrietta in quite some time."

I nearly choke on a laugh. "You name your instruments?"

"Duh." She gives me an incredulous look before tuning it. I relax back into the couch, waiting until she takes a deep breath and settles the violin under her chin. Zara's eyes flip to mine, and I give her an encouraging nod before the first notes hit me.

I'm not a musician. I've never been into the arts, as that was always Ellie's thing. But hearing Zara play for me? I understand why people love music. The symphony has nothing on her.

The notes have a haunting quality to them as she starts to pick up speed. She sways in time with the notes as the music flows through me. It's fast then slow. Heavy and light all in the same breath.

Zara is absolutely breathtaking. She's a dream playing this song for me. I have no idea who wrote it, but I'll always remember it.

When she's done playing, her eyes are heavy. Hazy. It's like she was making love with the song, and damn, if that doesn't turn me on.

"Well?" She holds her violin in front of her, like she's guarding herself from criticism from me.

"I have no words." Her face drops for a moment before I stand and take a few quick steps and pull her into me. My lips are attacking hers with no finesse. I'm hungry for her. It's all teeth and tongues clashing. Hearing Zara play for me peeled back another layer to her. This person who is so passionate about her music and her life's calling to teach it.

"I have no words for how incredible that was, love." My thumbs tenderly brush her cheeks.

"Yeah?" Her voice is soft.

"Yes." I drop a kiss on her forehead. "It was beautiful." A kiss on her nose. "Better than the orchestra we went to." A ghost of a kiss on her lips.

She laughs, looking up into my eyes. Her brown eyes are swimming with warmth. "Now I know you're lying."

I smile against her lips. "Not a lie. I'd rather listen to you any day of the week, Zara."

She sets her violin down before wrapping her arms around me. "Did I tell you my mum taught me to play?"

I shake my head.

"She was a brilliant violinist. Also played the cello. I don't remember much about her since she died when I was little, but I remember her teaching me to play."

I squeeze her tighter to me. "And the violin that was destroyed was hers?"

She nods against me. "I know I shouldn't be so attached to it, but it's one of the last things I have left of hers."

I fucking hate that the paparazzi destroyed something so cherished by Zara. I don't know how I can make it right, but I have to fix her violin. No matter the cost.

"I know she would be so proud of you." Zara's face is soft as she turns those gorgeous brown eyes on me that I can get lost in. "You are pretty incredible." I run my hands down her cheeks, before placing a chaste kiss on her lips.

She steps out of my arms, biting down on her lip. God, she's the sexiest woman I've ever met. She wraps her hand in mine. No words are said as she leads me upstairs to her bedroom. It's dark, the curtains blocking out any light from the houses behind hers. Zara stops in the centre of her room, and I step into her space, letting my fingers drift lazily up her arms.

An anticipation like I've never known buzzes through me. Zara's hands grasp my waist as I trail hot, wet kisses up her neck to her jaw. I linger, nibbling just how she likes, before moving to her lips. She opens for me the second my lips are on hers. The soft tangle of our tongues makes my dick impossibly hard. I've never known a need like this before. I crave her with every fibre of my being.

Her warm hands fist in my shirt as I guide us back to the bed. She sits, looking up at me with all the love in the world. Fuck, this woman is absolutely doing me in. Pulling my jumper and T-shirt off, I kneel in front of her. My hands drift up her legs, stopping where she's trying to get friction. I pull her forward and lift her jumper over her head. Pushing her back, I trail warm kisses up her soft stomach.

Zara is arching into my touch. Her nipples are diamond hard through the lacy cups of her bra. Teasing her, I run my fingertip over the tight bud of one nipple while sucking on the other through the fabric.

"James." Her voice is husky, laced with want. I pull back, hovering above her. Lightning trails through my body as her fingers drag down my chest, hooking into the waistband of my jeans.

Our eyes lock. Her brown eyes are dark with need and lust and want. And love. There is so much love shining out of them that I don't feel worthy of it. Instead of dwelling on these new emotions that Zara is bringing out in me, I crush my lips to hers.

The soft, wet heat of her mouth is driving me crazy. We battle for control as our tongues sweep into each other's mouths. I don't remember kissing ever being this good. There's something about Zara that overwhelms me.

I flip onto my back, and she deepens the kiss, grinding over my rock-hard dick. I love that she takes control like this, but I want her naked and writhing beneath me.

"Mmm, Zara." All thought leaves my mind as her lips trail down my neck and chest. I should stop her once she gets to my jeans, but I don't. Her soft hands unzipping and pulling them down my body is too much, yet not enough at the same time.

My cock springs free, precum dripping from the tip. Her smile is downright evil as she licks me from base to head, swirling her tongue about the crown. "Fuck, Zara. That feels too damn good."

She takes me to the back of her mouth, and I can't help thrusting up. She gags but doesn't stop. Her eyes are hooded with lust as she continues sucking and licking me, playing with my balls. Fire is racing down my spine as my release threatens. Threading my hands through Zara's silky locks, I pull her off me with a pop.

"I'm not ready to come in your mouth. I want to be buried inside of you as I make you come."

Zara stands, dropping her bra, and her gorgeous tits are put on display for me. "Damn, you are so fucking sexy." I pull Zara down onto the bed, stripping her of the rest of her clothes. Her pussy is glistening for me. Swiping my finger through the wetness, I drag it down towards the tight pucker of her arsehole. She squirms into my touch.

"You like that? You want me to fuck this gorgeous arse of yours?"

"Yes, James! God yes!" Her voice carries around the quiet room as I dip down and take her clit in my mouth.

"Your wish is my command, my Queen."

I continue sucking on her clit, ignoring the aching throb in my dick. Thrusting two fingers inside her hot, wet channel, I bring her closer to orgasm. Zara is writhing beneath me as her pussy starts clenching around me, her release coating my fingers. I don't relent as I stay on her until she comes down.

Her skin is flushed from her orgasm. I lean back on my heels, her sated body laid out before me. She's beauty in its purest form.

"Do you have any lube?" My voice is husky. I'm ready to explode and have to stroke myself a few times to hold back my release.

"Bathroom cabinet. Bottom drawer."

I waste no time finding exactly what I need and returning to Zara. She's up on her elbows, watching me jog back to her.

"Someone's eager." She's got a condom in her hand that I pluck out, rolling it down my hard length. Coating my fingers with lube, I rub it up and down my cock, before I spread her legs apart.

"Fuck. You look so sexy laid out like this for me." I slowly push a finger inside as she takes a deep breath. Getting past the tight ring of muscle, she relaxes against me. "That's it, love. You're doing great."

Zara takes my finger to the knuckle as I start moving in and out of her. Her groans tell me she's ready for another finger. I want to make this as good for her as possible.

"How is it possible that this feels so good?" Her voice is breathy as she bears down on my fingers. Knowing she's ready, I pull my fingers out and line my cock up.

"If you want to stop, just tell me." I lean down over her, resting my forehead against hers.

"I'm ready."

I skim her lips with kisses as I push inside, giving her a moment to adjust. Once she starts moving underneath me, I push all the way in, inch by slow inch.

I have to silently sing "God Save the Queen" so I don't

blow my load immediately. It's heaven. Nothing has ever felt better than being inside Zara like this. She consumes me as I start moving, shallow thrusts at first. But the more she moves under me, the faster I go. Hiking one leg over my shoulder, I deepen the angle.

"James. I'm so close. So damn close." She's chewing on her bottom lip as a bead of sweat trails down her temple. I pick her other leg up and wrap it around my waist. I watch, my own orgasm racing down my spine, as Zara starts massaging her clit.

"Fuck. I need you to come right now." Thrust. "I'm not going to last much longer." My thrusts are hard and unrelenting as Zara starts to come apart around me. Her screams of ecstasy take me over the edge with her. I pump my release into the condom as I start to still above Zara. She holds me to her as I collapse on top of her. There is no better feeling in the world than being wrapped in this woman's arms.

The thundering of her heart under my head matches my own. It has nothing to do with what we just did and everything to do with the woman I did it with. I've gone and fallen irrevocably in love with my future Queen.

Chapter Sixteen

ZARA

"Why do I feel like I'm back in primary school and being summoned to the headmaster's office?" For once, James and I didn't have any plans. No events. No galas. Nothing. We were going to have a lazy Sunday afternoon at his house. But a call came from the Queen, requesting our presence at the palace.

"Because whenever the Queen wants to see you, there's usually a reason," James answers.

James pulls into the gates of Buckingham. The last time I was here, I was nervous. But after getting to know James's family better, I feel more comfortable here.

"Did she tell you why we needed to come here today?" James grabs my hand as we head inside.

"We'll find out," James says, his face uneasy.

"Your Highness. Lady Zara. The Queen's advisor greets us. "James. Your mother is waiting for you in her quarters. Miss Cross, please come with me."

"I guess I'll meet you back here when we're done?" James says as he turns to me, his brow creased in confusion.

"Sounds good." He drops a quick kiss on my lips before leaving me behind.

"Please, follow me, miss."

I follow the advisor, heading deeper into the palace. She opens a heavy set of wooden doors, and the perfumed smell of flowers greets me.

"Lady Zara. It's a pleasure to meet you." A woman in a form-fitting red dress greets me. "I'm Thea and I will be assisting you with the wedding plans."

"Wedding plans?" I can't hide the shock in my voice.

"Yes. We need to get started with plans, as there will be a lot of moving parts on the day of."

"But we're not even engaged yet!" My voice comes out higher than I expected.

"Not to worry. That will be taken care of soon."

"Taken care of soon?" James and I have been seeing each other for a few months. An engagement is not something that should be "taken care of."

"Yes. Your engagement should be announced within the next two months, so it's best we start preparations now."

The room is getting hot around me, the heavy perfume of the flowers doing nothing to help. I never thought much about my wedding growing up. Not having a mum made it hard to think about my wedding. I always wished I had my mum here to share in my special day. Not some tightly wound royal wedding planner.

"We'll need to decide on flowers and cake today. Dresses will be for a later time, once we have a list of approved designers to choose from." So much for the magic of planning your wedding.

"Shouldn't James be here for this?" The grand room we're in is filled to the brim with flowers. Cakes that are taller than I am line one wall.

Thea laughs, pinning me with a look that tells me this is for women only. Figures. "He is otherwise preoccupied. Now, if you'll please come with me."

I follow her farther into the room. "Now, the flowers will need to make a statement," Thea starts. "Orchids and roses are acceptable. We don't want anything too out there. We don't want to offend anyone."

"Heaven forbid the flowers I choose for my wedding offend anyone."

Thea gives me a piercing glare, her tight bun making her features even more harsh. "A great deal of research has been done as to the proper bouquets for royals. One misstep and everyone will remember your wedding for those reasons."

I try to listen as Thea goes into far more detail than I ever needed to know about flowers, but my mind is spinning. When James and I were summoned to the palace today, I never thought it would be to start planning my wedding.

"Zara? Which of these do you like?" Thea sweeps her hands to four different bouquets laid out in front of me. All are a combination of white flowers. The differences are subtle.

I chew on my bottom lip. There has to be a test in here somewhere. Did they put the unacceptable flowers in here to see if I would pick the right one? Why is there so much pressure on this one decision?

"Am I able to decide later?" My voice is hardly a whisper.

"I'm afraid the flowers and cake must be decided upon today. To get everything scheduled for a royal wedding requires quite a bit of time." Thea's voice is curt. From the look she's giving me, I doubt she likes me very much.

"How about this one?" I grab the one closest to me.

"I think this one would be best." She points a different one out to me.

"Then that one will be fine." I don't know why I'm needed here. It makes no difference to me which flowers or cake I have at my wedding. If Thea is just going to tell me my decision is wrong and guide me towards the correct decision, I really don't need to be here.

"Fab. We will incorporate these flowers throughout the abbey and will also have them as the boutonniere flowers."

I give her a small smile as she leads me in the direction of the cakes.

"You'll love getting to taste these cakes. Some of Britain's best bakers have been hard at work these last few weeks to prepare these for you."

"How is this not all over the tabloids right now?" Cakes of all different shapes and sizes are laid out before me. Some are lined with gold leaves, others with intricate flowers covering them.

"We have very strict policies as to who we can work with. All sign non-disclosure agreements. If it were leaked, we'd know."

I guess there can be one good thing to be said for being a royal.

"Want to have a taste?" Thea's face is in direct conflict with mine. Whereas she is beaming, I'm dreading this.

I try to put on a happy face, but this is just a bit overwhelming for me.

"Just tell me where to start."

James

"Mother. What did I do to be beckoned to the palace today?"

"Why must it be anything bad?" She gives me a peck on the cheek. As I move to sit down, she grabs my arm, leading me in the opposite direction.

"Where are we going?" I have a guess as to where we're going, but a feeling of dread starts to wash over me.

"Well, with the engagement being announced soon, it's about time we got Zara a ring, don't you think?"

"Mum! We've barely been dating a few months!" My voice echoes around the empty hall.

She stops, turning to face me. "James. You knew what was going to happen when you met Zara. You can't tell me you're surprised by this."

I open and close my mouth, like a gaping fish. "But things have been going well for the two of us. I guess I just assumed that maybe you might back off this whole arranged marriage thing."

"If I were to back off, you'd likely dump that kind girl in a heartbeat and be out at the clubs within the hour."

"Ouch. Thanks, Mum." I turn away from her, scrubbing my hand down my face. As crazy as it sounds, I haven't wanted to go to the clubs in weeks. Not when I have Zara. But does she really deserve to be brought into this crazy life?

"You've been doing a marvellous job lately, and I have no doubt it's thanks to Zara. But this marriage is moving forward as planned." Her tone leaves no room for argument. Her no-nonsense attitude causes my blood to boil.

"Fine, Mum. Lead the way." My jaw ticks in anger. My teeth could crack I'm so upset.

Following Mum down to the vaults here at the palace, I try to push my anger aside. The vaults are dark, lights shining on the jewels inside.

"I've taken the liberty to pick a few out that Zara might like."

"Of course you have," I mutter under my breath.

I walk over to her, looking at the rings laid out before me. Christ, I'm really doing this, aren't I?

"All of these have been in the family for centuries. It will be the perfect ring to symbolize the past but also signify a new future for the two of you."

"I thought my past is what got us in this situation." Bitterness undercuts my tone.

"There's no need to be rude, James."

I slam my hand down on the table in front of me. "And there was no need to ambush me today about picking our engagement rings, but here we are."

"Will you please excuse us?" Mum motions to the guards behind her and they leave. Once they're gone, she fixes me with a look that could strike down a lesser man. A lesser man wouldn't be gearing up for a fight today.

"You need to lose this attitude. Like I said before, you've come a long way since Zara has entered your life, and solidifying your union will secure your place in the eyes of our country as a steadfast King. I will not hear another word about it."

I screw a fake smile on my face. "Fine, Mum. Being forced to pick out an engagement ring when I was hoping I could do this down the road on my own sounds brilliant." I turn to look at the rings laid out before me. "This one should do." I don't even care what it looks like.

I know I'm acting like a child, but when Mum keeps shoving her agenda down my throat, I can't help it. If they want to have me pick a ring for Zara that means nothing to me, I'll do it. Zara would love the stories behind these rings, but there is no way I'm going to give her something that I was forced to pick by my mum.

"Are you actually going to look at any of them?" Mum's voice is angry now.

"I looked. This one is fine. Do you have ideas as to when I should propose? How?"

It's a shitty comment, but at this point, I'll do anything to be dismissed from her presence.

"We'll be announcing your engagement in a few months. How you want to do it before then is up to you."

"Is that all then?"

She turns, giving me a soft look. "I'm just looking out for you. When you're a parent, you'll understand."

I don't give her another word, turning my back on her and leaving the vault. I know my behaviour back there was appalling, but Mum just brings it out in me. I was hoping that with time, I could do this on my own.

The more I've gotten to know Zara, the more I wanted to be able to do this the right way. I wanted to talk with Marnie and find the perfect ring for her. Plan an elaborate ruse to make her think I'm going to propose, but then do it in the quiet of our home.

But it's tainted now. Tainted by Mum forcing rings upon me. Pushing our dates up. Zara and I are doing so well, and I hate to think what she's going to think of all this.

Zara is pacing in front of the car when I find her. "Ready to go?"

"Yes." She wastes no time getting in. If I was bombarded with ring options, I can only imagine what her day was like.

"Want to talk about it?" I put the car in gear, wanting to put as much distance between the palace and us as possible.

"Did you know there is such a thing as an offensive flower?"

Christ. Her day was just as bad as mine. "I'm assuming you know all about it?"

She turns, her face not showing any of the usual emotion I've come to find from her. "Yes. And I know all about the different kinds of cakes and what is appropriate for a royal wedding."

"Bloody hell. I can't believe this is happening."

"Oh, it's happening. The flowers and cake Thea chose for our big day will be wonderful." Her tone is caustic. "'Zara, please choose which flowers you'd like, but oh, not that one because it might offend some people. And chocolate cake might stain your dress. We can't have that.'" She mimics this Thea person she's talking about.

"I can't believe she did this."

I go to grab Zara's hand, but she pulls it away from me. "Can you just take me home? I'm just overwhelmed right now and need to be alone."

I don't want her closing herself off, but given my own mood, I can't blame her. It just hurts more than it should. What started as a nice afternoon with Zara has turned into a nightmare. I can only hope this wedge between us goes away. Because whether we like it or not, this wedding is happening. And possibly sooner than we both had hoped.

Chapter Seventeen

ZARA

"Are you sure I'm dressed appropriately for this?" Looking down at my stylish blazer, jeans, and wedge heels, I'm not so sure I'm going to fit in. After the week James and I had, it's nice to be out in a neutral environment. Neither one of us wanted to talk about being bombarded with the wedding at the palace, but it's been a cloud hanging over us. The pressure facing both of us at our pending nuptials isn't something we want to think about.

"Are you planning on trying out for the team?" James's heated stare moves up and down my body. "I'd give you the captain's position without question."

I smack his hard chest. "Of course you would."

James pulls me into his side before we walk out of the tunnel. "You look sexy as sin. Trust me, today it's all about George and his family meeting the team. They won't even know we're here."

"And he just thinks he's getting a tour of the stadium?" James told me all about the sweet boy he met touring the hospital. Seeing how happy he was to make this happen caused my heart to flutter.

"Yes. He has no idea he's meeting the team and will get to go to the match tonight."

I pull James to a stop, tucked away in the darkness of the tunnel. "He is going to lose his mind." Wrapping my arms around James's neck, I drop a sweet kiss on his lips.

"Maybe I can make you lose your mind tonight." His breath ghosts over my lips. Rolling my lips between my teeth, I stifle the moan that wants to escape.

"One thing at a time." Patting his chest, I walk towards the growing voices.

"This place is brilliant!" The excited voice of a young boy floats towards us.

"Do we get to go out onto the pitch?"

"C'mon, love. Let's go give him the surprise of his life." James grabs my hands and drags me away from the dark cove we were hidden away in.

"Mr. and Mrs. Smythson. George. Victoria. I'm so happy you all could join us today." James shakes hands with the parents before getting down on George's level. A bright blue cast hugs his leg in the wheelchair. "Are you excited today?" George is wearing his best Chelsea jersey and hat. I've never seen a brighter smile on anyone in my life.

"I can't wait to see where they play! I just wish I didn't have to be in this wheelchair," his voice squeaks out.

"It's easier for you to get around, love. You'll still get to see everything." His mum pats him on the shoulder.

"Well, what are you waiting for? Let's go!" James grabs the chair and wheels him down the tunnel.

"What's your name?" The dark-haired girl stands back as James leads us all out onto the field.

"I'm Zara. And you're Victoria?"

She nods at me. "I'm not a big football fan."

I bend down on her level, sticking my hand out to her. "Want to know a secret? I'm not a big football fan either."

"You're not?" She grins. "I like music more."

"I do too." Victoria chats my ear off as we follow everyone out onto the pitch. "I love the piano. But I'd love to learn the cello. And the flute. Lizzo plays the flute."

"Maybe you could be the next Lizzo."

"No way!" George's excited voice carries through the quiet stadium. "The players are here?"

"Prince James, this is too much." Mrs. Smythson is almost in tears as James gives them a big smile. The players jog over, crowding around George. A few of the trainers and coaches are with them.

"Do you want to meet them while we're here?"

For not liking football, Victoria seems a little starstruck. I walk her over, and the players swarm around her too. Stepping back, I let the family have their moment.

Looking around to find James, he's talking with one of the coaches. One of the female coaches. Jealousy flares up deep inside me. I shouldn't let it bother me. The connection between James and me is real. At least I thought it was real. It's been real for me.

And when she touches his arm? James gives her his thousand-watt smile. My stomach falls to my feet. It doesn't mean anything. Even though it's been a weird week for the two of us, I know what we feel for each other.

James is always affable with everyone he meets, but for the first time, his past slams into our present. Into our future. Is this what it is going to be like? Women flirting and throwing themselves at him everywhere we go? There's no way I can compete with the likes of these women.

"What do you say? Want to be our special guest

tonight?" George's loud shriek pulls me out of my morose thoughts. James catches my glance and gives me a wink. Instead of settling me, it just puts me more at odds with my emotions. Here is this incredible man, doing this amazing thing for this family after meeting them at the hospital. And all I can think about is how that woman was flirting with James. And he wasn't doing anything to stop it.

"Can we, Mum?" George turns eager eyes to his parents.

"Of course we can, darling." She rubs his shoulder, and the team cheers for him.

"Alright, how about a tour of the locker rooms?" George starts wheeling himself out of the centre of the huddle and follows a few players, chatting their ears off about plays. It's nice to see both of these siblings are passionate.

"Well, I'd say that went very well." James comes over to me, throwing his arm over my shoulder. The woman he was talking to gives him the side-eye, but he doesn't pay her any mind. Maybe it's all in my head. But James has always been called the Playboy Prince, and it's hard to shake that image. Women throw themselves at him, and maybe it's something I need to get used to. But if this has any chance at working, I need to accept that and move on.

"You're great with kids." I wrap my arm around his hips as we bring up the rear of the group. "James. This is what you should do for your patronage."

We're in the middle of the pitch when James stops, looking around him. "Bringing kids I meet in hospital to their favourite football club?"

"No, you wanker. Kids and sports. This is for one kid. Think of how many amazing things you could do for more children."

The wheels are turning. "You really think this could work?"

I grab his hands, giving them a firm squeeze. "You're so good with kids. And you have access to places that most people would only dream about. Why not combine the two?"

"Would you be there to help?" James pouts his lips at me. "I don't know if I could do it without you."

His tone is vulnerable. It quiets my doubts about him. "James, everyone was enraptured by you today. You have so much power to do good in this world."

James wraps his arms around me, settling his head in the crook of my neck. A heavy breath leaves his lips. "You're the first person to ever have so much confidence in me."

Shock slams into me. "There's no way that's true."

"Do you know what it's like to be the spare? The bar was set so low for me, that eventually there was no bar."

"So you just started doing whatever you wanted."

"Yes. Clubs. Women. I really didn't give a flying fuck what I was doing." James lets go of me, pacing in front of me. "It was all about Ellie. And don't get me wrong, I love my sister, but if they weren't grooming her to take over the throne, then it wasn't on their radar."

James looks so small walking around this massive field. "Where is all this coming from?" I ask softly.

"I'm just tired of the fucking paparazzi dredging up my past. When do I get a fresh start? When do *we* get a fresh start?"

"Hey." Placing a hand on his chest, I stop him and his racing thoughts. "What makes you think we didn't get a fresh start?"

His heart is racing under my palm. "Because you wouldn't be here if we did."

"Ouch."

"Look, I really don't want to talk about this right now. Let's just go enjoy the rest of our afternoon with the Smythsons." Shoving his hands in his pockets, James stalks away from me.

His mood is giving me whiplash today. He is his usually sparkling self one minute, and then worrying about our entire future in the next breath. James's shoulders are slumped as he heads back into the bowels of the stadium.

What in the world just happened?

James

THE MATCH SHOULD BE HOLDING my attention. It's tied two-two with ten minutes remaining, but all I can think about is the conversation with that coach earlier. I'm used to women hitting on me. But the way she propositioned me this afternoon even though Zara was there? It left a bad taste in my mouth.

She said she assumed I'd be down for a shag because I'd fucked so many other women before. Her words, not mine. And then Zara telling me she had faith in me? I couldn't handle it.

I wish I could sit here with George and talk strategy, but he's cheering his little head off. At least someone's day has been made. Zara has been an absolute charmer all afternoon. After we finished the tour, we were given a private box, and she kept Victoria entertained.

Zara has fit so seamlessly into my life that I didn't think twice about it. But now, my past is kicking my arse. I should've known better than to expect everything to fall into place.

"Goal!" The crowd erupts around me as George stretches his hand up for a high five.

"That was the best goal I've ever seen!" His excitement is infectious. It's hard not to be when someone is this energized. "Did you see that, Prince James?"

"I did. It was excellent." Players are celebrating on the field as the crowd goes wild. Looking over at Zara, even she and Victoria are cheering along. She shoots me a smile as we go back to watching the end of the game. Chelsea squeaks out a win over a tough team.

"This was the best day ever!" George's voice is happier than I've ever heard someone.

"Prince James, we can't thank you enough for everything you've done for George. You've truly made his dreams come true." Mrs. Smythson is giving me a warm smile. "I don't think anything will ever live up to meeting his heroes today."

"I'm glad I could give him this experience. It's given me a lot of great ideas."

"What sort of ideas?" Her husband has left her to help move George along, still talking about the match.

"Just thinking of how this could maybe become a new project of mine. Broaden the reach and help more children. Not just things like this, but bringing sports to areas that may not have the funds to support local teams."

Her face lights up with a smile. "That is absolutely brilliant. I can only imagine how many children will benefit from that. I know George is itching to get back to playing."

"Hopefully he'll get his cast off soon." He had me sign it before, but it didn't compare to having all his favourite players sign it.

"Are you ready to head home, Victoria?" She's still talking Zara's ear off as they walk over.

"Mum. I have all sorts of new songs I want to try. Can we go to the music store tomorrow?"

"Of course, love." She runs a hand down her daughter's hair in a loving manner. "Thank you again, Prince James, for such a wonderful afternoon and evening. Everyone is so happy."

"Thanks, James! This was brilliant. No one at school is going to believe I got to meet the players. They'll all be so jealous!"

"Now George, we don't want to go bragging. You wouldn't like it if your friends did that." His father takes a tone that sounds just like Mum's. Christ, is there a school all parents attend to master that?

"Thank you again, Your Highness." Mr. Smythson shakes my hand as they all head out. George is recapping the entire match on their way out as Victoria rolls her eyes. It's reminiscent of Ellie and me.

"What are you thinking about?" Zara wraps her arms around my waist, resting her chin on my shoulder.

"Just reminds me of Ellie and me when we were little."

I pull her in front of me. It's been a weird night, and these feelings floating up inside me don't have anywhere to go. I love this woman, but it seems no matter what I do, my past will always be rearing its ugly head to remind me why I'm in this situation with Zara. Doesn't she deserve better than a man who can't escape his womanizing past?

"You alright? You seem off today." That's one way of putting it.

"Taking stock of a few things. Nothing to worry about, love."

"Pretty heavy for a night at a football match." Zara drags the tips of her fingers over my cheek, before sliding into the hair at my neck. Her fingers rub soothing circles there. Fuck, what was I thinking about?

"Want to go back to your place and make it unheavy?"

She laughs at me. "Wow, what a charmer you are. You must get all the ladies with that line."

It stings, but I don't let her see that. "Why don't you charm me then?"

"Mmm, that sounds like a nice idea. Want to come back to my place and make it unheavy?" She throws my words back at me.

"Consider me charmed. Now let's get moving."

Chapter Eighteen

JAMES

"And how is my favourite son doing today?" Dad's voice precedes him into my office.

"Mum sent you?" I sigh, dropping the pen in my hand. Since Mum called us to the palace last week, I haven't talked to her. Every time I think about what she did, I'm seething with anger.

"Can't I just come for lunch?"

"Fine. Can we make it quick? I've got a lot of work to do." After Zara's idea about the new charity, I hit the ground running. It's the only thing that I've been able to focus on lately. It's the perfect distraction with a very real wedding staring me down.

"I've already called down to the kitchen. Should be here soon." Dad sits in the chair across from my desk. "What are you working on?"

"It's a proposal for a new charity I want to start. There's a lot of fine details to work out, but I'm hoping it'll pass muster with Mum."

Dad gives me a quizzical stare. "You're serious about this."

"I wouldn't be doing it otherwise." It also made me realize how much I still have to learn.

"Zara's been a good influence on you."

A smile I can't control spreads across my face. Just the thought of Zara has my pulse quickening. No woman has ever made me feel like this. "She has. I know it wasn't the most orthodox situation, but she's fit herself quite nicely into our world."

The door to my office opens and lunch is wheeled in. I didn't realize how hungry I was until just now. I give a slight nod as the staff leaves us.

"Your mum is quite pleased." My dad brings us back to the conversation we were having.

A sigh slips out before I can stop it. "Is she though? It just seems that every step forward is two steps back, and that I'll never live up to this standard she has set for me."

The clank of his silverware dropping has my eyes meeting his. It's like looking into a mirror when I get to his age. I'm the spitting image of him. "I'm not saying this to upset you. We're both quite pleased, shocked really, at how quickly you took to this whole situation. We thought there would be more pushback from you."

"Because who expects to actually fall in love with the person they're arranged to be wed to?"

Bloody hell, did that just slip out? I haven't even told Zara I love her, and now I'm blabbing to my dad. The smile on his face tells me he didn't miss my slipup.

"You two remind me of your mum and me at your age. Except of course we had twin babies to look after."

"Does that mean there's hope for me yet?" A wave of relief rolls through me. I can't be doing that badly if I remind my dad of himself.

"There was never a loss of hope. If it seemed that way, it's because your mother has the weight of the commonwealth on her shoulders. We've always been in your corner. And with this new charity you plan on starting, the rest of the nation will be as well."

I feel like I'm fifteen again, wanting my dad's approval. I'm almost thirty for Christ's sake, but it feels like another piece is falling into place. Whereas before they were all scattered, now it finally feels like I'm settling into who I'm meant to be. To become.

My throat is tight with emotion when I squeeze out the words, "Thanks, Dad."

He gives me a brief nod, trying to control his own emotions. "I didn't just come here to get on you. Your mother has requested Zara to attend the Garden Show with us tomorrow."

Of course she has. I haven't picked up her call, so she sends Dad in her place, knowing I'd refuse her.

"But it's a school day. She'll have class all day." Her nights and weekends are already dominated by events I'm dragging her to. I don't want to disrupt her life any more than it has been.

"It'll be a good opportunity for her to get to meet more of her citizens. See more of what will be required of her when everything is made official."

"I'll call her once we're done," I relent. I know this will eventually be her reality, but I want her life to be as normal as possible until then. Even if her version of normal has shifted.

Finishing up lunch, Dad stands to go. I stand with him, but before he can leave, I pull him in for a hug. "Thanks, Dad."

He squeezes me in a little tighter. "I'm proud of you, James, and I know your grandfather would be too." He pulls back, giving my shoulder a squeeze before leaving. Fuck if my emotions aren't getting the best of me today.

When our grandfather was alive, Ellie was the one expected to eventually be on the throne. She was always the one that was given the attention. I hate to admit it, but it's one of the reasons I slacked off. There was never any pressure on me. I was never going to be leading the country. But now that I am, hearing those words affects me more than I thought they would. My grandfather was arguably the best King our country has ever seen, so to have those words said to me? My heart swells in my chest. And the only person I want by my side when I do this is Zara.

I need to hear her voice. Even if it is to invite her to another event.

"Hi." Her voice is muffled when she answers.

"Bad time?"

"Sorry, just trying to finish eating before lunch hour is over."

Here I am, worried about pulling her away from school when I'm calling her in the middle of the day. "Sorry, love. But just have a quick ask."

"Is it about the Garden Party tomorrow?"

"You're in the wrong profession if you guessed that." Shock colours my voice. How in the world would she know about that already?

"It's the same time every year, so I only assumed I'd be going. Good press for the two of us." She sighs. "Is that why you're calling?"

"You don't have to come if you don't want to. I can tell the Queen to bugger off."

This gets a laugh out of her. "I'm not going to make you tell your mother to bugger off, even if I'd like to tell her that right now. I've already requested the day off. I'm just worried because the week after is our end of term concert and I want to get all the practise time in with the students that I can."

She doesn't have to say it, but I know what she's thinking. That as soon as we get engaged, she'll have to quit her job. That she'll no longer get to teach music but will start training for her new role as princess. I hate that I'm taking her away from her life, but at the same time, I want her by my side.

"You're wonderful, you know that?"

She laughs, soothing the sting to my soul. "So you've told me. Do I just need to come to your place tomorrow?"

"If you want to come early, we can do lunch."

"Mmm, sounds like the start to a perfect day."

More like the perfect life.

Zara

"WOW, do I love a man in uniform." James opens the door in full military dress. I never thought I was one for a man in uniform, but apparently, I am. Or maybe it's just James. He's swoon-worthy in the black coat with white belt. "Did you earn all of these?" Medals decorate his chest.

"Some I did, but some were handed down at the behest of the King. But I'm most proud of the ones I earned in service." His voice is proud as he sweeps me in for a kiss.

"I'm thinking you might need to wear this more often," I whisper against his lips, trailing my fingers down the brass buttons of his uniform.

"You aren't looking so bad yourself, Miss Cross." His eyes trail down my flowing dress, which is a light sage colour with a scalloped hem that hits just above my knees. It has plenty of spin to it for the warm summer day. The fascinator, complete with feathers and a mesh twist, is intricately woven into my hair.

"I wish we didn't have to go to this event. I could stay here with you all afternoon." My words are heated. I love this side that James brings out in me.

"If you aren't too tired, I plan on bringing you back here and doing exactly what you're thinking about right now."

"Then you best feed me now so I don't faint this afternoon." James grabs my hand, pulling me into the kitchen. A simple spread of sandwiches and crisps are spread out.

"Anything else to drink?" James hands me a water bottle as he sits next to me.

I shake my head. "I'm fine. So tell me, what can I expect this afternoon? All the pictures make it seem like such a high-end affair."

James's laugh echoes around the large kitchen. "Not as high-end as you would imagine. Today is in honour of the vets who served, so it will be the Queen shaking hands and meeting everyone. We'll be doing some of that, but not on Mum's level."

"Will you know anyone there?" I point to his uniform. "You know, since you served?"

He shakes his head, finishing the bite he shoved in his mouth. "No. These are typically higher-ups, and I never made that rank before I finished my service. You can only go so far in military service if you're royal. I went into active war zones, which is not typical for royals."

"Why did you get to serve?" I finish the sandwich I have and grab another. I can't say I'll mind the perk of having others cook for me.

"Because I was third in line to the crown. If I was

Reckless Royal

second, I never would have gotten to serve in the Middle East. I'm so proud of my service and was humbled to do it, but if I tried to do it now, I'd be laughed away."

I cover his hand with mine. He turns his to take mine. It's an instinct. Whenever I reach for him, he holds on tight. I love the feel of his hand encasing mine. His warmth spreads through me. "I'm glad you got to serve."

James brings my hand to his lips, dropping kisses on each knuckle. "It's the one thing I'm proudest of. I'll be the first to admit, I've made some poor decisions in the past, but not about that."

"I'm glad I'll get to see a glimpse of that world today."

James tugs me closer to him. "Well then, we best finish up here and get a move on. It's good form to never keep the Queen waiting."

FROM THE MOMENT we arrived at the palace, James was whisked away. We had a few moments together when we entered behind the Queen, but I feel so out of place. Standing on the sides in the massive outdoor space, nerves are flowing like electricity through me. It seems everyone here knows someone but me.

I'm trying not to hide, but with the large crowd, I blend in.

"Can you believe he brought that excuse for a woman?" My ears perk up at a group of women who are at a nearby table.

"She's a poor excuse for a girlfriend. I can't believe James is dating her."

My stomach drops to my feet.

"It'll be over before the holidays. He knows how good

we were together. They look terrible together in the news." A passing waiter offers me another glass of champagne, and I use it as an excuse to get a good look at these women.

Blonde hair, tight dresses, overly done makeup. The exact opposite of my tall, willowy frame.

Pricks of wetness coat my eyes. Will it always be like this? Women cutting me down because James chose me?

But he didn't choose you. That small voice of self-doubt kicks in. Just because our parents cooked up this whole arranged marriage doesn't mean I love James any less. Because I've fallen deeply in love with him these last few weeks.

It just worries me that he doesn't feel the same way. We've gotten closer than I ever thought we would, but is it all a ruse to him? The thought cuts through my heart.

"Excuse me, Zara?" A beautiful, curvy woman with long, dark hair and olive skin comes up to me, breaking through my morose thoughts. Red lipstick stains her lips. She's stunning.

"Yes, hi." I extend the free hand, the one not clutching my champagne glass like it's a lifeline.

"I'm Charlotte, James's cousin. You looked like you needed someone to talk to."

I blow out a deep breath. The sun is beating down on me, sweat prickling on my back. "Yes. I'm still learning the ropes, and it's quite unsettling."

Charlotte links her arm through mine. Her shoulders are exposed in her white sleeveless dress that billows around her ankles. A colourful fascinator adds several inches to her height. "It's very overwhelming some days, and I grew up around all this. How are you faring so far?"

I instantly like Charlotte. I'm surprised our paths haven't crossed sooner. "I'd say okay, all things considered.

I got a crash course in all things royal much sooner than I would have liked."

"Those bloody paparazzi. I can't believe what they did to you. But you've stuck around. That I find quite unbelievable. Not that you would've run, mind you, but most would have." Charlotte steers us to one of the high-top tables. Flowers of all kinds and colours fill the vase on the table.

"Honestly? I'm surprised that didn't send me running to the country." My eyes seek out James. He blends right in with the vets he's chatting with. A smile plays at my lips, one I try to hide. "But James is worth it." I put a little too much force behind my words.

"You don't have to prove it to me, Zara. I can tell."

"You can?" Shock drips from my voice. After those harsh words of the women earlier, it's hard to know.

"Everyone is going to try and tear you down. But believe in what the two of you have. I know how hard this life can be, and finding the right person isn't easy. I'm happy you two found one another. How did the two of you meet? I don't think I've heard the story."

I smirk. "You wouldn't believe me if I told you."

"Charlotte, thanks for keeping Zara company." James had wandered over to us while we were talking.

"Why have you been keeping Zara all to yourself?" Charlotte punches him in the shoulder.

"Because I didn't want you giving her any ideas about how she could do better than me."

Charlotte's laughter is light, as James only stares at her. "Give yourself more credit than that. Half the people here only wish they were as good as you."

I don't miss the shy look on James's face. This wonderful, kind-hearted man does not get enough praise for all he does. He might not have started out doing the best job he could, but it's clear as day on his face how he wants to do a good job, not only for himself, but for his family. His country. I hope for me.

"If you'll excuse us, Charlotte, I was hoping to take Zara on a tour of the palace."

She gives him a side-eye. "Is that what the kids are calling it these days?"

"Piss off." He kisses her cheek before taking my hand in his.

"It was so wonderful to meet you, Charlotte. Maybe we can grab drinks soon?"

Her eyes glimmer with excitement. "That sounds fab. Get my number from James." He's tugging on my arm to move faster. "I don't think a tour is necessarily what he has in mind," she whispers in my ear. Giving her a double cheek kiss, I fall in step behind James. His pace is hurried.

"Where on earth are you taking me?" I jog after him. He pulls me into the gazebo tucked into the private area of the garden. There are no photographers back here.

His lips hungrily seek mine. He tastes like champagne and desire. Of heat and lust. It swirls around us in the warm London air as I open to him. There's a sense of desperation behind this kiss. James likes taking command, and I easily give it to him. He nips at my bottom lip, tugging it between his teeth. There's something in the way he's taking this kiss that sets me on edge.

"Are you alright?" I bemoan the loss of his lips on mine, my voice breathy.

His thumb soothes the sting on my lip. "Just don't like not having you by my side at these kinds of things."

"Nothing's going to happen to me while we're inside the palace grounds." My heart balloons inside my chest for this man.

"You can't blame me for worrying about you, love."

His fingers stroke my cheek, heat sliding through me. I lean into that feeling.

"I'm stronger than you think I am. I can handle it." I say it just as much for him as for myself. I don't tell him that I worry about the paparazzi every time I leave the house. Or that those comments from the women earlier affected me more than I wanted them to. That I hoped I had a smile plastered on my face for the photographers at the event.

"Sometimes I just want you all to myself."

My hands trace the medals decorating his chest. "Think that's something we can make happen sooner rather than later?"

"Anything for you, my queen."

Chapter Nineteen

JAMES

The heat in Zara's eyes has me racing into the palace. I don't mind the royal garden party. I actually enjoy it. Honouring those who have served is always special to me since I served. But with Zara looking exceptionally sexy today in that green dress and fascinator, all I've wanted to do is cut and run as fast as possible. To strip her down and have my way with her.

With hands shaken and stories shared, I lead Zara through the maze of the palace to my office here. My need for her is boiling in my body so high that Egypt feels closer than my office.

Coming upon the right door, I throw it open and pull her inside. She's on me immediately. Her lips capture mine. This kiss is messy. It's passionate. It's everything a kiss should be. My cock gets hard beneath my zipper as her tongue tangles with mine. Running my hands up her thighs, I carry her to my desk, setting her on the edge.

There's a fire in her eyes. Hundreds of people have come out to be recognised by the Queen, and we're up in my office, acting on the desire we both feel for one another.

"I guess once a playboy, always a playboy." Zara's smile is playful as she unbuckles my belt. It's a harsh reminder of why we're in this situation. That situations like this one are precisely why Zara was thrust into my life. But when she slides her dress up her delectable thighs, it's hard to have any thoughts.

Dropping to my knees, I push the fabric of her dress farther up, exposing my end goal. Her thong is wet as her thighs spread open, beckoning me forward.

"Fuck, you're gorgeous." I tongue the wet spot on her lacy thong. Her needy moans tell me she wants more. Brushing the fabric to the side, I suck down on her clit. She's a writhing mess beneath me as I pleasure her with expert strokes of my tongue.

The heels of her shoes are biting into my shoulders. When I thrust two fingers inside of her, she clamps down on me. She's pulsing with need as my cock thickens in my pants. I need to find my own release, but I'm not coming before Zara does.

"Yes! Right there!" Her loud voice carries through the quiet office.

"Fuck, Zara. I need you to come now." I pull my fingers out, thrusting three inside of her. Her hands fist my hair, the spikes of pain mixing with the pleasure I'm driving her towards.

"Oh James!" Her voice is soft as she starts to come. I lap up her release, savouring it on my tongue. It's the sweetest nectar, I think as I drink it in.

When she starts to come down, I stand. Her once pristine hair is messy, and the fascinator lies on the floor behind my desk. When she turns her eyes on me, my heart stops in my chest. The emotions pooling in her eyes cause them to come pouring out of me.

"I love you, Zara. You're the best thing that's ever

happened to me. Fuck, I shouldn't be telling you like this." She pushes up onto her elbows, her skirt still hiked around her waist. She looks utterly defiled. And positively beautiful.

"I know this thing between us was arranged by our parents." I wave a finger between us. "But Christ, I can't help how I feel."

She doesn't say anything. The silence stretches like an ocean between us. I don't think I've misread this situation. The looks. The touches. She has to feel the same way, right? Just when I'm about to go run and hide, a smile cracks her lips. A smile that tells me all I need to know.

"I love you, James." She sits up, wrapping her hands around my neck as she brings me closer to her. "We had the strangest start of anyone I know, but it doesn't make it any less real."

"It's our story." I drop my forehead to hers. My heart could burst from my chest at the love I have for this woman.

"Our story. Think of what we can tell the kids."

I smirk at her. "Kids? Planning ahead now?"

She drops a sweet kiss on the corner of my mouth. "I'm thinking four, at least. Maybe we'll get lucky and have some twins too."

"As long as they all look like you, I'm happy."

A sigh escapes her lips, ghosting my cheek. "As long as they look like you, I'm happy," she parrots my words.

"Maybe we should start practising?" I lean into her, pressing my erection into her centre.

"We'll need all the practise we can get." She stands, giving me her back. I work open my pants, pulling my aching cock out. Pressing her down on the desk, I line myself up with her, before thrusting into heaven. Zara is perfect. This woman is absolutely perfect, and I don't know how I got so lucky to have been given the gift of her.

Zara shakes her arse against me, letting me know to get moving. "Someone's eager, aren't we?" I pull out before slamming back into her. I set an unrelenting pace as she moves underneath me. Her knuckles are white as she clings to the edge of the desk.

"Fuck, you feel incredible." My movements are hurried as I drive into her. Her moans are the only sounds permeating the rush of blood in my head. I lose all coherent thought when I'm around this woman.

"Kiss me." Her voice is breathless, full of need. I wouldn't deny the woman I love anything. I press my weight into her back, seeking her lips with my own. I nibble on her full bottom lip as she starts to come apart around me.

"Don't stop!" Zara screams as her pussy clamps down around me. Heat and desire are coiling at the base of my dick. I'm ready to blow, but I want to draw out Zara's pleasure as long as possible.

Pulling out, I spin Zara around, taking her in my arms. Her legs wrap around my waist as I carry us over to the loveseat. I sit, her on top of me. Finding the zipper in the back of her dress, I inch it down before freeing her breasts. Her nipples are diamond hard as I draw one into my mouth.

"How are you so good at that?" Zara arches into my touch.

"You make it easy, love." I move to her other nipple, as Zara grinds herself over my dick, spreading her wetness around. "But I'm going to need you to fuck me now."

Zara's fingers find my hair, pulling my head back. Staring into my eyes, she lowers herself down. Once she's fully seated, she takes a few settling breaths. I mirror her. It feels good. Too good.

Zara rises, sliding back down, spinning her hips to find her own pleasure. Bloody hell, it feels amazing. She continues to ride me, my own orgasm just out of reach. Her eyes are blazing with fire as she doesn't break contact. Drawing one hand down, I find her clit. Rubbing tight circles around the bundle of nerves, I can tell when she starts to crack. Her movements become more erratic.

I try to fight the heat raging through me, but it erupts from me as she starts to pulse around my dick. I growl as I come, thrusting up into her. Her movements start to still as our orgasms take over. I clutch her to me, needing to stay grounded.

This woman drives me wild in the best way. She makes me feel something I've never felt before. And damn, if I won't spend my entire life trying to make her feel the same.

I slip out of Zara, dropping her on the loveseat at my side. I'm spent. Sated. Happier than I can ever remember being.

"I guess we should return to the party?" Zara pokes my still clothed side. Her breasts are exposed, and her dress is around her waist. My dick is hanging out of my pants. We're quite the picture.

"Like this wouldn't make front page news tomorrow. Future King and Queen naked at current Queen's Garden Party." I throw my hands up, mimicking the news.

"I'd be thrown out on my arse if that were to happen." She says it in jest, but I can't help but grow concerned.

"You know if anything happens, I'll protect you, right?"

She shifts in my arms, looking up at me. "I know." There's doubt in her voice. I don't know why she would think I wouldn't protect her from everything this life brings with it. "It's just hard to predict what they are going to say about us."

I swing her legs over my lap, righting her dress around her before tucking myself back into my pants. This conversation feels too heavy to be doing it partially clothed.

"You have nothing to be worried about. You're the most stand-up person I know. Hell, that's why Mum picked you."

She winces at that statement. "I know, but what if someone were to sneak in here and take pictures of us right now?"

"You know that's not going to happen."

"I know. It's hard to shut off the worry sometimes. I'm not used to this crazy life, and some days it seems really hard."

Is she doubting me? Why would she tell me she loves me if she were going to turn around and dump me? Fuck, this nagging feeling starts tugging at the edges of my brain. I've never been a one-woman kind of man, because I didn't see the point. But with Zara? She's all I can see.

"Hey." Cupping my chin, she turns me to face her. "It's the press I'm worried about. Not you. You and I are solid. Don't doubt us."

Easier said than done.

Chapter Twenty

JAMES

"This is the charity you'd like to set up?" Mum's voice is quiet as she reviews my proposal for her. I'm usually not one to worry about things like this, but for once, I'm taking an active role in my future instead of letting someone hand it to me. I'll be the first to admit I've been acting like a shithead to her these last few weeks, but I was angry.

"Yes. After we took the Smythsons to the football club last week, Zara said it'd be perfect for me. I love sports and children, so why not mix the two? We can help those who are in hospital and set up some programs with local clubs."

Mum stands, rounding her desk to stand in front of me. "This is what I've been looking for from you, darling."

My eyes shoot to hers, confusion no doubt written all over my face. "Really?"

"Yes." Her hands cup my cheeks, a sense of pride emanating from her. "For so long, you did whatever you wanted because you could. And I'm afraid that's partially my fault for focusing so much on your sister. But I wanted you to find something you were passionate about. And this is it."

"You really think so?" I hate that my voice sounds timid and scared. But needing her approval is key to making this happen.

"Run with this, James. I have no doubt you'll see all the success in the world. And I'm so pleased to see Zara helping you with this."

I let out a breath I didn't realize I was holding. "Thanks, Mum." I stand, giving her a hug. It feels pretty damn good having her seal of approval on this.

"I'll always support you, my sweet boy. Sometimes, you just need a good kick in the arse to get there."

I smile at her as I get a shove out the door. I didn't realize how much I needed her validation in this project. So much of what I've done in the past has been because it's been handed to me. But for once, I don't want to do something just because I'm told. I don't want to skate by just because I was born into this life. I want to thrive. My grandfather was perhaps the best King we've had in centuries. I not only want to live up to his legacy, but to surpass him.

Finding my way back to my own office here at the palace, my advisors stand upon my arrival. "We've got some work to do."

"PARDON ME, sir, but if you don't leave now, you'll be late for your dinner with Miss Cross." Charles is at my shoulder. Checking my watch, hours have gone by. With no events on the schedule for today, I took full advantage of working on my new charity. I have so many ideas, and all I can think about is sharing them with Zara.

"Where are we meeting her?" Standing, I slip into my blazer and follow Charles out the door.

"You were going to cook for her tonight." His voice is even as we descend the stairs from my office.

"Did you get takeaway for me?" He gives me a knowing stare as I get into the car.

"Italian is waiting for you at home. Zara will arrive a few minutes after, so it will look like you prepared dinner yourself."

"Excellent." I clap him on the shoulder as we head off. My cooking skills are lacking. As much as I'd like to impress Zara, I don't want to poison her with my nonexistent abilities. Except, I don't think Zara is labouring under the delusion that I know how to cook after Oliver let it slip about my burnt pasta in uni.

Pulling into the grounds in Kensington, my mind eases. It's been a long few days. Things have never been better with Zara. We were off after the wedding was thrown in our faces, but after the Royal Garden Party, we're on the same page. We're connecting more. We easily tell one another how much we love each other. And we definitely show it. I can't get enough of her sexy body. I long for the day when I can wake up to her snuggled up against me.

The paparazzi are eating our every appearance up. I can't remember the last time my picture was on the front page of every tabloid, but there I am. With Zara by my side. I know she hates it, but I love having her there.

The heavy scent of Italian greets me as I walk in the door of the apartment. Heading to my room, I change into something more casual before coming downstairs for a drink.

Eggplant parmesan. Lasagne. Chicken Alfredo. It all

looks delectable. Whoever put this together did a brilliant job.

"James?" Zara's voice carries throughout the house. It's settling. Like she's seeking me out after a long day. That this is something we do on a daily basis. I like that thought more than I should.

Walking out into the formal living room, I find her setting her things down on the back of the couch. "Hi, love."

Her face softens as she looks over at me. The space of the living room separates us. I hate any distance between us.

"You seem to be in a good mood."

"Let's eat and I'll tell you about it."

She nods, walking over to me. Wrapping an arm around her shoulders, I pull her into me. "Where'd you get dinner from?"

"You don't believe I worked all day to make you a feast fit for a queen?" Her hand comes down on my stomach, warming me from the contact.

"If you cooked, we might get food poisoning. And you'd want to make it look like you did, so I'm guessing you had someone get takeout instead of anyone else cooking."

I stop, pulling Zara in front of me. "How the hell could you have guessed that?"

Zara drags her fingers over my cheeks. "I love you, James, and I know you better than you seem to think. Besides, it's what all men do." She walks away, a little more sway in her hips.

"Someone's in a cheeky mood tonight," I whisper, following her into the kitchen.

"It smells delicious." She tucks her hair behind her

back, as she takes a deep inhale of the dishes set out. "Are we eating in here?"

"Good a place as any." She grabs the dishes as she heads for the small table in the corner. I rarely eat in here, but it feels normal with her. I grab some wine for her and settle in beside her.

"So, how was school today? Teach the kids any pop songs?" She cuts into her eggplant, her lips closing around the fork. Fuck, if I don't want to be that fork right now.

"They do like the classics too."

"Do they?" I waggle my eyebrows at her.

"Well, they do when I tell them they have to in order to get the pop songs." She sighs, swirling her wine in her glass. "At least they enjoy playing, so I'll take that most days."

"Kids just don't appreciate the good things in life."

Zara peers at me over her glass. "Oh? And what are those good things in life that you appreciate?"

I reach for her hand, the small rings cold against my skin. "Having a beautiful woman to have dinner with me. Good Italian food. Fine wine."

Her hand flips under mine, holding it in her grip. "What's gotten into you today?" Her fingertips caress my palm. Heat radiates up my arm at the small contact.

"I talked to Mum about the charity idea." Her movements still as she sets her wine glass down. She stands, moving to sit on my lap. Dropping my own fork, I hug her close to me.

"I'm so proud of you. Tell me everything."

The confidence this woman has in me blows me away. It's more than I have in myself some days.

"You really want to hear about it?"

Zara's hands are warm on my face. Emotions swirl in her

eyes—exasperation with a whole lot of love. "Of course I want to hear about it. This is big. I know it can't be easy to tell the Queen you want to blaze your own trail, but you did it."

"I don't deserve you," I blurt out. Fecking hell, this woman is ruining me. Dropping my head to her shoulder, I try to calm my now racing heart. Zara is one of the most beautiful people I have ever met. Not just on the outside, but the inside too. I've never met anyone who loves their job like she does. She has such a passion for what she does, and a love for those around her, that it's hard not to want to be around her.

"That's just not true. Look at me." Her fingers under my chin bring my gaze to hers. Her eyes are soft. "There is a heart of gold under all this bravado. You don't want people to see the real you, because you don't want to be rejected."

"Coming with the big guns," I say on a laugh, trying to diffuse the tension of the moment.

"Stop it." This time, her fingers grab my chin, holding my focus to her. "If you didn't care, you wouldn't have taken the Smythsons to Chelsea. You wouldn't have gone above and beyond for them. If you didn't care, we wouldn't be here. You would've said fuck it and renounced the crown like your sister."

It's a staggering thought. Would I have given this all up if I didn't care? Would I have lived life in the fast lane until I ran out of gas?

"You are showing up whether you want to believe it or not. You are going to do amazing things as the prince and future King. Don't doubt yourself."

"You make it sound so easy."

"If there's one thing I've learned these last few weeks," her voice comes out soft, "is that none of this is easy. You learn to deal with the hard as it comes, and you get better at it."

"And are you getting better at dealing with the hard?" Zara had the worst crash course with the paparazzi, and it's difficult not to worry about her anytime she's out on her own.

She doesn't answer right away, causing my heart rate to increase. I keep waiting for the other shoe to drop. For her to decide that this life I lead isn't worth it. That I'm not worth it.

"Some days it feels easy. Some days it's hard. Really hard. Like I worry about what would happen if the paparazzi got into school or did something to one of my students."

Fuck. I never thought about that. About what could happen if someone crossed the line. It's not just Zara I need to worry about.

"But the security officers help. Being around you helps. I know people in the past have used you for leverage to increase their station in life, or a quick screw with the prince, but that's not me." Her eyes are gentle as she drops her forehead to mine. "I want you to know you're worth all this craziness, James. Even on the days I doubt myself, I never have any doubts about you. Or us. I love you more than I thought possible."

My heart swells in my chest. No one has ever said that. Like Zara said, they either want to sleep with the prince or try to get ahead in life. But Zara has never been that person. And it's taken meeting her to realize that I don't have a lot of people like her in my life. Most people are passing acquaintances. I have a tight-knit circle, but it's remained small because I haven't found anyone worth bringing into the fold.

But Zara is worth it. I love her so much, it hurts sometimes. Even if we met under the strangest of circumstances, I know I'll do everything in my power to keep her safe. Even if it means keeping her safe from me. I never want to dull this light that she has.

There are no words that can be said, so I simply wrap her in my arms. This beautiful, perfect, amazing woman that I am not worthy of. Zara may not have her doubts about us, but right now, in this moment, I'm full of them. Wondering if there is any future between the two of us that doesn't end in heartbreak.

Chapter Twenty-One

ZARA

"Alright, everyone. Sit up straight and instruments at the ready." Snickers break out across the room. "Okay, okay. Let's go."

From the moment they first sat down, they've been antsy. Whispering amongst themselves throughout class. If they weren't playing so well, it'd be more grating. Thankfully, it's the last class of the day.

Tapping my baton, the music starts to rise, and the practice of this week is noticeable. It's coming together and not a moment too soon, with the end of term recital coming up in the next week.

As the song starts to crescendo, the headmaster of the school makes his way into the back of the classroom. His face is drawn tight in dismay as he looks at his watch and then me. Nerves settle deep in my stomach. What in the world is he doing in here? Outside of formal evaluations, it's rare to see him in our classrooms. And considering we have them once a year, and mine was at the start of the term, his presence is unnerving.

We work through the piece a few more times before it's

time to pack up for the day. A few students are lingering before they're dismissed by the headmaster. They shoot curious glances back at me as he closes the door behind the last student.

"Miss Cross. I need a word with you."

Ice settles in my stomach at his tone. "Okay." I sit at my desk, taking in his discerning stare.

"Effective immediately, you are suspended for conduct detrimental to the terms of the contract you signed upon hire."

"What?" I explode out of my seat. "What conduct are you referring to?"

He slaps a magazine on the desk in front of me, and all blood seems to drain from my body. My stomach is somewhere near my feet as I read the headlines.

Our future Queen riding the Prince too hard?

BELOW THE HEADLINE is a picture of my first night with James. I'm on top of him as our naked bodies are exposed. "I don't understand. How did they get this?"

"There's more," he says, taking the magazine from my hands and flipping it open. There are more pictures from that night. The night that James took me to the orchestra. The same night I realized I was falling in love with him.

His words are distant as the pictures in front of me assault my eyes. Of James's hands all over me. Of his kisses. Of me stroking him off. Every single moment from that evening is plastered all over this gossip rag for the world to see.

"As you can see, these are rather disturbing. And this

goes against the contract you signed when you started here."

"This is an invasion of privacy!"

"And yet I can't ignore these images. I've already had several calls from parents concerned about the level of scrutiny these photos will bring down on the school. Until this dies down, we can't have you teaching."

I can only shake my head in dismay. Grabbing my purse, I leave the room without another word.

"Miss Cross. Please wait until we can have the car brought around." My security officer stops me at the side door.

"Is it bad?"

He pins me with a look that tells me it is. "Prince James is awaiting your arrival."

I nod as the door is pushed open and a wall of sound hits me. Flashbulbs are popping in my face as I'm guided out of the school. Bodies are pushing on all sides of me. It's worse than when they attacked me outside my house. They're screaming at me left and right.

"Is this how you plan to run the country?"

"Did you only want James because he's going to be King?"

"Are you just doing this for the attention?"

"How is the prince in bed?"

Bile is thick in my throat as I make my way into the awaiting car. Tears threaten as I pull out my phone. Hundreds of notifications are awaiting me, but I ignore them all. I know I shouldn't look at the damage, but I have to see what is being said.

I don't have to search hard. The images are at the top of every major news headline. At least some have the decency to blur out some of the more risqué photos.

Most of the photos are from that night at the orchestra

with James. But there are a few others. Us in my garden one night. Laughing in the kitchen. They're tame. I'm sitting on his lap while we had drinks. Nothing devastating like the ones of us having sex in my room.

I can't figure out how they took those photos. I'm in a quiet neighbourhood, surrounded by houses on all sides. Aside from misplaced post, my neighbours are quiet and keep to themselves. Who in their right mind would do something like this?

A fierce ache settles in my bones. I knew it wouldn't be an easy life, stepping into the royal spotlight. But I never thought my life would be invaded in such a drastic manner. The fact that my privacy was violated in such an epic fashion, in my own home no less, has doubts about this new life swirling in my head.

Will it always be like this?

Will they be able to protect us from the press?

How far will they go to get a story?

Kensington is swarming with press as we pull through the gates. Never in my life have I seen so many people crowded into such a tiny area, all hoping to get the money shot of the disgraced prince and his girlfriend. Is this really what I have to look forward to now that James and I are together? It's a sickening thought as we pull up to his apartment. He's outside waiting for me.

James eats up the distance between us as soon as the door is open.

"Zara. I'm so sorry this happened." He pulls me into his arms, his heart thundering in his chest.

"Let's talk inside." His brows are furrowed, and distress mars his handsome features.

Shutting the door behind us, the scent of James overwhelms me. Tears prickle the back of my eyes as I take in his distressed stance.

"How did this happen?" My voice is quiet as we move into his living room. "How could someone release photos like that?"

"They don't care about the damage they do. Only that they hit us where it hurts most."

"Well, they've certainly done that," I say on a huff.

"It will all blow over, I promise. This has happened to me before, and it'll leave the news cycle in a few weeks."

"A few weeks? I was suspended from school today because it's detrimental to the students I'm teaching!" I shriek. "I'm sorry I can't brush it off as easily as you, but our sex life is out there for everyone to see!"

James winces as he starts pacing again. "I didn't mean for you to brush it off. It's just this sort of thing will always be a threat as a royal."

"You mean I should always be worried that we'll be photographed having sex and it'll be released for the world to see?" I hit him with my most indignant glare.

"No, I don't mean that, Z." He approaches me, but I pull away. "Zara, love. Please, sit down and I'll tell you how I'm handling this."

I turn, settling my hands on my hips. "And how are you handling this?" I'm in no mood to be told what to do.

"You don't need to be so defensive."

"Oh, I'm sorry. You're right. No big deal that my tits are out there for the entire world to see!"

Walking over to the window, I see that clouds are starting to move into the city, much like my mood.

"Zara. I'm sorry. We have people looking into this. I don't know how the pictures were taken, but the palace will certainly get to the bottom of it."

"And how do you plan on preventing this from happening again?" I don't turn to face him. Dread hangs heavy in the air.

Dread that this can happen again.

Dread that I won't be able to recover from this.

Dread that my life has been altered beyond recognition.

"We'll just have to be more careful next time." James's hands wrap around my waist, pulling me into him.

"Weren't we being careful the first time?" I twist out of his hold. His arms, that are always so calming, only cause tremors to wrack my body.

"Zara, please. We'll get through this."

"Will we?" My voice cracks. I don't know how I'm going to be able to handle this. Or anything like this in the future.

"It's one scandal."

"This week. What about next week? Or next month? Or next year? What if I can't handle it? The paparazzi follow me everywhere. I'm already losing so much."

"What are you saying?" Pain is evident in his eyes.

"I just don't know if I can do this, James."

He sinks down onto the sofa, holding his head in his hands. He looks so despondent sitting there as the world weighs me down.

"You knew that this would be part of the risk of getting involved with me." James's voice is hollow. I've never heard such emptiness come from such a happy person.

"Maybe I didn't have the full picture. I never expected to have the paparazzi attack me outside my own home or invade my privacy inside my home." My hand goes to the healed cut on my cheek. "I just, I don't know if I can handle this life."

James shoots up and crosses to me in a quick stride. "Please don't say that, Zara. We love each other. We can work through this."

His hands are warm on my cheeks as the tears finally

fall, carving hot paths down my face. "What if we can't? What if it only gets worse?"

"All I can do is promise to protect you with everything I have. I don't want to lose you."

The guilt in his eyes is crushing. "I'm sorry, James. I just need time."

"How much time?" The crack in his voice splits my heart in two.

"I don't know." Grasping his hands, I kiss his knuckles before stepping out of his hold.

"That's not reassuring, love."

"I'm sorry, I'm not sure what else I can do right now." James's presence is overwhelming. So much so, I can't stand to be here a moment longer. Rushing to grab my bag, I try to leave as fast as possible.

"That's it? You're just leaving me here without another word?"

The break in my heart is too much. The tears tracking down my face are endless. "I told you I need time."

"Bullshit. You're running scared. Time is never a good thing, and you'll find every excuse to not be with me because you're not ready for everything this world is."

"Can you blame me? I'm sorry, but after today, I don't think I'm asking for too much."

"Well, it's too much for me. Because if you walk through that door, we're done."

The finality of his tone hits me square in the chest. "Fine. If that's how you want this to go, then we're done." Just saying those words causes another crack in my heart.

"Then I guess we are." Opening the door, my security officer offers me an umbrella in the now rainy skies. It matches my own misery. I run through the rain to the awaiting car. I'll no longer have the security officers to protect me from the paparazzi. My life is a pendulum, going from complete anonymity to being in the public spotlight with James, to losing the sense of comfort I have with him and being thrown to the wolves on my own.

And as we pull away, the palace grounds getting farther and farther behind us, the ache in my heart deepens. I wanted time. James couldn't possibly expect me to bounce back after an hour, could he?

But now, now I don't even have the option of bouncing back. Because he was swift to cut me out of his life. Just like all the bimbos he's ever been with. I really did fall for the playboy prince.

Chapter Twenty-Two

JAMES

The pounding in my head is getting louder. Bloody hell, why won't it go away? Sitting up, I realize it's coming from my front door. Just what I want, to be around people right now.

The sun is blinding as I get off the sofa. The room spins ever so slightly. I yank open the front door, and my mum, my grandmum, and Ellie greet me. "Oh goodie. Just who I wanted to see right now." I stalk back to the living room, not bothering to wait for them to come in.

"James, we need to discuss what happened." Mum's voice is firm as she takes a seat across from me.

"What's there to discuss? Someone took photos of Zara and me having sex and leaked them to the press." I'm wallowing, and I know it. "Zara was the best thing to ever happen to me, and now she's gone."

"Is she though?" Ellie's voice is hard as she shoves me from the side. "Have you talked to her?"

I collapse back onto the sofa, my head resting in my grandmum's lap. It's like I'm five years old again. "She wanted time, but you know what that means."

"Perhaps that she needed time to wrap her head around this?" Grandmum has always been straightforward. "I never had to worry about my naughty bits being strewn across the news for the world to see."

I huff out a laugh. "Thank God for that!"

She pinches my side. "I didn't ask for your cheek, darling. Why did you push her away?"

Why did I push her away? "Because I was scared. I was scared she was going to run and be just like everyone else who used me for my title."

"That's a load of crap and you know it. Anyone who saw the two of you together knows how in love you were." Ellie smacks me on the arm.

I rub my hands down my face. My beard is getting scraggly. I haven't left the house since Zara walked out on me. I didn't want the paparazzi to get a shot of the haggard-looking prince.

I shift my gaze to Mum. "I was trying. I was really trying to be better." My voice breaks.

"Oh darling." Mum walks over, crouching down to face me. "You don't have to be better. You just have to be you."

"Isn't being me what got us into this mess to start with?"

Her hand is warm on my cheek. "No. You had it in you this whole time. You just needed someone to see it in you."

Zara was that person. She saw me for me. I wasn't just someone with a title to sleep with. I wasn't just a prince to her. I was just James. Why couldn't I see that?

"How am I going to get her back?"

"Well for starters, you might want to shower and shave." Grandmum tugs at my beard. "No offence, but the beard isn't a great look for you."

I laugh. "Thanks, Grandmum."

"I'm not going to make it easy for you." She lifts me off

her lap, my eyes tearing up at some of the most important people in my life surrounding me at one of my lowest moments.

"Have you thought about what you want to do with your charity?" Mum starts cleaning up the empty bottles from the table.

"I have a general idea of what I want to do. Why?"

Mum shifts her gaze to Ellie. "Has he always been this clueless?"

Ellie laughs, shaking her head at me. "Of course. He's a man." Her hand is mindlessly rubbing her baby bump.

"I really hope you have a girl," I tease.

"James. Move up the kick-off of the event. Don't let the press beat you down. Instead of rebounding by going to the clubs—"

I cut her off. "I haven't been to the clubs in ages. It's never even crossed my mind."

"Aww, my baby brother is finally growing up after twenty-nine years."

"Piss off," I say on a laugh. I give her a weak smile.

"You may be down, but you're not out. Counter this scandal with starting your charity. People will see the good in you, and it'll become this wonderful thing."

I pull Ellie in for a hug. I've clearly had too much to drink, because I'm more emotional than I usually am. "You're going to make a great mum, Ellie."

Her eyes are wet when she pulls back. "Okay. Plan of attack. Throw a huge gala and invite Zara."

"Just need to plan a whole gala in only a few weeks?"

"Oh, however will you manage?" Mum comes back into the room. "Whatever you need, whoever you need to help you, they are at your disposal. Perks of the crown." She smirks at me.

"I better get started then."

"Fab. Do you have a name for this new charity you are starting?" Ellie asks.

"Sporting Kids?" I blurt out. It's the first thing that comes to mind.

"Sporting Kids? Are you set on that?" Ellie turns her nose up at the name.

"You really going to kick a man when he's down?"

"Not what I would've picked, but have at it. I need to get to the school. Let me know if you need help." Ellie drops a kiss on my head before leaving.

"Thanks, El." She winks on her way out the door.

"I think we've got you all sorted out." Grandmum stands, following Ellie. "Just make sure to close the curtains next time."

"Grandmum, I don't need you telling me that."

"How do you think your granddad and I kept it under wraps all those years?"

"Mum!" Mum's voice carries over the room.

"I'm scarred for life." If a hole would open up and swallow me down, I'd be forever grateful right about now.

"Katherine, are you joining me?"

"Give me a minute." Grandmum heads outside, leaving me with Mum.

"Are you going to be alright?" Mum's voice is quiet as she sits next to me.

My happiness shouldn't be so dependent on one person, but I can't help it. I've never met anyone like Zara.

"I'm sorry for all the trouble I've been lately. I know I haven't been easy on you these last few weeks, and I'm sorry."

"I'm the one who should be sorry. I didn't have enough faith that you could make a name for yourself. I was so worried that you would renounce your place in line to the throne like Ellie that I held on too hard."

Tears linger in her eyes. What is in the air today that is making everyone so emotional? "If it wasn't for you, I wouldn't have met Zara. I hated the idea of you finding my wife, but now I can't imagine my life without her."

Mum takes my hand. "Then tell her that. Tell her how much she means to you. Don't lose your chance at a once in a lifetime love over something that won't mean anything in a few weeks' time."

I stand, giving Mum a crushing hug. "I think that's the best idea you've had in a long time."

Chapter Twenty-Three

ZARA

"Zara! Are you home?" Dad's voice echoes throughout the living room. I've sequestered myself here the last few days, curtains drawn, so no one can see me.

"Hi Dad." I peer up from my spot on the sofa as he shuffles into the room.

"Why in the bloody hell are you moping about like this? I thought you'd be happy."

I shoot up as he sits next to me. "Happy? Why in the world would I be happy about any of this?"

"I figured with the paparazzi getting ahold of those photos, you'd be let out of your arrangement."

I give him a puzzled look. "Why would I be let out of it?"

"Because you never wanted it in the first place."

On top of everything else, I'm a terrible daughter. I was so wrapped up in my anger at my father that when things became serious with James, I didn't tell him. Tears burst from my eyes. I can't stop them. They're uncontrollable, as Dad pulls me into a hug. Deep sobs escape as I try to get them under control.

"I fell in love with him." My voice shakes, and my dad squeezes me tighter. "Not only was I a terrible daughter for ignoring your calls because I was upset with you, but I also fell in love with the prince and didn't bother to tell you."

"My darling girl." He pulls back, wiping the tears from my eyes. "You remind me so much of your mum. She could stay mad at me for days. No matter how much I buttered up to her, she'd freeze me out."

My tears lessen at the mention of Mum. "Apparently I learned that from her."

"You learned quite a lot from her. She was the most talented violinist I'd ever heard until you came along. It's like a piece of her is still with me whenever I hear you play."

"I hate that her violin was destroyed. I guess I don't have to worry about the paparazzi doing that again."

"Do you love him?" His brows furrow together, as if it's the worst thing in the world for his little girl to fall in love.

"Yes,"—I bite down on my lip, trying to stop the quiver—"with all my heart."

"As much as I hate that I drew you into my mess, I can't say that I'm too upset that you found the person you wanted to spend your life with."

I pull back, piercing him with a fiery look. "Why did you agree to this arrangement in the first place?"

A harsh look crosses his face. "For the money."

I roll my eyes. "I should've known. But if you were hard for money, why didn't you come to me?" It's not like I make millions teaching, but I would never want my dad to be out on the street.

"It's embarrassing. Being in debt and having no way out. And when the Queen came to me, I thought it would be the perfect solution. But I just hate the pain I've caused you."

I throw my arms around him. "I'm only in pain because I fell in love. So as upset as I want to be with you, I just wish there was a way to get him back."

Just as he's about to respond, a knock at the door stops him. "Aren't they supposed to stay back on the other side of the street? Don't you still have protection officers?"

I just shrug my shoulders as Dad goes to get the door. My protection detail hadn't disappeared like I thought it would. It was some comfort that I wasn't totally on my own with the madness of the paparazzi. But I still only felt safe in my own home.

"Your Highness. It's a pleasure to meet you." My heart clutches in my chest. But why would Dad say it's a pleasure to meet James? They've met before. A belly precedes the former princess into my living room. A short, black dress swings around her knees, clinging to her adorable baby bump. Her appearance is striking. Long pink hair and bright blue eyes. So similar to James it makes my heart ache.

"Ellie? What are you doing here?"

"I was hoping to have a word with you about my brother. May I?" She points to the chair next to me, and I nod for her to sit. "Thanks. This baby is really starting to wear me out."

"I'll let you two ladies talk. Call me if you need me." Dad drops a kiss on my head and heads to the door.

"I love you, Dad." He gives me a smile before the noise outside briefly permeates my bubble of safety. I turn my attention back to Ellie, feeling just a tad better.

"How much longer?" Her hands are resting on her bump. She's glowing.

"About three months. And it can't come soon enough. I'm ready to meet this little one."

"And you still haven't found out what you're having?" I

want to keep her talking about anything other than James. I need to know how he's doing, but I also don't want to hear that he's moved on without me. I've been doing my best not to check the news about him. The only thing that comes up is if we've had sex in a new place. But I want to see if he's doing okay.

"It's one of the last few surprises in life. Sean is dying to find out, but as long as he or she is healthy, I'm happy. But I didn't come here to talk about my baby, as much as I love to. Why are you still here and not at the palace with Jamie?"

My face twists in confusion. "What do you mean, why am I not at the palace? I'm assuming you spoke with James. He couldn't give me the time I needed to come to terms with everything that happened, so he said we were done."

I draw my quivering lip between my teeth. I don't want to cry in front of Ellie. I've done enough of that this week.

"But why did you need time? Why didn't you rely on James to help you come to terms with what happened?"

I must look like a fish, opening and closing my mouth, but no words come out. It's a harsh statement, but one I needed to hear. Why didn't I rely on James? It's not as if he hasn't faced his own scandals in the past. Did I cut and run because it would be easier than facing a life in the press?

"Look, I am not the role model in how to handle the paparazzi. But Jamie needs someone to be there when the going gets tough. If you can't handle it, you need to make a clean break of it now."

"James already made a clean break of it." My heart sinks at the thought. Just the mere idea of an arranged marriage with the "playboy prince" had me balking. But now? Now, it's hard to imagine my life without him.

"Would I be here if he did? He's a sodding mess.

Cancelled every event until the fundraiser event for his new charity. Sporting Kids, I think?"

My eyes shoot up to hers. "He named it?" My heart falls to my feet. He was so excited about this idea. It was his passion project. And I wasn't there for this. "But Sporting Kids? Really?"

Ellie turns her nose up. "Definitely not his best work, but he's not functioning properly."

"Is anyone going to be there for him?" It's not my place anymore, but my mind goes to supporting him. Even if we're not together anymore.

"You are. I don't go to any events where the press is, and it's you he wants by his side."

Tears blur my vision. "He really wants me there?"

Ellie stands, moving to sit next to me. Taking my hands in hers, she brings them to her lap. "He didn't explicitly say it, but I can tell. It's a twin thing."

I give her a sad smile. "Will he even take me back?"

Her grip is firm as I look into her clear, blue eyes. "Show him he's worth it. Every person up until this point in his life has only wanted to be with him because he's the prince. You didn't stay. He thinks that he's not worth it."

I shoot up out of her grasp. "But he is! He's the most wonderful person I've ever met in my life, and I can't imagine not being with him. He's never been the 'playboy prince' to me. He's James, the soft, caring man who will be the best King this nation has ever seen."

Ellie's face is warm as she looks up at me. "And you'll be the perfect Queen by his side."

"Am I able to attend the event for his charity?" There's no way I can miss this.

Ellie pulls a card from her bag. "Here's all the details. I've talked to Charlotte, and she'll send someone over to help you out with a dress and your hair this week. A car will pick you up, so you don't have to worry about getting there."

"I appreciate all that, but I think I can take care of my dress and hair."

And I have just the outfit that will hopefully bring James to his knees. And hopefully bring us back together.

Chapter Twenty-Four

JAMES

There are hundreds of people in this room, and I've never felt more alone. Sure, a few friends are lingering here and there, but there's no one at my side.

The dull ache in my heart roars to full strength. Tonight will be a good night. The official start of Sporting Kids. My very first, and my very own, charity. And the one person I want by my side isn't here.

"Things seem to be going well. There are a few more donors we'd like you to speak with before your presentation." Charles has been at my shoulder all night, reminding me of everything that needed to be done. Typically, the royals wouldn't be in charge of fundraising, but with this being my passion project, I wanted to be involved in every aspect.

"Start with Lord Browning. I hear he's wanting to diversify his charity holdings this year."

I nod, sipping on the champagne in my hand. It's an open bar, but I don't want to get pissed like I have been for the last few weeks. As I start making my way to the lord in question, whispers break out across the room. Can't I just go one night without some scandal?

"Your Highness. I would suggest heading to the press area. Miss Cross is here, and we don't want anything to happen tonight."

Zara's here? But how in the world did she know about this? The charity was only in the beginning stages when I talked to her last. Cutting a path through the crowds, my beautiful Zara is making her way into the room. The click of cameras is louder than anything else in the room.

Zara is wearing the dress. The same red dress she wore to the orchestra that night that hugs every curve and dip of her sexy body. Her long, dark waves fall around her shoulders. She's a life raft for someone who has been drowning in his own misery these last few weeks.

We invited the press tonight to help boost the visibility of the charity. Not that it wouldn't get out on its own, but I wanted the work we're doing to be covered here tonight as well.

"Zara! Where have you been hiding since the scandal broke?"

"Zara! Is it true you're addicted to sex?"

"Care to give your side of the scandal?"

Oh, for fuck's sake. Handing my glass to Charles, I head to Zara's side. She's stiff. She's not the easygoing Zara that I'm used to.

"Thank you all for coming. I appreciate you being here, but I need Miss Cross." I go to pull Zara away from the press, but her hand on my bicep has me stopping. Her eyes are clear. She gives me a small nod and turns to the press.

"Thank you all for being here to show your support for Prince James and his new charity, Sporting Kids." Zara's lips quirk up in the barest hint of a smile. Damn, she's giving me grief over the name too. Really not my best work.

"As for a statement, I will give one, and one only." Her fingers tighten on my arm, and I cover her hand with mine. "What was leaked to the press was a private moment between two people in love. It was a violation of our privacy, and the person who took those photos was trespassing on private property."

She turns to me, her eyes steely as I can see she's gearing up. "It was inappropriate for them to be released, and they should not have been cycled through the news. I hope more care is taken to spreading the good work that James is doing here tonight, and not illegally taken photos of us. Our focus will always be on the work we can do to better our country and our people, and not our private lives."

Damn. I don't think I've ever heard anyone put the press in their place better than that. The royal family is not one to give statements based on rumours or gossip they spread, but I know how hard it was on Zara being thrust into the spotlight. And this was her taking back control. My future Queen. I'm bursting with pride at the woman before me.

"Zara. What role will you play in the new charity?" She turns to me, her eyes now sparkling.

"That's up to the prince to decide."

"James?" A microphone is thrust my way.

I don't see who is talking to me. My sole focus is on Zara and that she's here tonight. That she stood up to the press, for herself. For both of us. That has to mean something, right?

"She'll have whatever role she wants. Now, if you'll excuse us." I take her warm hand in mine, leading her away from the press.

"What are you doing here?" I whisper, grabbing a glass of champagne for her from a passing waiter.

"I was told you might need some support tonight."

My heart swells. She came here for me. I don't want to read too much into it, but it's hard not to. "Fuck, it's good to see you, Zara." The words burst out before I can stop them.

She pulls on my arm, leading me away from the crowds. "We have a lot to discuss. Maybe I can come over tonight so we can talk?" Her voice is small.

"It's going to be a long night."

She shakes her head. "I don't care. I don't have anywhere to be tomorrow."

I wince. I know she was suspended from school, and I hate that. "Yes. I'll wait up all night if it means I can talk to you."

"Excuse me, Your Highness. But I was hoping I could have a word with you?" A tap on my shoulder breaks the moment between me and Zara.

"A prince's work is never done." She gives me a bright smile, telling me she's okay with me being pulled away.

"Save me a dance later?"

"I'll dance with no one but you."

Clutching my hand to my heart, I follow the man who wanted to talk to me, counting down the minutes until I can have Zara in my arms.

Zara

"Now before we turn you all loose for the rest of the evening, Prince James would like to say a few words."

My nerves have been getting the better of me all night. Sidelong glances from people here tell me they've all seen the pictures of us. I hate that a private moment between us was splashed across the news for the world to see.

But after talking with Ellie, I accepted it's part of this life. One that I knew I'd have to come to terms with if it meant keeping James. So I came here tonight, armed with a confidence I don't fully feel, and said my piece. The awe in James's eyes was worth it.

"Good evening." James clears his voice, looking out amongst the crowded room. His eyes settle on me. He takes a deep breath and turns back to the audience.

"I'm incredibly thankful that all of you came out here tonight to help launch Sporting Kids." Claps break through his speech. "It's been an interesting few months for us royals. I never thought I'd be the one to ascend the throne after my mum, and I'm sure not many of you thought that either."

People laugh at his self-deprecation. I only wince, knowing how those words ate away at him.

"It's the honour of a lifetime to serve this wonderful country. And in doing so, I wanted to follow my own passions in life. And that led me to Sporting Kids. After a visit to the new hospital wing in my grandfather's memory, I met the Smythson family, who were kind enough to join us this evening." They have a seat of honour at the table in front of the stage.

"As a child, it's hard being in hospital, and I wanted to make that easier for George. When his love of sport came to light, it gave me the idea for this charity. For children who are sick or are suffering, I want to give them the gift of sport. By working with national and local teams, we are hoping to have this program off the ground and throughout the country by next year. Because keeping kids' spirits up through the love of the game is something we can all agree on. Thank you."

Tears leak out of my eyes at James's beautiful words. His eyes find mine as he hops off the stage, giving George a high five. This incredible, wonderful, kind-hearted man. Why did I ever think I needed time from him?

James is pulled in different directions as people talk and ask him questions about the charity. The band starts to play as people head onto the dance floor.

"Lady Zara, may I have this dance?" Lord Paxton, the older man from the museum charity, is at my side. Pasting on my best smile, I accept his proffered arm.

"It would be a pleasure."

He guides me out onto the dance floor as couples spin and float around us.

"And how are you doing this fine evening, Lord Paxton?" My voice is sugary sweet. This man's ego loves to be inflated. "Did your lovely wife join you this evening?"

"She did. I believe she is off talking to some of the young footballers." Sounds about right.

"It was quite nice for James to have the support of the local London teams." James's eyes track mine, finding me across the dance floor. He excuses himself as he makes his way towards me.

"And your support. I thought you'd hide away after the scandal, but stiff upper lip and all. I'm pleased to see you two weathering the storm together."

"That's very kind of you to say." And I mean it. Instead of him leering at me like he did at the museum and like others have tonight, his show of support means more than I can say. An ally in a group of people who will become my peers.

"And you should know that James has my support with

Sporting Kids. However I can help. I hope for nothing but the best for you both."

"Thank you. We truly appreciate your support. And now if you don't mind, I think there's someone who would like to cut in." He turns to see James waiting patiently with his hands tucked into his pockets.

"Ahh. We shall not keep the prince waiting any longer. Your Highness." He dips into a bow as he kisses my hand.

"It was a pleasure, Lord Paxton." James steps in, his hand on me a comfort I've missed these last few weeks.

"I see you've taken quite easily to the schmoozing portion of the evening."

I give his hand a squeeze, tucking my chin on his shoulder. I love how evenly matched we are. "It's easy to sell schmooze when you believe in something wholeheartedly. You are going to do amazing things with Sporting Kids."

"Tell me the truth. You hate the name?" His laugh is hot on my cheek. It reverberates through my body.

"Is there still time to change it?"

"Guess I shouldn't make big life decisions when I'm bloody well pissed then, eh?"

My heart hurts at the thought. "And why were you drinking so much?"

James's warm hand slides up my back between my bare shoulders. Heat radiates from his touch. I've missed his touch. The way his face lights up when he sees me.

"Christ, I've missed you, Zara. Letting you walk out of my house was the worst mistake I've ever made."

"James, I—"

"Your Highness, we have a donor that would like to speak with you." Charles appears out of thin air at our side. James lets out a deep breath.

"To be continued?" he asks, his face lined with sadness.

"I'll meet you at your place later." Kissing my knuckles, he walks away.

This time, when he walks away, I don't worry it's going to be the last time. We didn't have the most normal start to our relationship. Most people meet and decide to date before wanting to get married. I was so against this whole arranged marriage, but now I can't imagine my life without James. And all I want is a future with him.

Chapter Twenty-Five

JAMES

It's late, after one in the morning. The kickoff event for Sporting Kids went better than I ever could have imagined. We raised more money than I thought possible, and the icing on the cake? Zara was there. I had no idea what it meant, but it was more than I could have hoped for.

A soft knock at the door has my palms sweating. A brick of nerves settles heavy in my stomach. I don't know what's going to happen, but Zara showing up tonight had to be a good thing, right?

"Zara." I open the door. Her long legs are bare beneath her trench coat. Her stride is purposeful as she walks by me into the living room. "Can I take your coat? Get you a drink?"

"Gin and tonic, please."

Mixing Zara her drink, I sit on the sofa. She's standing before me, finishing her drink in two gulps. Our combined nerves hang heavy in the air.

"Zara—"

She cuts me off. "Me first."

She comes and stands in front of me, running her

hands through my hair. Christ, that feels good. "I'm sorry I panicked after everything that happened. Nothing like that has ever happened to me before, and I didn't know what to do."

"And I'm sorry I didn't prepare you for something like that."

Her fingers cover my lips. "How could you have known something like that would've gotten out? It was such a violation of my privacy that I didn't know what to do. But I shouldn't have run away."

"But you weren't running away." My words are muffled against her hand.

"I was, I just didn't realize it at the time. But Ellie helped me see that instead of running, I should have leaned on you."

I'm shocked. "Ellie talked to you?" When they came to see me, I never thought she'd seek out Zara.

She nods. "You've been through this before. You know how to handle the press. And I ran scared instead of coming to you. No amount of time could ever get me prepared to handle the paparazzi." Her lips start to quiver. "By running, I was like every other woman who just wanted you for your name only."

"Zara, no. Absolutely not." Gripping her hips, I pull her between my legs. "Having your privacy violated like that isn't something anyone should have to worry about." I rest my head on her belly. "If it helps, we caught the guy. He paid off your neighbours to sneak onto their roof to take pictures."

She shakes her head. "I guess it's going to be hard to know who to trust in this life."

"Yes." I look up into her eyes. I don't want to lie to her. "It's going to be hard, and you'll stumble and make mistakes along the way. But I'll be there to help you. Right by your side, where I should've been to start with."

"I still don't think I'm prepared for this role, but I know you'll help me."

My breath catches. "Are you saying what I think you're saying?"

She smiles, her eyes shining with tears. "James, when our parents told us we were to be married, I never thought I'd fall in love with you. But I have. And there's no one else I want in this world. I know what it comes with. As long as we're together, we can weather any storm."

"Fuck, Zara." I drop my head to her stomach, pulling her close to me. Her hands are holding me there. For the first time in weeks, I can breathe easy. "I love you so damn much. These last few weeks have been bloody awful without you."

"Who would've thought that the two of us would've ended up here?" she asks.

Her fingers find my chin, tilting it upward. "Only us." She dips her head down, giving me a soft kiss. Fuck, I never thought I'd get to feel these lips again. I run my tongue along the seam of her lips, and she opens. Her gin-soaked lips are bliss. The velvety softness of her tongue has my cock hardening behind my joggers.

Pulling her onto my lap, my hands drift up her legs. The higher my hands go, the less material they encounter.

"Zara, love?"

"Yes?" I can feel her smiling against my lips.

"Are you wearing anything under this coat?"

"Why don't you find out?" She sits back on my thighs, the belt of her coat drawing my attention. Untying it, the sides fall loose at her side. A small swath of fabric covering her beautiful pussy is the only thing she's wearing. Her tits and hard nipples are on display for me.

"Fuck me."

"That's the point."

Slipping her arms out of the coat, I lift her into my arms, carrying her up the stairs to my room. Her lips are trailing a hot path up and down my neck. I'm ready to combust if I don't get her under me.

Throwing her on the bed, I slip out of my T-shirt and sweats. My dick is tenting my briefs. I crawl towards her on the bed, her heated gaze drawing me in. My world revolves around this woman. She's the sun, and I'm helpless to do anything but spin around her.

"Are you just going to stare at me, or are you going to fuck me?"

"Are you trying to kill me?" My voice is filled with heat and need.

Kissing my way up her legs, I rip that tiny excuse for underwear off her in one pull.

"Gah!" Her pussy is glistening with need as I swipe a finger through her folds. Zara arches into my touch. Goose pimples break out on her skin as I lower my lips to her clit. Pressing her legs wide, I lavish attention on her pussy. Licking and sucking on the tight bundle of nerves, I press two fingers into Zara's tight channel. Her walls are already pulsing with need.

"That feels incredible." Zara's voice is greedy as her hands grip my hair. The sting of pleasure has me finding friction on the bed. I can't wait to be in her tight heat. "I'm so close."

Pulling off her, I leave her riding the edge of orgasm. "I want to feel you come on my cock, Zara."

"No condoms."

"What did I do to deserve you?" Dragging my fingers down her flushed cheeks, I stare at her. If someone had told me a few months ago that I would have met my future wife, I would've said they were crazy. But somehow, we found our way to each other.

Shucking my boxer briefs, I settle over her. Notching myself at her entrance, I slide in slowly, savouring the feel of her heat around me. It takes everything I have not to explode inside of her. Her legs move up my hips, holding me in place as I wrap my arms around her.

I don't want any space between us. There's not a breath of air separating us. I've never been so close to a woman. I've never felt more connected to someone in my life. This woman is everything to me.

"You going to get moving there?" Zara's fingers trail down my back, fire in their wake. The slightest touch from her lights me up from the inside out.

Pulling out, I set a steady pace. Diamond hard nipples brush my chest on every stroke. My own release is racing down my spine. Need is coiling tight as I try to stave off my orgasm as Zara gets closer.

"Kiss me."

I didn't think it could get any better, but this kiss is everything. Fuck, it's the greatest kiss of my life. It's messy. It's needy. We're pouring every single emotion we're feeling into this kiss. I can't believe I thought I could do without this woman in my life.

"I'm so close, Z. You need to come." My thrusts are erratic as Zara's legs tighten around me. Whimpers escape from her lips, as I free an arm to find her clit. A ghost of a touch on that tiny bundle of nerves sets her off. Her pulsing around me is the greatest heaven I've ever known.

"Fuck." I groan out my own orgasm, pulsing deep inside her. Our lips graze each other as we savour the moment of being together again. To think, I almost lost this woman.

I go to pull out, but Zara keeps me locked in place.

"Not yet." Her hands are soft on my neck, tracing my frantic pulse. She clasps me to her, the soft pillows of her breasts the best place to land.

Dropping a kiss on the side of her chest, I slowly pull out of her. Getting up to go to the bathroom, I grab a warm washcloth to clean her up. A lazy smile dances on her lips.

"Would it be too cheesy to give you something right now?" I ask as my fingers trace circles on her stomach.

"What could you possibly need to give me after the best orgasm of my life?" Her eyes are closed, a sated look on her face.

I don't say anything, just throw on my sweats and go to grab my surprise for her. "I've been meaning to give this back to you for a few weeks now, but with everything that happened, I was a little lost."

Zara grabs my shirt and puts it on, the hem flirting with the tops of her legs. Taking the box, she pierces me with a puzzled look before taking the lid off.

"You didn't." Her hand is covering her mouth as she tearfully gazes at her violin. And not just any violin, but her most cherished one. Her mother's. "You replaced it?"

I shake my head. "No. I spoke with the company, and they were able to repair it."

Her eyes fly up to meet mine. A war of emotions is playing out in her soulful gaze. "But how? You just can't repair an instrument like this." Her hands are running over the wood and strings in a loving manner.

"I wasn't above dropping my name to get what I needed."

Setting it to the side, she stands, wrapping her arms around me. "I don't know what I did to deserve you."

"In your defence, you wouldn't have needed to replace it if you hadn't met me."

She pinches my side. "Such a smart arse."

I release my hold on her, not wanting to let her go, but wanting to hear something more. "Play for me?"

"Anything for you, my love."

I clutch my hand to my chest. I love hearing those words from her. She grabs the bow and stands before me. Light sparkles in her eyes as she starts playing. It's soulful, deep. It starts to pick up and gets more playful in the middle before taking on a sad tone again. I don't recognize it, but it touches me. I never understood music before, but Zara's love for it is infectious. She pours everything she has into the music she makes.

The piece turns happy again as Zara moves with the song. My heart catches in my chest as tears stream down Zara's cheeks. Her eyes are closed as the final note is played. There are no words for the beauty of that song. For as long as I live, I will remember this moment. Zara, looking like a goddess in my T-shirt and mussed hair, playing this beautiful song for me. And only me.

Taking the instrument from her hands, I set it down with the utmost care. Knowing the value of this violin, I don't want to take any chances with it. I pull her into my arms.

"What's the name of that song?" I want to lock in every part of this memory. I'll be old and grey and still remember this song she played for me.

"It's called James."

"James?" My brows are furrowed in confusion.

She tucks her head under my chin, wrapping her arms around me. "For the last few months, I've been trying to write music, but nothing has been coming to me. Even these last few weeks, bits and pieces were there, but always out of reach. Until today."

"And what happened today?" I squeeze her closer to me.

"Today I realized what true love is. The hard times. The fun times. The sexy times. And I get to experience all of that with the man I love."

I have to take a few steadying breaths so my emotions don't overwhelm me. "No one has ever done something so wonderful for me."

Zara turns to look at me. "You're worth it, James. Don't you ever doubt it. And if you do, I'll always be here to remind you. You're worth everything that comes with this life. Not the title. Not a way to get ahead in life, but you."

"That's music to my ears."

Chapter Twenty-Six

ZARA - TWO MONTHS LATER

I don't think I've ever been so nervous in my life. My palms are sweaty as my stomach roils.

"Is everyone ready? We'll be starting in just a few minutes." My students barely give me a second look. I can't be the only one who feels like they're going to pass out.

"Miss Cross, Prince James will introduce you, and then you'll give your speech before the show starts."

"Thank you, Alice." After everything that happened with the scandal, James and I decided I should start my own charity work. Instead of going back to school, I dove headfirst into launching my own foundation. Alice, Ellie's old advisor, was assigned to me in my new role. And with James by my side, it's gone better than I thought.

"Thank you everyone for joining us this evening. It is my great honour to introduce the head of the newest royal patronage, Lady Zara Cross."

Leaving my students on the stage, I join James out front. "Good luck. You'll do great." He gives me a peck on the cheek as I turn to face the crowd. Taking a deep breath, I start my speech.

"Thank you everyone for being here tonight. I'm thrilled to have you here at the launch of my new foundation, The Power of Music. As a former music teacher at the Hammersmith Conservatory, I know firsthand the power of music. I've seen how it can impact the lives of students and those around them." The spotlight is bright, blurring all the faces in front of me.

"My hope with The Power of Music is that we can bring music to those who wouldn't otherwise have access to it. Not just in London, but throughout the United Kingdom. And with your support, it will not only help children gain confidence, but skills to take them further in life than they ever thought possible."

Applause breaks out. "And on that note, I would like to introduce the secondary orchestra from the Hammersmith School to play for you this evening."

I leave the podium and head to the stage, the curtains now drawn. My students are all sitting, ready with their instruments. I lift my baton, and everyone sits up straight as the melody starts. All my nerves of the evening fade away. The piece is the one we were working on for the end of term concert that I never got to participate in. Even just this small event makes it worthwhile.

The students have never sounded better than they do tonight. My face is glowing as the song comes to an end. Happy, smiling faces are staring back at me. I couldn't be prouder of them than I am right now. I give them a thumbs-up as I turn to bow towards the audience. Raucous applause greets me.

One of the other conductors from the school comes on stage. As I'm off to wine and dine all of our guests, she'll take over the music portion of the evening.

Heading backstage, I let out a deep breath.

"Z! That was magnificent." James sweeps me into his arms. He swings me around, laughter bubbling out of me.

"I just don't know what to say." His eyes are alight with love and happiness. "I've never been so nervous in my life, but it went so much better than I thought."

James's lips crash down on mine. The love he gives me on a daily basis is unmatched. I love him more than life itself.

"Are you ready to get out there and win them over?" James drops his forehead to mine, his lips giving me another quick kiss.

"James." I grab him before he starts to pull me out to the main hall. "I couldn't have done this without you."

The love shining out of his eyes mirrors my own. "You did it all on your own. This is just the beginning for you, Zara." James squeezes me to him. "Everyone is going to fall in love with you. Just like I did."

I drag my fingers down his jaw, tracing over his kiss-swollen lips. "You were easy. They might be harder to win over."

"C'mon. Let's go win them over."

James

ZARA'S big night couldn't have gone better for her. The performance was incredible. Everyone was fighting to get a word with Zara. I was forgotten, and I couldn't be happier about it. And I hope the night will only get better now that we're home.

Zara hasn't officially moved in—heaven forbid two adults cohabitate—but we spend the majority of our time together.

"James. Why am I blindfolded?" I'm leading Zara through the dark gardens. There's some light from the park, but it's quiet back here.

"Just wait." My hands on her waist, I guide her towards the sunken garden surrounding the apartments here. Finding the spot, I stop and pull the blindfold off.

Her eyes go wide at the scene in front of her. A blanket is laid out before us, a bottle of champagne chilling. "What is all of this?" Awe is in her voice.

"You had this incredible night, and we need to celebrate you." I take her hand, sitting down on the blanket. I pull her between my legs as I pop open the bubbly.

"You are too much sometimes." She turns in my arms, leaning on my leg.

"Z. I am so fucking proud of you." My voice catches. It's hard to put into words just how proud of her I really am. "You shone like the brightest star tonight."

She closes her eyes as I drop a kiss on her temple. My nerves are starting to get the better of me. I take a large gulp of champagne.

"I can't wait to see how much money we raised tonight. I'm so happy that I get to do this." She looks at me, love filling her eyes. "I couldn't have done it without you."

"Bollocks. You didn't need me at all."

"Whatever you want to tell yourself." She sips at her champagne.

I take the glass from her hand, turning to face her. "Zara, there's something I want to ask you."

Her eyes widen. "Okay."

I take her hand, warm in mine in the cool London night. "I love you more than life itself. When our parents introduced us, I never thought I would fall in love with you, but I did. Hopelessly. I saw what my life would be like without you, and I never want to be without you."

Tears are glittering in her eyes.

"I want to wake up to you every day. I want to have kids with you. I want to support everything you do. I want to go to bed with you every night." I pull the ring from my pocket. Not the ring I picked out from the vault, but a ring given to me by my grandmum. "Zara Cross, will you make me the happiest man on earth and marry me?"

Zara leaps into my arms, crashing her lips down on mine. Her tongue licks at the seam of my mouth, and I open to her immediately. Love and passion swirl around us in the night.

"Is that a yes, love?"

She smacks me in the chest. "Of course, yes!"

I pull the ring out of the box and slide it on her finger. "James, it's absolutely gorgeous."

She holds her hand out in front of her face.

"It's from my grandmum. It was what Granddad proposed with." The ring isn't extravagant but has three stones set on a gold band. Nothing over-the-top, but perfect for Zara.

"If we have half the love they do, we're going to be just fine."

"That we are, love. That we are."

Epilogue

ZARA - FIVE MONTHS LATER

I hardly slept a wink last night. Butterflies threatened to overtake me anytime I thought about today. It is the day people have been looking forward to since James and I announced our engagement a few short months ago.

"You doing alright?" Charlotte's voice brings me back to the hotel room we're occupying before the service.

"Little nervous." My voice is quiet as I run my hands over my dress.

"Any second thoughts?" Marnie's voice is filled with laughter. "If he really isn't up to snuff,"—she waggles her pinkie in my direction—"you can back out now."

"Gross. Things I don't want to know about my brother." Ellie's pacing the room, swinging her new bundle of joy in her arms.

"You look stunning. James isn't going to know what hit him." Charlotte clasps my hand in hers, settling my nerves. "I don't know how anyone will ever compare to you."

I look in the mirror. The high-necked embroidered gown with cap sleeves is perfect. It hugs every curve before the skirt fans out around my hips. The veil covering my face has elements from all the countries of the commonwealth woven in. The tiara, loaned to me by the Queen, completes the ensemble. In short, I look like a Princess.

I don't know how my designer managed to create this masterpiece in a matter of a few months, but it's everything I dreamed it would be. James and I moved fast. After he proposed to me after the launch of my charity, we thought a winter wedding would be perfect. We had joked we'd be getting married fast when this whole arrangement started. And now, we didn't want to wait another second to start our lives together.

A knock at the door has everyone quieting down. The wedding coordinator pops her head in the suite. "The carriages are here. Are you ready?"

"We'll be down in a moment."

She looks down at her clipboard. "We need to leave in five minutes to stay on schedule." Her lips are drawn tight.

"They won't start without her. We'll be down in a moment." The Queen dismisses her. "Girls, would you mind heading downstairs? I'd like a moment alone with Zara."

"You look beautiful. Don't let her scare you off," Ellie whispers in my ear as she follows Charlotte and Marnie out the door. It shuts with a soft click.

"I know we need to get downstairs, but I didn't want you to leave without giving you a small something." She pulls a long, velvet box out of her bag that sits on the bed.

Opening it, I find a diamond halo bracelet in white gold. A gasp escapes my throat. "This is beautiful."

"May I?" She takes it out as I extend my hand to her. "My father gave it to me on my wedding, and I would like you to have it today."

Tears glisten in my eyes as I try to hold back my emotions of receiving such a thoughtful gift. "I will cherish this. Thank you." I spin my wrist, the light catching the diamonds from the sun shining in through the window.

"Thank you for being the woman my son needs." She cups my cheeks. "I know most people don't know how the two of you met, but you are the epitome of strength and grace. It will be many years to come, but you will be the Queen James needs at his side when the time comes. And I rest easy knowing that you two have each other to take on all that this life throws at you."

A single tear trickles out, carving a hot path down my cheek. "Thank you for saying that. I love James with all that I am. Whatever is thrown at us, I'll be ready." Hearing those words from her means more than I could ever say.

She sucks in a deep breath, trying to calm her own emotions. "Come now. We best get downstairs. I don't want to be blamed for your makeup being messed up on a day like today."

I let out a bark of laughter. "She is rather scary, isn't she?"

"All good wedding planners are. Now, let's get you to the church."

"YOU READY, DARLING?" Dad's voice is barely audible over the cheers as I step out of the carriage at the entrance to the abbey. The ride from the hotel to the church took no time at all. My cheeks hurt from the smile pasted on my face. The wedding planner told me hundreds of times that any break in my face would be captured on film for the entire world to see.

"As I'll ever be."

I give a small wave to everyone outside the church, and

cheers explode from the crowd. I take Dad's hand as we prepare to walk into the church. Marnie's behind me, fluffing out the back of my dress. She gives me a wink as we start to walk inside. The noise of the crowd dies out as soon as the heavy wooden doors close. As the music starts, everyone stands.

I don't recognize half the people here. Nods and bows are directed my way as we make our way down the aisle. We practised this only last night, but it didn't feel so endless then. When we make it to the archway, dissecting the church, James finally comes into view. He's wearing his military uniform today, his hair slicked back.

He's never looked more perfect to me than he does right now. I start to walk faster, but Dad slows me down. "You'll get there soon enough, darling." I turn to face him and see tears in his eyes. "Just let me have one more moment with my daughter before the entire world gets you."

I stop, right there in the middle of the aisle, and wrap my arms around him. "I'll always be your little girl."

He squeezes me a little harder before pulling back. "I know your mother would love James." His voice breaks a little, as I hold on just a little tighter.

"Come now, time to get you to your groom. He's looking a little antsy." James is rocking side to side as I catch his eye. He gives me a smile.

Linking my arm through my dad's, we make it to James. "Take care of each other." Dad clasps James's hand before giving me a kiss on the cheek. He goes to take his seat as James takes my hand.

"You think you could speed it up next time? I've been waiting here all day."

"Sorry. I'll be sure to hurry it along the next time we

get married." I squeeze his hand as the minister calls everyone to be seated.

Now to make it through the next hour without fainting and I'll be okay.

James

"HOW DO YOU FEEL, my darling wife?" We finally have a quiet moment on the dance floor. It's been a whirlwind of a day. From the moment I saw Zara walking towards me, I've been in a state of pure bliss. She looks like an angel, unlike anything I've ever seen before in my life.

From the carriage ride through the city, to our very public kiss on the balcony with people screaming from the streets, it's been nothing but insanity. But insanity of the best kind.

"Hmm, I'm kind of hoping we get to leave on our honeymoon soon."

I twirl a loose lock of hair around my finger. "Oh yeah?"

She tucks her face into my neck, dropping a kiss there. "We've been around people all day. I'm ready for it to just be the two of us."

I spin her away from me, pulling her back in a dip. "Only a little while longer, my love."

I haven't left her side today. After a huge party for all the foreign dignitaries, we came to Clarence House for a smaller gathering of family and friends. One that I'm ready to cut and run from.

"It has been a pretty spectacular day." Zara is glowing.

"That it has, my beautiful wife." I can't get enough of it. Calling Zara my wife. I never thought the day would come, but here I am. I'd lay down my life for this woman.

"Excuse me. Prince James. Princess Zara. The fireworks are about to begin and then you can take your leave." Charles is at our shoulder. Zara beams at him.

"Thank you." I tuck her hand in mine, following the guests outside. "I believe that is the first time someone has called you princess."

"You would be correct." She wraps her arm around my waist as Marnie hands her the fur stole to keep warm. The temperature has dropped, but it cools my heated skin. Everywhere we've been today, people upon people have been congratulating us and wishing us well.

As we step out onto the balcony, fireworks burst into the dark February sky. Oohs and aahs echo around us. Pulling Zara in front of me, I wrap her in my arms, resting my chin on her shoulder. She leans into my touch.

"You know, I never imagined my wedding day would be like this."

"Oh yeah?" I ghost my lips along her ear. It's been too long since I've been able to touch her how I want. We've spent the last few nights apart while the final preparations were done for the wedding. Several people told us it would be crass if people saw either one of us leaving the other's home in the morning. We knew it, but we didn't like it.

"I thought it would be just a few close family and friends. Nothing broadcast all over the world for everyone to see."

"Any regrets?"

"Not a one." My heart picks up as the fireworks continue to explode across the London sky. "This was better than I ever could have dreamed."

"I never thought I'd get married, but then you came along. I couldn't have wished for a better person if I tried."

She laughs, the sound warming me from the inside out. "Not bad for an arranged marriage, huh?"

No, not bad at all.

The End

Want to find out what James and Zara are up to? Signup for my newsletter for an exclusive bonus epilogue!

Be sure to check out Royal Roots…a continuation of James and Zara's story now!

And join my Facebook reader group to stay up to date on all the news!

Author Note

Book four is officially out in the world! I absolutely loved writing James and Zara and hope you love them as much as I do!

It never ceases to amaze me how amazing the romance community is. All the love and support from this community keeps me going! And to my Accountability Tribe… Norma and AK…you two are amazing and keep me laughing on the days where I want to cry!

To the best beta readers…Audrey and Tara…thank you for helping me make this book what it is! To my ARC team…thank you for all the love and support you give me.

And to all the amazing readers out there…thank you for picking up my book and helping make all my author dreams come true!

xo, Emily

Royal Relations

AN AINSWORTH ROYALS NOVEL

ROYAL
Relations

EMILY SILVER

TRAVELIN' HOOSIER BOOKS

Prologue

CHARLOTTE

"You made it!" Ellie wraps her arms around me as I rush into the sitting room at the palace.

"Sorry I'm late. Lost track of time working."

"I'm just happy you were able to come." Ellie loops her arm through mine and pulls me farther into the crowded room.

"I thought you said this was going to be a small celebration."

Ellie rolls her eyes. "Sean's mum planned everything, and then my mum sort of took over."

"As she does. But it does look pretty good in here."

Flowers decorate all the surfaces in the family room in the palace. A table is overflowing with gifts in the corner. "Presents? I thought you didn't want any."

I turn my gaze back to Ellie. Her pink hair is braided around her head. She's wearing a long, white dress that clings to her baby bump. She's absolutely glowing.

"I didn't. Sean and I need nothing, but everyone brought something." Ellie's eyes shift to find Sean. He's standing next to someone I haven't seen before, but the stranger's eyes pull me in. Bright blue eyes that are filled with laughter. White teeth hidden behind plump lips.

"Who is that—" I'm cut off.

"Charlotte. I'm so pleased you could join us today." Aunt Katherine, better known as the Queen, pulls me in for a hug.

"I just can't believe Ellie is having a baby." I squeeze Ellie's shoulder. As cousins near the same age, she's been one of my closest friends for as long as I can remember. "I can't wait to meet this little baby."

"I just wish we knew what she was having." Katherine gives Ellie a look.

"Mum. You'll meet them soon enough," Ellie reminds her.

"Katherine. Stop bothering Eleanor." My mum appears at my side. "Hello, darling."

"Hi, Mum." I give her a quick side hug as a server with champagne walks by.

"Just you wait until Charlotte begins having kids. It will drive you just as crazy."

I choke over my sip of champagne at Aunt Katherine's words. "I'm not even dating someone. Let's not talk about that."

"Better you than me," Ellie laughs.

"I'm sure they'll be asking when baby number two will pop out before long."

The mystery man crosses my view, talking to James and Zara. My mum and Aunt Katherine get carried away into a conversation about the baby and who will have another child first. A conversation only mums can have.

"Who's that talking with James and Zara?" I whisper over the top of my drink to Ellie. No need to broadcast who I'm looking at.

"Who, Pierce? That's Sean's brother."

It's as if he hears his name. Pierce turns and looks over at Ellie and me. A small smile plays on his lips. Flutters erupt deep in my belly, something I haven't felt in a long time.

Before I can make my way over to him, my attention is pulled away and he's gone.

I need to meet this man.

Chapter One

CHARLOTTE

"I'm sorry, Your Highness, but it's just not possible."

I give my advisor, Jasper, a blank stare. "Why is wanting to create a charity to help women not possible?" I keep my voice even.

"The Queen thought it would step on too many toes." Jasper doesn't give me a passing glance as he moves to the next item on today's agenda. "You have lunch with the new Canadian ambassador next week, and tomorrow—"

"I'm sorry." I throw my hand out to stop him. "What does she mean by that?"

"Only that your proposal to start a new women's charity covers too much." His voice is dismissive. He's not even looking at me.

"Can you get more information?"

Jasper gives me a piercing look. I guess that answers that question. I don't hear another word of what's said. Wanting to help women would step on too many toes? Cover too much? I fight the eye roll that wants to come with being told no. It seems like anything I try to do these days is met with resistance.

Being in my position is a privilege, and one I don't take lightly. I love being able to do the work I do. But lately, it's been draining. Wanting to start my own charity to help women is something I'm passionate about. It's frustrating that I'm shot down with little explanation.

A knock on the door pulls my attention away from Jasper. "Excuse me. Can I steal Charlotte away?" Zara's head pops in through the door.

"Absolutely. Thank you for your time, Jasper. I hope you'll get me more information from the Queen, as this is something I want to pursue." I give him a withering stare, but it gets me nowhere.

"Thank God. I was in need of a rescue," I say as soon as we're out of my office. I link my arm through Zara's. "And why are my services required today?"

I'm nearly a head shorter than Zara, even in heels. I loved my cousin James's fiancée, Zara, immediately. With his twin, Ellie, renouncing her place in line to the throne, it's nice to have someone in the battlefield with me. If you want to call it that.

"James ended up going to Wales for the day for an event for Sporting Kids and left wedding tastings to me."

"Well, his loss is my gain. Are we tasting desserts?"

Zara laughs as we make our way down to the kitchens. We both have offices here at the palace. With James taking over more responsibility, he wanted Zara close by. Since we all work together, my office was moved here as well. It's nice to get to see her as often as I do.

"Please. The cake has been decided on for months. Apparently that takes much more skill than cooking the meal. We're tasting our dinner options today."

I shrug. "Still better than what I had planned for the rest of the afternoon."

We make our way down to the study overlooking the

gardens where lunch is being served. The kitchen staff is already bustling around, making sure everything is perfect.

"Your Highness. I didn't realize you'd be joining us." The head chef curtsies to me.

"James is otherwise busy today, so I figured it'd be helpful to have a second opinion."

"Excellent, Lady Zara. I'll bring over the first option and get your wine pairings."

"Remind me to thank James the next time I see him." My day had been droning on. Seeing the good work that James and Zara are doing with their charities makes me want to carve out my own space in the world. I don't want to be content doing what the Queen hands me, but it appears that's all I'm good for.

"Seems you could use a good distraction," Zara states matter-of-factly as the wine is poured and dishes are set before us with a flourish.

"For our starter, we have two options. Your guests may choose between marinated salmon, crab, and langoustines served atop a fresh herb salad, and quenelles served in a lobster sauce. Both pair well with the Sauvignon Blanc that you have now."

I nod to the waiter as he scurries away. "Cheers, Zara."

The wine is refreshingly crisp on this dreary London day. "Just what I needed," Zara remarks. "Now, tell me why you need distracting."

"God, this food is the perfect distraction. This salad is incredible," I moan around the tongs of my fork. The marinade on this salmon is delicious.

Zara gives me her teacher look. The one that used to scare her students into obeying her every word.

"I was told no on my charity idea."

Zara slumps back in her chair, taking a large sip of wine. "She said no?"

I nod. "All I got from Jasper is that I was trying to cover too much."

"You want to help too many people?" Her voice is as angry as I feel. "That's a load of bollocks."

I snort into my glass. "You are starting to sound just like James."

A blush creeps over Zara's face. "What can I say? He does rub off on you."

If I didn't like Zara so much, I'd be jealous of the happiness she's found with James. I thought I'd found my happily ever after with my last boyfriend, Michael, but he couldn't stand the spotlight. It's been two years of going to events on my own and seeing all my friends from uni fall in love and get married.

Not as if that's the only thing I want in my life. But lately, it seems that something is missing. I was hoping this charity would fill that void, but even that is a closed door for me.

"Would you want to help me with my patronage?" Zara spears a piece of crab into her mouth. "Oh my God. This is incredible. This is definitely going on the menu."

"I would fight you if you didn't include it." I sigh, taking a sip of my wine. "But no, I don't want to be a part of your charity. You and James are already doing such good work. I was hoping to have something of my own that could do the same."

Zara leans across the table, taking my hand in hers. "But you already are doing good work. The people love you. Do you know I was most scared that I couldn't live up to you?"

"That's just crazy." I shake my head, taking another sip of wine.

"It's true. I know Ellie was first in line, but the people love you. Don't sell yourself short."

Royal Relations

This is why I love Zara. She's one of the kindest, most caring people I know, and I couldn't be happier for her and James.

Servers come to clear our plates, and the chef brings out the next course.

"For the first meal option, we have a Chardonnay paired with a lobster mousse stuffed chicken with seared asparagus on the side. Please make note of anything you like or don't like, and we can adapt the food accordingly."

Zara clinks her fresh glass to mine. "Have you thought of maybe trying to focus more on women in the charities you do currently have?"

I shake my head as I take a large bite of the chicken in front of me. "How does the kitchen come up with these meals? I'd gain a stone in a week if I ate such decadent food every day."

"I let them have free rein. If it were up to me, James and I would get married in our backyard, but that can't happen."

"You know you'll be the most beautiful bride there is. I can't wait to see your dress."

A smile lights up Zara's face. "Oh, Charlotte. I really do love it. I thought I would hate having to choose a specific designer, but I fell in love the moment I saw the dress." She points her fork at me. "Nice try trying to distract me."

I sip my wine, giving her a coy look over the glass. "I thought I had you. Most of my charities right now don't really apply to women. I wish I could make them, but they focus on kids, and I love those too much to give them up."

"Well, I don't think you should stop trying. Just because the Queen says no, does that really mean no?"

Zara and I lock eyes before laughter bubbles out of both of us. "Good one, Zara."

The chef is back at our side. "For the second meal option, we have a rich Cabernet Sauvignon served with lamb and seasonal vegetables."

Zara and I chat, passing the time during each tasting. By the time the third course comes out, Zara and I are giddy from the wine.

"Will we get to have all this wine with dinner?"

"You know we can't!" Zara says on a hiccup.

"It would make the day that much more enjoyable."

"It's going to be enjoyable because I get to marry James and then we can shag all we want because we're living together." Zara's laughter is masked by her hand going to her mouth. "Oh, bugger. I didn't mean to say that."

"Things I don't want to hear."

"I'll gladly hear all about yours once you find a beautiful man to bed." She clinks her glass a little too hard against mine. "What about Oliver? You could fancy him."

I try to keep in the laugh, but it's hard. "Ollie, James's friend from uni? Are you serious? I wouldn't touch him in a hazmat suit. He's worse than James."

Zara winces, and I speak quickly to apologize. "Sorry. I'd kill to have someone look at me the way James looks at you." James was the biggest playboy of all not long ago. But now, he's the happiest I've ever seen him with Zara.

"Much better. Don't worry. I'm determined to find you a proper man."

I can only shake my head.

It'd be easier finding Neverland than a man who would want to take on the royal life.

"Thanks, Zara, but I think I'll pass."

"And what's your alternative? Moping around the palace? You look miserable."

I stab the remainder of the lamb on my plate. "Gee, thanks. Just what every girl wants to hear."

"Sorry, but have you ever considered taking a break? You look exhausted. I know you've been pushing yourself since Ellie renounced her spot in line to the throne."

"As much as I would love a holiday, I could never get one right now. Not after the way Ellie left."

Zara gives me a shocked look. "You mean they wouldn't just let anyone run away again?"

Laughter bubbles out of me, bringing me out of my sombre mood. "I guess you'll just have to make do with having me and my mopey self around."

"Well, if it means I get to drink wine and eat indulgent food with you throughout the day, then I'll keep you around."

Chapter Two

PIERCE

"Goal!" Liam runs around the pitch, pumping his arms.

"What the fuck, Hunter?" I glare at our goalie. "My grandmum could have blocked that shot."

He flips me the bird. "Why don't you come play goalkeeper and then we'll see just how good you are."

"Got your knickers in a twist because you're losing?" Liam drapes his arm over my shoulder.

I shove him off. "Just you wait. We'll come back and finish you off."

"I'd like to see you try, Davies." He jogs back to the centre of the pitch, getting ready to take the ball.

Fucker. Liam comes at me dribbling the ball. He tries to fake me out, but I don't bite. I steal the ball from him and take off down the field, his cursing following behind me.

On a breakaway, I don't hesitate to shoot. The goalie has no chance of blocking my shot as it sails into the back of the net.

"Fuck, yeah!" My team is cheering on the sidelines.

"You're acting like you just won the World Cup for England." Bitterness coats Liam's voice.

"Oh, I'm sorry. Are you being a sore loser?" I mock a whiny voice to him.

Liam and I have been playing football together for years. We met during a pick-up game and have been best mates ever since.

"Don't get so cocky over there. Still plenty of time left in the game." Liam flips me off as we take our positions.

The game continues at a fast pace. Guys switch out on and off the pitch. It's a relaxed game. We don't have a lot of the same rules as the big leagues. We're just playing for the fun of it. I've met some of my best mates out here.

The ball bounces back to me, but I lose control, nearly wiping out when Liam comes out of nowhere.

"You fucker!" I yell, chasing him down the pitch. He gets an easy shot on goal, but Hunter blocks it with ease.

"Yes! Take that!" I give him a shove as I go to congratulate Hunter. He sails the ball out of the box towards the other end of the field.

"Get your head in the game, Davies. We need to beat these arseholes." He pushes me back into the game, and I can only shake my head at him.

God, I love being out here with these guys. Whenever anything is going wrong in life, this is the distraction I need. Running around like a kid, playing the game I love.

"I CAN'T BELIEVE you wankers won," Liam chokes out into his beer. The local pub across from our small pitch is always our post-game hangout spot. Half the time, the waitresses comp our drinks.

Royal Relations

"You're lucky we don't play for tattoos. Can you imagine inking Hunter's face on your arse?" I snort over my beer.

"Dude. That's not even funny." Horror mars his face.

"Anyone would be lucky to have this mug marked on them for life." Hunter, with his curly blond hair and bright blue eyes, could be a model. No one actually knows what he does.

"It'd scare my girl off anytime we fucked."

"Ahh, Liam. I think we've discovered the reason you don't have a girlfriend."

He pierces me with a questioning stare. "Because I'm so handsome, they would die of pleasure?"

"Because you're a wanker who says things like 'anytime we fucked.'"

Liam shrugs his shoulders. "I'm not ready to be tied down and become a miserable old sod. Too many beautiful women in London."

"You lads doing all right?" The waitress comes by, dropping off another round of drinks. Even though we didn't order them. This is why we keep coming back here.

"Doing better now that you're here." Liam winks at her.

"Don't piss where you eat, mate." I slap him upside the head.

She walks away, shaking her head. "What if she's my soulmate and you just ruined my chance with her?"

Hunter coughs out the gulp of beer he just took. "Don't make me laugh. If she's your soulmate, then I'll bloody be married to Princess Charlotte next year."

A bark of laughter escapes me. "Oh, like you could date a princess."

"Your brother managed to snag one."

"How my brother ever got a princess to fall in love with him, I'll never know."

Ellie, formerly Princess Eleanor, ran away from royal life and straight into my brother's tattoo shop. No one had any idea who she was. Dying one's hair pink tends to do that. But after Sean discovered who she was when her grandfather passed, she renounced her place in line for the throne and is now happily expecting a baby with my brother. I've never seen him so damn happy.

"If there's hope for him, there's hope for us all." Hunter raises his glass in cheers.

"Except Pierce. He's going to end up moving back to the country and living with his mummy."

"Fuck off, you wanker." I snag Liam's beer, draining it before he has the chance. "As much fun as hanging out with you lot is, I'm heading home. I've got an early appointment tomorrow."

"Aww, finally going to see a doctor about your tiny dick?" Hunter joins in on giving me shit now.

"Remind me why I'm friends with you?" I flip them both off, before slapping their backs. "See you next week for drinks?"

They raise their glasses as I head out into the cold London night.

"SO YOU LIKE THE DESIGN?" I show the cover-up piece I've been working on for the last week to the man in my chair. When the old guy came into the shop, he was looking for Sean, but got me instead. I shouldn't let it bother me like it does, but everyone always wants my brother. He runs one of the best tattoo shops in all of

London. But sometimes, it feels like I'm playing second fiddle to him.

"Damn. You do some great work, kid. Are we good to get started?"

"Absolutely. This is going to look great."

I get to work, readying my station. For someone who feels like he gets lost in his brother's shadow, choosing to go into the same line of work as him was odd. But when Sean gave himself his first tattoo, I was hooked. I've been learning about the art of tattooing ever since.

And cover-ups have become my favourite. What people wanted at one point in their life and what they want now is always cool to see. Sometimes, I'm covering up some fucked-up shit. Other times, old girlfriends' names. I've even covered up a few mum tattoos. Those are always awkward.

"You coming over tonight?" Sean's voice pulls me away from the work at hand. The person I'm tattooing doesn't even notice. His heavy breaths tell me he's asleep. The big burly man has no qualms about needles. Looking at the clock, a few hours have gone by. This is why I love what I do. I can get lost in the work.

"Why do I need to come over tonight?" I wipe the excess ink away, tracing the needle over the stencil.

"Because Ellie and I need to talk to you."

"And if I have plans?"

He doesn't say anything until I glance up at him. His arms are crossed over his chest. "Cancel them. This is important."

I huff out a breath, pulling the needle away from the body laid out before me. "Fucking hell. I'll say yes if you piss off and let me work."

"Ouch, someone's in a grouchy mood," Trevor pipes

up from the booth beside me. Christ. I love working with these two guys, but some days they wear me out.

"Why are you in such a mood?" Sean leans against the wall of my space in the studio. Sean doesn't want to hear about staying out too late after football. He's all loved up at home while some of us still enjoy hitting the pubs.

"Would you two leave him alone?" Pink shoos them away. Her bright pink hair, hence the nickname, is plaited over one shoulder. Trevor goes back to his own work while Sean lingers over Ellie. She's seven months pregnant, and he worries over her. She shoves him away. "Sorry about your brother."

"Not sure why he's got his knickers in a twist about dinner tonight."

"Great design. Did you draw it yourself?" Ellie draws attention away from Sean, gazing down at my work.

"Of course I did. Only the best."

"Will you please come to dinner for me?" She bats her eyelashes at me.

Any fight I had leaves my body. "You know I can't say no to you, Pink."

Her eyes sparkle. "Fab. I promise, you won't regret it."

Chapter Three

PIERCE

"Pierce. You've made my night!" Ellie's bump greets me before she does, wrapping her arms around my shoulders.

"You're pretty hard to say no to." I drop a kiss on each cheek, hanging my coat on the rack. Ellie and Sean live in a posh neighbourhood near Shoreditch. While I thought it would be overly stuffy, Ellie has made it into a cosy home.

"Glad one of us could convince you to come over." Sean greets me with a beer.

"Will you stop being such an arse to your brother?" Ellie pleads with him, smacking him on the chest.

"You're lucky I like you so much." I give her a wink, as the door swings open behind me.

"Sorry. I'm not late, am I?" A curvy brunette slams into me. "Oh crap, sorry!" She rights herself on my chest, and a spark of heat moves through me.

"No problem. I'm Pierce, this wanker's brother." I extend my hand to her.

"Charlotte. Ellie's cousin." Her smile is bright, dark red

lipstick staining plump lips. This woman is gorgeous with her deep brown eyes the colour of molasses.

"Come inside before you freeze." Ellie pulls her in for a hug as best she can. The late fall air is colder than normal.

I can't take my eyes off this woman. I've always known who she was. Living in London, you can't escape the royals. But in the time I've known Ellie, I've never met Charlotte. Only saw her at the baby shower. Even though I didn't meet her, I was aware of her. Anyone in their right mind would be. She's fecking gorgeous.

"How was your day?" Ellie wraps an arm around her shoulder and drags her into the kitchen, but not before my eyes find hers. I give a small waggle of my eyebrows, my eyes fixed on her as she leaves the room.

"Things go better at the shop this afternoon?" Sean sips his beer, flopping down on the sofa in front of me.

"Once you lot let me get to work."

"I wasn't trying to bother you."

I sit next to my brother, kicking his leg with my foot. "Relax. I'm not mad."

At least, I'm not anymore. I love him. But growing up, I was always following in his footsteps. Teachers and coaches alike asked me why I couldn't be more like by brother. Sean was always considerate and thought everything through.

Me? I was always more rambunctious. Still am. Don't really think twice before making a decision. It's served me well, but sometimes, it makes me feel like I'm lacking.

"Your piece looks great. You'll have to show me how you did the cover-up on it."

My chest puffs out with pride. Sean rarely asks for help, but I love when he comes to me. "Who decides to get a skull and crossbones on a cupcake? It doesn't make the cupcake more badass."

"From your lips to God's ears. People get the weirdest shit tattooed on them."

"Keeps us in business." Sean tilts his beer bottle towards mine in agreement.

"Until then, we're here for all the weird shit people want," he says with a smirk.

"Okay, now that everyone is here"—Sean jumps up as soon as Ellie and Charlotte walk in the room—"we can tell you the reason we brought you both here tonight." I'm not sure which one of them is glowing more. The baby isn't even here, and Sean is beaming.

"Don't drag it out." Charlotte sits down on the loveseat next to me. Warmth radiates from her, causing chills to wrack my body. My palms start to sweat. Christ, I've barely said more than two words to this woman and I'm acting like an altar boy who's seen a girl for the first time.

"We wanted you both here tonight to ask you to be the godparents to our little one." Ellie's face is nervous. "You both mean so much to us, and we want our baby to have you both in their life."

Charlotte jumps up, screeching, as she rushes to Ellie. Tears are in both their eyes as they hug one another.

"You want me to be the godfather?" Shock colours my voice as I stand, making my way over to Sean.

"Is it that big of a shock?" He does a good job hiding the hurt.

"Sorry. It's just, fuck, I'm not a great influence, am I? Shit, do you really want your baby's first words being a curse word?" I run a hand through the scruff on my jaw. "Godfather? Really?"

"If anything happens to us, God forbid, there's no one else I want taking care of my kid. You'll be the best uncle and godfather, Pierce."

"Shit." Emotion chokes up my throat as I pull my

brother in for a hug. "I still can't believe you're going to be a dad."

He pulls back, looking over at Ellie, who's now staring at the two of us. "Fuck, I can't believe it myself. Would you have thought a couple of years ago that this would be happening?"

"That the princess would fall madly in love with you and leave her life behind for you? I'd say you were bloody well pissed."

"You're such a dick." He wraps an arm around my neck, pulling me down and rubbing my head.

"Oh, very mature, Dad."

"Okay, boys. Sean, come help me with dinner. Let's leave our godparents to get to know one another." Ellie winks, pulling Sean behind her. He goes willingly. He would follow her to the ends of the world. And damn, if that doesn't make me jealous. I want to follow after someone like my brother does.

Charlotte

GODMOTHER. Joy threatens to bubble out of me as I stare at the handsome man in front of me. "Can you believe we're going to be godparents?" I clap my hands in front of me.

"I can't believe my brother is going to be a dad. Like who decided we're ready for that responsibility?"

"There's actually a class you take. Parenting 101. Ways to not completely screw up raising your kid."

He quirks a brow at me. "Aren't you the funny one."

"Better than having any other labels." I plop down on the sofa next to Pierce. His sculpted chest and arms fill out his jumper. He props an ankle over his knee, his thighs bunching as he settles back into the sofa cushions.

"Fight a lot of stigma as a princess?" Pierce sips his beer, the liquid glistening on his lips. With bright blue eyes and dark brown hair that has me itching to run my fingers through it, Pierce is one of the sexiest men I've seen in a long while. Not that I've been looking. Ever since my ex left me, it's been hard to find anyone willing to take on this life.

"Just have to toe the line."

"Seems like you 'toe the line' just fine." He makes air quotes around the line I just gave him.

"Just because I'm a princess doesn't mean I don't rebel in my own ways. I'm not an idiot like my cousin James was, but there's more to me than meets the eye."

"Okay. If you don't toe the line, what's one of your most embarrassing moments?"

"Most embarrassing moment?" I tap my lips with my finger.

"You can't have that many embarrassing moments, can you?" Pierce's handsome face is puzzled, with pursed lips, eyes wide in wonderment.

"It's hard to tell you who it's more embarrassing for, me or the First Lady of France."

He snorts. "Only you could have a story involving a head of state from another country."

"You asked what the most embarrassing thing to happen to me was." I quirk a brow at him. "I was visiting France on behalf of my grandfather, and I was attending a state dinner with the president. They were welcoming me at their home when I tripped on the cobblestones and ended up falling into the First Lady."

Pierce winces, sipping on his beer. "This can't be good."

I nod my head. "I ended up grabbing her chest and ripping her gown. It was plastered all over the French news by the end of the night. Said I was trying to start war with France."

"A war?"

"They were all very dramatic about it. Thankfully, she didn't flash anyone. I was utterly mortified, but the First Lady was very kind."

"And you didn't start a war with France. Cheers to that." Pierce clinks his beer bottle against my wine glass. An easygoing smile spreads across his lips. He looks like he's up to no good. I should turn and run in the other direction, but for the first time in a long while, someone isn't talking to me like I'm the princess, but just a regular woman. It's refreshing.

"What's your most embarrassing moment?" I ask, sipping on my wine.

"I got pantsed at a football match once." Pierce doesn't hesitate.

I nearly choke over my sip of wine. "You play football?" My eyes peruse his body. He doesn't look like a footballer.

"A few mates and I play together every few weeks. We're hardly the national team, but it's fun."

"And getting pantsed while playing is fun?"

Pierce chuckles to himself, setting his now empty beer bottle on the coffee table in front of us.

"It's fucking awesome. I mean, not the getting pantsed part. My mate did it to steal the ball from me. Flashed everyone."

His laughter is contagious. "This doesn't really sound embarrassing to me."

"Eh. Could've been worse. Just us taking the piss on the pitch."

I roll my eyes at him. "So just boys being boys."

"Hey!" Pierce shoves my shoulder. "It's a very spirited match, and we all play to win. It's very serious."

"Oh, yes, I'm sure it is. And what do you win if you win the match?" I sit on my knees, moving closer to Pierce. Something about him draws me in. Scruff lines his square jaw as his eyes focus on me.

"Free drinks at the pub." Pierce says this like I should know.

"Who wouldn't want their drinks paid for?"

"How about I pay for your drinks sometime?" The easy way Pierce says this catches me off guard.

"Like a date?"

Pierce shifts closer to me, his knees bumping into mine. The small contact causes goose pimples to break out on my skin. "Yes, Charlotte." The way he says my name has heat licking up my spine as I lean farther into him. "When a man asks you out for drinks, typically that means it's a date."

"Smartass."

Pierce tucks a piece of hair behind my ear. His fingers linger. "What do you say? Date with the smartass?"

"A date it is."

I couldn't wipe the grin off my face if I tried.

Chapter Four

PIERCE

Fuck me, she's beautiful. Charlotte is walking towards me, skin-tight jeans and a jumper hugging all her delicious curves. The early evening light makes her look like an angel. I don't know how I got her to agree to a date with me.

"Hey, handsome." She's got a swing to her hips as she walks towards me. Her red painted lips are bright with a smile.

"Hi." Words fail me. This woman is looking at me like I'm dessert. She's running her hands down my leather jacket. Only the best for Charlotte.

"So where are you taking me tonight?" She swings her hair over her shoulder, exposing the gentle slope of her neck. It takes everything I have not to bite down on the pulsing vein there. To trace my lips over the gentle thrum of her pulse.

"How does mini golf sound?" I pull her into my arms, loving the feel of her curves under me.

"Mini golf? I don't think I've ever played mini golf before." Her eyes are sparkling.

I can't keep the flirting out of my tone. "Well then, stick with me, love, and I'll show you a good time."

"A good time, huh?" Charlotte wraps her arms around my neck, playing with the hair at the nape of my neck. "You think you can show me a good time?"

This time, I don't hesitate. I capture those red lips with mine—those alluring, pouty lips. She licks my lips and I open to her. Bloody hell. This is hot. Charlotte is taking control of this kiss, and I'm at her mercy as she leans farther into me. My hands drift lower, settling just above her perfect arse, and pull her closer to me, sinking deeper into this kiss. I could stay right here all night, wrapped up with her.

"Fuck, Charlotte." The wind blows her hair around us, as I tuck it behind her ear. Her cheeks are red, her lips swollen. All I want to do is toss her over my shoulder and go back to my flat. But I have the perfect date in mind. Something away from the spotlight that I'm sure she's going to love.

"C'mon. Show me where this amazing place is." She takes my hand in hers, walking backwards. I'm helpless to do anything but follow.

"SWINGERS? Should I really be at a place called Swingers?" I can see the question lingering in her eyes.

"I promise, I'm not going to pimp you out to someone who doesn't deserve you." Fuck, I don't even think I deserve her, but here I am.

I push the door open, and we're swept away to a different world. Flowers line the wall near the bar, as music plays throughout the old warehouse. Colorful plants, windmills, and all sorts of contraptions line the holes.

A few eyes turn to Charlotte, but her security officers wave them off. I guess I've gotten used to them since Ellie still has them. The last thing I want is for her face to be splashed all over the headlines, but her smile at me says she doesn't have a care in the world.

"So, you going to teach me how to play?" She grabs the scorecard from my hand.

"Not sure how much I'll be teaching you. I'm not the best at this either."

Charlotte sidles up to me. "Well then, best start stretching, because I'll teach you a thing or two."

She winks as she walks over to the bar. Bloody hell. I say a silent prayer that no one can see the semi I'm now sporting. Charlotte is unlike any girl I've ever met. I've only known her a few days, but I know she's different. Whereas Ellie shied away from the spotlight, Charlotte has no problem being in it.

"What'll ya have?" the bartender asks, not looking twice at Charlotte.

"Moscow mule for me, and…" she trails off.

"Same."

I lean against the bar, watching as she turns into me. "So how'd you find this place?"

The bartender slides our drinks across the bar and goes back to the couple now in front of her. I take a long pull on the drink. Damn, that's good. "A client told me about it. Said his boyfriend loved coming here because he feels like Alice."

"Alice?"

"Alice in Wonderland."

Charlotte looks around the space. "I see it. Let's go see if we can wander down the rabbit hole."

She grabs my hand and leads me in the direction of the first hole. Setting my drink down, I grab two putters and balls from the stand behind us. I hand Charlotte hers, our fingers grazing. It sends a zing of electricity moving through me. Fuck. This woman does things to me that no other woman has done before. And judging by the look on her face, she feels it too.

"Alright, ladies first." I gesture for her to go. A Ferris wheel sits at the end of the hole. Flowers line the bricks on either side of the fake turf. The lights are low overhead.

"Okay." She takes a readying sip of her drink, and hands it to me. She sets her ball down and takes her stance. The wiggle of her hips is intoxicating. So intoxicating I miss seeing her hit the ball.

"Hey, not bad!" she cheers, reaching for a high five.

"Beginner's luck." I smirk at her, taking a sip of her drink. I eye her as she watches me.

"So we're sharing a drink now?"

She walks up to me, taking a drink right where my lips were. Who is this woman? How did I get so lucky to find her?

"Figured I'd get some of your good luck." I drop a kiss on her cheek as I set up my shot.

"Your hips are all wrong. And the way you're holding the club isn't how it's done."

My eyes meet hers. It's as if we're the only two people here. "And since when did you become a world expert in golf?"

"Since I can do this." Charlotte moves to stand behind me and angles my hips. I doubt either of us know what we're doing, but I don't care. "I think that works much better, don't you think?" She squeezes my side and moves away as I hit the ball into the wall. It bounces off, landing only a short ways away from where I started.

"Christ, you're not playing fair, woman." I give her my best hard look. But the smile on her face would melt even the world's hardest person.

"Never said I would." She hops by me on her way to take her next shot. It's going to be a long night.

Charlotte

"THAT'S NOT FAIR. You can't drop your ball in the hole and say you win the hole." My hands are fisted on my hips as I stare at Pierce. We've been cheating all night. We aren't playing by the rules, and I love it.

"What are you going to do about it?" I have half a mind to walk right up to him and kiss that smug smile off his face, but we're in a crowded area of the club. As much as I want to kiss him, I don't want it splattered all over the news. Damn paparazzi taking pictures of every single thing.

Instead, I play dirty.

I walk right up to him, my eyes at his shoulders. Even in my heeled booties, I'm still shorter than he is. "If we weren't in the middle of a crowded area, I'd kiss the ever-loving piss out of you. Make you so dizzy with need that you couldn't see straight, so I'd win the next five holes."

"Only five?" His voice is gruff with need. I've hit my intended target.

I graze my fingers up his chest. "There's only five left." I walk off to the next hole. "You coming or what?"

His growl hits my ears as I approach the next hole. It's

tucked behind a wall. A flower-lined pergola sits over the hole.

Pierce's heat overwhelms me as he stands at my side. "You think you're going to get away with that?"

"Pretty sure I already did." I'm not looking at him. My focus is on the pergola ahead of me. Pierce's lips land on my neck, just below my ear.

It takes everything I have not to let out a groan. The scruff on his face does things to me that I shouldn't be thinking in public. This is getting out of hand and getting out of hand fast.

"What are you waiting for? Going to take the shot?"

His voice sends shivers down my spine. The ball hits the short wall on the course and bounces up and over, clanking off the metal walls of the building.

"What a shame." Pierce steps back, and I lament the loss of his heat. "Time to learn from the master."

I stalk off to grab my ball as Pierce takes his shot, directly into the pergola and in the hole.

"Holy shit!" he yells, grabbing me around the waist and swinging me around, all earlier jabs forgotten. "I aced it! World's best mini-golfer right here."

My laughter is bubbling out of me as he sets me down and lays a kiss on my cheek. "You really are good luck for me, Charlotte."

"Next time just taunt me the entire time, and then you'll ace it on the fourteenth hole."

"I'd be annoyed at that, but I got a hole in one! I should sign up to play golf with the professionals." He struts to the hole to grab his ball.

"Pretty sure the professionals don't act like this when they get a hole in one."

"You're right. They're probably way worse and throw

their clubs into the water. But seeing as how we're in the middle of London, we'll get dinner to celebrate."

"Sounds fab."

Pierce drapes his arm over my shoulders as we walk to the next hole. "And since you're the loser, you must buy."

Now I'm laughing for a whole other reason. "I'd say you're so full of shit that you should buy dinner, but I can't even help it. I'll buy you whatever you want."

I CAN'T REMEMBER the last time I've had so much fun on a first date. Or any date for that matter. Most people tend to steer clear of anything that might be too public, with me being a princess and all. Pierce found us a private booth in the back for dinner and drinks. After going through the entire course, it's nice to be away from prying eyes.

"We might have to come back here and try again." I grab a street taco and take a bite. I'd say I kicked Pierce's arse, but that would mean I did well. Neither of us has much game.

"We'll have to set a wager next time." He takes a long drink of his beer, not turning his eyes from mine. They're blue like the sea. So deep, I could get lost in them.

"You know royalty can't gamble." I give him my best smirk. His eyes find my lips this time. What I wouldn't give to kiss him again. He has the softest lips. So sensual that it's hard to keep my mind off them. I want a repeat—any chance I can get.

"I didn't say we'd be doing it with money." His eyes are heated with lust. It drives me mad.

"Oh yeah?" I slide closer to him in the booth. It's quiet

back here. My security officers are close by, so I know we're okay here. "What do you have in mind?"

"I was thinking something like this." His lips take mine in a soft kiss. He tastes like the beer he was drinking. He pulls back slightly, and it's like my lips are magnets to his. I follow, the butterflies in my belly not wanting to lose this contact with him.

I slide my hand up the soft fabric of Pierce's shirt, wrapping my hand around his neck. I capture his lips, teasing them with my tongue. His groan grants me access to his mouth. My ex used to hate that I liked to take control when kissing, but there's something so powerful about it. It turns me on. And Pierce gives it to me.

The soft velvet of his tongue has my core tightening with need. It takes everything I have not to move into his lap and rock my hips over him. He breaks the kiss, lips moving along my jaw, back to my ear.

"Bloody hell, Charlotte. We can't keep doing this, or you'll be in the papers tomorrow." I have to bite back my groan. All I want to do is go home with Pierce. I'm a woman who knows what she wants. And right now, I want Pierce. If only I wasn't a princess and could act on this desire flowing through me.

"I wish this was like any first date, and we could go home together." I drop my forehead to his.

"Thank God we have a table to hide how hard you're making me right now."

I giggle at his words. "Pretty sure that could be said of how you've been feeling all night."

A pinch at my side has me throwing my head back in laughter.

"Sorry I'm not more of a gentleman."

"Someone who isn't a gentleman wouldn't admit that." I trace my fingers over his swollen lips. This is bad. I think

I could fall for Pierce. With his intense blue eyes, innocent face, and those tattoos. I never thought I'd be a woman who enjoyed tattoos, but on Pierce? I want to learn every intimate detail about each of them. Trace them with my fingers. With my tongue.

Pierce is lighting a fire in me that I long thought was dead. After Michael left, it felt like there was something wrong with me. That no matter what I did, no one would be able to love all sides of me, both the private side and the very public side. Everyone says they're okay with my position, but once they face that public side, they sing a different tune.

But Pierce didn't shy away from it. Instead of taking me on a palace-approved date, he brought me to my new favourite spot in London. Who knew mini golf could be such a turn-on?

And the man who brought me here is fast turning into my new favourite person.

Chapter Five

CHARLOTTE

The grin on my face has been plastered there since this morning. I can't remember the last time I've had such a good first date. A fun first date. I keep trying to rework the charity idea I have, to be better suited to talk about with the Queen again, but my thoughts keep drifting back to Pierce.

To the way his eyes lit up when he first saw me. And the excitement in his voice when we went mini golfing. Who knew mini golf could be so much fun?

And that kiss? I still feel it, all the way down to my toes. Nothing can wipe the smile off my face today.

"Your Highness. The Queen will be in shortly to discuss a few matters with you." My advisor dips low before leaving the room.

Damn. It's never good if she wants an impromptu meeting. But maybe this will be a good chance to discuss the new charity I want to start. She's been rather evasive anytime I want to speak with her.

"Charlotte. How are you today?" Aunt Katherine, or

Queen Katherine as most call her, sweeps into the room in a bubble of floral perfume and a finely pressed suit.

"I'm well. And you?" I give her the customary double kiss, cheek greeting before sitting back down. Nerves are fluttering in my belly.

"I want to talk to you about this boy you're seeing."

"Pierce?"

She nods. "Sean's brother, no?"

"Yes. We had dinner at Sean and Ellie's the other night. He was here for the baby shower."

"And then you proceeded to have a date?" She sets a few magazines down in front of me. There, plastered all over the pages of gossip rags, are images of Pierce and me on our date. Anger churns inside me. I hate that we can't have a normal first date. Even being third in line, every move I make is documented for the entire world to see. It hasn't been as bad with the pending royal wedding, but they always find me.

"We weren't doing anything wrong." There's a defensiveness in my tone. Pictures of Pierce standing behind me, hands on my hips, while helping me swing, grace the pages of these magazines. Us having a drink. It's nothing that any other person wouldn't be doing on a first date.

"He's a bad influence, and we have a certain image to uphold as the royals of this nation. We can't be seen drinking and carrying on like this in public."

"Carrying on? It's not like we were having sex in the middle of the course for everyone to see!" I throw the magazines down and stand to match her. "It was two people having fun and getting to know one another."

"Be that as it may, you cannot see him again."

I rear back, as if she slapped me. "I'm sorry? I can't see him again?"

"With everything we go through with the press, I can't have another scandal coming down on us."

I cross my arms, levelling her with a stare. "And what makes you think there will be a scandal?"

"Ellie renounced her place in line to the throne for Sean. Look at what James and Zara are still going through."

"The press paid off their neighbours to get compromising photos of them!" I shout. Images of them having sex were leaked to the press. It was devastating. They almost broke up over it, but thank God they didn't.

"It's only a matter of time before something happens, and we can't handle another blow like that this early in my reign. I'm sorry, but no."

"And if I don't stop seeing him?" Every second of my life is already controlled. Every move monitored. Every place I go carefully vetted. Don't get me wrong, I love my life. I love getting to help and support the people in my country. But why can't I have one thing for myself?

"It's either the crown or him. And I know you'll make the right decision."

"That's it?" The air leaves my lungs on a huff.

"I will not discuss this any further, Charlotte." Her voice is clipped, ending the conversation. Anger boils up inside me as she spins on her heel to leave.

"Wait! Can I talk to you about the charity I want to start?"

She turns to face me, her lips pursed in a grim look. "Why are you still on that, Charlotte? I have set up plenty of events for you these next few weeks that are perfect for you."

"I'm sorry, you've set up events for me? Why am I just now hearing about this?"

"Your advisors were made aware. These events are much more conducive to helping the people of this country."

"Are women not people of this country? Do they not deserve our help?" I can't keep the ire from my voice.

"Charlotte." Her voice is stern. I'm not going to like what she says. "You have an idea, but it's too broad. I commend you for wanting to help the women of our nation, but you're wanting to do too much."

"What if I change it? Narrow my focus. Would you consider it then?"

"I would take it under advisement, but you are to continue with the events I've set up for you this week for our current patronages. Now, if you'll excuse me." She waves me off.

Aunt Katherine leaves the room without another backwards glance at me. My heart sinks at the thought of not seeing Pierce again. The few men I've seen these last few years were more interested in the crown than anything else. Trying to date with the weight of a crown hanging over your head is impossible.

But Pierce didn't think twice before asking me out. Sure, he knows Ellie and knows what she's dealt with in the past. All I can think of is how gutted he'll be when I tell him I can't see him again.

It was one date, but it was so different from anything I'd ever experienced. We had the best time together, and I don't want to lose out on that feeling.

Anger fuels me as I pick up the phone and dial someone who I hope can talk some sense into the Queen.

"Hi darling," my mum's voice rings.

"Mum. I need your help." Despite Mum marrying into the Ainsworth family, she's always been close to Aunt

Royal Relations

Katherine. Thick as thieves back in the day, from what I heard.

"Everything okay?"

"Well, I met this man, and he is—" I don't even get to finish my sentence.

"You met someone? Where? Tell me the details." Mum's voice goes high with excitement.

"That's the problem. It's Sean's brother. And the Queen doesn't approve of him."

"Did she say why?"

"Only that he would be a bad influence on me."

"Maybe she's just trying to protect you."

"Protect me from what?"

"You know what the press can be like if someone doesn't fit the mold."

I want to scream. "Does it not matter what I want?"

"Darling,"—Mum's voice takes on a soft tone, but it sounds pitying—"just because you want someone, doesn't mean they are ready for royal life. I grew up the daughter of a duke, and it was an adjustment even for me."

"So because Aunt Katherine decides he'll be a bad influence, I don't even get the chance to see if we'll work out?"

She sighs, long and heavy. "Charlotte, this is between you and your aunt. I don't want to get involved and be put in the middle. I love you both, and I don't want to hurt either one of you."

Damn my mother for wanting to be so reasonable. I sigh. "You're right. I guess I'm just upset. I'll let you get back to work."

"Stop by for dinner this week, love."

"I will. Love you, Mum."

"Love you, darling."

I hang up the phone. Frustration over my situation surges through me. That smile that I was walking around with all morning is gone. First my charity and then Pierce? You've pissed off the wrong princess.

Chapter Six

PIERCE

I can't remember the last time I was nervous to have a woman over to my flat. When Charlotte called today to change our plans, nerves took over. This woman is a princess, for fuck's sake. Sure, our first date went off without a hitch, but we were on a level playing field. Now she's coming to my flat.

My flat is fine, if not on the small side. Artwork I've done over the years covers the walls. My bedroom barely fits a bed, and a small sofa takes up most of the living space. It's never bothered me before because it's exactly what I want. But when an actual princess is coming over? It's hard not to see the differences between us.

A knock at the door ratchets up my nerves. Swinging it open, I have to step aside as one of Charlotte's security officers sweeps inside. Charlotte's standing outside with another officer.

"Sorry about this. Standard protocol." A blush creeps up her face as they search my flat. No doubt she hates this as much as I do.

"All clear. We'll be waiting downstairs should you need

anything, Your Highness." They clear out as fast as they came in.

"Hi." Charlotte walks up to me, wrapping her arms around my waist. It calms the earlier panic that was rising inside of me.

"Hi, love." I squeeze her closer to me. The soft scent of her perfume wraps around me, setting me at ease. "Care for dinner?"

"Mm, it smells great in here. You cooked just for me?" She steps out of my arms, walking into the kitchen.

"Just for you." Charlotte lifts the lid off the pot, sticking her nose in the pot roast I'm making.

She turns her head, eyes wide and sparkling at me. "There is something very sexy about a man who knows how to cook."

"Oh yeah?" I step into her space. I haven't known her long, but I need to feel her under me. To feel her curves. To feel her soft skin. Need, need, need.

"Of course, you could be a terrible cook, and then we'll both be fucked."

Laughter escapes out of me as I bury my face in Charlotte's neck. "I'll have you know I'm an amazing cook."

"Whatever you say, Pierce." Fuck, I love the way my name rolls off her tongue. Sensual and sweet all at the same time. I grab the wine I picked up for us and pour us each a glass.

"Cheers." I clink my glass against hers as I take a steadying sip. Just being around this woman has my heart beating faster.

"So, why the change of venue this evening?" I plate our dinner, as Charlotte moves to the small table. She's wearing yoga pants and an oversized jumper. No makeup. She's absolutely stunning all the time, but even more beautiful when she's like this.

"Why don't we wait until after dinner? Not let it ruin the mood."

My skin prickles. Not ruin the mood? "Well, that's not going to put a downer on the evening." I set her plate of food in front of her and take the seat next to her. She's not looking at me but focusing too hard on her dinner.

Charlotte cuts herself a piece of meat, her delicate fingers holding her knife and fork the proper way. Her lips wrap around the fork, taking a bite. What I wouldn't give to be that fork right now as she moans around it.

"Pierce. That is so good." Her eyes are closed as she savours, and fuck, if that doesn't make me hard. My gaze narrows on her lips, and I picture the way they would be wrapped around my dick as I thrust into her mouth. As she takes control over me by sucking me down.

"Pierce?" Charlotte startles me out of my thoughts as I shove a bite in my mouth. I smile at her, trying to rid my brain of the images of her on her knees in front of me.

"Sorry. Just drifted off there."

"How was the shop today? Any new tattoos?" I don't miss what she's doing, trying to steer the conversation away from my earlier question. I'll give it to her, but not for long.

"Good. Nothing overly exciting. Just some walk-ins who wanted butterfly tattoos."

"Do you not like butterfly tattoos?" She sips her wine, her gaze drifting over my exposed ink.

"Eh, not my favourite. I like more challenging pieces." I shrug my shoulder. "Once you've moved on from butterflies, they aren't the most fun thing to do."

"Would you tattoo a butterfly on me?" Her eyes are dark with lust. Fuck, if I wouldn't love to put my ink on her. I now understand why Sean is so possessive of being the only person to tattoo Ellie.

"Would you want a tattoo?" She slips the fork between

her lips, pulling it out slowly. Damn. The image of her doing that to my cock has me tenting my pants. Again. This woman is driving me crazy in the best way.

"I can't say that I do. Unfortunately, I don't like needles."

"Most people who get tattoos end up not minding needles."

Charlotte gives me a small smile. "I'm pretty sure it's you that helps them through that fear."

"Me?" I don't think anyone has ever said that to me before.

Charlotte pushes her plate away from her and stands, moving to sit on my lap. Her eyes are soft. Big, brown pools that I can get lost in.

"You. You have a way about you that sets people around you at ease. I knew it from the minute I met you. Most people would've been putting on a show for Princess Charlotte, but not you." Her fingers play with the hair at the nape of my neck, and I lean into her touch. The gentle scrape of her nails is electrifying. My entire body is on edge with need for this woman. "I can only imagine how you make the people you tattoo feel. I'm sure if they've never done it before, they must be scared, but you can put them at ease. Make them feel comfortable."

"I don't think anyone has ever described it like that." A shy smile plays on my lips. "Most people would just think I ink people and move on. Nothing like saving lives."

"Don't diminish what you do. Just because you aren't saving lives, doesn't mean you aren't helping people through a hard time with your work. Or helping them move on from a dark time." Charlotte grips my chin, forcing my gaze to hers.

"I like the way you see me." I lean up, claiming her lips with mine. It's a soft kiss. No one has ever looked at my job the way Charlottes has. They see my tattoos and think I'm a bad boy. But that couldn't be further from the truth. And thinking about Charlotte's view has my chest swelling with pride.

"You know, if this whole princess thing doesn't work out, you could be a therapist. You're really good at talking to people." I tuck a loose strand of hair behind her ear.

"Maybe that's what makes me such a good princess," she teases, as I pull her in tighter.

"It also makes you really good at dodging the reason we're here," I whisper into her ear.

She stands, making her way over to the windows. An unease settles over me. "What is it, Charlotte?"

She turns, her arms clutching her stomach. Her eyes hold a sadness that belies the happiness we felt earlier. "I've been told I can't see you anymore."

Shock colours my face. "Can't see me anymore? Says who?"

I stand, crossing the short distance to her. She rears back from my embrace. "The Queen."

"I'm sorry. The Queen says we can't see each other? Why the bloody hell not?" I don't keep the disdain from my voice.

"She seems to think you might be a bad influence on me."

Fuck me. I drag my hand down my face, trying to keep my anger from boiling over. From unleashing it on Charlotte when she isn't the one keeping us from seeing one another. "How am I a bad influence on you?"

I'm pacing around my flat. There's not much room to move, but I keep moving until Charlotte settles a hand on my shoulder. The warmth radiates over me.

"I didn't say I agreed with her." Her voice is soft, but firm. "Why would she get to have a say over my love life?"

"She's the Queen. Kinda seems like she can make you do a lot of things you don't want to do." I step out of the bubble Charlotte's seemed to wrap me in. "I don't know why you had to come all the way over here if you're just going to break things off."

I slump down on the sofa. Fecking hell. I shouldn't be this upset. It was only one date. It's not like we've been dating for years. Just one more person to add to the list of people who think I'm not good enough.

"Pierce. Do you really think I'd come over here to tell you I couldn't see you anymore?" Charlotte's standing in front of me, her arms crossed and her lips turned down in anger.

"Shit. I don't know."

She laces her hands through my hair, tilting my gaze to meet hers. "Do you really think I'd come over here and have dinner with you and kiss you if I was going to break up with you?"

Charlotte straddles me, resting her arse on my thighs. She presses closer into me, as I lock my arms around her waist.

"I don't want to stop seeing you, Pierce." Her breath caresses my cheek.

"You don't?" I hate the need in my voice, but it's there.

She shakes her head. "I don't care what the Queen says, but it does make seeing each other slightly more difficult."

This time, I pull back to meet her gaze. I don't think I've ever heard someone talk about the Queen like this. "It seems like it would be a lot more difficult if we can't be seen together. You live your life in public."

"I do. But it just means we'll have to be careful. Hanging out here together."

"You mean hiding our relationship?" I'm skeptical this

will work. She's a public figure, and the paparazzi are terrible here.

"I don't want to hide you from anyone, Pierce. But if it means that we get to see each other, then I'm all for it."

Her eyes are dancing over my face, trying to get a read on me. I know this will make her life that much more difficult, hiding this. Hiding us. But I've never met anyone like her. Someone that I ache to see after just meeting them. Wanting to hold her in my arms. To hear about all the mundane things she does every day and not get tired of it.

"So sneaking around and staying at my flat because if anyone sees us together...shit, what would happen?" I'm thinking out loud at this point.

"It'd be off to the dungeons for you."

"Think you'd come with me?"

Charlotte leans in for a kiss. Her taste is intoxicating. It's wiping out any annoyance I have at having to keep what we have together a secret.

"You have to admit. We'd probably be the sexiest couple in the dungeons." Her laugh seeps into me, settling me.

I roam my eyes over her face, studying her closely. Her eyes give her away. She's nervous about this. About having to hide or about possibly being caught, I don't know.

"Are you sure you want to do this?" she asks. She's playing with the collar of my shirt, not looking at me.

"Charlotte." My voice is firm. I wait for her to look at me before continuing. "If you're asking if I want to hide away my relationship with you, I don't. I hate that the Queen thinks I'd be a bad influence on you. But if hiding away means we get to be together, then let's do it. I'd stay in my cramped flat for months on end if it means I get to spend time with you."

"I don't know why anyone thinks you'd be the bad

influence." Charlotte kisses me, moving down my jaw. I groan, trying not to rock into her at how good she feels sitting over me. Her hands skate over my arms, tracing the tattoos there.

"You're the bad influence. And I, for one, can't wait for you to corrupt me."

Chapter Seven

PIERCE

Charlotte's scent lingers over me as I lie on the sofa, staring at the ceiling. My mind is still working on overdrive, replaying the conversation we had. Charlotte wants to keep seeing me, but the Queen is against it. It didn't seem to faze her. But guilt lingers in my gut. Is this something I'm really cut out to do?

When she was here, the decision was easy. That confident smile of hers told me she knew exactly what she was doing. The soft way her lips moved over mine made it easy to forget why continuing on with her is a bad idea.

Our first date was unlike any first date I've ever had. It was perfect. I'd never had more fun in my life. But that's what got us here in the first place.

Except my fingers remember what it felt like to have her luscious curves under them. I wish I could have curled around her all night, feeling her against me. But if she were to be seen leaving my flat, it'd be bad. Very bad.

Christ. Why is this a good idea again?

CHARLOTTE
Hey, handsome. Care to sneak away tomorrow night?

Is that really a good idea?

CHARLOTTE
Where's your sense of adventure?

Just trying to play by your rules

CHARLOTTE
I like a man who knows how to follow instructions

Bloody hell, and now I'm hard. To think, I've seen this woman everywhere for most of her life, and now I'm getting to see this side of her. I shouldn't like her as much as I do, but damn, if she isn't casting a spell on me.

CHARLOTTE
Come on…I want to see you

How can a man turn down an offer like that?

CHARLOTTE
Brill. I'll make it worth your while

Excitement replaces the guilt I'm feeling in my gut at the prospect of seeing Charlotte tomorrow night. Oh, right. This is why I agreed to Charlotte's plan.

We're playing with fire, and it's only a matter of time before we're incinerated.

I FEEL LIKE JAMES BOND. Looking around the pub, I see Charlotte stand from a secluded booth. Her long hair is tucked away in a hat that hides her face. If you weren't looking closely, you wouldn't know it was her. The dingy pub outside of London wasn't the kind of place I expected Charlotte to know about.

Hell, I didn't even think we could come to someplace like this. When she told us we had to keep our relationship a secret, I assumed it would be a lot of nights hidden away in my flat.

"Wanted to live on the wild side tonight." Her arms wrap around my waist, and she places a kiss on my lips.

"I don't think I've ever heard of this place before." The place is completely empty. Aside from one or two people hunched over the bar, the dark restaurant holds two extra patrons. Us.

Charlotte slides into the booth, and I sit next to her. "How'd you find this place? Doesn't seem very princessly."

"Princessly?" Charlotte eyes me over the pint glass she's sipping on. "I overheard some of the security guys talking about it. They come here after shift and aren't bothered, so I figured it was a good place for us."

"What'll it be?" A gruff voice comes from behind me.

"Another pint and two steak and ale pies." I don't turn to face him as he shuffles off.

"Pretty presumptuous there that I'd like a pie for supper." Charlotte takes another sip, licking the amber liquid from her lips.

The server drops the pint, sloshing it on the table. He doesn't pay any attention to us. It's the perfect spot for us.

"Guess I should've asked. Do you like pie for supper?" I cock an eyebrow at her.

"Anything with gravy, yes. How do you think I get such great curves?"

The beer does little to cool me as my eyes drink her in. The memory of those curves is ingrained in my head after feeling them while playing mini golf. I wrap a hand around her waist, tugging her closer to me. My hand lingers before pulling away.

"You're quite surprising."

"Why do you say that?" Her piercing eyes hit me square in the chest. I should not be feeling this way about her. Not when we've only seen each other a handful of times.

"You say what you're thinking. You don't hold back. I like it."

Charlotte props an elbow on the table, resting her chin in her palm. "You might be one of the only people to say that."

I nod, gulping down my beer. "Because you're a princess?"

She taps a finger to her temple. "Sneaky like James Bond and smart. Quite the package."

"What can I say?" I give her my best smile. "I aim to please."

Charlotte slides closer to me, her breath ghosting my face. "Keep doing what you're doing. You're quite pleasing."

Fecking hell. If I make it through this evening without having to whack one off in the loo, I'll consider it a win. This woman is driving me mad with need.

"Would it please you if I did this?" I slant my mouth over hers. Her deep red lips are soft and pliable under mine. Charlotte deepens the kiss, her tongue sweeping into my mouth.

Everything about this woman is unexpected. I expected someone quiet. More worried about how the media portrays them, like Ellie. But Charlotte is a breath of fresh air.

She takes what she wants. She doesn't hide who she is. She's a lioness, ready to strike when she finds her prey. I'm just glad it's me.

"Right. Enjoy." Dinner is dropped onto the table without ceremony, as I drag my lips from hers. Charlotte's biting her lip, staring at my mouth.

"To be continued." She pulls her dinner in front of her but stays glued to my side. The heat from her body does nothing to douse the raging inferno burning through me.

"What's your favourite flavour of ice cream?" Charlotte takes a steaming bite of pie, licking her fork clean.

"Random much?" I eye her over my own bite. Long lashes flutter against her cheeks as she swallows her bite.

"Not random. I want to get to know you. Twenty questions style."

"Isn't twenty questions supposed to be yes or no questions?"

She pokes her fork in my direction before taking another bite. "Yes, but I want to get to know you better, and yes or no questions don't cut it."

"But your favourite flavour of ice cream does?" Gravy sits on the corner of Charlotte's mouth. I thumb it off, licking it into my mouth. Even the gravy tastes better with her.

"For all I know, you could be a monster and not like ice cream. What kind of person doesn't eat ice cream?"

"Someone who doesn't eat dairy?"

She rolls her eyes at me. "Fine. But you still haven't answered my question."

"Mint chocolate chip. You?" I take another hearty bite. "Bloody hell. This might be the best pie I've ever had. Don't tell my mum I said that."

"Aww, I won't tell her. You know I have her number now."

My fork clanks down on the plate in front of me. "Of course you do. She has no boundaries."

"It's sweet how much she loves you guys. She does throw quite the party."

"I should say Ellie's mum throws quite the party. Mum was just going to have something at Sean and Ellie's. The Queen made it into so much more."

"And I remember thinking how upset I was I didn't get to talk to the handsome stranger."

A smirk plays on my lips. "Handsome stranger, huh?"

A blush creeps up Charlotte's cheeks. "I might have to take back those words."

"Are you sure? Even if I bring you ice cream?" I finger a lock of her hair, feeling the silkiness.

"Only if it's butterscotch."

My lips snarl on their own. "Butterscotch? That's the worst."

Charlotte shoves me to the side. "And here I thought you were perfect."

"Sorry to shatter any illusions. I should be given sainthood by being seen in public with you considering your terrible taste in sweets."

She leans in, giving me her best smile. "You're pretty sweet. I think that makes up for my abysmal taste in ice cream."

"Damn. And just like that, you're back to being pretty perfect."

"I try." She takes her last bite, the tines of her fork playing on her lips. "Coolest place you've ever travelled? Mine was Norway."

"And here I was expecting someplace more exotic."

Charlotte laughs. "I think I was ten. My granddad

went to visit with the king, and he took Ellie, James, and me along. They had kids our age, and we spent the whole time sledding and snowshoeing. It was the most fun I ever remember having."

"Sounds like I'll need to add Norway to my list of places to go."

"I'd love to go back. Traveling is much harder for me now. I have to get clearance to go, so it's much harder to go on holiday for the fun of it."

"So no beach holidays for you then?" The thought of Charlotte lying topless on a private beach somewhere slams into me. Sliding into her tight pussy while I sink my teeth into that lush bottom lip. Damn it. Now I want to whisk Charlotte away to the closest beach. A little hard considering we're not supposed to be seen together.

"How about you?" Her voice pulls me away from my dirty thoughts.

"Dixon, Idaho."

Confusion mars Charlotte's sexy face. "Idaho? Can't say I've ever been there."

I laugh. "I don't suppose you would have. It's where my mum grew up."

"I think having an American mum blows up the whole concept of perfection."

"Hardy har." I tickle her side as she tries to squirm away. I box her in the booth as she throws her hands up in surrender.

"Fine. Tell me about Idaho."

Memories of my childhood flash through my head. "It was perfect. We went every summer to stay with my grandparents. We have cousins that still live there, but it was everything a little boy could have ever wanted."

"Need anything else?" The server comes by, breaking my stare with Charlotte.

"Two more pints, please. Thank you." Charlotte gives him a warm smile before he heads back to the bar.

"What kinds of things did you do?"

"Fished. Hiked. Learned to make a fire. Horseback riding."

"That sounds like the best way to spend the summer."

"Sean and I used to get into so much trouble. My grandparents own a ranch out there, but they used to spend half the summer chasing us around to keep us from doing something stupid."

"Times like that make me wish I had a sibling." Her voice turns wistful.

I wrap an arm around her shoulders as our fresh drinks are delivered. "Did you ever get lonely growing up?"

She takes a long sip, her eyes staying on mine. "A sibling would've made being in the public eye more manageable. Having someone to lean on when times got hard. But I had Ellie. And James to an extent."

I adjust her hat, looking deeper into her eyes. Whenever I'm around her, my body calms. I never thought of myself as an overactive person, but she settles me.

"I always felt like I lived in Sean's shadow growing up. Even then, I wouldn't trade having a brother for anything."

"Did your parents want you to be like him?"

I snort into my glass over the sip I just took. "My dad's a professor. I don't think he thought his kids would turn into tattoo artists if he could've helped it."

"Then why do you feel like you were living in his shadow?"

"Every schoolteacher always compared me to Sean." My voice gets higher, imitating every teacher I've ever had. "'Why aren't you applying yourself like your brother? Why aren't your grades as good as Sean's? Sean was such an excellent student.'" It all bubbles out of me. I'm not one to talk about it, how I feel less than. But with Charlotte, it's easy. I don't feel the need to hide how I really feel.

"I guess that's the one good thing about not having a sibling. No one to be compared to. Although, everyone thought they knew who I was in school. It drove me crazy through primary school, but I learned to deal with it by the time secondary came along."

"Did they tell you your favourite colour was blue?" I say on a laugh.

"Black, actually. I went through a phase where all I wore was black. It was summer holiday, and the paparazzi swarmed us while we were in Scotland, so everyone assumed it was my favourite colour. It's actually purple."

I drop a chaste kiss on her lips. "So if I want to woo you then, purple flowers, not black, would be the way to go?"

"You think I need to be wooed?"

I shrug my shoulders. "Just need to see how much wooing I need to do."

Charlotte's eyes sparkle with mirth. "If this is you not wooing, I don't stand a chance with you."

I want to puff out my chest and beat on it like a caveman. "You best be prepared then. Because I can woo with the best of them. And Charlotte?" Her eyes are heated as they hold my gaze. "I plan to woo the shit out of you, love."

Chapter Eight

CHARLOTTE

The ballroom is crowded tonight. People on top of people, all hidden behind masks. Because of Halloween, Ellie planned a massive fundraising event for Sean's school with a masquerade theme. Masks required. She was wary about my presence drawing more attention to the event with both of us in attendance, but I wanted to come and support her. Even though she's my cousin, she's still one of my best friends. She and Zara are my team. Without them, I don't know where I'd be.

Growing up in the spotlight, it's rare to have someone know exactly what you're going through, so Ellie and I were lucky to have each other. And even though she gave up this life, my need to support her will never go away.

"Charlotte! You look fab!" Ellie appears, as if out of nowhere, beside me. She sweeps her gaze down my emerald-green dress. The material hugs every curve, dipping low in the front with a dangerous slit up the side to my thigh. My hair is twisted up, hiding the knot of the mask.

A gown like this would never be approved by the palace. But this is an unofficial event, and with my annoyance at Aunt Katherine at an all-time high, I wasn't ready to be told no.

"Me? *You* look incredible. I don't think I've ever seen you so happy." I wrap her into a hug, before she pulls me over towards the bar. The black material of her dress clings to her bump. The gold mask does little to hide her bright blue eyes. She's glowing.

"Please, I feel like a whale. This kid is dancing on my bladder, and it's killing me."

Pierce is with Sean by the bar, a drink in hand. My eyes peruse the suit he's wearing—a fitted blue suit, with a light blue pocket square. Pierce is handsome, there's no doubt about that. I could spend the entire night staring at him, and I wouldn't get my fill. What is it about a man in a suit that makes a woman lose her bloody mind?

"Charlotte. Nice to see you." Sean gives me a kiss on the cheek, but my gaze doesn't leave Pierce. His blue eyes spark with desire under his mask. I can feel the heat from here. How I want to be able to kiss him. Stand in his arms and not have anyone tell me it's wrong.

"You remember Pierce?" Ellie asks.

"I do." I extend my hand for him to shake. I never got to tell Ellie about our date before the Queen made it clear I couldn't see him again. She clearly doesn't bother reading the news. Heat snakes up my arm as he takes my small hand in his much larger one.

"Nice to see you again." He drops my hand, letting his fingers ghost over mine. The fine cut of his jaw and the perfect fit of his suit cause heat to build in my core. This man is pure temptation.

"We have to go mingle. Make sure to talk up the school to get as many donations as you can tonight." Ellie loops her arm through Sean's and drags him off. I turn to the bartender and order a glass of champagne.

"You look unbelievably sexy." Pierce's voice is dripping with lust as he stands at my side, his glass hiding his mouth.

"I can say the same about you." I take my drink, the cool liquid helping to calm my overheated body. Just being near Pierce is messing with my head.

"I didn't think you'd be coming tonight." We move to the side, standing close enough to talk, but not close enough to raise any questions.

"I wanted to support Ellie. She's still family, even if she has stepped away from her royal duties."

"I'm glad you came. But fuck, the things I want to do to you in that dress."

Fire licks down my spine at his words. "And what would you do?"

Pierce moves closer, setting his empty glass down beside me. "I'd kiss my way up your leg, and when I get to the top of that slit, I'd tear that dress right off you. Then I'd work my way up the other side. I'd show you pleasure no man has ever given you before."

Bloody hell. I rub my thighs together, trying to quell the building need in my core. I could come just from hearing those words from his lips.

I look around and see someone start to walk over to me. "It was nice to speak with you, Pierce. Hopefully I'll see you later?"

He gives me a questioning look, before seeing why I changed the subject. He turns, backing away from me. "To be continued."

ALL NIGHT. All night I've been filled with an aching need for Pierce. No matter whom I'm talking with, my eyes find

Pierce. The searing heat in those blue eyes of his have been driving me crazy. No matter where I go in this ballroom, we find each other, as if we're two magnets destined to connect.

"Thank God I found you." Ellie is at my side.

"Are you okay?" I look over her to make sure nothing is wrong.

"I just need to sit. I'm absolutely knackered. I forgot how tiring these events are, let alone doing it while almost eight months pregnant."

"C'mon then." I loop my arm through hers and drag her off towards benches on the side of the room.

"Do you want me to go find Sean for you?"

She gives me a sweet look. "Could you? I'm ready to head home. Would you mind staying a little longer?"

I drop a kiss on her cheek. "I'll take care of it."

"You're the best, Charlotte."

I give her a bright smile as I push my way onto the crowded dance floor. Drinks have been flowing all night, and the loud music has enticed people onto the dance floor. It's hard to tell who anyone is behind their mask.

A hand on my stomach pulls me back into a hard body. "Where do you think you're going?"

Pierce's gravelly voice washes over me. This simple touch has me itching to turn in his arms. To kiss him.

"Trying to find your brother so he and Ellie can leave."

His breath is hot on my neck. "And do you plan on going home with anyone tonight?"

Goose pimples break out over my skin. "I did see someone I'd like to take home. Not sure if he has any plans."

The masks were perfect for tonight. I'm not Princess Charlotte. We're just two strangers on the dance floor.

"The only plans he has tonight is to make you his."

Lust coils deep in my core. I bite my lip, stifling the moan desperate to break free at his words.

"I'll meet you back at your flat tonight." Desire hangs on every word.

"Wear the dress. I have big plans for you tonight."

Chapter Nine

PIERCE

The knock on the door has my dick perking up. I've been on edge all night. Being near Charlotte but not being able to touch her is the worst feeling. When I swing the door open, Charlotte stands there in the same dress, no mask.

I waste no time, pulling her into me and dropping my lips to hers. She opens, and our tongues tangle. I could get drunk off the taste of champagne on her lips alone. I'm hungry for her. To feel her bare skin against my lips.

"Fuck. You've been driving me crazy all night." I drop my forehead to hers, breathing in her scent.

"I hated not being with you tonight." Charlotte's fingers trace over my lips. I capture her thumb, swirling my tongue around the pad. Her teeth sink into her lower lip, stifling her moan. She steps closer, her hard nipples brushing my chest.

"You're here now." I back her slowly into my flat, until she hits the back of the sofa. "And tonight, you're mine." I flip her around, bending her over the sofa. I don't want to waste a minute of our precious time together. I hike her dress up, exposing her hips. I pull her thong to the side, running my finger up her slit.

"Have you been wet for me all night?" I dip my finger lower, running it over her clit.

"Yes." Her voice is breathy. "I want you, Pierce."

"Oh yeah?" I kneel down and sit back on my heels, squeezing the sweet globes of her arse together. "Did you imagine how it will feel when I sink my cock into your tight pussy?" I lick down her slit, savouring the taste of her.

She peeks over her shoulder, locking eyes with me, and shakes her head. "No. I imagined how it would feel while I was riding you. To see me bring you to release."

She plays the role of demure princess, but she's anything but. She's fierce. She's powerful. She's commanding. And she can bring any man to his knees. But somehow, I'm the lucky bastard that gets to worship this woman.

My teeth sink down into the globe of her arse before licking the sting away. Charlotte's gasp urges me on as I plunge two fingers into her hot channel. She pushes back, rocking her hips into me. My other hand wraps around her front, rubbing over her clit.

"Just like that." Charlotte's voice is low with need. My cock threatens to break free of my trousers, but there's nothing I can do about it as I focus on stroking her. I want to be inside her but want her orgasm more. "I'm close, Pierce."

Her pussy contracts around my fingers, as I thrust three fingers inside her. I'm dying for her to come on my fingers, but I want her taste on my tongue more. Pulling my fingers out, I lick down her slit, just as her orgasm slams into her.

"Pierce!" Her calling my name almost makes me come in my pants like a wanker. Fuck. Feeling her come on me and tasting her release is the best nectar.

Royal Relations

I pull back, steadying her as I stand behind her. She stands, turning to face me, peeling the straps of her dress off. The green silk pools at her feet. Charlotte stands on her tiptoes, taking my lips with hers. Her fingers toy with my hair, scraping along my scalp. I press my erection into her hip as I unhook her bra.

"So, are you ready to ride me?" I step back as Charlotte takes my hand, leading me back to my room. The soft sway of her hips is mesmerizing. Like leading a thirsty man to water. Her naked body is a sight to behold, as if someone created her from my dreams.

She drops her thong and kicks out of her heels as she lies back on the mattress. Her pussy glistens with her release.

"Bloody hell, do you even realize how sexy you are?" I undo the buttons on my shirt slowly, shrugging out of it. I feel her eyes everywhere.

"Do you realize how sexy you are?" She parrots back at me, rubbing her legs together. I grab her ankles, pulling her towards me.

"You don't get another orgasm unless I say so." Her heated gaze roams over me. She wags her finger, beckoning me over her. Charlotte's lips are soft, peppering kisses along my jaw to my ear. I've never been so fucking hard in my life. All I want is to sink into her sweet heat and feel her pulse around me.

"I don't orgasm until you orgasm." She flips us around, straddling my hips. Her fingers trace my tattoos, lighting my skin on fire.

"So you're in charge now?" I thrust my cock up towards her core, as her fingers drift down my chest. Her lips follow. I've never had a woman take control like this before, and it's a huge turn-on.

Her eyes hold mine as she starts to undo my belt

buckle. She drags my trousers and boxers down as my cock springs free. Her smile is downright wicked as she tosses them to the side.

Charlotte moves back up my body, taking my dick in her hand. A low hiss escapes, loving the feel of her nimble fingers wrapped around me. "I've been imagining this all night."

She takes the head of my cock in her warm mouth, and it takes everything I have not to come down her throat right then. Her tongue and fingers are magic as they work together to make me harder and harder. I fist her hair, loving the sight of her swallowing me down.

"Fuck, Charlotte." I try to pull her off me, but she keeps going. Pushing me closer and closer to release. Tears wet the corner of her eyes as I bump the back of her throat. "I can't be coming down your throat the first time we do this."

She pulls off me with a pop. "And what if that's what I want?" She keeps stroking my cock, slick with her saliva.

I reach over to my bedside table, grabbing a condom. "Next time, love. I want you riding me. Just like you said." She quirks her lips up as she grabs the condom.

"You are lucky you're sexy, otherwise I might just hold out on you." Charlotte rolls the condom down my length, giving me a hard squeeze. She rolls her pussy over my dick. It jumps, wanting to get inside her.

"You're driving me crazy, Charlotte." I squeeze her tits together, thumbing her hard nipples. She rocks over me faster. "I need you inside me." I pull her over me, crashing her mouth to mine. I need her lips on mine. I need to feel her everywhere as she slowly sinks down on my cock. My hands squeeze her arse, holding her still. I go over every step of tattooing to keep from blowing my load. Charlotte shifts her hips, starting to move over me.

"You feel amazing." I thrust up into her, meeting her pace. Her nails digging into my chest cause pain to mix with the pleasure. Heat races down my spine as my balls draw up tight, threatening to explode. I try to move her faster, but she slows down, dragging it out.

"Uh, uh, uh. Not yet." She throws her head back, rocking over me. Charlotte is a vision moving over me. Taking me right towards the edge but pulling back.

"You're such a tease." Charlotte peeks down at me, a smile playing on her lips as she starts to play with her clit. I love a woman who knows what she wants. And Charlotte is going for it.

"God damn it. I'm so close." My thrusts are erratic as I try to chase my orgasm. Charlotte is moving faster, the first flutters of her orgasm starting.

"Pierce. Yes! God, yes!" Charlotte pulses around me as I explode into the condom, thrusting up hard.

"Yes. Fuck, yes." My fingers dig into her thighs as we move through our release together. I've never seen a more beautiful sight than Charlotte, eyes half closed with passion and desire as she stays on top of me. I pull her down, chest to chest. Her sweat-slicked skin is flushed from her orgasm. The sweet scent of her perfume hits me and something settles over me. A feeling like coming home—something I don't think I've ever felt before.

No woman has ever made me feel like this. How can this woman I've only known for a short time make me feel so settled? Like I don't have to reach for more. Like everything in my life is okay. That I'm not living in someone's shadow.

"Thinking some deep thoughts there." Charlotte's voice ghosts over my chest. Goose pimples break out over my skin.

"Just thinking how right this feels."

And it does.
Being with Charlotte right now?
Well, it feels bloody well perfect.

Chapter Ten

CHARLOTTE

"Mm, what smells so good in here?" I push my way inside Pierce's flat. Pierce is in his kitchen, plates of food spread out before him. He looks delectable in that tight black tee of his. Ever since the night of the masquerade ball, all I've wanted is to be around him. Any free moment I get, I'm racing across town to his flat.

I want to be wrapped up in his comfort. Locked away from the rest of the world and those keeping us apart. The Queen. The press. Mum, to an extent. If only they could see the man I see. He's the furthest thing from a bad influence.

"Hi, love." He tosses a towel over his shoulder and greets me with a kiss. "I missed you today."

I press up onto my tiptoes, giving him another kiss. Longer. Deeper. "I missed you too."

He wraps an arm around my waist, tucking me into his side. Different plates of food are spread out in front of us. Asian. What smells like curry. Mini tacos. And… "Is that cereal?" I ask.

Pierce's smile is bright. "I figure since we can't go out to all these places, I can bring all the best of London to us."

My heart catches in my chest. One of the things I hate about having to hide our relationship is that we can't be seen together. I want to be able to go to all these places with Pierce, but they're too public. Prime for the Queen to catch us together.

"I love it. Where do I get to start?" I rub my hands together, leaning over and smelling all the different aromas.

"Relax, Charlotte." Pierce hands me a beer. "Plenty of time to enjoy everything I have. Now, sit so I can serve you."

He walks around the bar, pulling out a seat for me. "What did I do to deserve this tonight?" I can't stop beaming with happiness. One of my favourite things is going to all the fun restaurants around the city. With a city this size, there's no shortage of quirky places to try.

"Just because we can't go out, doesn't mean I can't plan a night that isn't boring."

"I'm finding things are anything but boring with you, Pierce."

I sip the cold beer as Pierce places one of the first dishes in front of me. "For your appetizer, ma'am." His face is full of sass, his eyebrows waggling at me. "We have Asian fusion pork belly tacos with a crème sauce. Pairs perfectly with the beer you're drinking."

Laughter bubbles out of me. "Will you accept tips at the end of the night?"

Pierce leans across the counter, capturing my lips with his. "Not in the form of currency, no."

"However will I afford my dinner then?"

Pierce's eyes sparkle with mischief. "I can think of a few ways to pay your server back."

He moves closer, hoping to sneak a kiss. I pull back. "I only pay for exceptional service."

"Better up my game then."

I grab a mini taco off my plate, my gaze locking with Pierce's as I take a small bite. The flavours burst to life on my tongue, and I let out a very unladylike groan.

"I don't think I've ever tasted anything more delicious than this." I shove the rest of it in my mouth. The sweet and spiciness of the Asian flavours are perfect together. "Where is this from? I want to eat only this for the rest of my life."

Pierce's face is lit up with satisfaction. "Circus. I had a feeling you would like them. If you're at the restaurant, there's this whole show they put on." He grabs one and puts the whole thing in his mouth. There's no bitterness in his tone that we have to stay here and can't experience the show together.

"I like that you know what I like," I say over the bite in my mouth. It's not becoming of a princess, but Pierce doesn't care. I can be myself around him. Not have to worry about anyone snapping an unflattering photo to be out in the world for the rest of time.

"Well, I hope you'll like this too." Pierce pushes a small bowl filled with cheese and bread towards me.

"Cheese? This doesn't seem very exciting." I tear off a small piece of bread, still warm, and drag it through the gooey concoction.

"The entire restaurant is cheese. It's all they serve. Who doesn't love cheese?"

The same could be said of Pierce and the adoring eyes he's aiming my way. Who would go to so much trouble to get all this food from restaurants all over the city? It's nights like these, with Pierce, that make all the sneaking around worth it.

"You're looking awfully thoughtful over there, love." Pierce's blue eyes focus on me.

My life isn't easy. People can't handle the press and the rigid standards we have to live by. It's what made Michael leave. Even though we have to hide, being with Pierce is easy. With the way he makes me feel, I'd gladly spend all my days tucked away here if it means I get to be with him.

"Just enjoying the company tonight. I love finding new places and now, I can't wait to go and visit them all." I take another dip of the cheese, but Pierce grabs my wrist, taking his own mouthful. The way his jaw works as he chews is mesmerising.

"Maybe it's something we can do some day." There he goes again. Making plans when I have no idea what our future holds. How long can the two of us sneak around like this? The thought is ice water in my veins. I love being with Pierce like this. Us in our own little bubble. But it can't last, right?

"Try this now." Pierce pushes a steaming, orangey soup towards me.

"What is this?" I inhale. "And why does it smell like peanut butter?"

"Because it is peanut butter. Peanut butter stew from West Africa."

I take a hearty spoonful. Peanut butter. Carrots. Sweet potatoes. "This seems like it would be weird, but wow." I take another bite, tamping down the errant thoughts.

"It's one of my favourites." Pierce has scarfed down half his bowl by the time I look up.

"Where is this from?"

"It's from a small food truck. The owner is from Ghana and came in for a cover-up. Told me all about making the dish from his country. I went the next day and tried it.

Been going every week since. Great mate of mine now. Even plays football with us now. "

I sink back into my chair, finishing off my beer as Pierce sits beside me. "I bet you meet a lot of interesting people."

He nods, sipping on his own drink. "Like you wouldn't believe. But you have to meet a lot of interesting people too."

He pulls my feet into his lap, rubbing the soles. "That is heavenly." His touch soothes away any thoughts on how this won't last. On how this won't work.

"I meet a lot of great people," I say, going back to his question. "But they always put on a front for meeting the princess. The kids are the only ones who don't have any airs about them when they meet me. They're my favourite."

"Do you see yourself having kids?"

I swallow the steaming bite of soup, washing it down with beer. "Two. I've always wanted them. What about you?"

"Never thought about it before. Wasn't with anyone serious. But I could be swayed."

The look in his eyes tells me what, or who, could sway him. "Oh, yeah?"

"Seeing how happy Sean and Ellie's baby makes them, and he or she isn't even here, makes me want that same kind of happiness."

"They are so good together." I take the last bite of soup, not sure what else Pierce has for me.

"Kind of makes you wish we could be together like that?" His voice takes on a melancholy tone.

"What do you mean?"

"That I could hold your hand in public. That I could

kiss you whenever I want to. That you could spend the night here."

I laugh. "Sorry to burst your bubble, but spending the night is frowned upon if you're a royal. Can you imagine the scandal?"

"*Princess Charlotte is a hussy! Seen leaving boyfriend's flat in the early morning hours!*" Pierce emphasises each word with his hands.

"Oh, so I'm a hussy now?"

Pierce pulls me closer to him. "Only for me. Now do you want the last dish?"

"I don't think I can eat anything else." I lean back in the chair.

"Are you sure? You haven't had dessert yet."

My ears perk up. "Is that the cereal?"

"Thought it'd be fun to try for dessert instead of breakfast." He leans across the counter to grab the colourful bags. I twist my fist into his shirt, pulling him back towards me.

"I can think of something else I'd like for dessert too."

Pierce's eyes darken with need. "Oh yeah? Perhaps a coffee? Tea?"

I smack his shoulder. "I guess you don't want what I'm offering up then. Guess I should just call it an early night."

I drag my feet out of Pierce's lap, feeling how hard he is for me. I stand, moving between his legs. "Guess I'll see you in a few days then?" I whisper in his ear.

Pierce pulls me closer, moving his hands under my jumper and running them along my bare skin. A cunning smile cuts his face.

"I guess dessert can wait."

Chapter Eleven

CHARLOTTE

"Okay, if you could have any job, what would it be?" My fingers trace the intricate tattoos on his chest. The peaks of the mountains that cross his chest.

"What makes you think I'm not doing my dream job?" Pierce is relaxed, his head resting on his arm against the pillows. Soft light filters in from the streetlights outside. His fingers are brushing through the tangles in my hair, no doubt put there by his hand being fisted in it while he was pounding into me.

"Did you always want to be a tattoo artist?" I ask. Pierce captures my hand, bringing it to his lips.

"I actually wanted to move to Australia and become a surfer."

I sit up, and Pierce moves with me. I crawl into his lap, and his leg bends, letting me rest against it. This intimate way we're together? It's relaxing. These quiet moments with Pierce are my favourite. I'm not the princess. We're just two people spending time together. Loving each other's company. No pressure from the outside world. No one telling us we can't be together.

"Can I ask the obvious question?" Laughter laces my voice.

His face lights up. "If I can surf?"

I nod my head, biting my lip to keep my laughter to myself. "Seems like something you would need to know how to do if you wanted to move to Australia and surf."

He shrugs his shoulder. "Mum took us to the beach in Nice when we were little. Dad was giving a lecture at a uni there, so we got to tag along. I remember seeing the surfers and wanting to be just like them."

I lace my fingers with his. "And have you tried surfing?"

"I did once. Total, absolute crap at it. Kind of killed the dream of moving Down Under."

I lean closer to him, my lips a breath from his. "I'm kind of glad you didn't move to Australia."

"Because you wouldn't be here with me right now?"

I nod, dropping a kiss to his lips. "And I'm rather enjoying your company right now."

Pierce's mouth claims mine, his powerful lips moving against mine, his tongue sweeping into my mouth. I lean into his touch, wrapping my arms around him. The easy caress of his tongue starts a fire in my belly. I can't get enough of this man.

He pulls back, his eyes hooded with lust. Will my desire for this man ever be sated?

"What about you, love?" He peppers my face with kisses. "What would you be doing with your life if you weren't a princess?"

"Roller derby girl." My answer comes without hesitation.

"Of all the things in the world, I didn't expect you to say that." Pierce tucks a loose strand of hair behind my ear.

"What, I don't look like I could be a roller derby girl?" I pull back, waving my hands over my body.

"If this is how a roller derby girl looks,"—his warm hands squeeze my breasts together—"then I've been missing out."

Arching into his touch, I try to quell the desire now racing through me. "We went to a roller derby once growing up—I can't remember why—but I remember thinking how badass those women were. I wished I could've been like them." There's a wistfulness in my tone that Pierce doesn't miss. "It's one of the reasons why I want to start this charity for women. To make them all feel like the badass women I know they can be."

"You're pretty incredible, you know that?" Pierce's eyes are soft as he meets my gaze.

"You're just saying that."

"Just because you're not a roller girl, doesn't mean you're not a badass. Your nickname should be Princess Badass."

I bury my laughter in Pierce's neck. "You know just what to say to make a girl feel good."

"Only good?" Pierce wraps me in his arms and flips us on the bed, his weight settling over me. "I must not be doing my job if I don't make you feel like the powerful badass you are every day."

This man. This man takes my breath away. Every other man I've been with made me feel like they were doing me a favour by being with me. I'm self-aware enough to know that my life is hard. That not a lot of people want to take on what the crown requires of them.

But Pierce did it without blinking. Can't be seen in public? *Come to my flat.* Not being seen together at the same event? *No problem.* How can one man be this good?

I run my hands down his spine, his skin pebbling

beneath my fingers letting me know how my touch affects him. "Would you be my cheerleader as I raced around a rink in a short little skirt? Tattoos covering my arms?"

"Tattoos? All this untouched skin you have…just think of the tattoos I could give you…" he trails off.

"What kind of tattoos would you give me?"

Pierce's face is thoughtful. "You'd have a sleeve of flowers. Soft and gentle. But vines of thorns for your badass side." His hand traces down my arm, as if he's imagining the ink there. He rests on his elbow, moving his hand between my breasts.

"And here, you'd have the female symbol." My nipples harden with his hands caressing the underside of my breasts. "Hidden so only I know it's there. Knowing that you're this badass woman who doesn't take shit from anyone, but wants to help everyone around her? Yup, total badass." He traces the pattern on my skin, his fingers lighting a fire inside me.

"What about your face on my arm?"

Pierce shakes his head. "Fuck, no. No names or faces. Shop policy."

My lips turn down in a frown. "So you'll never get your badass roller derby girl tattooed on you?" I trace an empty space on his side. "You don't want me in roller skates and a short skirt right here?"

"Fecking hell." Pierce rolls his hardening erection into me. "Now all I want is to put that bloody tattoo on me and be a cheerleader for you while you knock out other women on skates. You'd be the sexiest one out there."

"And I'd have the sexiest man on my side. All the women would be drooling over you."

Warmth washes over Pierce's handsome face. "I'd have eyes for only you. No other badass could sway me."

Our lips crash together. It's gnashing teeth and tongues

as we fight for control. I love the give and take that Pierce and I have. Some days he takes control, but most of the time, he relinquishes it to me. But now, we're fighting to dominate this kiss. I plant my feet to flip us, but Pierce pushes me down into the bed. His hips grind into me as I tear my mouth away. His lips trail down my neck, hot, searing kisses making me wet with need.

I grab a condom from the nightstand, rolling it down his hard length. He doesn't waste another second before thrusting deep inside of me.

"Pierce," I moan, desire and need evident in my voice. My fingernails dig into his back, urging him on.

"Fuck, Charlotte." He picks up speed, and I already feel my orgasm racing down my spine. His lips drift down my neck, nibbling and sucking. My hands move down his taut back, skirting the top of his arse, pulling him into me on every thrust.

"You." Kiss. "Feel." Kiss. "Amazing." Pierce's words are lighting me up from the inside out.

"Don't stop."

I'm on the edge of the cliff, ready to fall over, when Pierce slows down.

"I'm so close!" My voice is whiny.

"I can't have you coming too quick. What would you think of me if a few pumps and you come?"

I lean up to him, my lips tracing the shell of his ear. "That you're a fantastic lover."

"Damn it, Charlotte. You don't play fair."

I squeeze his arse. "I could say the same of you."

Pierce growls, picking up his pace again. It doesn't take long. I was on the cusp before, but a few thrusts and I'm exploding around him.

"Pierce. Yes!" Pierce surrounds me. His arms. His

scent. Everything about him swirls around me as he starts to come.

He's a sight to behold. The way his neck is tightly corded. How his chest ripples. The flush of his skin. Pierce is the sexiest man ever. And watching him come undone like this prolongs the need that's taking over my body.

Pierce stills inside me. His hair falls into his eyes. Tucking it back, I pull him to me, his lips meeting mine in an easy kiss.

"I wish you didn't have to go."

"I wish I could stay."

We laugh, our words spoken at the same time. No matter how long we're together, it's too short. I want more time with him.

"One day, Charlotte. One day we can be together. Just you and me."

I know it's not that easy, but for just one moment, I picture Pierce and me—holding hands, walking through the park, and attending events together. Just being together.

"Mm, one day." I hug him to me, not ready to let him go just yet.

"One day sounds pretty great."

Chapter Twelve

CHARLOTTE

The loud beat from the club vibrates through me. Even in the VIP section, it's loud. Tiny rooms make up this level of the club. It's one of the only places I knew Pierce and I could get some privacy. I was able to sneak in without anyone seeing me. Drinks, courteous of my security team, were waiting. Now all that's left is for the man of the hour to arrive.

Sipping on my champagne, I glance at my watch. He should be here any minute. We've camped out at his flat these last few weeks, but I could tell we were going stir-crazy, so I suggested a night out at the club. Pierce was hesitant, but I knew we could get away with it. James always was able to when he was here with the women he used to hook up with. But now it's me waiting for Pierce.

As if my thoughts conjured him, Pierce walks through the door, clicking it shut behind him. He is delicious. His mere presence takes over my every nerve as I get my fill of him. Dark jeans. White T-shirt that shows off all his tattoos. I never thought I'd find a man with tattoos so sexy, but Pierce is drool-worthy.

"I was getting antsy." I uncross my legs, setting my drink down as he approaches me. The clean scent that is all Pierce overwhelms me.

"Can't have that, now, can we?" He drops a kiss on my lips before sitting next to me. "Had I known you'd been waiting long, I would've gotten here much faster."

"Couldn't have you seen with me coming in." I hate that we have to hide what we have. Every part of me lights up the moment I see him. The moment I even think about him. I've never been so enraptured by someone before.

Pierce pulls me closer into his side. Not a breath of air is between us. "I get you now, though. That's all that matters." He pushes my hair over my shoulder as his lips find the spot on my neck he loves kissing so much. "Fuck, you are gorgeous." His hands roam over the short, leather miniskirt and silky tank top I'm wearing, one that shows off my curves nicely.

"I've missed you." It's only been a few days since I last saw him, but whenever I leave him, I can't help but feel I might not get to see him again.

"Long day?" He grabs a beer off the tray in front of me and pops it open.

I tuck myself into his side, needing to feel him. To finally relax. "You could say that."

Pierce's long fingers slide under my chin, tilting my gaze to meet his. "What happened?"

"You don't want to hear about my day. People have it way worse than I do." My fingers play with the collar of his shirt and the exposed ink there.

Pierce's eyes don't leave mine as I let out a breath. "On top of the Queen rejecting my proposal again, I was told by several people today how much they miss Eleanor, and how wonderful of a job she did with their organization. I

Royal Relations

know everyone loved her, but don't they see that I want to be there?"

"Maybe it'll just take some time for them to get to know you. They have to see what a big heart you have."

"I'm tired of everyone thinking I'm the sad, castoff princess." I gulp down the rest of my champagne.

Pierce tucks a loose strand of hair behind my ear, before dropping his hand to my knee. "I don't see you that way."

I pull back, looking into his eyes. "And how do you see me?" My voice is soft, barely heard over the bass pumping through the club.

"I see a strong, confident woman." He drops a hot kiss on my neck. "I see someone who sees what she wants and goes after it." A kiss on my jaw. "I see a woman so full of spirit that nothing will stop her from getting what she wants. Not even the Queen."

Butterflies swarm my stomach. Anytime I'm with Pierce, all the second-guessing goes away. I don't know what it is about him, but he calms me in a way I've never needed before.

My life was good. Even becoming third in line didn't change much. I was happy. But then Pierce came along and showed me exactly what I was missing.

"I wish everyone saw me the way you do." I trail my fingers over his face. This beautiful face that I'm falling for.

The flashing lights overhead change as a new song comes on. Pierce is tapping the beat of the music on my leg. Every beat sends a pulse racing through me.

I pull Pierce up. "Dance with me."

"Your wish is my command, princess." His lips quirk up into a smile. But his eyes belie him. Heat dances behind his darkened irises. Warm hands land on my hips, skating underneath the waistband of my short skirt.

I throw my arms over his shoulders, pulling myself closer to him. "You are the sexiest woman I've ever laid eyes on," he whispers in my ear as his hands drift lower, squeezing my arse as he tugs me to him. His erection is hard against me.

I sway my hips to the music, getting lost in the sensations around me. Of Pierce. Of the alcohol flowing through me. There's nothing but me and Pierce and the music. There're no worries about why I'm not good enough, who will see us, or why we can't be together. Everything fades to the background.

Pierce's lips ghost over my neck as I throw my head back. They drift lower and lower, driving my need for him higher and higher.

Throwing a leg around his hips, I grind into him, needing the friction. I've never felt so wanton in my life. Nothing has ever felt as good as when I'm with Pierce.

He starts to pull the cup of my top down, revealing more of my breast to him. He licks and sucks at the tender skin. I arch into his touch, wanting to tear my top off entirely to be at his mercy.

"Someone's needy tonight." His breath is hot against my overheated skin.

I pull his face to mine. "I need you." His eyes are dark with need, matching my own. Pierce's lips crash down on mine. This kiss is hard. Hot. Needy. I never want it to end. With one hand holding my body to him, his free hand drifts up my thigh.

"You want me like this?" His finger traces over the damp material of my thong, my need for him evident.

I bite down on my lip. I nod in response, my grip on his biceps tightening as he slips a finger inside me. "Bloody hell, have you been like this all night?"

"Whenever I'm around you." My voice leaves me on a

Royal Relations

gasp as he starts thrusting his finger in and out of me. The heel of his hand is grinding down on my clit.

My pleasure is ratcheting to new heights. I'm shamelessly riding his hand, wanting nothing more than to find release with Pierce at this moment.

"Do you know how sexy you look right now?" His eyes are locked onto mine. "You're every man's wet dream, and yet somehow you're mine."

I wrap one hand around his neck, bringing him closer to me. "I only want to be yours," I whisper to him. His lips are everywhere on me as he sinks two fingers inside me.

"Yes, just like that, Pierce!" Any decorum of how to carry myself in public is out the window at this moment. It's just me and Pierce as he's driving me closer and closer towards an epic orgasm.

When his lips come down on mine again, my release shatters through me. The noise of the club fades to the background as I hold onto Pierce for dear life. Not a breath of air is between us as he coaxes me through my orgasm.

When I finally come down, he pulls his fingers out and sucks them in his mouth, tasting my release.

"There's nothing like watching you come all over my fingers." His eyes are hooded with lust as he gazes down on me. "I don't know what I did to deserve you, Charlotte."

His voice betrays his eyes. It's laced with a need I feel down to my bones. I don't know where I found Pierce, but I'm not ready to let him go yet. Even if this game we're playing is dangerous.

He sits, pulling me down on top of him. I'm utterly spent. "I should say I'm the lucky one." My fingers brush his cheeks. "Making you sneak around like this. No one should have to do that." My voice drops, even as I try to hide the anguish that laces it.

Pierce lifts my chin, forcing my focus on him. "You are

worth it, Charlotte. Don't ever doubt that you are. I'd spend years sneaking around if it meant I got to have you. In any way."

There aren't enough words to express what his mean to me, so I pull his lips to mine. It's a sweet kiss. Easy, languid strokes of my tongue meeting his.

"You're too good to me, Pierce."

"You make it easy, love." He reaches forward, passing me my drink before grabbing his. The cool liquid is refreshing to my overheated body. We stay like this, in comfortable silence as the music and lights continue to pulse around us.

"Do you need to be home soon?" he asks. My fingers skate over the tattoos on his arms.

I shake my head. "Not Cinderella tonight. No events tomorrow, so I can stay here with you as long as I like."

"Fecking hell, if that isn't an invitation." His heated words are a fire licking my skin.

I nip at his earlobe. "I'd close the club down if it meant I got to be here with you all night, but you know we can't."

His breath escapes him on a sigh. "Just means we have to make the most of the time we do have."

"I like the sound of that."

His lips capture mine in the sweetest of kisses. Everything about this man should scream bad boy, with the tattoos and intense eyes that hide his emotions. But not to me. He reveals everything to me with one glance. I love that he doesn't hide from me. Most men wouldn't show their true colours to a princess. But not Pierce.

He lays everything out for me. I could never get enough of this man. His touch. I shouldn't want him as much as I do, but I can't help it. His touch has brought me back to life.

He grabs my chin, changing the angle. Deepening the kiss. I straddle his lap, grinding myself over his erection.

"If you keep doing that, I'm going to come like a teenager in my pants."

I pull back, giving him a naughty grin. "Then we can't have that, can we?"

Finding the zipper, I pull it down. Reaching into his pants, I find his hard cock leaking.

"Fuck, that feels amazing," he says on a hiss. Wrapping my hand around his hard length, I start stroking as he tips his head back in pleasure. He rocks into me as I pump, moving my hand up and down. I slide off his lap, kneeling before him. His eyes are hungry as I take the tip of his hard cock into my mouth.

Pierce's hips buck off the bench, as I take him deeper. I push up his shirt, trailing my fingers over the lines in his abs. His hands fist through my hair, guiding my motions.

My eyes lock on his, not pulling away. I move my hand down, gripping the base and working him in tandem with my mouth. The hard floor is biting into my knees, but I don't care.

I've never done anything like this. Never felt so dangerous before. I hollow my cheeks and take as much of Pierce into my mouth as I can. My eyes water as I suck him down.

"Fuck, I'm going to come." His voice is gravelly. Pierce tries to pull me off of him, but I swat his hand away as the first spurts of cum hit my tongue. I drink it down. I take every last drop of his orgasm before I pull off him. His eyes are closed, his chest heaving with his quick breaths.

I wipe the corners of my mouth before I settle next to him. "Damn, Charlotte." He tilts his head to the side, opening one eye to look at me. "That was...wow."

I pull him in for a kiss, not wanting to lose the connection with him. It's getting late, and I know we'll have to leave soon. Each time, it gets harder and harder to leave him.

"I have to say, tonight was a pretty good night." I drop my forehead against his. A small smile plays on the corner of Pierce's lips.

"We should definitely come here more often."

Chapter Thirteen

CHARLOTTE

"You seem really happy." Zara stretches up in a warrior pose. We've been getting together to do yoga on Saturday mornings as often as our schedules allow.

"It's just been a good few weeks." *And an even better night at the club.* I try to hide my grin, going into downward dog.

"The last time I saw you, you were moping about. What changed?"

It might have to do with a certain handsome man, but I can't tell her that. I hate that I have to keep my relationship with Pierce a secret from Zara. Seeing how happy Zara and James are, as well as Ellie and Sean, makes my heart ache that I can't shout about my relationship.

"Just reframing how I'm going about things. No sense in moping, as you say, when things won't change."

Zara drops her pose, sitting on the yoga mat in her study. "Just like that?"

I peer between my arms, her body upside down from my angle. "Just like that."

"And here I was worried about you."

I drop my knees to the ground, sitting back on my heels. "Why were you worried about me?"

A sheepish look washes over Zara's face. "You just seemed so unhappy. I know you went out on a date with Pierce and had a great time, but nothing came of it."

I try to school my features, but I can't keep the smile from spreading.

"Nothing came of it, right?" I hesitate, only for a moment, before Zara's eyes widen. "Are you still seeing him?"

I shush her, waving my hands in front of her. "Of course I'm not still seeing him."

"Then why are you blushing?"

I pat my hands over my cheeks, trying to quell the growing heat in my face. "It's warm in here."

"Bollocks. It's a drafty old palace, and it's barely five degrees outside. You're sleeping with him, aren't you?" Zara's voice echoes throughout the room.

"Shut it!" I slap my hand over her mouth, but her eyes are alight in amusement.

"Why are you keeping this a secret from me?" She pulls my hand off her mouth.

"We need drinks for this."

"SO LET me get this straight. You and Pierce had, and I quote, 'the most magical evening of your life,' and the Queen told you you couldn't see him anymore?"

I nod my head, sipping on champagne. It's still early, so we could justify mimosas this morning. "That's basically it."

Royal Relations

"All because she's worried that Pierce will take you away from the crown?"

"Yup." I pop the p. "Apparently I don't know how to make my own decisions and could easily be swayed by a man."

"So just like that, the Queen says no, and you hide your relationship?"

"It's either that or give up the crown."

"I just can't wrap my head around it. Why would she think you'd give up the crown?"

"Ellie met Sean and then gave up her place in line."

"But she never wanted to be the Queen in the first place!" Zara shrieks.

"Shh! Keep your voice down." Why couldn't I have just said I was happy because I was working on my own charity? "She hated royal life, but Aunt Katherine only sees what she wants to see. And Pierce is a threat."

"Have you tried talking to her about it?" Zara tries to reason with me, but it won't help.

"No. I can't bear the thought of having to tell her why I want to date Pierce and have her shut me down again." Pain settles in my chest. How could anyone dislike Pierce? With his easy smile that lights up his face, the way he listens to me, and the caring way he holds me. I've never felt with anyone else the way I feel with Pierce.

"I hate this for you." Zara's face is full of sympathy, and I get it, because I hate it too.

"I've only ever had one real boyfriend, and he wasn't cut out for this life." I drain the rest of my mimosa and pour another. This conversation took a heavy turn for a Saturday morning.

"Michael?"

I lick my lips, nodding my head. "I thought he was the one,

you know? Granddad loved him, and my parents loved him. Turns out he didn't love me enough to put up with the circus surrounding my life." Tears wet my eyes. Thinking about him now pushes my relationship with Pierce into a harsh light.

"I hate to ask the tough question,"—Zara pauses, squeezing my hand—"but what makes you think Pierce is the one?"

I try to swallow over the nerves bubbling up. "Maybe he's not the one." My words feel forced and fake, but I play it off. "We could decide tomorrow we have no chemistry and want to end things right now."

Zara slaps her hands down on the counter. "Now I don't believe that for a second."

"And why not?"

"Because when you talk about him, you look the same way I do when I think about James. You have love in your eyes."

Covering my eyes with my hands, I rest my head on the counter. "It can't be love. We can't even be together."

The ache in my chest starts to grow. What if Pierce wakes up tomorrow and decides this isn't worth it? That I'm not worth sneaking around for? I don't know if I would survive it.

"And what are you ladies discussing this morning?" James startles me as he makes his way into the kitchen, dropping a kiss on Zara's cheek. Her face warms over at the mere sight of my cousin. I wouldn't be surprised to see hearts coming out of her eyes. These two are so bloody in love, it kills me. Is that the same face that Zara was just talking about?

"Just discussing wedding plans."

"And it's driving you to drink this early?" James quirks a brow at us.

"You've met the royal wedding planner," Zara deadpans.

"Drink away." James leaves just as quickly as he came.

"I love that man, but any time the wedding is brought up, he fakes an emergency just to try and leave."

"Can't trust men with anything." I force a laugh.

"Charlotte, I love you like the sister I never had, so I'm going to give you some tough love."

My heart sinks at her words. Please don't let her tell me to stop seeing Pierce. I don't know what our future holds, but I'm not ready to give him up yet. I'm too selfish for that.

"You need to make a decision, one way or the other. I know you care about him. It's easy to see. But you're doing a disservice to you and to him."

"There's no easy choice here, Zara." I pick at the hem of my workout top, not wanting to feel the full force of Zara's words. It's too hard.

"No one said love was easy."

Chapter Fourteen

CHARLOTTE

"Aren't you just precious?" A woman with hair as white as a cloud pinches my cheek. It's one of the many reasons I love coming to retirement centres. I love the elderly. "We loved your grandfather. May he rest in peace."

"Thank you for your kind words, Edith." She beams up at me from her seat in the community centre. "We loved him dearly."

"Didn't hurt that he was easy on the eyes." Her friend smacks her on the shoulder.

"Don't mind her. She's been on the hunt for a new man since she got here."

I have to hide my laughter. "You would've had to fight Grandmum off for him. She's quite the feisty one."

"Oh, I think I could take her."

"I'd pay good money to see you try," her friend says on a laugh.

"Ladies, we need to show Princess Charlotte a few more areas." The director of the community, Martha, looks mortified at these two women's words.

"I had such fun chatting with you two. It's people like you that make my work so enjoyable." I drop kisses on both of their cheeks.

Edith beams with pride. "Thank you for making these old loons' day." She motions between her and her friend. "My family won't believe I met you."

"Oh, we snapped a few pictures," the photographer in the back pipes up.

"One more?" I step behind Edith, and he gets another photo. "Hopefully your family will believe you now."

After another pinch to the cheek, I'm led into another part of the building. "Thank you for humouring some of our more lively residents. At this age, they tend not to have much of a filter."

"It's quite alright, Martha. My grandmum is the same way. Some of the things she says…" I laugh. Grandmum always has an inappropriate story to tell. Ever since Granddad died, it's like she lost the filter. She no longer makes public appearances, so it's as if she doesn't care.

"She's quite the woman. We all miss your grandfather dearly. But Queen Katherine is doing a marvellous job."

"That she is. She had big shoes to fill, but the Queen is doing a great job."

"Do you know I met your grandfather once?"

I shake my head. "When did you meet him?"

Martha is an easy woman to talk to. With soft features, she has the perfect temperament to run a place like this. "There was an event at the palace to thank healthcare workers. I didn't think I'd get invited, but I was. Both he and your grandmother were quite welcoming. Must say, it was such a highlight to meet him. He had quite the personality."

I smile. "My grandparents were quite the couple. We

were lucky to grow up with them. Seeing them on tours of the world was always special."

"Do you remember when they went to Canada? You might have been too young."

I laugh. "I grew up watching highlights from that tour. They were at a children's hospital, and one of the kids wanted to have a wheelchair race with him. I don't think I've ever seen him so happy."

"It was truly brilliant. It's what made me want to go into this business. Seeing how kind and caring he was made a difference in my life. My mum and I were lucky to have good people in our life. Turned our lives around."

"Turned your lives around?" I give her a questioning look, hoping she'll enlighten me.

"Dad wasn't around growing up. It was just me and Mum. If it wasn't for some friends of hers, we would've been out on the streets. Thankfully, a few of them took us in and gave us what we needed to get started again."

A lightbulb goes off. It feels like a lifting of the fog. This is exactly what I've been waiting for. I pull Martha in for a hug. "Thank you for telling me that. Stories like that are why I love my work. I only hope I can inspire someone like that in the future."

Martha gives me a warm smile. "I can assure you, you are inspiring to a lot of people."

A blush creeps up my neck. I love my work, but I never hear these words enough. And now, with her story, I hope I can inspire and help even more people. "Thank you. I can only hope I will live up to the legacy that my grandparents leave behind."

Seeing how in love my grandparents were makes me yearn for that kind of love. It makes me think I might have found that kind of love with Pierce. It's only been a few weeks, but whenever we're together, I'm happy. Even though we stay in the safety of his flat, we're in our own bubble. But can we exist outside of our bubble?

Only time will tell.

Chapter Fifteen

PIERCE

The door to my flat swings open, and Charlotte stands there, looking as sexy as ever. She's bundled up tight in a winter coat. It's colder than it should be in November. But the pink on her cheeks and the cute hat she's wearing have me clutching her tightly to me.

"Hi, love. Good day?"

She shivers, her body shaking in my arms. "Fantastic. I've finally realised what I'm going to do for my charity." Her hands snake under my shirt, a cold contrast to my warm body.

"Bloody hell. Let me make you some tea to warm you up, and you can tell me all about it."

The lights from the street flicker into my apartment. It's dark out already. I love the early nights at the shop during the winter months. It means I get more nights like this with Charlotte.

"It's so simple in its brilliance, I don't know why I didn't think of it before."

Charlotte is bubbling with excitement. I don't think I've

ever seen her this happy. The kettle starts to hiss, as I make us each a cuppa.

"Tell me about it."

Charlotte drags me over to the sofa, settling next to me. "I met this incredible woman today, Martha, and she told me her story. How seeing my grandfather racing in a wheelchair with a kid made her want to go into the healthcare industry and help people. And how her mum struggled when Martha was growing up."

I listen, not wanting to interrupt her. She sips at her tea, setting it down before grabbing my hands. "I want to help women who are down on their luck like Martha and her mum. If they might not have a place to go, create shelters for them. If they need a hand up in getting jobs, help them that way. Organise job fairs at these different shelters as a way to lift them up."

"And you think the Queen would approve?" I know how much she's been pushing back on Charlotte and not wanting her to do it.

"It's a much narrower scope than what I originally had planned. I really think this could be it, Pierce."

Her eyes are searching mine, as if she needs my approval. I cup her cheeks, still cold. "I think it is absolutely brilliant." I drop a tender kiss on her lips. "I'm so happy you finally found the spark. It's perfect. I don't know how the Queen wouldn't greenlight this for you."

"Really?"

I nod my head. "I want to help. I don't know how I can, but you're the perfect person to do this."

Charlotte drapes her legs over mine, scooting closer to me. "I feel really good about this. Like I was told no before because I was just waiting for this idea."

I love her passion about her job. It shines through in how she talks about her day. She was born to do this work.

"Anyway, enough about me. How was your day?"

I pull Charlotte closer to me. She never wants to keep the spotlight on her. It's one of the things that makes her so wonderful.

"New cover-up piece today. Going to take a few sessions, but it's going to be great."

Charlotte sets her tea down, straddling my legs. "I'd love to see your work someday."

I lift my sleeve up, showing her the ink on my forearm. "I designed all of these myself."

Her fingers trace the ink. The soft touch lights me up. I want to bottle it up and never lose it.

We're quiet, soaking each other in. Her eyes follow her fingers on my skin. It's moments like this that make me think this could work. That Charlotte could have an amazing day at her charity and come home to me. That we could be together for real.

"I've got a question for you." Charlotte pulls me from my thoughts.

"Hit me." My hands run up her thighs. I love that she always wants to sit on me like this, her straddling my lap. The constant need for contact with this one is high.

"What's your favourite sexual position? Or one you've always wanted to try?" Her voice is heavy, desire hanging on to every word.

My cock thickens behind my jeans, pressing into the zipper. "Bloody hell. That's quite the subject change."

Her fingers trace the throbbing veins on my neck. It takes every ounce of strength I have not to throw her down on this couch and ride her until she screams my name.

"I had a conversation with Zara—"

"You were discussing me with Zara?" Panic undercuts any other emotion I'm feeling.

Charlotte looks sheepish, dropping her gaze to her

hands that are now playing with the collar of my shirt. "I couldn't hide it. She's one of my closest friends, and it just sort of came out."

"What if she tells someone?" I'm not ready for this to be over. Sure, I wasn't sure if I could do this at first, but it was a pretty easy decision. Charlotte makes it easy, and I'm not ready to give her up.

"She won't. I'd trust Zara with my life," Charlotte says, her tone forceful, leaving no room for argument.

"I trust you." And I do. It's easy to trust Charlotte, but there's still a niggle of worry that this could bite us in the arse.

"I wasn't discussing you specifically with Zara. She was telling me about this game her friend Marnie got her for their wedding night."

"A game? What kind of game?" My interested is piqued.

"You draw a card, and whatever position you get, that's how you're having sex."

Fucking hell. "And where do we get a copy of this game?" My cock is hard against Charlotte's heated core. There are far too many layers of clothing between us.

"I couldn't possibly go out and buy the game. But I thought it'd be fun to try the ones we want to try tonight." Charlotte's eyes are dark. Darker than I've ever seen them.

"Well then." I kiss her neck, sucking on the tender skin over her throbbing pulse. She tilts her head, giving me better access. "I say ladies first then."

Charlotte runs her hands down my chest. "I want you to tie me up."

"What are we talking about here? Arms? Legs?"

"Just my arms. I've never done it before, and I only trust you to do it."

My lips curl up into a smile. "I think I'm really going to like this game."

I pick Charlotte up, her legs wrapping around my waist. Her mouth moves over my neck as I take us into the bedroom. I drop her in the middle of my bed, watching as her gorgeous tits bounce under her T-shirt.

"I think mine will line up nicely with yours." Dragging a finger along the V of her shirt, I pull it away from her skin, getting a peek of the swell of her breasts.

"And what is yours?"

"I want to fuck these tits of yours." My voice is gravelly, my dick threatening to explode with the tension buzzing in the room. "You have the most beautiful breasts I've ever seen, and I want to see my cock sliding through them. Feel them surrounding me. Come all over your beautiful tits."

Charlotte gets up on her knees, crawling towards me. Her fingers hook into the waistband of my jeans, pulling me closer. The brush of her fingers on my warm skin has me ready to strip her naked and take her right here.

"Then let's get started." The clink of my belt echoes around the room. She pulls it out before moving to pop open the button of my jeans. Her fingers move the zipper down, the snick the only sound I hear. My boxers are tented, the need in me evident as Charlotte palms the bulge.

"Fuck. If you keep doing that, this little game is going to be over well before it starts."

Grabbing the back of my shirt, I pull it over my head and drop it on the floor. Charlotte's eyes track my movement. My skin heats under her stare. I love the way she looks at me. It's how I look at her. Like she's the best thing to ever happen to me.

Charlotte takes her shirt off. Her nipples are diamond hard through the lace cups of her bra. "I can't believe I get to fuck these." I squeeze them together, feeling their heavy weight in my hands. As my thumbs graze her tight nipples, Charlotte arches into my touch.

"What are you waiting for? Tie me up and get to it."

"Patience is a virtue." Hand landing in the centre of Charlotte's chest, I push her back on the bed. She lifts her back up to take off her bra as I take my belt in hand.

"I'll make these loose, in case you want to stop." I lean over her, bringing her arms up with one hand.

"I trust you." Her eyes lock on mine. There's no hesitation in them. I don't take this trust lightly. I claim her lips with mine. The need I have for this woman is undeniable. I thought we'd have a few fun dates and then call it quits because it was too hard.

But the only hard thing is how fast I've fallen for her. I've never had this connection with anyone else. Asking silly questions. And fun questions. Fuck, questions about what sexual positions we want to try. Only a deep sense of trust between two people would move a relationship like this along.

I link the belt around Charlotte's wrists, binding them together through the slats of my bed. "Feel okay?" She tests the strength.

"Perfect."

With a leg on each side of her waist, I gaze at the beauty beneath me. Long dark hair fanned out on my pillow. Lips a deep red. Eyes shining bright with trust.

Standing, I shuck off my pants and boxers, my cock hitting me in the stomach. I grab a condom and lube from the nightstand and go back to Charlotte, continuing my perusal of her body.

"You still have on far too many clothes." I run a single finger down her stomach. Goose pimples break out over her soft skin.

"Whatever shall you do about it?" Her voice is filled with lust. I undo the button and zipper on her pants, pulling them down her legs, a scrap of black fabric covering the pussy that I love so much.

"I think I'm going to fuck this pussy nice and hard. But right before I come, I'm going to fuck these tits." My hands go to them, pinching and rolling the dark nipples between my fingers. "I'm going to come all over your chest." My vision blurs with need. "Fuck. I'm going to claim them as mine. No one else gets these tits but me."

A possessiveness I've never felt settles over me. I've never said anything like that to another woman. But I know I want Charlotte for as long as she'll have me. I want to make her mine in every sense of the word.

Charlotte's legs are rubbing together, and I command, "I don't think so. Your orgasm is mine tonight." I pull her legs apart. Running a finger under her thong, I rip the material away from her body. Her pussy glistens with need.

"Pierce. I need you," Charlotte moans. Gazing up at her, I see she's pulling at her binds.

"Oh, you do?" I sit back on my heels, my gaze roaming over her naked body.

I've had my fair share of sexual experiences, but seeing Charlotte tied up like this is a new one. "Fucking hell, you're absolutely gorgeous."

Charlotte's eyes open, locking onto mine. The world stills around us. It's just the two of us in my bed. Charlotte's not a princess, and I'm not someone she has to hide away from the world. It's just us. Pierce and Charlotte. Charlotte, giving herself over to me in a way I never would have imagined.

Settling over her, I claim her lips. I need the connection. To be as close as possible to her. I kiss down her jaw.

Nibble on her ear. Suck on the elegant slope of her neck. Charlotte pulls against my belt.

"Doing alright, love?" I nibble on her collarbone.

"Ugh. I just want to touch you." I pepper kisses down her chest, lavishing attention on the swell of her breasts.

"I have to say, I like this. Getting to take my time and explore every inch of your body." I squeeze her tits together, flicking her nipples with my thumbs. Her leg is moving under my hard cock, and I have no doubt precum is leaking all over her leg.

"I might have to rethink this next time."

"If you're ready to stop, I have no problem doing so." I pull back, my hands resting on the curves of her hips.

Charlotte gives me a look that would bring me to my knees if I wasn't on the bed already. "If you stop, there will be hell to pay."

The corner of my mouth quirks up. "Your wish is my command then."

Kisses rain down over her stomach, sucking on every inch of creamy skin before nibbling on her hip bone. The smell of her need has me moving faster. Wanting to sink my cock into her tight pussy. To fuck her within an inch of orgasm and then take what I want.

Spreading her folds, I take my time, licking and sucking on her pussy. Swirling the wetness on her clit. Her moans and sighs are making it hard to go slow, but I love making her crazy.

"Are you going to fuck me yet?" I peer up at her, not moving my tongue from heaven. She tastes like the most forbidden fruit. Sinful and sweet, which is my Charlotte in a nutshell.

Sitting back on my feet, I grab the condom and roll it over my hard length. "Are you ready for this? I won't go easy."

I give myself a hard stroke, not wanting to blow my load before I'm between her tits. "I want it hard, Pierce. Fuck me hard."

I sink into her tight pussy. "Fuck. Fuck fuck fuck."

I don't know what it is about tonight, but Charlotte has never felt so good squeezing my cock. Setting an unrelenting pace, I drive into her. My thrusts are quick and hard. Grabbing the lube, I pop the lid open and coat her tits. While I'm playing with her nipples, her pussy flutters around me.

"You like that?"

"God, yes!" Charlotte's eyes are closed, head thrown back in pleasure. Seeing her like this, laid out before me, has my balls coiling up tight.

I pull out of her, taking the condom off. Moving up her flushed body, I take her tits in my hands, squeezing them together as my cock slides through the slickness. The tip bumps her chin.

"Fuck. This is hottest thing I've ever done." I play with the hard peaks of her nipples as I thrust between them, this time long and slow.

Charlotte's eyes connect with mine, and I couldn't look away if I tried. They're dark with need, but the trust there? It's like nothing I've ever experienced. The trust she has in me to do this, to give me control, is something I don't take lightly. The connection is strong. The desire swirling between us causes me to pick up the pace. I want to paint her with my release. To mark her as mine.

I've never felt so possessive of a woman. But Charlotte brings it out in me. She makes me feel things I've never felt before.

The soft moans from Charlotte and her own orgasm shuddering through her body pulls mine from me. Long spurts of cum land on her chest, rolling down her neck and chin. Fuck, if this isn't the sexiest thing ever. I pull back, her breasts thoroughly ravaged. Charlotte's body is soft, sinking into the mattress.

Climbing off her, I undo the belt, pulling her arms down. "I don't think I'll be able to move." Massaging the stiffness in her shoulders, I kiss my way down her arms, paying special attention to the red marks on her wrists.

"You okay?" I grab my shirt from the floor, cleaning her up. Charlotte snuggles into my side as she burrows under the covers.

"I feel amazing." Her fingers dance across my chest as we lie together. It's the perfect moment, soft and tender after what we just did. But it can't last. "I wish I could stay the night."

"I know." I kiss the top of her hand, brushing my hands over the silky locks of her hair. "Maybe just stay a little while longer?"

"Mmm. Okay." Charlotte's voice is soft as she starts to drift off.

This right here is everything. Exactly what I want in life. To have Charlotte by my side in every meaningful way. To protect her from the world but support her however she needs.

The woman I didn't know a few short weeks ago has now become everything to me.

Now, how do I keep everything from slipping through my fingers?

Chapter Sixteen

PIERCE

"You do realise Thanksgiving is usually celebrated on a Thursday, right?" Peering over Ellie's shoulder, I watch as she continues making dinner with Mum.

"Yes, thank you. But this was the only time your parents could make it, and I wanted to do it before the baby comes, so hush." She shoos me out of the kitchen, but not before I grab another beer.

"Pierce. Have I taught you nothing? Stay out of the kitchen while your mum is cooking." Dad shakes his head at me as I sit beside him in the living room. Ellie told Mum she wanted to learn how to cook a proper Thanksgiving meal, and that none of our input was needed. With an American mum, we grew up celebrating because it's her favourite holiday.

"I wasn't commenting on her cooking skills. I'm not that dumb." I take a long pull on my beer as Charlotte bursts through the front door. Charlotte's coming today? I don't know if I'm prepared to be in the same room as her and not want to touch her.

"I'm not late, am I?" Her cheeks are pink as she shrugs

out of her heavy coat. Christ, does she look beautiful in leggings that hug every curve and a cream sweater that hangs off one shoulder. Her lips are painted a bright red. It takes everything I have not to sweep her up into my arms and kiss that lipstick right off her.

"I'm so happy you could make it!" Ellie comes out of the kitchen, wrapping her arms around Charlotte as best she can. "Better than the rest of the family who couldn't make it."

"I don't think I've ever been to a Thanksgiving dinner before. Anything I can help with?" She gives me a shy look, before following Ellie into the kitchen.

"Are you listening to me?" Sean is giving me a strange look.

"Sorry, what were you saying?" I take another sip of my beer, trying to cool down. Anytime Charlotte is near, I can feel the heat coursing through me. I love what she does to me, but I hate that we have to act like we hardly know each other.

"Did you finish that piece you were working on yesterday?"

I nod my head. "Yup. Definitely not my favourite, but it's what they wanted."

"What'd they want?" Dad asks, attention still focused on the TV.

"It was a bear attacking a lion. Why people want what they want is beyond me," I say, shaking my head. "It was to cover up an old quote on their back."

"I'm sure it was the best bear attacking a lion out there." God love our dad. He's brilliant but doesn't always understand what we do.

"Dinner's ready!" Ellie calls from the kitchen.

The table is set for a feast. Turkey, potatoes of all kinds, rolls, corn. You name it, Ellie cooked it.

Royal Relations

"Is Thanksgiving dinner always this much of a to-do?" Charlotte asks, carrying the turkey out.

"In our family it is," Mum answers. "It was my favourite holiday growing up, so I made sure to continue the tradition with our kids."

"Pretty sure we were the only kids in our school who got a random Thursday off school to have dinner," I snicker.

"And yet, you never seemed to mind as a kid." Mum goes to her seat, as the rest of us take any open spot available. The only seat left is right beside Charlotte.

"So, your first Thanksgiving, huh?" I whisper to her.

"Ellie was very excited to make it, so I figured I'd come. Plus," she leans closer, lowering her voice, "good excuse to see you."

Bloody hell. I'm in way deeper than I should be with this woman. Not a soul in this room knows we're dating, and I hate it. I hate that Charlotte's life is controlled to the point where we can't be together. I want to be able to hold her hand and kiss her in front of my family. But we can't.

Because I can't kiss her like I want, I press my leg to hers, wanting the contact. Needing the heat from her to calm my raging storm of emotions.

"Before we tuck in, I'd just like to thank Ellie for making such an amazing meal for all of us. We're so pleased to have you in the family, and I can't wait to meet my future grandbaby." Mum's face is lit up with excitement.

"Cheers!" Everyone holds up their drinks in Ellie's direction.

"I'm so happy you all could make it. I love getting to be with all of you today, even if it's not really the holiday today." She takes Sean's hand as everyone starts to serve themselves.

"Pierce, when are you going to start giving me grandbabies?" Mum asks from her end of the table.

Oh, for fuck's sake. Charlotte coughs into her napkin beside me. "That's a bit of a ways off, Mum. Do we really need to have this conversation at the dinner table?"

She holds her hands up in defence. "Sean is giving me grandchildren. They'll want cousins to play with."

"He'd need to be dating someone before that can happen, Mum." Sean smirks at me from his end of the table.

"Thanks, bro. Appreciate that." I shake my head, hating where this line of questioning is going.

"Is there anyone you can set him up with, Ellie?" Mum asks.

"Christ, can we not have this conversation?" I really don't want to be talking about anyone setting me up when the woman I'm currently dating is sitting next to me.

"Maybe Ruby knows someone at school that would be good for Pierce." Ellie completely ignores me.

I lean back in my chair as Charlotte quietly eats her dinner without looking at anyone. I grab her knee beneath the table, giving it a squeeze. She pulls her leg from mine, uncomfortable with the conversation.

"I'm sure she knows lots of people. Maybe you can find someone for Charlotte while you're at it."

"Okay, Jacqueline. Enough of that. The kids don't need to be set up by their mum." Dad pats her arm, ending the topic. Thank fuck.

An ache settles in my chest. I can feel Charlotte pulling away from me even when we're sitting right next to each other. This fucking sucks. I've finally met someone I truly care about, and we can't be together. It isn't fair, but I'll take whatever Charlotte can give me.

And right now, she's not giving me much.

"Sorry. Just want all of my children to be as happy as we are." She gives Dad a sappy face before kissing him.

"Ugh, we're trying to eat," Sean groans, covering his face.

"Oh, like you two aren't going to kiss in front of your kid all the time. I know what you do in the office." I wave my fork between the two of them, before popping another bit of turkey in my mouth. Christ, that really is good.

"And what is it that you two are doing in the office?" Mum shifts her focus to Sean, thank God.

"Not cool, bro." He shakes his head. Ellie's face is redder than a tomato.

"You okay?" I whisper to Charlotte, the attention all on Sean and Ellie.

"Fine." Her voice is sharp, and she won't even look at me. She's anything but fine. Fine is the most dangerous word in the English language.

"Can we talk later? Maybe head over to my place after?"

"I'm tired. Maybe another night. I've got a busy day tomorrow, so maybe later this week." Fecking hell, Mum had to go and open her mouth, and now Charlotte can barely look at me.

"If that's what you want."

Charlotte

"MISS CHARLOTTE. Are you going to find a prince?"

Oh, bloody hell. Ever since Thanksgiving dinner this

past weekend, it seems everyone has an opinion on my love life.

"Maybe one day, darling. But not today," I answer the small child. I've spent my morning at a new children's hospital outside of London. Normally I love this, but a rain cloud has been following me around since Sunday.

Even the thought of Pierce's mum setting him up with someone caused a bone deep ache to settle inside me. I know it can't be easy sneaking around, but I still want to be with him. The thought of him with another woman causes a fury to ignite inside me that I can't contain.

"Sorry for all the questions. The children have been cooped up inside because of all the rain," the director tells me.

"No worries. I'm sure they're all ready to get home."

We finish the tour, and the director curtsies to me as we leave. The press is stationed outside, as usual.

"Was today a good visit, Princess Charlotte?"

"Any update on your love life?"

I give a polite wave, before heading into the safety of the awaiting car. I wish I could snap my fingers and just do away with everyone asking me about my love life. I should be used to it by now, but it's hitting harder than usual.

All I want is to find Pierce and curl up next to him. Bounce ideas off of him for my charity. Hold his hand in public and tell everyone that we're dating. Take him to events where I can show off what an incredible man he is.

But no. We're subject to late night dates at his place, where I can sneak in and out without the press finding out. All because the Queen needs to keep a firm grasp on the royal family.

Needing his calming voice, I pick up the phone and dial him immediately.

"Hey, love." He picks up on the first ring.

"Hi." I let out a deep breath I didn't realize I was holding. His voice is instantly calming.

"Everything okay?" The sound of the tattoo guns fades away, as a door clicks shut through the phone.

"Just needed to hear your voice."

He chuckles to himself. "Anything I can do to help. How was your morning?"

"Any chance you can get away this weekend?" I blurt out, ignoring his question.

"What, like a holiday?"

"Yes. Just a short weekend away from the city. You. Me. No press. Just be together without any interference from anyone else."

"What happened this morning?" His voice is concerned.

I can't blame him. "Just your average morning. Kids asking if I'll meet my prince. The press asking about my love life. I'm sick of it. I just want to be with you."

"How does Bibury sound? We can sneak away to my family's cottage we have there. No one is there this time of year. Just you and me." Pierce doesn't hesitate.

"Sounds like heaven." I settle farther back into the seat as we race through London.

"Perfect. A weekend away, just the two of us."

I could cry at how beautiful those words sound. Just Pierce and me together. It's music to my ears.

Chapter Seventeen

PIERCE

"So this is your family house?" Charlotte's eyes are wide as I pull up to the cottage in Bibury. Her smile is bright.

I nod my head. "We came here during summer holidays if we weren't visiting Mum's family. And celebrated every Christmas here."

"It's beautiful." Leaves are falling off the trees that line the front of the stone house.

"Wait until you see inside." I grab her hand, kissing her knuckles. "Let's go."

Charlotte's security officers came up earlier to ensure everything was safe. Not something I've ever experienced, but if it means we get to spend the weekend together, I'll suck it up.

"Can we move here?" Charlotte's voice is a whisper as we walk into the house. Wood beams cover the low ceiling. A small sofa sits in front of the fireplace. The kitchen takes up the back of the first floor before stairs lead up to the bedrooms. "This is perfect."

Charlotte walks up to me, grabbing my cheeks and

pulling me down for a kiss. It's soft. The barest hint of a tease. When she pulls back, her eyes are glassy.

"You alright, love?" I wrap my arm around her waist, tugging her into me.

She sighs, relaxing into my touch. "It's just been a hard few weeks. I hate having to hide what we have."

I drop a kiss on her head, breathing in the scent of her shampoo. God, this woman consumes me. Every thought, every feeling, every touch. "It's worth it. I know it sucks, but if it means I get to be with you, I'd hide out in every closet just to see you or touch you."

She turns, resting her chin on my chest and gazing up at me. "Aren't you just a charmer today?"

I smirk down at her, tucking a loose strand of hair behind her ear. "C'mon. I want to show you all the favourite parts of the village."

"Does one of them happen to be your room?" Charlotte waggles her eyebrows at me. Fucking hell, my dick is twitching in my pants.

"No. As much as I'd love to show you the bedroom,"—I drop a kiss on her lips—"there's a lot of fun things about this place that I love."

Charlotte straightens before me, grabbing her wide-brimmed hat and dropping it on her head. "I'm at your every whim today. Show me the Bibury you love."

God, I love this woman. I don't know how she feels, but I've gone and fallen in love with the woman that I'm not supposed to be seeing. Everything about her has pulled me in. Her laugh. Her smile. The way she lights up when she talks about the work she does. My heart beats for her. I want to do everything I can to make her life easier.

Because maybe we might get to be together someday. For real. Maybe. Hopefully?

Charlotte's tugging me out of the house, but I lead her to the side shed. "We're not walking?"

I laugh as I throw the doors open. "We're biking. Best way to see the entire village."

"I don't think I've ridden a bike in years."

"Good thing it's like riding a bike then."

She smacks my chest. "Aren't you the funny one."

I capture her lips with mine before hopping onto my bike. "I try. Now, let's go."

It's cold, but not as cold as it could be, as we start off towards town. Charlotte's security officers are following behind us in my car. Not the most obvious, but she still has to have them. I peek back at Charlotte, and the brightest smile paints her face. I feel it in my chest. Happiness is radiating off of her as she pedals behind me.

"This is fantastic!" she shouts at me. The old houses of Arlington Row pass by in a blur as we head farther into the small town. The river winds by on the other side, acting as our guide. I turn, finding one of the small footbridges to stop next to.

"Enjoying yourself?" I'm straddling the bike as Charlotte stops beside me.

"I get to stare at your cute arse. Of course I'm enjoying myself."

I shake my head at her. "And here I thought you were enjoying the town."

Charlotte grabs the lapels of my coat, bringing my face down to hers. "I'm enjoying myself because I'm with you. We could be in a shack on the sea, and it'd be fab. Your cute bum is just a plus."

I slant my lips over hers, licking into her mouth—needing to feel close to her. Her lips are cold from the wind. "Want to head into the coffee shop and warm up?"

Her eyes are hazy as she pulls back. "Mm, a tea sounds perfect right now."

We steer our bikes away from the footbridge and towards the small village. The main part of town has only a few shops, and even fewer people, so it's perfect for us. Charlotte tucks into a back booth as I grab us each a cuppa.

"Cheers." I clink my glass against hers.

Charlotte sips on hers, keeping her eyes on me. "Thank you for bringing me here. I didn't realize how much I needed to get away." Her hand lands on top of mine.

"It sucks not being able to tell people we're together, but I'm glad we're here. Even if only for a few days."

Charlotte's face is pensive as she looks at me. "The only weekend getaways we had when we were younger were to Sandringham. There's a small town there, but everyone knew us, so it's not like we could escape like here. I don't think one person has noticed me."

There's an older couple sitting at a table by the window, but no one else. "That's one of the perks. It's a small village. There were a few other kids here growing up, but it was mainly always Sean and me playing by ourselves."

"I can only imagine what it would've been like coming here as a kid."

"Yeah, but think of the places you got to see growing up. Not a lot of people could have travelled like that."

"I have a good life." Charlotte rests her chin in her hand, staring back at me. "But you still see a very polished version of wherever you go. They don't want you to see the bad bits."

I link my hand with her free one. "I guess I never thought of it like that."

"People only see what they want to see. It's a very

glamorised life, and it's mostly good. But people don't understand the hard parts."

"Like?"

"Like wanting to be with someone so badly, but you can't and have to hide it."

My heart aches for her. I want to shout it from the rooftops that we're together. That we love each other. But the idea that it could be a scandal is hard. We've been careful together. So careful. Even now, my eyes keep drifting to see if anyone has a camera.

"I want nothing more than to kiss you and hug you in public. But until then, I'm happy to be with you anyway I can."

Charlotte leans in for a kiss, tasting like the tea she's been sipping on. "You make me happy. So, so happy." Her breath is a whisper against my lips.

"And I'd do anything to keep you happy. Like bringing you to our family home in the tiniest village in England."

Charlotte lets out a quiet laugh. "Fordwich is actually the smallest town in England."

I roll my eyes at her, finishing my tea. "Of course you would know that."

"What can I say?" She shrugs her shoulders. "I know a lot of obscure facts about this country."

"Maybe we could find a way to go to a quiz night at the pub. You'd clean up there."

Charlotte laces her warm fingers through mine. "Consider it a date then."

WE TAKE the long way back to the cottage, stopping at the river for no other reason than to watch it float by. Kissing.

Touching. I love seeing Bibury through Charlotte's eyes. I've only ever come up here with family. No one has ever been special enough to bring here.

But Charlotte? I'd buy the entire town if it meant we could be together for real.

We drop our bikes off in the shed and head into the warmth of the house. "Want to get started on dinner?" My hands drift around Charlotte's back, warming up under her jumper. She squirms under my touch.

"You're mean!" She shimmies away from me, heading towards the kitchen. "Why don't you start the fire and I'll start dinner. I had the guys get everything I need to make you my special dinner."

"Special dinner? That sounds promising."

She strips off her hat and jumper, standing in a tight tank top. "Yes. So get comfortable, get us some drinks, and I'll make you a meal you'll never forget."

I don't think it's the meal that will be unforgettable, but the woman making it. Her eyes are sparkling with happiness as she leaves me to it.

I stoke the fire as the clattering of pans drifts out of the kitchen. Charlotte's soft voice is singing. It brings a smile to my face, one I rarely feel. That anxiousness at never being good enough falls away when I'm with her. I don't have to live up to any crazy expectations when I'm with Charlotte. We can just be.

With the fire started, I head into the kitchen to find the woman who is bringing me to life. Her dark brown locks are swept into a knot on the top of her head, and her cheeks are pink from the heat of the stove.

"How's it going?"

She turns her dark brown eyes on me, apron now tied around her waist. "It's going. Pour us some wine."

I brush by her as I grab the wine glasses. "Smells good," I whisper into her ear.

"Stop distracting me." She elbows me out of the way.

"Sorry. Anything I can do to help?" I pour us each a glass of red.

"Grab the veggies from the refrigerator so I can start on the sauce."

Getting what she needs, I hand everything over. Meat is simmering in a pot as spaghetti boils in another. "Spaghetti?"

"Hey." Her eyes swing to me, poking towards me with the knife in her hand. "It's the best damn spaghetti you'll ever have. A chef in Italy taught me how to make this sauce."

I wrap my arms around her shoulders. "I can't wait to have the Charlotte special." I drop a kiss on her nose before pulling back, not wanting to distract her. Charlotte's smile is happy as she goes back to cooking. I settle on a barstool, watching as she works. Her hips shake as she cuts and stirs, her hands moving quickly to slice the veggies as she makes the sauce. I move to set the small table, not wanting to be a useless wanker.

It's intoxicating, being swept up in this woman's world. We might not have a lot of moments together, but I cherish the ones we do get. And I'll love getting to wake up beside her tomorrow, holding her in my arms. It's the thing I hate most about this arrangement.

"We just need to let the sauce sit for a bit and then dinner will be ready." Hair is plastered to Charlotte's forehead, face red from cooking.

"Cooking looks good on you."

"Wait until you try it." Charlotte takes off the apron, setting it on the counter. "I promise, best meal you'll ever have."

"It'll be the best meal I'll ever have because you made it for me, love."

Charlotte's hand captures my chin, locking eyes with me. "You are such a charmer, you know that?" She brushes her lips against mine. "I don't know what I'm going to do with you, Pierce."

My eyebrows waggle at her. "Feed me and then I'll show you a thing or two."

Chapter Eighteen

CHARLOTTE

"I have a surprise for you today." Pierce's lips dance up my spine as he wakes me up. His voice is heavy with sleep. I never realised how good it feels to wake up next to someone. Going to bed with Pierce felt pretty good too.

"What kind of surprise?" I sit up, pulling the sheet with me. Pierce's hair is standing on end. Pillow lines decorate his face. We gave each other several orgasms last night and then passed out in spectacular fashion.

"If I told you, it wouldn't be a surprise. Now, get dressed and meet me downstairs." He pops out of bed, his fine arse on full display for me.

I drop the sheet, crawling on my knees over to Pierce. "I'm going to shower. Care to join me?" I drag my fingers across his chest as I saunter into the bathroom. His hurried footsteps are quick to join me.

"ROLLER SKATING?" My eyes are lit up with excitement at the bright pink roller skates in his hand. After a not so short shower together, Pierce dragged me downstairs for my surprise. He was like a kid at Christmas. He couldn't contain his excitement.

"I figure we can unleash that inner derby girl."

I can't help it; I jump into his arms and lay kisses all over his face. "This might be one of the most fun things anyone has ever done for me."

I've never told anyone about my desire to be a roller girl. When you grow up as a princess, you're not allowed to have dreams like regular people. We were raised in the royal ways and how to put our best foot forward. Always.

Wanting to roller skate? I would've been laughed at if I told people this was something I always wanted to do. But not Pierce. He went out and bought me a pair of skates and is going to spend the morning with me while I roller skate. What did I do to deserve someone as good as him?

Pierce squeezes my hip before setting me down. "I aim to please. Now, let's get going because I can't wait to see you in skates."

Walking outside to the small driveway, I find a typical cold and grey day. There's not much room to skate, but seeing as how I've only done this a handful of times, I won't need much space.

"Are you going to catch me if I fall?"

Pierce quirks a brow at me. "Have you ever done this before?"

I shove my socked feet into the skates. A perfect fit. "Only a few times as a kid. I wasn't the most coordinated of kids, so I think they didn't want me breaking any bones."

"Are you going to be breaking any bones today?"

I tie the bright green laces and reach out to Pierce to stand. "That's not the plan."

Steady hands lead me away from the bench as we start to move over the uneven surface.

"You know you actually have to use your feet to skate, right?"

"Feck off, you. It's not like riding a bike."

"Sorry. You're doing wonderful, and you'd win the Olympic medal of skating."

I tighten my grip on his hands, keeping my eyes on his feet. "No need to flatter me. I know I'm not going to be good at this."

"How about this." Pierce rolls me into his arms, wrapping me in his warmth. "For each lap you take around the driveway, I'll give you a kiss?" He drops a soft kiss on the corner of my mouth.

I eye him warily. "And what was that one for? Good luck?"

"You don't want my incentive?" He mocks being annoyed. "I'll have you know that's the best possible motivation to learn to skate."

I'm closer to eye level with Pierce in my skates. "I can think of a much better motivation than a kiss." I dip my hands under his jumper, warming my cold hands on his hot skin.

"Orgasms for laps? I guess I could get on board with that." An innocent smile stretches across Pierce's lips.

"Good." I shove Pierce out of my arms before he can give me another brain-swirling kiss. "Now, out of my way while I become the world's best skater."

It would've been a much more convincing statement had I not pushed off and immediately fallen on my arse. Pierce is doubled over in laughter. He goes to help me up, but I wave him off.

"No help! I want to earn my orgasms on my own."

"Alright, love. I'll just be sitting here watching you go."

I flip him the bird as I stand like a baby giraffe for the first time. This was much easier when I was trying to do it as a child.

Pushing off on each foot, I get a little momentum, circling part of the drive. Pierce's face is twisted in laughter. His laughter only makes me more determined.

Getting the hang of it, I take a turn and move slower than a turtle back to him. "Look at me go!" I throw my arms up in victory as I pass him.

"You'll be trying out for the Olympics in no time," he says dryly, his arms crossed over his chest as he watches me take another lap.

Turning on my next lap, I get cocky, and my foot catches on a rock. Thrashing my arms, I try to balance myself, but end up falling face first in the grass. "Shite!"

"Are you alright?" Pierce is on top of me as I flip over, laughter bubbling out of me.

"Why did I ever think I could be a roller girl? I'm bloody awful at this!" Deep, belly laughs take over. Pierce's face goes from one of concern to echoing my laugh.

"I'm glad you said it and not me." Pierce's voice is breathy with laughter. "And here I thought you'd be skating laps around me."

"Hey! I got in one lap. Even that incentive didn't do much, did it?" I pop a brow at him.

"Oh I don't know." He pulls my feet into his lap, untying the laces. "I could be convinced that you're sad your dream died today and make it up to you."

"Pierce. I'm so sad. I'll never be a roller girl, and I don't know what to do with my life," I say, dramatics lacing my tone.

"Poor Charlotte. However will I make it up to you?"

His eyes darken with need. He yanks the skates off my feet. As I wiggle my toes, he digs his knuckles into the arches of my feet.

"Mm. That feels amazing." I lie back on the cold grass, the morning sky still foggy around us. "I feel that we should go try to surf now."

"Charlotte, I say this with all the kindness I possess, but what makes you think you'll be able to surf?"

I poke his hard chest with my toe. "I meant for you. There's no way I'm ever getting on a surfboard."

"Alright then." Pierce lies down beside me, pulling me closer to him. "Where do you suggest we run off to and try to surf?"

"The river looked nice." I smirk at him.

"My balls would shrivel up and fall off if we even set a toe in that river. You're crazy, love!" A full body shiver wracks over him.

"Fine." I fist my hands in his jumper, pulling him closer. "But how about the next time we escape the city, we go somewhere warm, and you can try your hand at surfing?"

Pierce pulls me closer to him as he rolls onto his back. I throw a leg over his, cuddling into his side. The cold of the grass fades away as I'm wrapped up in his warmth.

"I like that idea. Learning how to surf. Lazing about on the beach. I can't remember the last time I've been on a true holiday."

"This is shaping up to be a pretty good one." I tilt my chin, gazing up at his handsome face. He's staring at me like he doesn't have a care in the world. That there is no other place he'd rather be. That watching me face plant in epic fashion on a pair of skates is how he wants to spend every morning.

"I'm glad you brought me here. This is just what I needed."

"I'll bring you here every weekend if it means we get to be together without the prying eyes of the world wanting to tear us apart."

"I hate that it has to be this way."

"I know, love, I know. But I'd do it a hundred times over if it means I get to be with you."

I don't know why Pierce thinks I'm worth it. Why putting up with my royal life is worth it. My last ex couldn't handle it. And he was someone the Queen approved of.

Now, here's a man who is putting up with sneaking around and we can't be together in a way I truly want. I want to shout our relationship from the rooftops and tell everyone how wonderful a partner he could be for me. I know he struggles with playing second fiddle to his brother and would hate for him to feel that way with me. But his words and actions do nothing but support me. He is the kindest, most caring man I've ever met.

Falling in love with someone you're hiding away isn't easy. It's getting harder and harder to keep our relationship a secret. I don't know how we'll get to stay together, but I'm going to do everything in my power to keep Pierce. Because he's the one.

I only hope he feels the same way about me.

Chapter Nineteen

CHARLOTTE

"Okay, next question," Pierce says, as he settles above me, leaning on his elbow. After another fantastic supper, we made a fort of blankets in front of the fire. I'm in nothing but his shirt, Pierce only in joggers. It feels like we're kids again, hiding from the world. Not a worry in sight of who is trying to keep us apart.

"You really like these questions, don't you?" I ask, tracing my fingers over his chest. The strong muscles ripple under my touch. I love seeing the reaction I cause in him. It stirs something deep inside me, knowing that this man craves my touch in a way no man ever has before.

"Yes. I don't think we've come even close to twenty." Pierce drops a chaste kiss on my lips, making no move to deepen it. "I'll never tire of your questions. Hit me."

"Where do you see yourself in five years?"

Pierce scrubs a hand over his stubbly jaw. "Are you my secondary counsellor? Asking what I see in my future?"

"It's a valid question." My fingers move lower, tracing the intricate ink that runs down his side. "My future has been planned out for me since before I was born."

"Does it ever bother you that you never had a choice?" Pierce's words are soft, the rippling fire the only other sound in the small cottage.

"When I was a moody teenager, yes. I thought the world would end if I had to be told what to do and where to be my entire life. That's when I went through my stage of wearing all black."

Pierce laughs, his fingers drifting down my stomach. "I can't imagine you being a sullen teenager. You're the happiest person I've ever met."

"It's not like I was likely going to ever become Queen, but I thought my life was over. It wasn't until I went to uni that I realized what a privileged position I'm in. How I want to make a mark in this world by creating my own charity."

"You will, Charlotte." Pierce's fingers drift over my cheek. "You've done incredible work on planning the women's charity, and I know it'll do great things for so many people."

Something settles in my chest. People always tell me how much my work means to them. That I make a difference in their lives. I hear it so often, that sometimes it's hard to believe. But when Pierce says it, it's as if everything settles into place. It's not a given yet, but it's affirming to hear Pierce say these words to me. Almost like the Queen can't say no. Won't say no.

"What are you thinking about, love?"

My fingers wind into the hair at the nape of his neck. His eyes are bright, the fire sparkling in them, his square jaw firm as he takes me in. "Just how happy I am to be here with you. You have no idea how much I needed this weekend."

Pierce lies on his side, shifting me so I'm looking directly into his eyes. "I hate how this is the only time I can wake up with you in my arms. All I want is to hold you every morning. Wake up beside you."

I trace my fingers over his plump lips. Lips that have brought me so much happiness. "Is that where you see yourself in five years? Waking up with me?"

His hand is firm on my hip, his eyes serious. "What would a future for the two of us look like? Would I be called Prince Pierce?" There's a lightness to his tone that belies the serious look on his face.

That piece that settled inside me feels like it's moving around in my chest. A living, breathing thing that threatens to ruin this happy bubble we're in.

"Yes. You'd be in the spotlight. Cameras thrust in your face every day. Your face plastered all across magazines across the world. Every move you make documented. People wanting to get tattoos from the famous Pierce."

"Is that all?" He chuckles. "Piece of cake."

"I'm serious. My last serious relationship ended because he couldn't handle the spotlight. Couldn't handle being a step behind me for the rest of our lives. The first time his photo was in a newspaper, I could see the struggle. He hated it, but it was as if he didn't know what to do. We were together a long time after that, but every day was hard. I was selfish and didn't want to end it. I thought I had finally found my person. But he left me high and dry."

"A lesser man then. I could never leave you like that. Would never leave you like that." He moves his hand off my hip and cups my face. His thumb gently strokes the apple of my cheek. "He didn't see how incredible you really are, Charlotte. The way you light up when you talk about your work. It brings out something incredible in you. That you want to serve your people like you do."

A few weeks with Pierce, and it's like he knows exactly what to say to me. Anytime I met someone, I compared them to Michael. Would they be as strong as him? Would they run scared before we even made it past a second date? One date with Pierce, and we were front page news. He's taken it all in stride, but for how much longer?

"I know it'll be hard, but we can make it work, can't we?" His words break me out of my thoughts.

I sigh, my breath ghosting his cheeks. He's moved closer to me, his skin hot on mine. "You know what it was like for Ellie. She gave up the throne to have what she really wanted in life. It's a sacrifice so few people would be willing to make. And Zara had a hard go of it, and she's the daughter of a duke."

"If it means I would get to have you by my side, it's a sacrifice I'd be willing to make."

I shove off of him, trying to lighten the mood. "You say that now. It's very different when the entire kingdom is bearing down on you."

"I've never had an entire kingdom's future on my shoulders. Could be fun to try."

This man. If he doesn't make my heart beat for him. "We'd just have to get your official seal of approval from the Queen."

"Are there prince lessons I could take? If so, sign me up." Pierce wraps me in his arms.

"Here's your first lesson." I push him back on the pile of blankets underneath our fort, straddling his hips. "What the princess wants, the princess gets."

A heated gaze sends shivers down my body. "That one is easy. What do I get for passing your lesson?"

I quirk my lips at him, his arms now propped behind his head. "I can think of an incentive." I drop hot, open-mouthed kisses down his chest, licking the swirl of colours on his pecs. When I draw the tight bud of his nipple into my mouth, he hisses.

"Damn, Charlotte. You know just how to make a man feel good."

"You'll be feeling really good." I move down his body, drawing his joggers down his thighs. His thick cock springs free, a bead of precum on the crown. I wrap my hand around the base, licking the white bead.

"Fuck, Charlotte." Pierce fists my hair in one hand, gently holding my head as I take him as far as I can. His hips jerk off the floor as I work his cock in tandem with my hand. I love taking Pierce like this. Feeling his need for me. Feeling him come apart under my touch is a powerful feeling and turns me on even more.

Pierce's hips move faster as he starts to fuck my mouth. My eyes well with tears, but I make no move to leave. I let him use my mouth. It's a heady sensation. The raw passion swirling around us pushes me closer to my own orgasm.

"Shit. I'm going to come." Pierce moves to pull me off of him, but I suck him down farther as the first spurts of his cum land on my tongue. I drink him up, loving the taste of his salty release. I take every last drop before pulling off of him.

"Is this what prince lessons are like?" His voice comes out on a huff, his chest rising and falling as he comes down from his high. I wipe the corners of my lips on the back of my hand. I pull his pants back up, as I settle my weight over his chest.

"With this princess, yes."

"Can I sign up for daily lessons?"

"I do lessons by the hour if that pleases you." I walk my fingers up his chest, then trace the features of his sexy face. I can't get enough of this man.

"Shit. Is death by sex a thing? Because I reckon you'll kill me if we do that."

The tight need in my core is bordering on painful. Bringing Pierce pleasure like that has me on the edge.

"If I don't get your mouth on me, I might die right now." Overdramatic, yes. But his lips landing on mine as he flips me over has me climbing closer and closer towards the edge of the cliff.

"You know, these prince lessons are easy. If you're going to quiz me, you should at least make it harder." Pierce draws his shirt up my body, exposing my bare pussy to him. The soft brush of his hands over my stomach has me arching into his touch.

"You seem to be catching on very quickly."

Pierce flattens his tongue against my slit, dragging through the wetness building there. "What can I say? I'm a quick study." The pressure of his tongue has me bucking my hips, riding his face. His strong hands hold my legs apart.

"Mm, Pierce. Just like that." My voice is rough, laced with need. Need for this man. His tongue is working my clit. Soft strokes. Hard strokes. Fast then slow. Heat is racing down my spine, an inferno ready to explode.

"You like my tongue? Or do you want my fingers too?" Pierce slowly, oh so slowly, sinks a thick finger inside my pussy. He crooks it, hitting that delicious spot deep inside me.

"I'm so close, Pierce. So close."

Pierce thrusts two fingers inside me, swiping his tongue over my clit. "I need you to come. I want to taste you on my tongue. Feel the way you use my mouth as you climax. Over and over again."

His words.

His fingers.

His tongue.

They drive a soul-shattering orgasm out of me. Stars

burst behind my eyes as I ride his face. The world could be ending, and I wouldn't know. Because right now, it's only Pierce and me, in this tiny cottage in Bibury.

My muscles shake as I come down from my high. My body is boneless. Pierce settles over me, a hand on each side of my head. My release glistens on his lips. He drops a kiss on my lips, but when he goes to pull away, I pull him back. The taste of me on his tongue is hot. Mix it with his release on mine, and it's downright sinful. Our tongues fight for control, but our bodies are languid. Sated after each of our releases. My legs wrap around his, keeping him close.

"Damn, Charlotte." Pierce shifts back from me, breaking the kiss. "That was the hottest fucking thing I've ever seen."

A satisfied grin plays on my lips. "It's only because of you."

Pierce growls. "Fuck. You know just what to say to turn me on." He rolls his hips into my core, his cock already hardening.

"Consider me the Pierce whisperer then."

"I love that you know exactly what I like. Fuck, it's so damn sexy having a woman who knows exactly what she wants and takes it. And gives it too."

"I should say the same about you. You know just what to say and do to make me feel so lo…treasured."

I know I love this man, but it's hard to get the words to come out. The words came easily with Michael. He was supposed to be my forever, but he cut and ran. I want Pierce. I want him with an ache that I've never felt before.

So why is it so damn hard to say those three little words to him?

Chapter Twenty

CHARLOTTE

"Why do I have to keep my eyes closed?" My hands are covering my eyes as Pierce moves around in front of me.

"Because it's a surprise. I promise, you'll love it."

"It smells like hot cocoa." The air smells sweet.

"Stop trying to guess."

We haven't left our blanket fort all night. We've spent our time here talking. About everything and anything. About my charity. About his work. I want to soak up every second with Pierce before going back to real life.

"Okay, open your eyes."

Pierce is sitting next to me with…something in his hands? "What is this?" I take it from Pierce's hand.

"Try it. I promise, you'll love it."

I take a big bite of whatever this is that is melting.

"This might be the best thing I've ever put in my mouth."

"That's what she said," Pierce says, a smirk covering his face.

"I don't even care. Why have I never had this before?"

Gooey marshmallow drips from my fingers as I take another bite.

"S'mores. They aren't a thing here. We used to have them when we visited my grandparents over summer holiday. They are my favourite."

Pierce takes another large bite, his eyes glittering with happiness. The joy shining out from him is like a light in my chest. I've never been this content before.

"I command you make these for me all the time."

He pulls me onto his lap. "You command me to?"

I rest an elbow on his shoulder, taking the last bite of this delicious treat. "I'm a princess. I can command you to do my bidding."

Heat flares in his eyes. "Is that right?"

I nod, licking my lips. "Yes. I command you make me s'mores every night from here on out."

Pierce grabs my hand before I can lick the sticky goo off my fingers, sucking them into his mouth, his eyes now dark with need. Heat floods my core as his tongue circles the pads of my fingers.

"Can you also command me to do other things?" He pulls my fingers out of his mouth, kissing down my arm. My pulse is racing beneath his lips.

"Like to fuck me right here on the floor?"

A growl escapes his lips before they crash into mine. He tastes like marshmallows and chocolate and Pierce. I rise on my knees, deepening the angle of the kiss. I want this man with a fire I've never known.

Pierce's hands drift up my stomach, his fingers ghosting my breasts. A low moan escapes as he tweaks a nipple between his fingers. His lips move down my jaw, my neck, before he rips the shirt off of me, leaving me completely exposed to him.

"Fecking hell, you're the most gorgeous woman I've

ever laid eyes on." Pierce's words cause my heart to stutter in my chest. This man. I don't know what I did to deserve him.

His hands roam over my body, fire left in their wake. "God, I need you." Desire drips from my voice as his lips take my nipple into his mouth. I rock over his erection, throbbing beneath me. I'm shameless as I grind over him. Pierce moves to my other breast, lavishing it with the same attention.

My hands drift lower, his chest flexing beneath them as my fingers skirt the waist band of his joggers. Pierce pulls the taut bud of my nipple into his mouth as I dive my hands into his joggers, meeting the hard flesh of his cock.

"Fuck," he moans on a long breath. He throws his head back in pleasure as I brush my fingers over him.

His hands drift up my thighs, his thumbs grazing my clit. It lights an inferno in me. "I need you inside me, Pierce."

Pierce flips us around, laying me out on the soft blankets. The orange light from the fire casts him in a gentle glow. He's studying my face like I'm studying his. Memorising it. Taking in every feature lest we forget one another.

His lips meet mine in a sensual kiss. Pierce's tongue demands control, and I willingly give it. The powerful, yet languid, strokes cause a fire to burn low in my belly. Heat floods my core as he deepens the kiss.

I've never been kissed like this before. Like a merging of two souls. I lean into Pierce's touch, craving more of his lips on mine and needing his hands on me. Using my feet, I shove his joggers down his legs. I want to feel every bare inch of his body on mine.

Pierce's lips move down my neck. Hot, open-mouthed kisses nibble at my skin and at the swell of my breasts before he pulls a diamond hard nipple into his mouth. My hands fist in his hair, keeping him there. His teeth and tongue are working me into a frenzy.

"Pierce. Please." My voice is breathy, coming out on a long moan as Pierce shifts to my other nipple.

"Not yet, love." His eyes drift up to mine as he toys with the tight bud, swirling his tongue before taking it in his mouth. I can't keep my eyes off him. He knows how to bring me pleasure as if he were a professor studying my body.

His hands drift lower, swiping through my slick folds. I arch into his touch. I want his cock, but his fingers on my clit ratchet my pleasure up. The mix of pressure is dizzying. My orgasm is racing down my spine, just out of reach.

I'm writhing with need as Pierce slips a finger inside me. His lips smile against my hot skin as he works his way down my stomach. "God, I can't wait to feel you come on my tongue." Pierce's voice is gravelly with need as he tongues my clit.

"Please. I'm so close," I beg. I'm needy and wanting and don't care how desperate I sound. "I need to come."

"What are you waiting for?" Pierce sucks down on my clit as he starts thrusting his fingers in faster, pulling me over the edge.

It's an orgasm like I've never felt before. The intensity racks my body. It's powerful in the way it colours my vision and slows time. Like Pierce and I are the only two people on earth.

Pierce's lips on mine bring me back to reality. My body is still high on his as I taste my release on his lips. "I've never seen anything so beautiful as when you come." His voice is heavy with reverence. His hands worship my body as he shifts us to our sides. Pierce grabs the condom from his sweats, but I still him.

"No. I'm clean, and I want to feel you, all of you,

inside of me."

"Christ, Charlotte. I'm clean too." Pierce takes my mouth in a hot kiss, his tongue stroking over mine.

Pulling my leg over his hip, Pierce notches his cock at my entrance. Wrapping my arms around him, I bring him closer, feeling him slip inside. His eyes don't leave mine as he sinks all the way.

I bite down on my lip. The pleasure is already so intense from my earlier orgasm. Pierce's eyes are hooded with a desire that matches my own.

"You feel incredible. Fuck, I don't think anything will compare to this." He sets a slow pace, his thrusts steady and measured. An ache to be closer to him washes over me as I bring him nearer to me. His forehead drops to mine as he squeezes me to him.

This isn't sex. This is making love. This is slow and passionate and everything I've always dreamed of. This connection, this unspoken connection, with another person that binds you to them.

I feel it with Pierce. Every touch, every word, every kiss.

"Charlotte." His voice is needy as I start to feel the pulses of his release. It takes me over the edge with him. He buries his face in my neck as we ride out our orgasms together.

The stillness in the air surrounds us, lying wrapped up in one another. Pierce pulls out and takes me in his arms. The only sound is the fire crackling. His fingers drift down my spine. I've never felt more at peace. A blissed-out smile spreads on my face as the slow steady rhythm of Pierce's heart pulls me under.

IT'S EARLY. Or late. I'm not sure what time it is when I wake up. The fire is out, and I'm wrapped around Pierce like a koala. His breathing is easy, his hand clutching mine to his chest. We're lying mixed up on the blankets and pillows. It's dark out, and a howling wind cuts through the quiet of the small cottage.

Things are perfect right now with Pierce. This weekend away was exactly what we needed. It's been a hard few weeks with the pressure of hiding our relationship from those closest to us. And it'll get even harder these next few weeks with the holidays coming up.

I try not to think about the future of our relationship. This sweet, thoughtful, tattooed man is everything I've ever wanted. He didn't think twice when I asked him to keep our relationship a secret. All I want, all I crave, is to be able to share our love with the world.

But tomorrow we go back to the real world. The real world won't care that we want to be together. Pierce stirs next to me, his heavy breaths ghosting my face.

He's the most beautiful man I've ever seen. Long eyelashes. Defined jaw. Plump lips. I never want to be without this man, but the longer we're in hiding, the stronger I sense that we're somehow moving closer to imploding.

The thought is so terrible, it steels something inside of me. I can't let Pierce go. There has to be a middle ground we can find. To be together and still support the Queen's work. Nothing will be figured out tonight. All I can do is enjoy these last few hours away with Pierce and hope that whatever plan I come up with allows us to be together.

Because I can't lose him.

It has to work.

It just has to.

Chapter Twenty-One

PIERCE

"What the actual fuck, Pierce?"

Ellie comes waddling into the shop, her belly making an appearance before her.

"What are you talking about, Pink?" I'm cleaning my station after my last appointment of the day.

"This." She thrusts a paper in my arms, her pink hair a wild halo around her head. On the front cover is a picture of Charlotte and me leaving the cafe in Bibury.

Princess Charlotte has a new love interest. See page 5 for all the details.

FUCK. Fuck, fuck, fuck! We were careful. No one in Bibury cares about status, so I thought we were safe. We couldn't be seen together, or the Queen would be furious. Shit.

"Care to explain any of this?" Ellie's words break

through the chaos swirling in my head. I can only stare at her. I flip to the designated page, and across the entire magazine is pictures from our weekend away. Pictures from biking. Sitting along the river. Kisses in front of the cafe. What I thought was a safe trip could end up destroying Charlotte. Destroying what we have.

"I need to talk to Charlotte." I push past Ellie, heading to the back offices. Sean is restocking supplies when I brush by him.

"How did I not know you two were seeing each other?" Ellie calls after me.

"Who's seeing each other?" Sean asks, his gaze moving between Ellie and me.

"Charlotte and Pierce."

"I thought you were setting Charlotte up with someone?" Sean's eyebrows furrow in confusion. I love my brother, but sometimes he can be a real wanker.

"For fuck's sake, Sean. We were seeing each other," I belt out.

He turns to Ellie. "Did you know?"

She shakes her head. "No, but now the entire world does." She hands Sean the magazine, and he looks at it before turning back to me.

"What in the world have you done?"

Anger boils out of me. "Oh, so I'm the only one who can't date who he wants to? Only you two are allowed to do that?" I wave my finger between the two of them.

"That's not fair, Pierce." Ellie's voice is quiet when she looks at me, a blush spreading across her face.

"Yeah, well, it's pretty unfucking fair from where I'm standing. You two can be together, but Charlotte and I can't?" I'm pacing the tiny space. All I want to do is talk to Charlotte, but who knows if that's even possible now.

Ellie grabs my arm, halting my movements. "It's different. I'm no longer a princess. She is. There's a different standard."

Ellie's words cut deep. "Wow. Thanks for thinking I'm not good enough for Charlotte."

Her face turns soft, and Sean comes to stand behind her. "It's not that at all. When you're a royal, you don't always get a say in the matter."

"How did we not know about this?" Sean asks.

I scrub my hands over my jaw. "We were being careful." Sean snorts.

"Seriously?" I'm ready to punch my brother in the face.

Ellie turns to Sean, giving him a similar look to mine. "Can you give us a minute?"

He drops a kiss on her forehead and heads out front. "What's your goal here, Pierce? Is this some fling? Are you in love? What?"

Ellie crosses her arms, piercing me with a punishing stare. It's the face that says *I may not be a princess anymore, but I can still get what I want out of you.*

"Of course she's more than a fling." I'm fucking in love with the woman, but I don't want to tell her cousin that before I tell her. "We wouldn't be sneaking around if it were a fling."

"So then what do you plan on doing?"

"Can I not just fucking talk to Charlotte first?" I boom. I can't control the anger bubbling up inside me. "Look, I'm sorry, Ellie. But I just can't be here right now. Tell Sean I'll see him tomorrow."

"Wait, Pierce!" I don't give Ellie another glance as I leave the shop. Pulling out my phone, I dial Charlotte's number immediately. It goes straight to voicemail. Fuck. This can't be good.

Charlotte

NOTHING LIKE GETTING a summons from the Queen first thing in the morning. A lead weight settled in my stomach from the time I left my apartment to getting here at the palace. The knowing faces of the staff tell me whatever I was called here for can't be good. And she's making me wait.

"Your Highness. Her Majesty will see you now." The Queen's advisor opens the door to her office, allowing me to enter.

"Thank you." Nervous energy is crackling through the air. Or maybe it's just my nerves.

"Charlotte. Thank you for coming on such short notice." Aunt Katherine is sitting behind her desk, looking every bit the regal Queen she is this morning.

"What was so urgent that it couldn't wait?" I take a seat in front of her, my hands twisting in my lap.

"I wanted to talk to you about this." She throws down several magazines and newspapers on the desk in front of me. All of them have Pierce and me on the front page of the paper. Forget nerves. Every terrible feeling I had of being found out is crashing into me. I can't hear anything around me. I can only focus on the images in front of me. Of Pierce and me in Bibury. Of us sneaking off to the cafe. Stolen kisses.

"Do you have anything to say for yourself?" The tight draw of her face sticks me harder than I thought. No words come out.

"Did you honestly think you could get away with this? The press knows everything!" Her voice gets higher, carrying around the room.

"But I'm not a senior royal. Why does anyone care about who I date?" My voice is quiet, still flicking through the magazines spread out in front of us.

"Don't be naive, Charlotte. The press doesn't care about that. You're a royal, therefore you are ripe for the picking."

"But we weren't doing anything wrong!" I force myself to meet her gaze. It's punishing. Something I've never felt from her before.

"Did you see the last article?" She pulls one from the back, dropping it on top of the pile.

Another royal abandoning her duties for a Davies brother?

"THEY CAN'T HONESTLY BELIEVE THAT." I push it away from me, unable to look at the horrid news any longer.

"And yet, there is now a pool on the odds of you renouncing your place in the line of succession."

Tears wet my eyes. This can't be happening. "Of course I'm not going to renounce my place. I'm not Ellie."

"I never thought Ellie would, but here we are. It's hard enough keeping the press from releasing photos of James's past, but now I have to worry about talk of another royal leaving. Next thing I know, they'll be calling to abolish the monarchy all together."

"Who is talking about doing that?" Sure, there are people who don't like the monarchy in the modern age, but to abolish the monarchy? It's never been given any real thought.

"The number of scandals since I ascended the throne reflects poorly on me and upon us all. If the people think I can't control my own family, how will they think I could be a steadfast force for this nation?"

For the first time, I see the worry my aunt carries around. Being Queen isn't easy. Being the fifth in line growing up, it was never a worry for me of actually taking the throne. But with Grandfather dying, Ellie renouncing, and James's past causing him all sorts of problems, the stress she bears breaks through.

"I didn't think who I dated would be that much of a problem."

"Yet you continued to date Pierce behind my back, against my wishes. I won't allow it anymore. You will stop seeing him. I know you take your royal responsibilities seriously and will do the right thing."

I rear back, her words a slap to the face. "You can't be serious. There's no salacious gossip being spread. I still continue to do good work in the name of you and the crown. There has to be another way."

She slaps her hands on the desk, rising before me. It takes everything I have not to flinch away from her. "You will end things at once. You're dismissed."

I don't waste another minute, scurrying from her presence. By the time I escape down the halls, tears are flowing freely.

Pierce and I had the best weekend in Bibury. I thought it was just the two of us, no need to sneak around. But I was wrong. Now that the Queen knows, there's no more sneaking around. The press knows. I'm sure by now, Pierce knows.

My heart is tearing in two at the thought of ending things. There has to be another way. I'm not like Ellie. I have no desire to give up my role as a working royal. I love what I do. I love seeing the people I get to help.

But I love Pierce. I know he loves me. I could feel it in his actions. In the way he held me. Made love to me. I was worried I wouldn't get to keep him. This is why.

How in the world am I supposed to just end things with the one man who has become my entire world?

Chapter Twenty-Two

PIERCE

I'm staring a hole in the wall. Charlotte texted that she was going to come over so we could talk. I can't imagine what kind of day she's had. My entire family has been blowing up my phone all day, Ellie included, but I've been ignoring them all. The only person I want to talk to should be here by now. I have no idea what's going to happen. I can't imagine the Queen reacted well.

A soft knock at the door has me leaping off the sofa and throwing open the door. I don't waste a moment before pulling Charlotte into my arms. She's stiff. Not her usual relaxed self. Fuck.

"How are you?" I squeeze her tighter to me, not wanting to let go. Her perfume is calming. The first time I've been calm all day.

She pulls out of my arms, taking off her coat and dropping it on the sofa. She doesn't respond to my question. My nerves ratchet up.

"I have to end things with you."

"What?" Her voice is so quiet, I couldn't have heard her correctly. Charlotte looks up at me, tears glazing over her eyes. Her face is bare of any makeup. She's a shell of the vibrant Charlotte she usually is.

"You heard me. It's already causing a scandal."

"But how? How has it come down to that?" I go to her, trying to take her in my arms, but she pulls back.

"Because there are now odds on if I'll leave the royal family. On whether or not I'll follow in Ellie's footsteps."

My brows pull together in confusion. "But you don't want to leave the royal family. Why is it an issue?"

"Because Ellie left. Because they think I'm going to follow suit. That you Davies brothers are bad news for the royal family and will try to overthrow the monarchy!" She throws her hands up in exasperation.

"Can't you tell her that's not the truth?" My heart is beating a rapid pace against my ribs, trying to escape my chest.

"You have to see it from her perspective. She's been rattled by one thing after another since she became Queen. It hasn't been an easy road, and she's trying to control what she can."

"I don't bloody well care! It shouldn't come down to this. She shouldn't get a say if we continue seeing one another. That's fecking insane."

Charlotte winces. I have no idea what's going through her head. She's always been an open book, so easy to read. But for the first time, she's closed off.

"What are you thinking?" I try to find her gaze, but her eyes are moving all over my flat. Like she's seeing it for the last time and trying to memorise it. Fuck. Fuck, fuck, fuck.

This woman. This beautiful, kind, wonderful woman that I've fallen in love with is going to choose the crown over me.

There's no way she could give up the royal life for me. It's not even a possibility. I've seen the way Charlotte lights

Royal Relations

up when she's talking about her work. She loves it. She was made for it.

The ache in my chest grows. If Charlotte gave up her life for me, she'd regret it. She might be happy for a while, but it would end with her resenting me. And that thought is too much for me to bear.

"There has to be a way around this." Charlotte's words are said more to herself than me.

The hurt in her eyes is evident. But with my next words, it will be a torrent of pain.

"I guess it's as good a time as any to end. Not like we were in love or anything." I'm surprised my voice stays steady. I know the moment the words register because Charlotte's face goes ashen.

"What?" Her voice shakes.

I shrug my shoulders as if this isn't ripping me apart. "We both knew this thing between us wouldn't last. I'm not royal material, and you need someone who is ready to lead by your side."

"You don't believe that." Charlotte presses the heel of her hand to her chest, as if willing her heart not to break.

"There's a reason the Queen didn't want us together. Best to move on with people in our own social standing. It's obvious I could never meet the standards expected to be with a royal."

Charlotte rounds the sofa, stopping in front of me. Her small hands wrap around my forearms. It takes everything inside of me to not pull her into my arms and tell her we can run off together. "Where is this coming from? You can't possibly mean this."

"If you really wanted to be with me, we wouldn't have had to hide our relationship."

"Pierce." Her voice breaks. Tears gather in the corners of her eyes, and fuck me, I can't stand to see her like this.

But it'll be better this way. She can meet someone who the Queen will approve of, and I can live out the rest of my lonely life living in my brother's shadow. "You know I would've shouted our relationship from the top of The Eye if we could have," she implores.

"That's just it." I shake her off, pacing in front of the small window. Londoners are going about their night on the street below, while our world in here is crashing down on us. "If you weren't ashamed of me, we never would have had to hide our relationship."

"You know I was never ashamed of you. Pierce, look at me." Charlotte plants a hand over my heart, stopping my movement. I can't look at her. My eyes will give me away.

"Is what it is, Charlotte. We had fun. Good sex, but that's not enough to stick around, is it?"

Charlotte's gasp has her pulling her hand off me. Looking at her face, I know exactly what heartbreak looks like. Like telling the woman you'd die for that she's nothing more than good sex so she ends up hating you. "That's all this was to you? Good sex?"

I steel myself, going in for the kill. "What man wouldn't like putting his bare dick in a woman's pussy?"

The sting of her slap reverberates through my body. "You bloody bastard! I never want to see you again."

Charlotte spins on her heel, grabbing her coat and taking what's left of my heart with her.

I couldn't keep her, and now, she'll never be mine.

Chapter Twenty-Three

CHARLOTTE

"Miss Charlotte. Would you like to play football with us?" The tiny hand tugging me towards the pitch is happy, not a care in the world.

"I would love to. Do you like playing football?" All the students are crowding around me as we make our way outside the school.

"I love it. The boys don't like me playing with them because I'm better than them."

Figures. "Do you hope to play for the national team someday?"

Her baby face is excited. "It's my dream. I want to beat all the boys."

I give her a high five. "I know you can do it!"

"You can play offense with me. You look like a good runner."

I can't help but laugh at her. She'll have a career in coaching if football doesn't work out.

The teacher blows the whistle, and all the students start moving around me. It's not your standard pitch size, but the kids are running around, passing the ball. I try and stay back out of the action, letting the kids have the fun, but I get passed the ball and take off down the pitch. "Shoot it!"

I hit the ball towards the net, and it goes sailing in. "Goal!" All the students converge on me. Hugs and high fives are given as joy takes over. I haven't felt this good since…Bibury. The thought strikes me down as a bone deep ache settles over me. The pain is constant, Pierce's words on a loop playing in my head. I can't turn them off, no matter how hard I try.

"You all did brilliantly! Now let me see you all play and I'll watch." The excitement is palpable on their faces.

"You're quite good with them." The teacher is on the sidelines, watching as the game takes off.

"They make it easy. You have a great group of students here."

"We appreciate all you do for our school. Your support makes all the difference here to be able to achieve our goals."

Another goal is scored, and students run around the pitch in excitement. The excitement of the students is why I love what I do. Seeing how we can support them in achieving their dreams, whatever they may be, is why I could never give up the crown.

It doesn't make the pain of not having Pierce by my side any less. I guess you can't have everything you want.

"ZARA. WHAT ARE YOU DOING HERE?" Zara's at my door, bottle of wine in hand.

"You seem like you need a friend right now." The kindness in her eyes has mine welling up.

"Thank you." I waste no time pulling her in for a hug.

It's been a long few days. I've done everything I can to keep myself distracted from the pain that threatens to split me in two. But it's no use.

Every night I come home to my empty apartment at the palace, and it thrusts everything I'm missing in my life into a harsh light. The charity I want to start? In the Queen's hands. Pierce by my side? Think again.

"How are you doing?" Zara follows me into the kitchen, grabbing two glasses and pouring the wine.

"Would you believe me if I said I was right as rain?" I plaster a fake smile on my face. It seems like it's all I can muster lately.

"If you're anything but devastated, I won't believe you. I saw how you talked about Pierce."

"And how is that?" I swirl the wine, not looking at her.

"Like you lost the love of your life." I risk a glance at Zara. Her deep brown eyes are sad. "You look exactly how I felt when I thought I lost James."

"Oh bollocks." Tears leak from my eyes unchecked. I cover my face, trying to hide them, but it's not use.

Zara's arm comes around my shoulders. "It's going to be okay."

"How do you know that?" I bark out, feeling like it will be anything but okay.

"Because it was for James and me. What could he have done that was that bad?"

"All I was to him was a warm pussy to wet his dick." Zara blanches and leans back. "His words, not mine." The anger that was simmering comes back in a rushing tidal wave. "I mean, who says that to someone? How could I have been so stupid to believe that he was in love with me?"

"Based on how he treated you, from what you've told me, it was love." Zara's voice is quieter this time.

"Just because he took me to his family cottage and bought me skates to live out my dream of being a roller girl, doesn't mean he loved me."

"He bought you skates?"

I nod, gulping down my wine. "Doesn't mean he was in love with me."

"Oh, Charlotte." Zara pats my arm. "Don't hate me for saying this, but I saw those pictures in the tabloids." I pierce her with a vicious stare. She throws her hands up in defence. "When your advisors make it their business to know, they tell you. Beside the point. Pierce was in love with you."

I sigh, dropping my head down on my arm. "It's no use. There's no way we could be together even if that were true. The Queen forbids it. You should have seen her face when she saw the papers."

"Honestly? I know she's going to be my mother-in-law, but the woman still scares me. She has this face that you don't want to mess with." I lift my head up as Zara shudders.

"That's exactly the face I got." I throw my hands up in the air. "See! It's useless. I'm going to die alone."

"Well, you will with that attitude." Zara gulps down her wine before rubbing her hands together. "You need a plan to take on the Queen with. I know you have it in you."

"Zara, I love you, but I really *don't* have it in me right now. I just want to be sad. Even sending her my updated charity idea didn't make me happy."

"Why didn't it make you happy? You've been working on that for ages."

"Because Pierce was helping me with the final idea."

"It's still your idea. Your plan." Zara's voice is firm. "I just have a good feeling about it."

"I wish I had your positive attitude right now."

Zara shoves my shoulder. "If I kept up that attitude, I wouldn't soon be marrying the best man I know." The smile that plays on her lips is nothing but love.

I'd hate her if I didn't love her so much. "Zara, I love you, but can you please drop it?"

Zara gives me her teacher face. I know I'm not going to like what comes next.

"Fine. I'll drop it for now, but I won't let you lose the love of your life because of the Queen."

I laugh, watery from the tears still streaming down my face. "You make it sound so easy."

"Oh, I've got a master plan ready to go." She taps her temple like she's a genius.

"And what do you plan on doing?"

"Withholding grandchildren. If you're not happy, then no grandbabies for her."

"And your husband would be okay with this?"

Zara rolls her eyes at me. "How do you think we'll get the Queen on board with our plan?"

Evil genius indeed.

Chapter Twenty-Four

PIERCE

"You bloody wanker. You're dating the princess and you didn't tell us?" Liam sounds pissed.

"Were dating," I mumble to myself, pulling my socks up. These last two weeks have been absolutely miserable. I get no relief from my misery. Every person who comes through the shop asks me if I was the guy spotted with Princess Charlotte. At home, everything reminds me of Charlotte. From meals eaten together in my small kitchen to sex in my...well, everywhere. I can't even escape to Bibury, because that reminds me of her too.

"You broke up with the princess?"

I stomp my cleats on the pitch, ready to play. I need the physical activity to calm the constant ache churning in my gut. It's dark, the bitter cold sweeping through London. It matches my mood. Dark, cold, and bitter. "Yes. Now let's play."

"Hold up." Hunter stops me before I get two steps out on the pitch. "You were dating the princess and didn't tell us. What the fuck happened?"

"Christ. Can't you two let this go?" My gaze shifts

between Hunter and Liam. "We dated. Now we're not. End of story."

"You're one of our best mates, Pierce. Based on how you're acting, it's not exactly 'end of story.'"

Fucking intuitive prick. "We never would've worked out. People were against us from the start, so it was better we called things off before anyone caught feelings."

"This is you not catching feelings?" Liam waves his hand over me. "Because, fuck, mate. You look like someone told you Santa isn't real."

That gets a laugh out of me. "What do you mean, Santa isn't real?"

Liam pulls me into a side hug, like only a man can do. "Seriously. Were you happy with her?"

More than I ever admitted to her. Maybe if I grew a pair and told her how I felt, we wouldn't be in this mess. But I saw how she talked about her work. How it lit her up from the inside out. And no matter how much I loved her, I couldn't take her away from that.

"What does it matter now?" I grumble, shoving away from Liam and jogging out onto the pitch.

"What does it matter now?" Liam parrots back to me, still not giving this up. "I've never seen you so cranky before. Shit, were you in love with her?"

That stops me in my tracks. And by the knowing look on his face, he knows it.

"Bloody hell, mate. We need to get her back."

I crack my neck, ready to be done with this. "Why bother? If we couldn't be together before, we can't be together now."

Liam shakes his head, kicking one of the balls over towards me. "Not with that attitude."

"How would you suggest I win her back? It's not like we ended on good terms." I'm humouring him. The look on Charlotte's face when she left is burned into my mind. I won't be able to forget it as long as I live. It was the face of someone who never wanted to see me again. Cutting down the woman I love like that was more brutal that I ever could have imagined.

"We can't rely on your charming personality." I kick the ball back to Liam with more force than necessary. "Can't you just tell her you made a mistake?"

I laugh, for probably the first time in two weeks. "Yes, Liam. If it were that easy, I'd ring up Charlotte, tell her I made a mistake, and all would be forgiven. Christ, no wonder you've never had a girlfriend."

"Just saving all this for that special someone."

Hunter claps him on the back. "Just keep telling yourself that. Now, are you two done? I'm ready to kick some arse tonight."

"LET'S GO GRAB A DRINK. Commiserate our collective loss." We got our arses handed to us tonight. 5-0. It's like we'd never played football before in our lives. Just more bitterness to add to my ever depressing mood.

"Drinks on the moody wanker," Hunter calls out, jogging off the pitch.

"Which one is the moody wanker? We all lost tonight."

"The moodiest of us all. You." Liam tosses his bag over his shoulder, getting ready to leave.

I grab my phone from my bag and see dozens of missed calls from Sean. "Shite."

I dial his number, panic settling over me. Did something happen to Ellie or the baby?

"Where the bloody hell have you been? Ellie's having

the baby!" His voice is loud. So loud I have to hold the phone away from my ear.

"Are you serious? It's two weeks early!"

"No shite. Babies come on their own time."

"Where are you? Which hospital?" I start grabbing my stuff, throwing it into my bag.

"St. Stephen's. Get here as fast as you can."

"Is everything all right?" He wouldn't be calling me like this if something was wrong, right?

"It's fine. Just need my brother here." He clicks off, a happy feeling bubbling inside me. I can't stop the smile from spreading across my face.

"Was that Charlotte calling to beg you to take her back?" Liam quirks his eyebrows at me.

"Fuck, let it go, man. I'll be fine."

"You won't be, but whatever you need to believe." His face is dead serious as the words leave his mouth.

"Fuck off. Ellie's having the baby, so I've got to go." I give him a brief hug, excitement at meeting my new niece or nephew coursing through me.

"Shit. You're going to be an uncle? Get outta here, Uncle Pierce. We'll toast to the new little baby." Liam's smile is almost as big as mine.

"Uncle Pierce. That does have a nice ring to it."

I wave to all the guys, running off the pitch. Of all the directions I thought my night would take, meeting my brother's baby wasn't on the list. But now, it's the only thing that's bringing me happiness. I've been a sad sack since Charlotte left, so seeing this new person will be the highlight of my day. Hell, my week.

Royal Relations

"SO WHO'S GOING to give you your first tattoo?" Ellie gave birth to a healthy baby boy, Edward, who's now curled up in my arms. "Dad shouldn't be allowed to do it."

"Fuck off, you wanker." This is going to be a fun way to rile up my brother.

"Could you please not talk about tattooing my baby? And maybe lay off the swear words. I don't want his first word being F-U-C-K." Ellie enunciates each letter, driving home her point. Her voice belies her exhaustion. She's tired. She's snuggled next to Sean on the bed, while I hold my new nephew. He's got a full head of brown hair. The tiniest set of fingers peek out over the blanket he's wrapped up tight in.

"It's going to be so easy to tease your dad." Edward is quite possibly the cutest baby I've ever seen. Granted, my experience is limited, and I'm biased.

"I'll be your favourite uncle." His little face screws up, and he lets out a loud cry. "Ouch, kid." Sean walks over, grabbing him from my arms. He's a natural, cuddling him into his neck.

"It's okay if you don't like Uncle Pierce. I didn't like him much when we brought him home."

"I really hope you don't give him another brother." I lean down and drop a kiss on Ellie's head. "I should get going. The shop isn't going to run itself tomorrow."

"I appreciate you helping out while I'm gone." Seeing the way Sean looks at Ellie further shatters the pieces of my heart. What I wouldn't give to be able to have a moment like this with Charlotte. It was hard to see the big picture when we were sneaking around, but it's as if everything became clear the moment she left my apartment.

Charlotte is all I want in life. It would be hard to be in the spotlight. To have people want to be my friend for no other reason than what I could do for them. But it would be okay. Because she's worth it. Charlotte is worth everything I'd be giving up in order to support her in her life's work.

"Pierce, are you okay?" Ellie gives me a despondent look. Shit, I'm not doing a very good job at hiding my feelings lately.

"I'm good. Promise."

Before Ellie can respond, a security officer walks into their private room. I guess being a former royal still has some privileges.

My stomach drops to the floor. Would Charlotte come to the hospital? Whatever clarity I just had goes into hiding. I'm not ready to face her yet. Would she even want to see me?

Panic runs wild as the Queen enters the suite Ellie is staying in.

"Mum! What are you doing here?"

"Isn't this what normal mums do?" Her smile is easy as she enters the room. She's wearing jeans and a jumper under her coat. I don't think I've ever seen the Queen so dressed down. But it is well past two in the morning.

"Would you like to hold him?" Sean's voice is steady as he sets the small baby in her arms, not even awaiting an answer.

"He's beautiful. Have you decided on a name yet?"

"Edward." Ellie's eyes well up, mirroring her mum's.

"You'll have a lot to live up to, little one."

With the Queen here now, it feels like I'm intruding on a family moment. But the security officers are blocking the door. Fuck. All I want to do now is leave.

"Mum. You remember Pierce, Sean's brother?" Ellie's words are soft. I love her for trying to bring me into the mix, but all it does is remind me what I don't have. That

Royal Relations

Charlotte isn't here with me. That both of Edward's godparents weren't here to welcome him into the world.

"Yes. Pleasure to see you. I hope you're doing well." She gives me a small nod. One that sets me off.

"I'd be doing much better if Charlotte were here." The Queen's eyes are hard as she turns to me. She's not a woman to be messed with. But I don't care. Because of her, I lost the love of my life. I pushed her away because she couldn't give up her life's work.

"Pierce. Now is not the time." Sean's voice is stern.

"I don't bloody well care. Because of her, Charlotte and I aren't together anymore. It's not fair that you two get to be together and we can't."

"And this little outburst of yours tells me all I need to know." The Queen turns back to the baby in her arms.

"Mum. That's not fair." Ellie's voice is hard as the tension in the room thickens.

"Excuse me if I'm having a hard time containing my emotions. I only lost the love of my life." I scrub a hand down my face. Christ, I've made this all about me. "I need to go. I'm sorry. Congrats, you two. I can't wait to come over and see him." I drop a kiss on Ellie's cheek, but a voice stops me. One I wasn't expecting.

"Come see me at the palace on Tuesday promptly at noon. You and I need to have a discussion." This time, the Queen's eyes aren't as hard.

Bloody hell, they don't still behead people, do they?

Chapter Twenty-Five

PIERCE

"Anyone home?" I call out, pushing open Ellie and Sean's front door. They brought Edward home from the hospital last night, and I was already itching to see him. That and sitting at home by myself waiting to meet the Queen has me antsy.

"Are you insane?" Sean whisper-yells. "What if Edward was sleeping? You could've woken him up."

"Was he asleep?"

"Well, no. But you just can't come yelling into the house anymore."

I raise my hands in defence. "Sorry. Lesson learned. Where is the little bugger?"

"Is that your Uncle Pierce I hear?" Ellie walks out from the kitchen, baby in her arms. Her pink hair is pulled up in a messy bun and her eyes are tired. But I've never seen her happier.

"Wanted to see my nephew." His eyes are wide as Ellie moves the tight bundle into my arms.

"Can you at least call before you come over?" Sean's voice tries to be annoyed, but it's anything but.

"Don't listen to your brother. Anytime you want to come over is fine. Just be warned, you might not see me because I might be napping."

"That's just fine. I can hang out with my new buddy," I coo. Big blue eyes meet mine. Christ, if this isn't the cutest kid in the world.

"Good to know you don't need to see us."

I look up, Sean now wrapped around Ellie. "Tough shit. You'll have to get used to people wanting to see Edward and not you."

"Again, with the swearing. I would like it if our son's first words were mama or dada and not fuck or shit."

"Pink. How dare you cuss in front of Edward." I cover his little head, shifting him away from her. "Sorry, Edward. I'll make sure no one uses such foul language around you."

Ellie shakes her head. "Unbelievable."

A knock at the door has Ellie leaving us behind.

"Oh, Charlotte. I forgot you were coming."

My heart stalls in my chest. Charlotte's here? Sean gives me the same panicked look that is currently pulsing through my veins.

Charlotte and Ellie appear from the entryway, and Charlotte stops cold.

"Sorry, I didn't realise you had company. I'll come back later."

"Charlotte, wait." My voice is thick. All I want to do is talk to her, but I have no idea where to start.

Charlotte is out the door before I can get in another word. "Let me go talk to her. I'll see you guys later." I pass Edward over to Sean and run after Charlotte. She's halfway in the car before I can get to her.

"Please don't go," I plead. "Charlotte. We need to talk. Please."

I don't know where this courage is coming from, but

I'm ready to tell her everything. That I love her. That I didn't mean a single word I said. That I broke my own heart as much as hers when she left my apartment that day.

"I can't be here, Pierce. Please. Just let me go." The pain in her voice cracks me in two. My already shattered heart breaks even more.

"No. You stay and visit. Meet your godson."

Her brown eyes are dull and lifeless when she looks up at me. Her face is devoid of any makeup, her usually dark red lips natural.

"I can't stay if you're here."

"I'm going. But Charlotte?" Wetness hangs on her eyelashes as she peers up at me. "We need to talk. Maybe not now, but later. This can't be the end for us."

She steels her spine, straightening as she steps back out of the car. "No. The end for us was when you crushed my heart in your flat." She spins on her heel and walks back into Ellie and Sean's. The slam of the door reverberates through me, rattling all the broken pieces. Christ, I don't know if she'll take me back. Even getting the Queen's approval won't mean anything if she can't even look at me.

What have I done?

Charlotte

"ARE YOU OKAY?" Ellie's voice is quiet as we sit on the sofa. Baby Edward looks just like Pierce. His bright blue eyes. Full head of dark hair. Looking at him makes me ache.

"No." I rub a finger over Edward's chubby cheeks. He's staring at me with wide eyes, like he isn't sure who I am.

"Don't you even want to hear him out?" Ellie moves closer, wrapping an arm around me.

"How can I? I can't even be in the same room as him without wanting to cry." I bite down on my quivering lips. Whenever I've had a quiet moment these last two weeks, tears flood my eyes. I'm sick of crying over Pierce. I loved him, but he clearly didn't love me. I should be able to move past that. But my heart won't let me.

"Oh, sweetheart." Ellie smooths a hand over my cheek. Such a mothering gesture. "I know he didn't mean those words."

I called Ellie in tears when I left Pierce's flat. She tried to talk through it with me, but I was too distraught. My heart has never been broken like that. Crushed. Shattered.

"You didn't see his face." Edward starts to fuss, so I bring him to my shoulder, rubbing his back.

"But I've seen him almost every day since." I love Ellie for not picking sides. Hard to when she's with his brother. "That's not the look of a man who isn't in love."

"Then why did he tell me I was nothing more than a p-u-s-s-y for his d-i-c-k?"

Ellie tries to contain her laugh but can't. "I know you're in pain, but thank you for not cussing in front of my sweet boy."

A smile pulls on my lips. "I try."

"But Charlotte. I don't know why he said that, but it's the furthest thing from the truth."

"And how do you know that?" I rest my head on Edward's. At least he'll never turn on me.

"Because he looks at you the way Sean looks at me."

I suck in a breath. I want someone to look at me the

Royal Relations

way Sean looks at Ellie. Like I am the centre of his world. That he wouldn't know what to do if I wasn't in his life.

"He can't look at me like that." I shake my head. It's impossible. "I saw the last look he gave me. Not possible."

"Then you're seeing what you want to see. He went toe to toe with Mum the other night."

"What?" No one in their right mind would want to face the Queen. I'm a blood relative, and even I can't push back.

"But you're right." Ellie waves off my earlier comments. "He doesn't love you. He's just taking on Mum for the sake of it."

Edward starts crying, and Ellie takes him from my arms. "I guess you'll just forever wonder why Pierce is taking on the Queen for you."

Why on earth would Pierce talk to Aunt Katherine? He told me he didn't love me. But the man outside looked as broken as I feel. Pierce knew the position I was in. Him or the crown. Did he fall on his sword for me?

That night has been playing like a bad movie through my head nonstop. But Ellie's words have me seeing it in a new light. Did Pierce break up with me so I wouldn't give up my life?

Confusion swirls in my head. If only I knew which way was up and how to move forward.

Because right now, it feels like the only way forward is with Pierce.

And I'm not quite sure I'm there yet.

Chapter Twenty-Six

PIERCE

"Damn. You do great work. I should've covered this old piece up years ago."

The man is admiring the piece I just finished. It's some of my best work. "Thanks. Need the aftercare instructions, or you know them by now?"

"Nah. I know them." I wipe off the oozing ink, taking another minute to look at my latest piece. "Thanks again." I pull my gloves off with a snap, taking the cash from his hand.

"Hopefully you won't have any need to cover this one up in the future."

He shakes his head. "Not a chance in hell."

"Cheers." I wave him off, going about clearing my station.

"He seemed quite happy." Sean's head pops over the wall.

"What are you doing here? Shouldn't you be at home with Ellie and the baby?"

A loved-up look washes over his face. My chest aches at the thought of never getting that feeling again with Charlotte. The look of pure anguish on her face yesterday gutted me. I couldn't let her give up her work, but hopefully, after my talk with the Queen tomorrow, we might get that back.

"Wanted to talk to you about something." He nods his head towards the back, and I follow him.

"What's up?" He closes the door behind me before sitting behind his desk.

"I wanted to talk to you about becoming a partner in the shop."

Shock doesn't even begin to describe what I'm feeling. "A partner?"

"Why do you sound so surprised?" Sean leans back in his chair, grabbing a bottle of gin and pouring two glasses.

"I just never thought you thought that highly of my work." I sip the drink, wincing through the burn.

"Why the fuck would I keep you here if I didn't?"

"Because I'm your brother."

Sean stands, coming around to where I'm sitting. "I'm still a businessman. If you sucked, I wouldn't string you along." I eye the clear liquid, swirling it in the glass. "You're one of the best cover-up artists in the city, and I want to make you a partner. Expand on the business."

"You really want to do that with me?"

"Of course I do. Do you know how many people come in here and ask for you?"

My eyes fly up to meet his. "Are you fucking with me? Everyone always comes in here asking for you."

Sean shakes his head, sitting in the empty chair next to me. "I guess I don't do a good enough job telling you how good you're doing. I have people coming in here all the time asking for you. It's almost giving me a complex."

"Welcome to my life," I mumble to myself.

"Pierce." Sean claps me on the shoulder, shifting my

gaze back to him. "I'm sorry that I haven't told you how good you are and made you question your work. You're one of the best tattoo artists I've ever worked with, and I set the bar pretty high. I wouldn't be asking you to do this if I wasn't serious."

"You'd really want me to be your partner?"

"Fuck, yes. There's nothing that would make me happier. Is it what you want?"

"I mean, yeah." My voice is quiet, not quite conveying how I feel.

"Wow, way to sell me that you want to be here." Sean's voice is easy.

I run a hand down my scruffy face. I haven't bothered to shave the last few days. "Sorry. I just can't get Charlotte out of my head."

"Do you think meeting with the Queen tomorrow will help?"

"Fuck, I don't know." I stand, pacing the room. "I have to try though. All I want is to be with Charlotte, but I can't let her give up her work. It lights her up."

"Even if you get approval, it won't be easy. People still follow Ellie around, and I wish I could do more to protect her, but I can't. You'll never get an ounce of privacy again. Is that really what you want?"

"Yes." I answer without hesitation.

Sean smirks. The bastard. "Then that's what you need to tell the Queen. You're not some bloke off the street." His smile widens. "You're a partner in a thriving business, and anyone would be lucky to have you as a member of their family."

Hope blooms in my chest for the first time in what feels like ages. "I don't think I've ever gotten quite the pep talk from you. Maybe I need to be mopey more often."

Sean sets his drink down, crossing his ankles. "I hate

seeing you like this, but I promise it'll be okay. I have a feeling things are going to fall into place for you. Here and with Charlotte."

"Well, at least I know I'll always have my work."

"Does that mean you'll be a partner with me?"

I give Sean a big smile. "Someone has to keep you in line."

The faith and trust my brother is putting in me is huge. We're on the same playing field. All this time I've been focusing on why his work is better than mine, why I play second fiddle to him, but I was wrong. We both shine in our own ways. His words mean more to me than he'll ever know. And I can't wait to see where this takes us.

Sean stands, pulling me in for a hug. "I love you, Pierce. I know things will work out with Charlotte. They did for me and Ellie."

I just pray those words are true.

Chapter Twenty-Seven

PIERCE

I don't think I've ever been so nervous in my entire life. Sure, I was nervous when I did my first tattoo, but nothing compares to this. I apologised profusely to Ellie for making such a show when Edward was born. But she said she understood. She knows the pain I was in from losing Charlotte.

But now, I'm sitting in the Queen's office, waiting for her to arrive. I'm so nervous I could puke.

"Mr. Davies? Her Majesty will see you now." I stand, buttoning my jacket, as I'm shown into the fanciest room I've ever seen. Portraits older than generations of my ancestors hang on the walls. Heavy purple drapes block the grey London skies from piercing through. A chandelier hangs overhead. I'm afraid if I touch anything, it might break.

"Pierce. Thank you for joining me today."

I bow. Her presence is more overwhelming in here than I thought. I'm surprised I haven't passed out yet. "The pleasure is mine, Your Majesty." At least Mum would be proud of my manners. As much as I want to tell the Queen off again, I know it's not in my best interest.

"I'm sure you're wondering why I called you here today."

I give her a tight smile. "First let me apologise to you for my outburst at the hospital. It was inappropriate. I wasn't in a good place at the time, and it wasn't right to do that at such a happy moment."

She sighs, shaking her head. "I was hoping I could apologise to you."

Shock colours my face. "Apologise to me?"

She gives me a stiff nod. "I'm afraid I was wrong about you, Pierce."

"Wrong how?" My palms are starting to sweat under her watchful eye.

"As you know, it's been a hard year. With Ellie renouncing her place in line to the throne, and James and Zara's scandal, it's been hard to lead the country as I want to."

"Is that why you've been so hard on Charlotte?" I blurt out. Shit. I want to take the words back as soon as I say them.

She gives me a warm smile, one that sets me at ease. "You're astute, Pierce. I'm afraid when I saw the photos of you and Charlotte together, I thought I'd have another Ellie situation on my hands."

"Even though Charlotte loves what she does and wants to contribute more, you thought I was going to make her give up her place?" Bitterness laces my tone. Nice to know how they really feel about you.

"And that is why I'm apologising. A Queen can admit when she's wrong."

"And that's it? I go back to my life and be a miserable sod because I can't have Charlotte?"

Royal Relations

The Queen stands, coming around her desk. "I'm going to be frank with you, Pierce. This life is hard. A camera is shoved in your face daily. Any wrong move and it's fodder for the entire world. I'm shocked you two weren't discovered before. Is this really how you see your future?"

"Yes," I answer without hesitation. "I know what Charlotte's life is like. I know what Ellie still goes through. I know people probably take one look at me and make a snap judgment on what I'm like, but I want this. I want to support Charlotte on the hard days and keep her moving forward in the work she does. I want to be with Charlotte more than I ever thought possible. I love her."

"And you're ready to give up your privacy? Stand by Charlotte's side while she serves her country?"

I nod my head. "If you're trying to scare me away, it won't work."

She crosses her arms, giving me a knowing look. "And is that why you broke up with Charlotte in the first place?"

"How in the world do you know about that?"

"It doesn't matter."

"I broke up with her because I wasn't going to make her give up everything she loves just for me. She would resent me if she had to."

"That's very noble of you." The Queen goes back around her desk and scribbles something on a piece of paper, before dropping it in a file and handing it to me. "Meet Charlotte at this address at seven sharp tonight. Don't be late."

I stand, taking the folder. "What, that's it?"

"I think you've proven that you know what you're getting yourself into. Unless you have something else to say?" She raises a perfectly manicured brow at me.

"Thank you for your time." I bow, trying not to run out of her office. I don't want to test her patience any further.

Did she really just give me permission to date Charlotte? Hope blooms in my chest.

I only hope Charlotte will hear me out.

Charlotte

SNOW SWIRLS around me as I step out of the car and head into the restaurant. I didn't want to come tonight. It's taken all my energy to make it through each day this last week, so meeting someone at the Queen's request isn't my first idea of a good night. I wanted to curl up and eat my weight in ice cream. But no. When the Queen wants something, you're at her every whim.

"Ahh, Princess Charlotte. It's a pleasure to have you here this evening. Your party is awaiting your arrival." The hostess curtsies to me before leading me through the dimly lit restaurant. Dark cherry wood lines the walls, casting long shadows from the old lights hanging overhead. "Here you are." She gestures towards the booth in front of me and I stop.

All the breath leaves my lungs as Pierce stands in front of me. If my feet weren't stuck to the ground, I'd be running out of here right now.

"I'm sure you're wondering why I'm here." I hate that his voice washes over me, causing heat to erupt in my veins. That his bright blue eyes are pleading with me to sit down. The hostess's eyes are flitting back and forth

Royal Relations

between the two of us. Not wanting to cause a scene, I take a seat, as Pierce drops down across from me.

"How have you been?" His voice is quiet as he takes me in. He's not the same Pierce I'm used to seeing. Purple shadows hang under his eyes. His smile isn't happy like it usually is.

"Oh, I don't know. Just trying to figure out why I make such terrible life choices. Why men don't want to stick around."

Pierce winces. I should feel bad, but I don't. Not after he made love to me and then ripped my heart out.

"If you let me—"

"Good evening. Can I start you off with something to drink?" comes a cheery voice as our server interrupts him.

"I'll take a whisky neat." My voice is curt, my eyes not leaving Pierce as he orders a scotch.

He holds my gaze, not speaking until our drinks are dropped off. The waiter seems to be ready to take our order, but one look at my face and he scurries off. I'm not in the mood for playing games tonight. I take a steadying gulp of my drink before focusing on Pierce.

"Why are you here tonight?"

"No one told you?" Confusion mars his handsome face.

"I was given explicit instructions to be here at seven sharp." By the Queen. Why would she want me to meet Pierce here?

"I met with the Queen today." His voice is quiet, as if he's unsure if the ground he's treading on is safe.

"You what?" Shock colours my features. "How did you get a meeting with her?"

He takes a sip of his drink, the liquid glistening on his lips. Oh, how I've missed kissing those lips. The way they'd make me feel. Bring me pleasure. Make me feel loved.

"I sort of yelled at her at the hospital, and then she told me to meet her at the palace."

This time, I can't keep my shock to myself as a laugh bubbles out of me. "You yelled at her? Not many people can get away with something like that."

Pierce shrugs. "I must've caught her at a good moment. She had come to the hospital to visit the baby."

"And what did you discuss with her?" My nerves are frayed. The longer I sit here, the more I want to be swept up into this man's arms. But he rejected me. In the worst way. And now all I want to do is go home and let out all these emotions that are coiling up inside of me.

"How I want to be with you."

I roll my eyes, finishing off my drink. "Right. Why would you want to be with me when I'm nothing more than a nice pussy?" I throw his words at him. He at least looks ashamed. Good. Now he knows a tenth of what I'm feeling.

"You know that wasn't true. How could you even begin to think that?"

"It's not like you ever told me you loved me." I'm staring at my glass. I can't look at him as tears well up in my eyes. I don't want to cry over this man anymore, but it's hard not to.

Pierce is at my side, sliding into my side of the booth. "Look at me, Charlotte."

I close my eyes, gathering the strength to make it through this conversation. When my gaze meets his, those eyes I love so much are heavy. Weighed down with emotion.

"I didn't mean a word of what I said to you. You had to know that as much as it broke your heart that day, it decimated mine."

"Then why would you say such a horrid thing?" My voice wavers.

Pierce's warm hands cup my cheeks, keeping my eyes on his face. "Because I couldn't make you choose. Me or the crown. If I made you choose me, you'd resent me for making you give up your life. You love what you do. I couldn't be the reason you walked away from it."

Pierce thumbs away a tear that falls. "Why didn't you just tell me that?"

He drops his forehead to mine. "Because she was making you choose. She was against us from the start, and no matter what we did, she wasn't going to support us."

I pull back, clasping my hands on his wrists. His pulse is beating a rapid tattoo under my fingertips. "And why is she going to support us now?"

"She is no longer convinced that I will be a bad influence on you." A skeptical laugh leaves my lips. Pierce smiles down on me. "She thought you would follow in Ellie's footsteps and renounce your royal title."

I shake my head, disbelief taking over. "I don't know why everyone thinks I can't make up my own mind. I'm not Ellie. Sean didn't convince her to give up the crown. She was unhappy. What do I have to do to prove I'm not going anywhere?"

"I also told Queen Katherine how I know what your life is like and how people will always make snap judgments about me. About how I always want to be with you. I know I'm giving up my privacy, but I want to be by your side while you serve this country."

"What?" My voice is quiet. My eyes rake over his face, trying to find doubt there. But there is none. His face is strong.

"Charlotte, I love you. I love you more than I ever thought possible. You are brilliant at what you do. I could never take you away from the people that need you. I guess the Queen just needed to hear it from me that I would support you in everything you do."

"What are you saying?"

Pierce licks his lips, threading his fingers through the hair at my neck. My heartbeat is erratic, waiting with bated breath for what he says next.

"I also told the Queen how I knew what I was getting myself into. That I'm prepared to support you for the rest of my life. How you need a partner to keep you moving forward on the hard days. Someone willing to live a very public life in order to be a part of your life."

I can't control the tears now. "You said that to her?"

He nods, his tongue darting out to lick his bottom lip. "I did."

I shake my head. "But I'm not worth all of that. The paparazzi following your every move. Nothing about your life will be private. You have to know that."

"You're wrong." Pierce's lips ghost over my cheek, my jaw. They find the shell of my ear. "You are worth it. More than you'll ever know. My life would be incomplete without you. When you walked out of my flat that day, you took my heart with you. You own me, Charlotte. Completely. No one else can compare to you. You're it for me."

I bury my head in his shoulder, hiccuping over the tears. No one has ever said anything like this to me. Made me feel so treasured. So valued.

"I can't believe you went toe to toe with the Queen." I wrap my arms around his waist, needing to feel him. I can't believe I'm here, listening to the words I've been aching to hear from him.

"After seeing Ellie and Sean with Edward, there was no doubt in my mind that I had to fight for you. I would've gone to the palace every day until she listened to me."

Royal Relations

I drop a kiss on Pierce's neck before pulling back. His eyes are glassy. "You know you probably would've been arrested for harassing the Queen?"

He lifts a shoulder, as if it's no big deal. "She would've known I was serious."

"You're ready to walk into this chaotic life and be with me? Never having an iota of privacy again?" My head still doesn't believe it. My heart? His words are mending it, stitch for stitch, word by word.

"Love, I'd do anything for you. You and me. That's all I need in life."

I trace my fingers over his face, memorising every detail. I never thought I'd find the kind of love like my cousins have. To feel a love so fierce for someone else, that some days it hurts to breathe. But I've found that with Pierce.

"I love you, Pierce. So much. You broke my heart, but I knew I couldn't be happy without you. Seeing baby Edward reminded me so much of you and it gutted me, thinking we could never have that." A watery smile is painted on my face as Pierce claims my lips.

I lean into him, my tongue tangling with his. I don't hide the groan that escapes. I don't care that we're in the middle of a restaurant. I thought kisses like this were gone when Pierce walked away. But feeling the hunger and passion behind his kiss makes need coil throughout my body.

"That's not the only news I come bearing tonight." Pierce pulls back, his thumbs stroking my cheeks. Nothing but love shines out of his eyes.

"What more could I need?"

"How about a new charity to run with your boyfriend?"

"Mm, I like the sound of that."

"Running a charity?" His voice is playful.

"No, my boyfriend. Doesn't seem to fit with how much I love you."

Pierce wraps an arm around my shoulder as we sink into the booth. The scent of his cologne wafts over me. I forgot how calming it was.

"Don't you want to know about the charity?" His voice is a whisper in my hair. He passes a folder I didn't notice on the table over to me.

"I'm sure it's something the Queen is dumping on me because no one else wants to do it." I'm more than a little skeptical of her motivations, even if she sent me to Pierce here tonight.

"What if it has to do with the women's foundation you've been wanting to start?" I pull back out of his arms, my mouth gaping open in shock.

"You mean…are you serious?" I plant my hands on his chest, keeping him at arm's length. "This would be a really mean joke if you aren't serious."

He shakes his head, pulling me back to him. "I'm serious. I know how badly you want this, and I'm invested in it. I want to see this succeed. If you'll have me." I flip open the folder and my proposal, the one I worked on with Pierce, has notes from the Queen on advisors who can help make it work. I can't believe it.

Everything about this night is surreal. I didn't expect to see Pierce here. I didn't expect to get my charity that I've been fighting for. Everything is falling into place.

"I can't believe you got her to change her mind on this." Pierce's wide smile is bright. Butterflies break out in my stomach. "We really get to do this?"

"I had nothing to do with it. It was all you, love."

"I don't know what magical powers you have, but you've somehow pulled the Queen under your spell. I might just have to keep you around." I pull him towards me, taking another kiss. Needing to feel his lips under mine. To know that this moment is real. That I'm not dreaming.

Pierce's lips are soft as they move against mine. I could sit here in this dark restaurant all night if it means I get to stay here with Pierce. I don't want him out of my sight.

"Excuse me." Our server clears his throat. "Can I get you an appetizer to start your meal?"

"Just the cheque." Pierce doesn't look away from me. He drops his mouth to my ear. "I'm ready to take you home and show you just how much I love you."

I shake my head. "My home. I want you to see where we'll be living."

Pierce lifts an eyebrow at me. "Where we'll be living? Pretty presumptuous of you to assume I'll be moving in."

"I have big plans for you, Pierce. I don't want to waste another day without you. I want to marry you and have lots of babies."

"Little princes and princesses running around? Sounds pretty good to me."

"Thought so. Now, take me home and show me just how much you love me."

Pierce drops some pounds on the table, not bothering with the cheque. He pulls me up, my hands colliding with the muscle in his chest. "Your wish is my command, princess."

Chapter Twenty-Eight

CHARLOTTE

The door hasn't shut behind me before Pierce is attacking my lips with his. It's all teeth and tongues. His lips soothe away the sting of the words he said that I haven't been able to get out of my head. But seeing him tonight, the look of love on his face, I know he is it for me.

"Fuck, I've missed you, Charlotte." Pierce picks me up, wrapping me in his arms. His hard length presses into my core. Tears prickle his eyes. "I thought I'd never get to see you again."

"You were doing what you thought was right." My thumb smooths the furrowed line between his brows away. "But it's you and me now. This will be our life." I look around the grand halls of the palace I call home.

Pierce's smile is blinding. "I can't fucking wait." His lips crash down on mine. I wrap my arms around him, holding him as close as possible to me. My nails claw down his chest, fumbling to release him of his shirt.

Giving up, I rip the material away. One button pings off. The rest haven't moved. "Huh. I always thought that would work."

"I'm glad you're so eager, but I want you laid out beneath me. Bedroom?" Pierce's voice is playful. I drop my legs, leading him towards my oversized room. His eyes don't leave me. They don't take in the grand staircase. Or the paintings on the stairs that are centuries old. Family history bearing down on us.

I grab Pierce's hand and lead him to the bed. Sitting on the edge, I work his belt buckle free. I run my hands over the obvious bulge in his pants.

"If you keep doing that, I'm going to come in my pants, and we can't have that." Pierce pushes me back onto the bed. His weight settles over me as his lips blaze a trail of hot kisses down my neck.

I'm a writhing mess beneath him, wanting more, but not wanting his lips to leave mine. Pierce links our hands, stretching them over my head.

"I'm going to strip you bare and feast on you. All I've dreamed about is getting to taste you again." The heat in his eyes has my release barrelling through me. My need to come has never been so high.

"What are you waiting for?"

A smirk dances across Pierce's face. His fingers work their way down my body. Unbuttoning my slacks, the snick of the zipper echoes through the quiet room. I lift my hips, giving him better access to pull them down. He throws them behind me before grasping my ankles and pulling me towards the edge of the bed.

"Looks like someone is ready for me." His lips ghost over the tender flesh of my inner thigh. My thong is wet with need. Pierce is slow with his lips, grazing them over my flesh. Nipping and sucking everywhere but where I really want him.

"You are such a tease." I roll my hips, trying to get him to my aching core.

"Is this where you want me?" His finger trails down my thong before he swipes it to the side.

"God, yes!" I shout.

"I should make you beg." His voice is heated.

"Please, Pierce. Please put your mouth on me." I tilt my head up, his grin downright evil.

"I don't know. It doesn't sound like you're desperate enough." He pushes my shirt up and over my head. Those plump, sinful lips move down my arms. Over the swell of my breasts. Down my belly. He nips at my hip.

"Oh my God. If you don't fuck me, I'm going to die."

"Well, we wouldn't want that, now would we?" His finger slides under the poor excuse for underwear and tears it from my body. "Fuck. You're soaked."

"I need you." No sooner do the words escape than Pierce sucks my clit into his mouth. A deep groan bursts from my lips. My skin is vibrating with need as Pierce laves me with his tongue. He thrusts two fingers inside my pussy, and I'm practically coming apart at the seams.

"Pierce! Don't stop." I thread my fingers through his hair, keeping his mouth on me. The pressure is building, racing down my spine, like a cannon ready to go off.

"Are you ready to come for me, love? I want to feel you come on my tongue and fingers."

His words pull my orgasm from me. Pleasure washes over me as I arch into Pierce's touch. His fingers continue their ministrations through my release. The pressure in my belly eases, a happiness settling over me. I've entered a state of pure bliss.

"You still with me, love?" Pierce kisses his way up my body, his tongue flicking over my hard nipples.

I peek one eye open. His lips are wet with my release, his hair mussed from my hands. "Barely."

"Think you can handle more?" His hand splays over my stomach.

I sit up, moving over him. "If I don't have you buried inside me tonight, I might combust."

Pierce kisses me. Long, languid strokes. I forgot how good kissing him was. "I just got you back. I can't have you combusting on me."

I push Pierce back on the bed, pulling his briefs down his legs. His hard cock springs free. Licking my lips, anticipation builds at the thought of having him inside me.

I grip the base of his cock, giving the vein underneath a long lick. His hips buck off the bed, as I suck his tip into my mouth. "Fuck, Charlotte." His hands wrap around my hair, pulling it away from my face.

Precum leaks onto my tongue, driving my own pleasure higher. "If you keep doing that, love, I'm going to come down your throat, and that's not what I want tonight." I pull off him, wiping my lips.

Pierce's eyes are glazed over as he takes me in. He looks small in my bed. I love having him here in my space. He looks so at ease, so natural, that it makes my heart swell.

Pierce pulls me over him before flipping us to the centre of the bed. The look in his eyes is nothing but love. I can't believe how lucky I am to get to be with this man. To not have to hide our relationship any longer.

Pierce reaches for his jeans, pulling out a condom. "Just in case?"

I nod. "You're in the good graces of the Queen now. Can't have an unplanned pregnancy giving you the boot."

Pierce sheathes himself before sliding inside of me. Wrapping my arms and legs around him, I pull him close to me. Running my fingers through his hair, I stare up into his eyes as he moves inside me.

"God, I've missed you," he whispers against my lips, as he continues moving. Long, slow thrusts.

My heart is so full in this moment, that I get to be with the man of my dreams. A single tear slips out, as Pierce kisses it away.

"You okay, love?"

"As long as I'm with you, I'll be okay." The orgasm that rolls through me is quiet, but powerful. It's how it always is with Pierce.

He drops his forehead to mine as he groans through his own release.

"Promise me it'll never stop being like this?" I whisper against his lips.

"Never."

Pierce pulls out, taking care of the condom before wrapping me in his arms. I could stay like this forever. But my stomach seems to have other ideas.

"Hungry?" Pierce asks, my belly growling again.

I pull Pierce's T-shirt on to cover myself. "Come with me. I've got a little surprise for you."

Pierce smirks, pulling on his briefs. "Didn't you already have something sweet?"

"Aren't you funny." I wrap my arms around his bare chest, his muscles flexing under my fingertips. I drop a kiss over his heart, before threading my fingers through his.

"Are you going to give me a tour?" Our footsteps are quiet as we head down towards the small kitchen I use most days.

"You'll get a tour another time." I grin at him over my shoulder. The soft lights of the apartment are reflected in his eyes. Pierce pulls me back, his chest colliding with my back.

"I like the sound of that." His lips find my neck.

"The sound of what?" Butterflies threaten to burst in me at the slightest touch of his lips on me.

Cupping my chin, Pierce turns my gaze to him. "Next time."

My heart threatens to burst from my chest. God, I love this man.

I lead the way towards the kitchen, turning on a small overhead light. "Sit."

"What's the surprise?" Pierce stretches out in the booth by the window. His abs ripple under the soft light. Long legs stick out from under the table. I don't think I'll ever get used to seeing him here in my space. I grab the small bag and hide it behind my back as I saunter over to Pierce.

"Can you guess?" A sly smile spreads across my face.

"Twenty questions?"

I laugh. "Only twenty."

"Can we make this strip twenty questions? Each question I get wrong you lose an article of clothing?"

I smack his chest. "I'm only wearing a shirt. You'd ask if I had an alien behind my back if it meant you could see my tits."

Pierce's eyes grow dark. "They are very nice tits." He squeezes them together, and it takes everything I have to remember why I came down here.

"Slow down. You don't get these"—I wave in front of my chest—"until you guess what I have."

Pierce snarls at me. "You really don't play fair."

"No." I kiss the corner of his mouth. "Now, start guessing."

"Is it an alien?"

I pinch his side. "You little shite."

"Fine." His hands snake under my shirt, his thumbs rubbing soothing circles at the base of my spine. "Is it chocolate?"

I shake my head, dropping a kiss on his lips. "No."

"Do I get a kiss every time I get one wrong?"

"No, because then you'd never actually give me a real answer."

Pierce leans farther into me, pulling me under his spell. Next thing I know, the bag is ripped from my hands, and I'm sprawled out on the table under him.

"Marshmallows?"

I can't help the giggle that bursts forth. "I haven't been able to stop eating them since we came home from Bibury. And when you..." I can't finish my thought. We're together now. I never want to think of being without him. "Those and wine are all I've been eating the last week. I've been a sodding mess. But marshmallows made it better."

Pierce drops the bag, caging me in under him. "Am I allowed to make it better?"

My fingers rake through the scruff on his jaw. "You've already made it better."

"So these are just the icing on the cake?"

I nod, biting my lip. Pierce takes one, holding it out to me. I sink my teeth into the sugary goodness. Instead of eating the other half, his lips graze mine. His tongue licks the seam of my lips and I open to him.

"Fuck, you taste amazing." His voice is a growl.

"I'm pretty sure that's the marshmallow."

I sit up, pushing Pierce back into the bench. He pops the other half in his mouth, smiling at me.

"You know, this is pretty great," I say with a grin.

"What is?" He grabs one from the bag, and I steal it from him, shoving the whole thing in my mouth.

"Sitting here in my kitchen. Eating marshmallows with you."

Pierce runs his hands up my bare thighs, settling on my

hips. "If this is all you need, I'll promise to always bring home marshmallows."

"Yeah?"

"If it'd make you happy, I'd buy you an entire factory of marshmallows. I never want to see you sad."

"Well that's impossible. No one can ever be that happy."

Pierce pulls me down into his lap, wrapping his arms around me. "As long as I have you, I'll have everything I need in life."

"And as long as I have marshmallows and you, I'll have everything I need in life."

Pierce smiles. "Sounds like a damn good life to me."

Epilogue

CHARLOTTE - ONE YEAR LATER

"Are you nervous?" I smooth the lapels of the suit Pierce is wearing. I love him in anything, but he wears a suit well.

"Love, I think you're more nervous than I am." He grabs my hand, kissing my engagement ring. The pink sapphire set in a burst of diamonds on a rose gold band is my favourite. Pierce picked the perfect ring for me.

"It's going to be a long few days, and I just want to get them over with."

He tips my chin up to look him in the eye. "You want to get our wedding day over with?"

I sigh, wrapping my arms around him. "I don't care about some big wedding. I just want to be married to you. To get to live together and start our life here."

After our engagement, the Queen gifted us a cottage on the grounds of Windsor Castle. We wasted no time making it our own, even though Pierce won't officially live here until after the wedding. It's been lonely without him here.

"You know what I'm looking forward to?" His lips kiss down my jaw.

"What's that?" I close my eyes, relishing his touch.

"The honeymoon."

A laugh escapes my lips. "Of course you are."

We're leaving for the Maldives the morning after the wedding. Ten days in a secluded over-the-water hut. Ten days in paradise with my new husband.

"Hey." I open my eyes to see Pierce's gaze fixed on me, a small smile playing on his lips. "We've been working hard this last year. It's about damn time we get a break."

Pierce has been working with me on my women's charity, getting it off the ground. I don't know where I'd be without him. His endless support makes me fall deeper in love with him every day.

"Before everyone gets here, I've got something for you."

"I like the sound of that." Pierce drops a hot kiss to my neck, making me forget what I'm doing.

"Stop it. Everyone will be here any minute." I shove him off of me and grab the small velvet box off the dresser.

"What's this?"

I roll my eyes. "It's a present. You need to open it." Pierce sits on the end of the bed, opening the small box.

"Love, these are beautiful." He pulls out the gold cufflinks.

"They aren't fancy or new or anything. But my granddad wore them on his wedding day, and I figured they'd be good luck. I won't tell you what else Grandmum said when she gave them to me, because I'm scarred for life."

"I'll treasure these." He closes the box and pulls me

between his legs. "Makes what I got you seem a little cheesy." He pulls a small book out of his jacket pocket.

I flip it open. Each page has a picture and a memory Pierce wrote out. Telling me why he loves me. How happy he is to be marrying me. I try to quell the tears, but they fall freely.

"Do you like it?" Pierce's voice is quiet.

"Oh, Pierce." I slant my lips over his, pouring all my emotions into this kiss. I've never been given anything so thoughtful. Pierce pulls back, wiping the tears from my cheeks.

"I'll cherish this forever." I flip through a few more pages, before setting it next to him on the bed and sitting on his lap. "I might need to go freshen up before everyone gets here now."

I revel in his handsome features. My breath catches when I see him for the first time every day. I've never felt a love like this before. To be so taken with someone, that they become your whole world. I can't imagine my life without him. He supports me in ways I never dreamed of, and I've been doing everything possible to help him adjust to royal life.

"Oy! Is anyone home?" Sean's voice carries up the stairs. I sag against Pierce, wanting just one more moment with him.

"Give us a minute!" Pierce calls down to him. "Wanker. Just letting himself in the house."

"I'm pretty sure we told everyone they could come right in after the rehearsal."

The afternoon was spent doing a walkthrough of the ceremony tomorrow. It was almost longer than the wedding itself will be. We invited our families back to our cottage for a small dinner. With how lavish everything will be tomorrow, we didn't want anything grand.

"We best get going then." Pierce drops a kiss on my lips before standing and taking my hand in his.

Pierce has been the picture of calm leading up to the wedding. I can't imagine being thrown into the public spotlight like he has and having your wedding broadcast around the globe. But he's taking it all in stride. Thinking of him by my side for the rest of our lives makes my heart flutter. I can't believe I got this lucky.

"Pierce! Charlotte! Can you believe tomorrow is the big day?" Jacqueline is in the sitting room, sipping on champagne as she comes to wrap me in a hug. Getting Jacqueline as a mother-in-law might be one of the best things about marrying Pierce.

"I can't wait to get the show on the road."

She laughs, wrapping me in her arms as Pierce takes Edward from Sean and into his arms. The love Pierce has for his nephew floors me. Seeing how good he is with him makes me anxious to start our own family. Pierce is going to be the best father in the world.

"I couldn't wait to marry Pierce's father. We were supposed to spend the night apart, but I snuck into his room." She wags her eyebrows at me.

"That doesn't surprise me." She hands me a glass of champagne, clinking her glass against mine.

"I can't wait until you're officially a part of the family."

I pull Jacqueline back in for a hug. "Not many people could handle the troubles that come along with their two sons' partners being royal."

Jacqueline cups my cheek, a warmth washing over her soft features. "Seeing how happy you make my Pierce is worth more than any troubles we might face. You two are going to have a wonderful life together."

Tears wet my eyes as I try to choke back the emotions threatening to bubble over. I sneak a peek at Pierce. He's making faces at Edward, who is giggling at his uncle. "He makes me so happy. Some days I have to pinch myself to believe this is really my life."

Jacqueline drops a kiss on my cheek. "It's going to be a wonderful life. But I wouldn't mind you popping out some more grandbabies for me. I'm not getting any younger."

I throw my head back in laughter. "That's something I can say I wouldn't mind having sooner rather than later."

"Excuse me, Jacqueline. I need Charlotte." Aunt Katherine is at my side.

"She's all yours." She pats my cheek, before I'm led over to where Pierce is talking with Sean and Ellie.

"Pierce. I need you and Charlotte so I can say a few words before dinner is served."

Pierce hands Edward back to Ellie and takes my hand, as we follow Aunt Katherine to the front of the room.

"Can I have everyone's attention for a moment?" She doesn't even have to raise her voice. When the Queen starts talking, everyone listens.

"With tomorrow being a crazy day, I want to take a moment to welcome Pierce into our family."

Pierce wraps an arm around my shoulder, pulling me in closer. His eyes are locked on Aunt Katherine as she continues.

"I know it wasn't an easy start to your relationship, and I'm afraid that's my fault. But seeing the love you and Charlotte have and the respect of duty to this country brings me great pride."

I glance up at Pierce and his eyes are wet. It wasn't an easy road for the two of us. But tomorrow, the whole world gets to see the love we have for each other.

"And as an early wedding present, I bestow the title of Duke and Duchess of Clarence on each of you."

"What?" My voice is startled. Dukedoms for married royals don't come until a few months after the wedding.

"I know I wasn't welcoming like I should have been. Pierce has been a wonderful addition to this family, and I can't wait to see how the two of you further the monarchy."

"Thank you." I wrap my aunt, the Queen, in a hug. Tears track down my face. There is no better acceptance of Pierce and our marriage than receiving this gift from the Queen.

I pull back, and she wipes the tears from my eyes. "You are such a wonderful young woman, and I couldn't be more proud of you."

My lips quiver as she wraps Pierce in a hug. Words are whispered between them that I can't hear.

Edward breaks the moment with a loud wail. "I guess we're all hungry." Ellie's eyes are wet as I look over at her and Sean. Beaming smiles radiate off everyone in the room.

"Let's give these two a moment. We'll see you in the dining room." Katherine ushers everyone out of the room, as I'm left standing in awe of what just happened.

"Did you know that was going to happen?" Pierce asks.

"It usually doesn't happen until after the wedding."

Pierce pulls me into a hug, squeezing me tight against him. I push up on my toes, peppering his face in kisses.

"I guess that means the Queen likes me." His voice is breathy as it leaves him.

I cup his cheeks, wiping a single tear that escapes. "Of course she does."

"But now I know she does. I know I don't need her acceptance, but I felt like I had to get it. Because you're worth it. And knowing she approves of me…it feels like a weight has been lifted off my chest."

"Oh, Pierce. You sweet, wonderful, kind man. I am so in love with you, it hurts some days. Never doubt that you are just the man I want you to be. Nothing more and nothing less. You're perfect."

Pierce buries his face in my neck, keeping us close together. "Christ, you have no idea how good it is to hear you say that."

"It's the truth."

Pierces kisses my neck, my jaw, my lips. "I love you more than I ever dreamed of." His smile is bright. "I have a question for you."

Laughter bubbles out of me. "And what question might that be?" We still pepper each other with questions. They're fun and lighthearted now.

"How are you feeling about tomorrow?"

"Like I'm the luckiest girl in the world."

The End

WANT to find out how Pierce proposes to Charlotte? Signup for my newsletter for an exclusive bonus scene!

JOIN my Facebook Reader's group, Emily Silver's Travelers, to stay in the know about all future books!

Note from the Author

Book five is now out in the world!

I fell in love with Pierce and Charlotte while writing Royal Reckoning, and just knew I had to write their book. It was a labor of love, so thank you from the bottom of my heart for reading this book!

I wouldn't be here without the support of so many people. To all the authors out there, who are too many to name... your support has made this journey one of the best I've been on! I have loved every minute of this crazy ride and only hope it continues. To my beta readers for helping to make this story perfect. Without you, I wouldn't be where I am today.

To my street team and bookstagrammers who shared and read this book...thank you! Your enthusiasm and love for my books puts a smile on my face every day.

And to all you readers who have picked up my books... thank you for taking a chance on my books. You're the best part of this journey for me!

<3 Emily

About the Author

After winning a Young Author's Award in second grade, Emily was destined to be a writer. A lover of all things romance, Emily started writing books set in her favorite places around the world. As an avid traveler, she's been to all seven continents and sailed around the world.

When she's not writing, Emily is working to pay for her next big adventure, trying to learn a foreign language and reading all the romance she can get her hands on!

Find her on social media to stay up to date on all her adventures and upcoming releases!

Also by Emily Silver

Get all my books on Amazon:

The Denver Mountain Lions

Roughing The Kicker

Pass Interference

Sideline Infraction

Illegal Contact

The Big Game

Dixon Creek Ranch

Yours to Take

Yours to Hold

Yours to Be - coming fall, 2023

Yours to Forget - coming winter, 2023

Off the Deep End — A standalone, MM sports romance

The Ainsworth Royals

Royal Reckoning

Reckless Royal

Royal Relations

Royal Roots

Royal Ties

The Love Abroad Series

An Icy Infatuation

A French Fling

A Sydney Surprise

Printed in Great Britain
by Amazon